Praise for *New York Times* bestselling author
B.J. Daniels
and The Montana Hamiltons

"The first book of Daniels' new Montana Hamiltons
series will draw readers in with its genuine characters,
multiple storylines and intense conflict set against the
beautiful Montana landscape."
—*RT Book Reviews* on *Wild Horses*

"*Wild Horses* is filled with action, intrigue, mystery
and romance; in other words a classic B.J. Daniels
book."
—*Fresh Fiction* on *Wild Horses*

"Forget slow-simmering romance…the second
Montana Hamiltons is always at a rolling boil."
—*Publishers Weekly* on *Lone Rider*

"*Lucky Shot* is third in a solid mystery series with
rugged cowboys and strong women who are smart
characters. Fans of the show *Longmire* will find a new
book to absoutely adore."
—*RT Book Reviews* on *Lucky Shot*

"Sure to have fans anxious for the next title in the
series."
—*Library Journal* on *Lucky Shot*

Also available from
B.J. Daniels
and HQN Books

The Montana Hamiltons

Wild Horses
Lone Rider
Lucky Shot
Hard Rain

Beartooth, Montana

Unforgiven
Redemption
Forsaken
Atonement
Mercy

B.J. DANIELS

NEW YORK TIMES
BESTSELLING AUTHOR

INTO DUST

ISBN-13: 978-0-373-78924-5

Recycling programs for this product may not exist in your area.

Into Dust

This book is dedicated to Kimberly Rocha
and Janet Rodman. These two women are the life of
any party. They have brightened many of my days
and have always been supportive and appreciative of
authors and what goes into writing a book.
Cheers, ladies, the next drink is on me!

CHAPTER ONE

THE CEMETERY SEEMED unusually quiet. Jack Durand paused on the narrow walkway to glance toward the Houston skyline. He never came to Houston without stopping by his mother's grave. He liked to think of his mother here in this beautiful, peaceful place. And he always brought flowers. Today he'd brought her favorite, daisies.

He breathed in the sweet scent of freshly mown lawn as he moved through shafts of sunlight fingering their way down through the huge oak trees. Long shadows fell across the path, offering a breath of cooler air. Fortunately, the summer day wasn't hot and the walk felt good after the long drive in from the ranch.

The silent gravestones and statues gleamed in the sun. His favorites were the angels. He liked the idea of all the angels here watching over his mother, he thought, as he passed the small lake ringed with trees and followed the wide bend of Brays Bayou situated along one side of the property. A flock of ducks took flight, flapping wildly and sending water droplets into the air.

He'd taken the long way because he needed to relax. He knew it was silly, but he didn't want to visit his mother upset. He'd promised her on her deathbed that he would try harder to get along with his father.

Ahead, he saw movement near his mother's grave and slowed. A man wearing a dark suit stood next to the angel statue that watched over her final resting place. The man wasn't looking at the grave or the angel. Instead, he appeared to simply be waiting impatiently. As he turned...

With a start, Jack recognized his father.

He thought he had to be mistaken at first. Tom Durand had made a point of telling him he would be in Los Angeles the next few days. Had his father's plans changed? Surely, he would have no reason to lie about it.

Until recently, that his father might have lied would never have occurred to him. But things had been strained between them since Jack had told him he wouldn't be taking over the family business.

It wasn't just seeing his father here when he should have been in Los Angeles. It was seeing him in this cemetery. He knew for a fact that his father hadn't been here since the funeral.

"I don't like cemeteries," he'd told his son when Jack had asked why he didn't visit his dead wife. "Anyway, what is the point? She's gone."

Jack felt close to his mother near her grave. "It's a sign of respect."

His father had shaken his head, clearly displeased with the conversation. "We all mourn in our own ways. I like to remember your mother my own way, so lay off, okay?"

So why the change of heart? Not that Jack wasn't glad to see it. He knew that his parents had loved each other. Kate Durand had been sweet and loving, the perfect match for Tom, who was a distant workaholic.

Jack was debating joining him or leaving him to have this time alone with his wife, when he saw another man approaching his father. He quickly stepped behind a monument. Jack was far enough away that he didn't recognize the man right away. But while he couldn't see the man's face clearly from this distance, he recognized the man's limp.

Jack had seen him coming out of the family import/export business office one night after hours. He'd asked his father about him and been told Ed Urdahl worked on the docks.

Now he frowned as he considered why either of the men was here. His father hadn't looked at his wife's grave even once. Instead he seemed to be in the middle of an intense conversation with Ed. The conversation ended abruptly when his father reached into his jacket pocket and pulled out a thick envelope and handed it to the man.

He watched in astonishment as Ed pulled a wad of money from the envelope and proceeded to count it. Even from where he stood, Jack could tell that the gesture irritated his father. Tom Durand expected everyone to take what he said or did as the gospel.

Ed finished counting the money, put it back in the envelope and stuffed it into his jacket pocket. His father seemed to be giving Ed orders. Then looking around as if worried they might have been seen, Tom Durand turned and walked away toward an exit on the other side of the cemetery—the one farthest from the reception building. He didn't even give a backward glance to his wife's grave. Nor had he left any flowers for her. Clearly, his reason for being here had nothing to do with Kate Durand.

Jack was too stunned to move for a moment. What had that exchange been about? Nothing legal, he thought. A hard knot formed in his stomach. What was his father involved in?

He noticed that Ed was heading in an entirely different direction. Impulsively, he began to follow him, worrying about what his father had paid the man to do.

Ed headed for a dark green car parked in the lot near where Jack himself had parked earlier. Jack dropped the daisies, exited the cemetery yards behind him and headed to his ranch pickup. Once behind the wheel, he followed as Ed left the cemetery.

Staying a few cars back, he tailed the man, all the time trying to convince himself that there was a rational explanation for the strange meeting in the cemetery or his father giving this man so much money. But it just didn't wash. His father hadn't been there to visit his dead wife. So what was Tom Durand up to?

Jack realized that Ed was headed for an older part of Houston that had been gentrified in recent years. A row of brownstones ran along a street shaded in trees. Small cafes and quaint shops were interspersed with the brownstones. Because it was late afternoon, the street wasn't busy.

Ed pulled over, parked and cut his engine. Jack turned into a space a few cars back, noticing that Ed still hadn't gotten out.

Had he spotted the tail? Jack waited, half expecting Ed to emerge and come stalking toward his truck. And what? Beat him up? Call his father?

So far all Ed had done from what Jack could tell was sit watching a brownstone across the street.

Jack continued to observe the green car, wondering

how long he was going to sit here waiting for something to happen. This was crazy. He had no idea what had transpired at the cemetery. While the transaction had looked suspicious, maybe his father had really been visiting his mother's grave and told Ed to meet him there so he could pay him money he owed him. But for what that required such a large amount of cash? And why in the cemetery?

Even as Jack thought it, he still didn't believe what he'd seen was innocent. He couldn't shake the feeling that his father had hired the man for some kind of job that involved whoever lived in that brownstone across the street.

He glanced at the time. Earlier, when he'd decided to stop by the cemetery, he knew he'd be cutting it close to meet his appointment back at the ranch. He prided himself on his punctuality. But if he kept sitting here, he would miss his meeting.

Jack reached for his cell phone. The least he could do was call and reschedule. But before he could key in the number, the door of the brownstone opened and a young woman with long blond hair came out.

As she started down the street in the opposite direction, Ed got out of his car. Jack watched him make a quick call on his cell phone as he began to follow the woman.

CHAPTER TWO

THE BLONDE HAD the look of a rich girl from her long coifed hair to her stylish short skirt and crisp white top to the pale blue sweater lazily draped over one arm. Hypnotized by the sexy swish of her skirt, Jack couldn't miss the glint of silver jewelry at her slim wrist or the name-brand bag she carried.

Jack grabbed the gun he kept in his glove box and climbed out of his truck. The blonde took a quick call on her cell phone as she walked. She quickened her steps, pocketing her phone. Was she meeting someone and running late. A date?

As she turned down another narrow street, he saw Ed on the opposite side of the street on his phone again. Telling someone…what?

He felt his anxiety rise as Ed ended his call and put away his phone as he crossed the street. Jack took off after the two. He tucked the gun into the waist of his jeans. He had no idea what was going on, but all his instincts told him the blonde, whoever she was, was in danger.

As he reached the corner, he saw that Ed was now only yards behind the woman, his limp even more pronounced. The narrow alley-like street was empty of people and businesses. The neighborhood rejuvenation hadn't reached this street yet. There was dirt and debris along the front of the vacant buildings. So where was the woman going?

Jack could hear the blonde's heels making a *tap, tap, tap* sound as she hurried along. Ed's work boots made no sound as he gained on the woman.

As Ed increased his steps, he pulled out what looked like a white cloth from a plastic bag in his pocket. Discarding the bag, he suddenly rushed down the deserted street toward the woman.

Jack raced after him. Ed had reached the woman, looping one big strong arm around her from behind and lifting her off her feet. Her blue sweater fell to the ground along with her purse as she struggled.

Ed was fighting to get the cloth over her mouth and nose. The blonde was frantically moving her head back and forth and kicking her legs and arms wildly. Some of her kicks were connecting. Ed let out several cries of pain as well as a litany of curses as she managed to knock the cloth from his hand.

After setting her feet on the ground, Ed grabbed a handful of her hair and jerked her head back. Cocking his other fist, he reared back as if to slug her.

Running up, Jack pulled the gun, and hit the man with the stock of his handgun.

Ed released his hold on the woman's hair, stumbled and fell to his knees as she staggered back from him, clearly shaken. Her gaze met his as Jack heard a vehicle roaring toward them from another street. Unless he missed his guess, it was cohorts of Ed's.

As a van came careening around the corner, Jack cried "Come on!" to the blonde. She stood a few feet away looking too stunned and confused to move. He quickly stepped to her, grabbed her hand and, giving her only enough time to pick up her purse from the ground, pulled her down the narrow alley.

Behind them, the van came to a screeching stop. Jack looked back to see two men in the front of the vehicle. One jumped out to help Ed, who was holding the blonde's sweater to his bleeding head.

Jack tugged on her arm and she began to run with him again. They rounded a corner, then another one. He thought he heard the sound of the van's engine a block over and wanted to keep running, but he could tell she wasn't up to it. He dragged her into an inset open doorway to let her catch her breath.

They were both breathing hard. He could see that she was still scared, but the shock seemed to be wearing off. She eyed him as if having second thoughts about letting a complete stranger lead her down this dark alley.

"I'm not going to hurt you," he said. "I'm trying to protect you from those men who tried to abduct you."

She nodded, but didn't look entirely convinced. "Who are you?"

"Jack. My name is Jack Durand. I saw that man following you," he said. "I didn't think, I just ran up behind him and hit him." It was close enough to the truth. "Who are *you*?"

"Cassidy Hamilton." No Texas accent. Nor did the name ring any bells. So what had they wanted with this young woman?

"Any idea who those guys were or why they were after you?"

She looked away, swallowed, then shook her head. "Do you think they're gone?"

"I don't think so." After he'd seen that wad of money

his father had given Ed, he didn't think the men would be giving up. "I suspect they are now looking for both of us." When he'd looked back earlier, he'd thought Ed or one of the other men had seen him. He'd spent enough time at his father's warehouse that most of the dock workers knew who he was.

But why would his father want this woman abducted? It made no sense, and yet it was the only logical conclusion he could draw given what he'd witnessed at the cemetery.

"Let's wait a little bit. Do you live around here?"

"I was staying with a friend."

"I don't think you should go back there. That man has been following you for several blocks."

She nodded and hugged herself, looking scared. He figured a lot of what had almost happened hadn't yet registered. Either that or what had almost happened didn't come as a complete surprise to her. Which made him even more curious why his father would want to abduct this woman.

ED URDAHL COULDN'T believe his luck. He'd picked a street that he knew wouldn't have anyone on it this time of the day. On top of that, the girl had been in her own little world. She hadn't been paying any attention to him as he'd moved up directly behind her.

The plan had been simple. Grab her, toss her into the van that would come speeding up at the perfect time and make a clean, quick getaway so no one would be the wiser.

It should have gone down without any trouble.

He'd been so intent on the woman in front of him, though, that he hadn't heard the man come up behind him until it was too late. Even if someone had intervened, Ed had been pretty sure he could handle it. He'd been a wrestler and boxer growing up. Few men were stupid enough to take him on.

The last thing he'd expected was to be smacked in the back of the head by some do-gooder. What had he been hit with anyway? Something hard and cold. A gun? The blow had knocked him senseless and the next thing he'd known he was on the sidewalk bleeding. As he'd heard the van engine roaring in his direction, he'd fought to keep from blacking out as whoever had blindsided him had gotten away with the blonde.

"What happened?" his brother, Alec, demanded now. He leaned against the van wall in the back, his head hurting like hell. "I thought you had it all worked out."

"How the hell do I know?" He was still bleeding like a stuck pig. "Just get out of here. *Drive!*" he yelled at the driver, Nick, a dock worker he'd used before for less than legal jobs. "Circle the block until I can think of what to do."

Ed caught a whiff of the blonde's perfume and realized he was holding her sweater to his bleeding skull. He took another sniff of it. Nice. He tried to remember exactly what had transpired. It had all happened so fast. "Did you see who hit me?" he asked.

"I saw a man and a woman going down the alley," Alec said. "I thought you said she'd be alone?"

That's what he had thought. It had all been set up in a way that should have come off like clockwork. So where had whoever hit him come from? "So neither of you got a look at the guy?"

Nick cleared his throat. "I thought at first that he was working *with* you."

"Why would you think that?" Ed demanded, his head hurting too much to put up with such stupid remarks. "The son of a bitch coldcocked me with something."

"A gun. It was a gun," Alec said. "I saw the light catch on the metal when he tucked it back into his pants."

"He was carrying a gun?" Ed sat up, his gaze going to Nick. "Is that why you thought he was part of the plan?"

"No, I didn't see the gun," Nick said. "I just assumed he was in on it because of who he was."

Ed pressed the sweet-smelling sweater to his head and tried not to erupt. "Are you going to make me guess? Or are you frigging going to tell me who was he?"

"Jack Durand."

"What?" Ed couldn't believe his ears. What were the chances that Tom Durand's son would show up on this particular street? Unless his father had sent him? That made no sense. *Why pay me if he sent his son?*

"You're sure it was Jack?"

"Swear on my mother's grave," Nick said as he drove in wider circles. "I saw him clear as a bell. He turned in the alley to look back. It was Jack, all right."

"Go back to that alley," Ed ordered. Was this Tom's backup plan in case Ed failed? Or was this all part of Tom's real plan? Either way, it appeared Jack Durand had the girl.

CASSIDY LOOKED AS if she might make a run for it at any moment. That would be a huge mistake on her part.

But Jack could tell that she was now pretty sure she shouldn't be trusting him. He wasn't sure how much longer he could keep her here. She reached for her phone, but he laid a hand on her arm.

"That's the van coming back," he said quietly. At the sound of the engine growing nearer, he signaled her not to make a sound as he pulled her deeper into the darkness of the doorway recess. The van drove slowly up the alley. He'd feared they would come back. That's why he'd been hesitant to move from their hiding place.

Jack held his breath as he watched the blonde, afraid she might do something crazy like decide to take her chances and run. He wouldn't have blamed her. For all she knew, he could have been in on the abduction and was holding her here until the men in the van came back for her.

The driver of the van braked next to the open doorway. The engine sat idling. Jack waited for the sound of a door opening. He'd put the gun into the back waistband of his jeans before he'd grabbed the blonde, thinking the gun might frighten her. As much as he wanted to pull it now, he talked himself out of it.

At least for the moment. He didn't want to get involved in any gunplay—especially with the young woman here. He'd started carrying the gun when he'd worked for his father and had to take the day's proceeds to a bank drop late at night. It was a habit he'd gotten used to even after he'd quit. Probably because of the type of people who worked with his father.

After what seemed like an interminable length of time, the van driver pulled away.

Jack let out the breath he'd been holding. "Come on, I'll see that you get someplace safe where you can call the police," he said and held out his hand.

She hesitated before she took it. They moved through the dark shadows of the alley to the next street. The sky above them had turned a deep silver in the evening light. It was still hot, little air in the tight narrow street.

He realized that wherever Cassidy Hamilton had been headed, she hadn't planned to return until much later—thus the sweater. He wanted to question her, but now wasn't the time.

At the edge of the buildings, Jack peered down the street. He didn't see the van or Ed's green car. But he also didn't think they had gone far. Wouldn't they expect her to call the police? The area would soon be crawling with cop cars. So what would Ed do?

A few blocks from the deserted area where they'd met, they reached a more commercial section. The street was growing busier as people got off work. Restaurants began opening for the evening meal as boutiques and shops closed. Jack spotted a small bar with just enough patrons that he thought they could blend in.

"Let's go in here," he said. "I don't know about you, but I could use a drink. You should be able to make a call from here. Once I know you're safe…"

They took a table at the back away from the television over the bar. He removed his Stetson and put it on the seat next to him. When Cassidy wasn't looking, he removed the .45 from the waistband of his jeans and slid it under the hat.

"What do you want to drink?" he asked as the waitress approached.

"White wine," she said and plucked nervously at the torn corner of her blouse. Other than the torn blouse, she looked fine physically. But emotionally, he wasn't sure how much of a toll this would take on her over the long haul. That was if Ed didn't find her.

"I'll have whiskey," he said, waving the waitress off. He had no idea what he was going to do now. He told himself he just needed a jolt of alcohol. He'd been playing this by ear since seeing his father and Ed at the cemetery.

Now he debated what he was going to do with this woman given the little he knew. The last thing he wanted, though, was to get involved with the police. He was sure Ed and his men had seen him, probably recognized him. Once his father found out that it had been his son who'd saved the blonde...

The waitress put two drinks in front of them and left. He watched the blonde take a sip. She'd said her name was Cassidy Hamilton. She'd also said she didn't know why anyone would want to abduct her off the street, but he suspected that wasn't true.

"So is your old man rich or something?" he asked and took a gulp of the whiskey.

She took a sip of her wine as if stalling, her gaze lowered. He got his first really good look at her. She was a knockout. When she lifted her eyes finally, he thought he might drown in all that blue.

"I only ask because I'm trying to understand why those men were after you." She could be a famous model or even an actress. He didn't follow pop culture, hardly ever watched television and hadn't been to the movies in ages. All he knew was, at the very least, she'd grown up with money. "If you're famous or something, I apologize for not knowing."

CASSIDY'S HAND SHOOK as she put down her drink. She could feel the buzz of the alcohol mixing with the adrenaline still flowing through her bloodstream.

Someone had tried to *abduct* her! She'd grown up

knowing something like this occasionally happened to the children of wealthy people in the public eye. But she'd never really been concerned because she'd grown up in Montana on a large ranch. After she'd left home, she hadn't made a habit of telling her friends who her father was—and not because she feared being abducted.

For years, she'd tried to distance herself from the notoriety that had always surrounded her family. She'd wanted her own life, which wasn't easy when you were an identical twin. She'd never felt like anything was truly uniquely hers. Add to that her infamous family and Cassidy just wanted to be free of what she considered a stigma.

But someone had found her. Not just found her, but had tried to kidnap her. She shuddered at the thought of what those men had planned to do with her.

"Look, I understand if you don't want to tell me," the Texas cowboy said. "It's none of my business. I'll just finish my drink and get on my way."

Cassidy looked at the man across the table from her and felt a rush entirely different from the alcohol or the adrenaline. This man had *saved* her. Gratitude alone would have made her feel close to him. But there was something about him… She'd grown up around good-looking cowboys. But this one was exceptional. His dark hair was long and thick. His blue eyes laced with thick dark lashes. Maybe it was the alcohol amplifying her vision, but Jack Durand was drop-dead gorgeous and she hadn't even noticed until this moment. Wouldn't her friends get a laugh out of that, she thought, forgetting for the moment what had brought them together. She finished her drink, her hand a little steadier.

"Whatever you decide to do, I would suggest you call the police," he was saying. "You aren't safe."

His words brought back the horrible minutes when the large man grabbed her and tried to put that stinking wet cloth in her face. Glancing toward the window to the street, she shivered. "You think they're still looking for me?"

"I'm afraid so."

Her gaze swung back to him. The bar was cool and dark and she felt safe sitting here with this cowboy. While a stranger, he'd risked his life to save her. "I don't know what I would have done if you hadn't come along. I haven't even thanked you."

"No need to thank me. After what you've been through… Whatever the reason, though, I don't think they're going to give up."

"Thank you and please don't leave yet." She was just so relieved he was here with her. What if he hadn't come along when he had? She looked around for the waitress. She was still trembling inside, but the alcohol was helping. She really could use another drink.

He signaled for the waitress and she was grateful when he ordered another round.

"It is strange, though, that someone would be that brazen as to try to grab you in broad daylight," he said.

Cassidy looked away for a moment. "I can't imagine why anyone would try to…" As she turned back and met his gaze, she saw his expression turn skeptical and knew that if she wasn't honest with him, he was going to let her deal with this on her own. Not that she could blame him.

"It probably has more to do with my father," she added quickly.

"Your father? Who's your father?"

"Republican presidential candidate Buckmaster Hamilton."

He blinked. Clearly, he hadn't connected the last name. Hamilton was pretty common so she wasn't surprised he hadn't made the leap. He pursed his lips, letting out a low whistle before he picked up his drink and drained it.

"That definitely puts things in perspective," he said after a moment.

This was why she didn't tell people about her father.

"I would think you'd have secret service watching you," he said.

She shook her head. "They only provide agents for the underage children of candidates after the primaries."

He looked surprised. "Well, I'm sure once you call the police—" The waitress returned with their drinks and took away the empty glasses.

She fiddled with her torn blouse. "I can't go to the police."

Jack seemed both surprised and maybe relieved to hear that. She didn't blame him for not wanting to get involved. After all, he'd hit that man who was trying to abduct her. He was a hero. But that came with police reports to fill out, followed by an investigation. Once the media got involved… She quaked at the thought.

"Why don't you want to go to the police?"

She took a sip of her wine before she said, "Do you have any idea what it's like being the daughter of first a senator and now a presidential candidate who, according to the polls, is headed for the White House?"

"Not a clue."

"I've been in the spotlight for one reason or another from as far back as I can remember." She could feel the alcohol coursing through her blood and felt stronger. She took another sip of her wine and continued. "The rule at our house was always 'don't cause trouble because a scandal will hurt your father's career.' Since I left home to go away to school, I've tried hard to live my own life. But even when I thought people didn't know who I was, I was still in my father's shadow. Buckmaster Hamilton casts a very large shadow."

"This friend you were staying with…"

"More like an acquaintance. But she didn't know who my father was. Or at least I didn't think she did." Cassidy frowned. "Her boyfriend, though… I think he may have known. That's the other thing about being… famous by extension. People are nice to you for the wrong reasons. It's hard to have true friends."

"Where were you headed earlier?" he asked, suddenly intent.

"To meet her and her…boyfriend." Cassidy felt her eyes widen as her heart dropped. "I was set up, wasn't I?"

JACK TRIED NOT to down his entire second drink. Cassidy was the daughter of the future president? What the hell was his father doing trying to abduct her? His father could be stubborn, worked too much, put too much value in making money and was a hard-nosed businessman. But to do something like this? It boggled his mind.

Worse, what was he going to do now? After seeing

that wad of money his old man gave Ed and knowing how his father was about employees who didn't do their jobs to suit him, Jack knew his father wouldn't stop.

Nor would Ed. He'd be more careful next time. He'd be more prepared. But like Jack had learned, you didn't let Tom Durand down or there would be hell to pay.

So how could he walk away now? Cassidy would be a sitting duck. And he didn't want to think about what his father would do when he found out that Jack was involved in fouling his plans.

"Look," he said to Cassidy. "You have no reason to trust me." On the surface, he looked like an urban cowboy today instead of the former rodeo cowboy who'd grown up on a huge ranch outside of Houston. His father had bought the ranch as a tax deduction and given it to him lock, stock and barrel when he turned twenty-one. But the deal had always been that he would take over his father's import/export business at some point.

Once he told his father he had no interest in doing that, that's when it seemed Tom Durand had changed. Now he wondered if he'd ever known his father at all.

Clearly, the last thing he could do was tell Cassidy who he really was or that he thought he knew who was behind her attack—at least until he had proof.

So he stretched the truth. "But if you'll let me, I'll try to keep you safe until we can find out who is behind this and why."

She took a drink of her second glass of wine. He could see from the shine in her eyes that she was feeling the alcohol. His plan hadn't been to get her tipsy, let alone drunk. He'd just needed a drink to calm his nerves and a place where they were safe so he could think what to do next.

"What do you have in mind?" she asked.

He wasn't that surprised that she was willing to trust *him*. She'd already proved she was too trusting given that she'd trust the acquaintance and boyfriend. But what *did* he have in mind? His thoughts raced as he considered how he could keep her safe—and yet find out the truth about his father's involvement.

"We're going to have to hide you out somewhere until I can get to the bottom of this. For starters, who knew you were in Houston besides this so-called friend and her boyfriend?"

"No one."

That surprised him. "Not even your family?"

She shook her head. "They think I'm still in New York with a Frenchman I met while studying abroad."

A Frenchman. Great. "So not even the Frenchman knows?"

Again she shook her head.

"Okay." He studied her. "Also, you're too cute and too blonde and too easy to recognize."

She grinned, taking it as a compliment. "How about if I was a redhead?"

"I'm thinking brunette. I don't know how you feel about cutting your hair…"

Cassidy shrugged. "I've been thinking about cutting it," she said as she pulled a long lank of her blond hair around to consider it. "A brunette, huh? So a disguise?" The idea seemed to appeal to her. He wondered if it would have before her last glass of wine.

Even with the changes he was suggesting, she'd still be adorable, there was no getting around that. She had one of those classic faces, huge blue eyes, a button nose and bow-shaped mouth. She looked so damned innocent that he felt a stab of guilt. He wasn't much better than her pretend friends she'd been staying with. Except that he wouldn't sell her out.

He recalled hearing his father talking about the election and the Hamilton family. Cassidy's mother, Sarah Johnson Hamilton, had returned from the dead about a year ago. Apparently, she'd tried to kill herself more than twenty-three years before by driving into the Yellowstone River. Her body was never found.

Then one day she just showed up—with no memory of the years she'd been gone. He remembered his father saying that her six daughters were now adults. He frowned as he recalled that the two youngest, twin girls, had only been a few months old when they'd lost their mother.

Going by age, that would have been Cassidy, he realized with a start. There was another one like her? He wondered where she was and if she was safe. His father had remarked that he couldn't believe how much that family had been through. Hadn't their stepmother died last year in a car wreck?

"You're sure you don't want to change your mind and go to the police?" he asked, feeling he had to give it one more shot since it was the smart thing to do—even if it would involve him and force him to lie. Whatever differences he and his father had, he wasn't throwing him under a bus until he knew the truth.

"If I go to the police, my name will be in every newspaper and so will my father's. And what is it you think the police can do to protect me? My father would insist I come home so he could hire guards. Or maybe I would get agents watching me 24/7. I wouldn't be able to leave the ranch. And for how long? Until after the election? Or until he was no longer president? No, thanks."

He'd forgotten for a moment that Buckmaster Hamilton was a Montana rancher, a former senator and now Republican candidate for president. Cassidy was one of six sisters. Was that another reason she didn't tell people who she was? He'd thought living under his father's domineering thumb was hard. Imagine what being one of Buckmaster Hamilton's daughters would be like if he was as protective as she said.

But without the cops or the feds, the two of them were on their own. And Jack had no idea what they were up against. All he knew was that he now had the assumed future president's daughter's life in his hands.

CHAPTER THREE

"Sarah, I don't understand." Republican presidential hopeful Buckmaster Hamilton paced the floor, his phone to his ear, his impatience wearing a path in the carpet. "I love you. I thought you were moving into the main house on the ranch. No more hiding, no more lying about how we feel about each other."

"Buck, can't we talk about this when you get home?"

"No, four months ago you went to your house to pack and the next thing I know you tell me you can't move in until after the primaries. Well, the primaries are over. I need you. I can't keep—" He heard the door open behind him. "I have to go." He disconnected and turned to face his campaign manager, who'd come in with a stack of papers, no doubt the latest polls.

"Sarah? Is that who you were talking to?" Jerrod Williston asked in an impatient tone. "Buck—"

"Don't start," he said, holding up both hands. "I'm trying to put my family back together. I know I've been a little distracted."

"You've been more than a little distracted. On top of that, all the media wants to know now is how your love life is going instead of talking about your platform. *You're the Republican presidential candidate.* If you hope to stand a chance in hell of winning this election, you have to start acting like a president instead of a lovesick fool."

"Tell me how you really feel." He waved a hand through the air, afraid Jerrod would only go off again. More and more he was having his doubts about this run for president. Was this his dream anymore? Or was he trying to do this for his father, JD Hamilton? JD had withdrawn from the race because of a woman. Wasn't Jerrod's fear that Buck would do the same thing?

He'd had so much trouble with his family since he'd thrown his hat into the ring last year. But last year there had been no chance of having Sarah. He was still married to Angelina. He had been ready to throw away everything he'd worked for and divorce Angelina before she'd been killed in a car wreck.

Buckmaster felt a wave of guilt. Angelina's death had worked in his favor, but he hated like hell how it happened. Now the only thing keeping him and Sarah apart was this damned election. That was why Sarah was dragging her feet, wasn't it? Unlike Angelina, she'd never wanted to live in the White House.

So he couldn't help questioning if bowing out now wasn't the best thing for them. He needed Sarah. Maybe if he quit he could pull his family back together again. Then his daughters might come around and get closer to their mother.

Sarah was disappointed that the girls never called her. Harper was making an effort, but Cassidy had barely said two words to any of them. Buck had no idea what was going on with his youngest. He hadn't heard from her either.

"You're tired. This campaign has been taxing.

You've had a lot on your mind," Jerrod said. "You just need some rest and then we'll—"

"I need my wife, I need my family."

Jerrod let out an impatient breath as if he'd heard this too many times. "Sarah *isn't* your wife. A wedding right now is the last thing you need. Win this election, then you can throw yourself a wedding on the White House lawn with all your daughters as attendants."

Buck raked a hand through his hair. He'd noticed this morning in the mirror that he was getting grayer. It was no wonder given what he'd gone through in the past year. If it hadn't been his first wife, Sarah, it had been his second wife, Angelina, or one of his six daughters. He was trying to keep his family together *and* run for president. He'd always felt that he owed it to his party, to his country. But right now he felt as if he had nothing left to give.

Jerrod came over to the desk in the room and put down the stack of papers he'd been holding. "You're doing well in the polls. You have this. Try to have a little patience. Even the voting public is on your side. So don't do anything to screw it up. Sarah isn't going anywhere."

He wasn't so sure about that, recalling how Sarah had been ready to marry Russell Murdock not that long ago. Murdock had almost run her over when she'd come stumbling out of the woods last year. Until that moment, she'd had no memory of the hours before— or the past twenty-two years. She knew only that she had jumped from a plane and parachuted into those Montanan woods. After landing in a tree, she'd managed to climb down and walk some distance to the dirt road where Murdock had almost hit her. He'd been her protector and probably still was. Buck didn't blame Sarah for agreeing to marry the man. Russell was apparently nice enough and at the time, Buck had been married to Angelina.

With Angelina dead for almost a year now, there was no reason he and Sarah couldn't be together. Even the media had taken it easy on him when he'd admitted to a woman on the plane—who'd turned out to be a reporter—that he was still in love with his first wife. He'd thought her dead for twenty-two years, so no one could blame him for remarrying. Angelina had supported his political ambition. She'd been determined to put him in the White House. But she hadn't lived to see that happen.

Now there was nothing standing in the way of him and Sarah being together. Nothing but this damned election.

CASSIDY AND JACK found a small market only a half block from the bar and bought what they needed. They'd grabbed a cab outside the store. Fifteen blocks away, the driver let them out at a run-down hotel.

Jack had looked over at her, his expression pained. "We can look for some other place if this is—"

"It's perfect," she said, gazing out at the large brick building. Maybe it was the drinks she'd had, but she felt as if she was a character in a thriller movie. "No one will be looking for me here," she said, thinking how true that was. The memory of the large man who'd grabbed her on the street seemed surreal now. It had happened so fast that it felt more like a nightmare she'd now awakened from. Had it really happened or had she dreamed it?

Wired on adrenaline and alcohol, she had leaped at the idea of a disguise. For so long she'd wanted to be someone different. Now she was getting her chance. It didn't hurt that a handsome Texas cowboy was her sidekick.

Jack chuckled as they got out of the taxi. "I hope you don't regret this."

Her whole life she'd been protected and pampered. She hadn't taken chances. Hadn't experienced any crazy adventures because scandalized behavior would hurt her father.

But now someone had tried to kidnap her—because of who her father was no doubt. She felt as if all bets were off. Had her whole life been heading toward this moment? Or was she deluding herself because she didn't want to face just how dangerous this still was?

Jack paid at the scarred desk and then led her to the old elevator. It cranked and groaned as it climbed to the fourth floor. The hallway they stepped out into needed paint and new carpeting badly. It had an odd smell, one she didn't recognize and didn't want to try to place.

Jack put the old-fashioned key into the lock, turned and pushed open the door to their room. Cassidy hadn't been expecting much, which was good. The hotel room was dark, dingy and sad.

"You sure this is going to work for you?" Jack asked, looking somewhat taken aback by their surroundings.

She laughed. "See why I don't tell anyone who my father is? They start treating me like I'm a princess. I've roughed it camping out in the Crazy Mountains as a kid. I can take one bad hotel room." She stepped in, going straight to the window. After she attempted to open it for what little fresh air there might be, Jack came up behind her and lifted it a few inches. Just the closeness of him sent a shiver of anticipation through her.

Cassidy wondered if he felt it as well and that's why he quickly stepped away. Hot air rushed in but it smelled better.

Turning, she spotted the bags he'd brought up. Digging out the scissors and hair dye, she headed for the bathroom, leaving the door open.

"I saw a used clothing place around the corner," Jack said from the other part of the hotel room. "I'll go get you something else to wear."

"Don't you need to know my size?" she asked, turning in the bathroom doorway, scissors in hand.

He grinned as his gaze took her in. She felt warmth flood her. "I think I have it covered. Keep the door locked. I won't be long."

JACK HURRIED, not wanting to leave Cassidy alone for long. Inside the used-clothing shop, he quickly went to what he believed was her size and sorted through the clothes for something appropriate. Appropriate would be something totally different from what Cassidy had been wearing.

All the time, his mind was racing as to what to do next. They needed somewhere to hide her while he tried to figure out what to do. If his father was as deeply involved in this as he suspected… He had to know the truth. Short of asking him outright, he realized there was only one way he might be able to find out what was going on.

Now, he knew that his father had secrets. It was something he'd suspected, he realized, for a long while.

When he'd worked at the warehouse, he'd discovered a locked drawer in his father's desk. When he'd asked him about it, Tom Durand had said he just kept a little spare cash in it. He'd joked that he better never find it missing or he'd know who had taken it. Even at the time, Jack had questioned why his father would keep spare cash at the office. Tom Durand always carried a couple of grand on him.

Now Jack wanted to know what was really in that locked drawer. Which meant he'd have to go to the warehouse tonight. He knew he had to move quickly. If he was right and one of the men had recognized him, then his father would try to cover up any improprieties.

But what to do with Cassidy? He couldn't leave her at the hotel. It didn't feel safe with her alone. But where?

With several outfits he thought would work for her, he checked out and headed back to the hotel. Before he'd left, he'd put his gun under one of the pillows on the bed. He didn't like walking around Houston with a loaded weapon even though he had a permit to carry it.

When he reached the hotel room, he used his key to open the door. He could hear her moving around in the bathroom and tried to relax. She was safe. At least for the moment.

He'd just placed the bag with his purchases on the bed when she came out of the bathroom. Her brunette hair was cut in a short bob that framed her face. The dark color brought out the tiny trail of freckles that arched over her nose and made her blue eyes look even larger. He stopped short at the sight of her.

"Is it that bad?" she asked in alarm.

He shook his head. "It's that *good*. You look… amazing."

She laughed, clearly relieved. "Isn't it wild?" Rushing toward the bed, she said, "Let's see what you got me to wear." She held up the skirt and peasant blouse that went with it. "Oh, these are great. I can't wait to try them on." With that, she turned and hurried back into the bathroom, closing the door behind her.

He stared after her, surprised by her excitement— and a little worried. The woman was excited about wearing hand-me-down clothing that hadn't even cost him twenty bucks? People reacted differently to fear, he knew, but Cassidy almost seemed to be treating this as if they were on some undercover adventure instead of probably running for their lives.

BUCK REALIZED HIS campaign manager was still speaking.

"What about your girls? Are they on board?"

He thought about his six daughters. He wouldn't exactly say they were on board when it came to his political career. They'd grown up used to politics being discussed at meals, they'd lived through his run for senator and the subsequent years of his being gone to Washington.

But he knew that as supportive as they'd often said they were, none of them wanted this kind of attention. "You don't have to worry about them."

Jerrod eyed him as if reading between the lines. "We need them with you the night of the election. The public will want to see them—and the solidarity."

The election was months away, Buck thought. A lot could happen between now and then.

"You have a big debate coming up," Jerrod continued. "I need you to be on top of this. You can expect questions about Sarah and your relationship. Maybe you should go home and get some rest. We can do a run-through as the date approaches. I want you relaxed, confident and ready to be president. Make sure Sarah understands how important that is."

He nodded, although he wasn't sure telling Sarah would make a whole lot of difference. The woman who'd returned after being presumed dead for twenty-two years looked like the Sarah Johnson Hamilton he'd known, but she didn't act like her. Maybe that Sarah was gone and he was a fool for thinking he could recapture the past and put his family back together. Sarah said she supported him, but if anything, she didn't want to live in the White House. Nor was she here with him now or waiting for him in their house back on the ranch.

"I'll be ready for the debate," he said, picking up his Stetson. The best thing he could do now was to go back to Montana. He needed to find out what was going on with Sarah and see his daughters. He missed them and worried about them all the time even though they were settled into their own lives. Olivia and Bo were each now happily married. Olivia was talking about a second child, Bo was expecting twins, and Kat and Harper were engaged.

Only Ainsley, his oldest, was still single, and his youngest, Cassidy. In truth, he had no idea where either of them was at this moment. Ainsley had taken a job scouting locations in Montana for film companies after dropping out of law school. Cassidy, as far as he knew, was still in New York dating some Frenchman she'd met while in Europe.

After Jerrod dropped him off at the airport, Buckmaster put in a call to his youngest twin. He felt badly he hadn't kept in touch. He'd spent so little time with them. He'd put his political career ahead of his family and was now doing it again.

When Angelina was alive, her driving ambition had been a tornado-like force that had kept him aloft. He'd gotten caught up in her dream of his being president. But Angelina was gone and he had a bad feeling that he should have dropped out before the primaries. Now he would hurt his party and possibly lose the election for the Republicans. He told himself he was just tired. Things would look different tomorrow. Unfortunately, he doubted that.

The call to Cassidy went directly to voice mail. "It's your father. Please give me a call when you have time. I can't remember the last time we talked." He hung up realizing that she hadn't been home in more than a year.

As he boarded the plane—unlike some candidates, he flew commercial since it was what Montana voters expected of him—he told himself he had to convince Sarah to come on the campaign trail with him. With her by his side, he believed he could do anything. But without her, without his family…

As soon as he landed in Bozeman, he called to tell Sarah he was on his way. He just had one thing he had to do first—make a call to the owner of a local jewelry store. The store had been closed for hours, but the owner promised to meet him there.

He had no idea what had happened to the first engagement ring—let alone wedding band—he'd given

Sarah, but if he hoped for a new beginning, it was time to put a ring on her finger.

As SARAH JOHNSON HAMILTON disconnected from Buck's call, she turned to look at the man standing with his back to her. He was dressed in a dated brown suit and tie, which made him look like a second-rate undertaker. Hardly anyone wore suits in Montana unless they were getting married—or buried.

As if feeling her gaze on him, Dr. Ralph Venable turned to look at her. He was in his early seventies, but didn't look his age. A tall, lean man with kind blue eyes, the doctor had unexpectedly shown up at her door back in the spring, something she'd kept secret from everyone.

"Was that Buck on the phone?" he asked now.

"He's landed. We have time." She'd been packing, planning to move in with Buck that night back in early spring, when the doctor had shown up at the old ranch house where she was still staying.

Seeing this man had frightened her, since, while she lived on Hamilton Ranch, she lived some distance from the main house—and everyone else, including her former husband and her six daughters.

"Who are you?" she'd demanded, telling herself that she didn't know the older man who'd appeared at her door without warning. But he knew *her*. And bone-deep, she realized she *did* know him. His name was Dr. Ralph Venable and he was the man who had stolen twenty-two years of her memory. Dr. Venable specialized in brain wiping. Not only had he stolen her memories, he'd also planted false ones.

"You made me forget my life," she had accused,

moving quickly to the kitchen, where she'd grabbed a carving knife and brandished it as he'd followed her. "You stole twenty-two years from me." Her voice had broken with emotion. "I missed seeing my babies grow up. Tell me why I shouldn't kill you."

"Because you need me."

"Who hired you to do that to me?" she had asked, terrified he would say it had been Buck, the father of her children, the man she loved. She hadn't wanted to suspect Buck, but the man who'd found her when she'd literally been dropped back into Montana, Russell Murdock, had been convinced that her husband had been behind the brain wiping. Russell believed that there was something Buck didn't want her to remember. Something so terrible that it had driven her to attempt suicide all those years ago.

"I *saved* your life, Sarah," Dr. Venable had said. "That winter night you drove into the Yellowstone River, your car breaking through the ice, the freezing water washing you downstream? I'm the person you called after that old hermit rescued you. You begged me to help you. The reason you called me was because you knew I was the one person you could turn to. The one person who understood and would help you."

"It makes no sense why I would try to kill myself. I *loved* Buck. I *loved* my children. I *loved* my life. What would make me agree to leave them for any reason?"

"You had your reasons, though misguided, and that is why I sent someone to pick you up and bring you to my clinic in White Sulphur Springs, a half day away from Hamilton Ranch. You and I are *friends*, Sarah. We've been friends for years—long before you met Buck."

"How is that possible? I don't remember any of it!" she'd cried. "You *stole* that from me."

"Only because you begged me to. You couldn't live with the memories. That's why you tried to kill yourself."

She hadn't believed him. She'd snatched up her cell phone, but his calm, reassuring voice had stopped her.

"Who are you going to call, Sarah? The sheriff? Your former husband? One of your daughters?"

She had looked down at the cell screen, her fingers momentarily frozen over the keys. Russell. He'd said to call him. He'd known Dr. Venable would come for her again. He'd known that Dr. Venable wasn't finished with her.

"Even Russell can't help you like I can," the doctor had said, surprising her that he knew about Russell. Knew that was who she was thinking of calling.

"I can clear this all up for you, Sarah. You want answers? I can provide them. I am the only one who can. Put down the phone. I've come back to help you—just as we planned."

She had looked from the phone to his face. Even as she'd tried to deny what he'd been saying, she'd known it was true. She *had* called him that night. She *had* trusted him. Even if she didn't remember, there was one thing she had known. Dr. Venable had all the answers she desperately needed.

That day last spring, she'd asked, "You know why I tried to kill myself?" The knife had wavered in her hand, the cell phone forgotten.

He'd nodded. "I know everything from the first time you and I met all those years ago."

She had begun to cry. He'd stepped to her, taking

the knife, then the cell phone and putting them aside before he'd taken her in his arms like a kindly father comforting her.

"It's all right, Sarah. You're going to be all right now. I'm here. I'm going to help you. It's time."

Now, months later, she still felt afraid and angry. She still wanted to kill him. But they both knew it was true. He *was* her only hope if she ever wanted to get the memories back. She needed answers before she could be with Buck as his wife again. Dr. Venable kept telling her they had to return her memories slowly. She wasn't sure she believed him, but she'd had little choice.

"I can't keep living like this," she said now. "I have to know what it is you're hiding from me before I can commit to Buck. I don't care if that's your plan or not." She dug her heels in. Just the fact that Dr. Venable was determined that she get back together with her husband made her resist.

He didn't just scare her. It was clear from the moment she found him standing on her doorstep that he wasn't just here for her. Whatever his ulterior motive was, it had something to do with her—and Buck.

Dr. Venable opened the small black bag he carried. He could have passed for a country doctor fifty years ago. He took out a tiny dark blue velvet bag. "I promise you that by the time he arrives, it will all be very clear."

Her mouth went dry. She stared at the bag in his fingers, suddenly terrified. "What are you going to do to me?"

"I'm going to help you remember everything you need to know so your husband will be the next president and you will be by his side. Right where you are destined to be."

Destined to be? Something in those words… Sarah felt her heart shudder. Suddenly, she wasn't sure she wanted to remember.

WHILE CASSIDY CHANGED into the clothing he'd bought her, Jack stepped out into the hall and called his father.

Tom Durand answered on the second ring. "Son, I didn't expect to hear from you."

Jack took a breath and let it out slowly. Had Ed recognized him earlier? Had he told his employer what had happened? "I didn't like the way we left things the last time we talked," he said, feeling his way cautiously.

"Neither did I. So I'm glad you called."

"How's LA?"

"Crowded compared to Texas."

Jack could hear something in the background. "Are you on a plane?"

His father laughed. "A boat. Headed for Catalina Island. I have a meeting out there."

It was several hours earlier on the West Coast, so not evening there quite yet. But still, there was no way his father could have gotten from Texas to California unless he'd jumped right on his private jet after Jack had seen him.

"How's the weather?"

"It's beautiful. Amazing sunset." Tom Durand sounded downright cheerful. Jack was beginning to wonder if he had misread what happened at the cemetery. Maybe the money had nothing to do with the abduction of Cassidy Hamilton. Maybe his father was in California. Maybe he was on a boat to Catalina Island. Otherwise—

"Jack, if you're at the ranch, could you do me a favor?"

He felt the hair rise on the back of his neck. "Sorry, I'm in town. Had to run a few errands. Is it something I can do when I get back there?"

"No, it can wait." The sound of the boat motor seemed to be getting louder. Or was it an automobile motor and the sound in the background wasn't waves but actually traffic on the highway? "I think I'm going to lose you. We'll talk later. I'm glad you called."

"Me, too." He disconnected, more confused than ever. His father had sounded too cheerful. Also, he couldn't shake the feeling that his father had only asked if he was at the ranch because he wanted to know where Jack was.

He was just putting his phone away when the hotel room door opened and Cassidy stuck her head out.

"I thought I heard you out here," she said, her expression tensing when she saw that he'd been on the phone.

"I had to cancel a dinner engagement I had."

"I'm sorry."

"No," he quickly assured her. "It wasn't anything important." Stepping back into the hotel room, he closed the door, winging his story as he went and hoping she bought it. "I was just verifying something. I saw a logo on one of the men in the van's jacket sleeve. It's a local warehouse company. It might be a place to start."

She raised a brow in admiration he didn't deserve. "Nice job. What company?"

"T.D. Enterprises Inc." He saw from her expression that she'd never heard of it. "You look nothing like Cassidy Hamilton," he said, glad to be able to change the subject. He'd picked up a pair of dark-framed glasses for her with clear glass lenses. The clothes, the hair, the glasses. The change was truly remarkable. No one would recognize her as the perky blonde she'd been hours ago.

Cassidy did a twirl, then smiling, asked, "So what's our next move?"

Our next move? "I'm not sure you should go with me for this part," he said, but she was already shaking her head before he finished.

"Like you said, I look nothing like Cassidy. So whatever you're planning to do, I'm going with you."

That was a bad idea on so many levels that Jack was at a loss for words. First off, they would be going to his father's business. He didn't want Cassidy knowing yet who he was or that his father might be behind this. Add to that the danger. They could be caught. They could even run into Ed.

"I'm going with you," she said, standing her ground. "I'm the one who got you into this. So stop trying to think of reasons I shouldn't." She looked around the dingy hotel room and hugged herself. She was still scared and didn't want to be left alone here. He couldn't blame her.

And it was true. She didn't look like the cute blonde Ed had tried to abduct earlier. Since he had a key to the facility, the two of them could waltz into his father's offices without being questioned should the night guard catch them. Also, he could tell by her determined expression that she wasn't going to sit tight and wait for him to figure this out.

If he hoped to help her, he couldn't keep her locked up in this hotel room. Which meant he had no choice but to take her to T.D. Enterprises Inc. with him later tonight.

But first he had to retrieve his truck. If Ed had found it, then Jack was pretty sure he'd be waiting for him. It was why they'd taken a taxi earlier. He couldn't leave the truck there overnight, though. Also, it was the best vehicle to take to the office. Which meant he was going to have to risk it.

CHAPTER FOUR

CASSIDY LICKED GUACAMOLE off her fingertips as she studied the man sitting across from her. Jack had taken her to a small Mexican restaurant in a funky neighborhood that went well with the clothing he'd bought her. She felt downright Bohemian. Her stomach had been growling by the time the waitress slid a huge plate of enchiladas, chiles rellenos, and beans and rice in front of her.

Earlier, he'd left her at the hotel, but only long enough to get his vehicle. He'd returned with a ranch truck. At first she'd thought he'd stolen it.

"I live on a ranch outside of Houston," he'd told her. "I have use of the vehicles."

"So what do you know about this company, T.D. Enterprises Inc.?" she now asked between bites.

"I gather it's an import/export business."

"What does that mean?"

"They buy and sell based on surplus, bringing in what Americans want and sending out what other countries want from us." He shrugged.

"Hmm," she said thoughtfully. "What would someone in the import/export business want with me?"

He shook his head.

She took another bite. Accidentally catching her reflection in a mirror across the room, she was momentarily startled.

"What?" Jack asked, sounding worried as he glanced over his shoulder.

"I just can't get over how I look. I'm shocked when I see my reflection, but not in a bad way. I think I look more…interesting." She touched her short hair, wondering why she'd never cut it. She and her twin, Harper, had had the same exact hairstyle since they were kids—long straight blond hair. "I like the clothes, too. I should shop flea markets more often."

He laughed at that. "You'd look good in anything, even rags."

She smiled at the compliment. Jack, however, seemed embarrassed, as if afraid it hadn't come out the way he'd meant it. As she studied him, she realized something. "You know everything about me, but I don't know anything about you."

"There isn't much to tell." He seemed to concentrate on the food on his plate, as if embarrassed to have the topic turned on him. "I'm an only child."

"I can't imagine how wonderful that would be," she said, only half joking. "Don't get me wrong, I love my sisters, but it's hard being one of the youngest and having five sisters bossing you around."

"It must have been fun growing up, though," he said as if truly interested. "You grew up on a ranch?"

Nodding, she said, "It *was* fun. We rode horses, swam in the creek, camped up in the mountains. The Crazies, at least that's what people call the Crazy Mountains, are right out our back door. But there were drawbacks, too. I'm sure you've read in the papers about my mother, who supposedly died when I was just a few months old. She returned over a year ago after being *dead* for twenty-two years." Cassidy shook her head, realizing that he'd turned the conversation back on her. "I bet your family is completely normal, right?"

He nodded. "Boringly normal. I was raised on a ranch, where I tried to ride any animal that would hold still long enough."

"You rodeoed?" she asked. He had the look of a bronc rider.

Jack seemed to relax as he grinned and nodded. "There wasn't a bucking horse on the circuit that didn't leave me in the dust. I realized finally that I wasn't born to rodeo. About then my father bought a ranch and I began to run it. It was my twenty-first birthday present. Don't look so impressed. It was a tax write-off for him."

"Still, nice present," she said. "So what do your parents do?"

"My father is a businessman. My mother was a homemaker."

"Was?"

"She died. A car accident."

"Oh, I'm so sorry."

"I miss her." He grew silent. "It's been a few years."

She could see that the years hadn't lessened the pain. She picked at her food.

"My oldest sister, Ainsley, pretty much raised us girls," she said into the silence that followed. "Dad was always involved in politics. When he became a senator, he was gone a lot."

"But you had a stepmother?"

"Angelina, the ice queen."

Jack laughed and she laughed with him. "I take it you didn't get along?"

"She ignored us, we ignored her. The only time we had to deal with her was when we got into trouble." She mugged a face. "Then we'd have to hear about how we were ruining our father's career with our selfish behavior," she said in a stern voice.

"What kind of trouble did you get into?" he asked.

"Kid stuff. You know, caught with some young neighbor boy in the barn or getting busted at a local underage kegger or taking one of the ranch vehicles without permission and ending up in a ditch on the way home. I remember once when she caught me trying to ride one of the wild horses."

"Seriously? You tried to ride a bucking horse?"

"You did the same thing."

He nodded. "But you're…"

"Female? You noticed." She grinned at him and realized she was flirting about the same time he did. Instantly, he turned back to his food.

Cassidy took a few bites of her meal. She'd been having fun a few minutes ago, enjoying Jack's company. For a while she'd forgotten why they were here and what was at stake and it had felt good.

But somewhere beyond this Mexican restaurant with its Latin music and wonderful smells were men who might at this moment be looking for her. She pushed her plate away.

"So how do we get into the offices at T.D. Enterprises Inc.?" she asked.

JACK GREW SERIOUS AGAIN as well. He couldn't remember the last time he'd had this much fun on a date. But this wasn't a *date*. He was Jack Durand, the son of a man who as far as he could tell had tried to abduct the daughter of the future president. If Cassidy even knew who he was or why he'd just happened to be around to help her...

He couldn't let himself think about that. Or what would happen if his father was really behind this. Instead, he concentrated on her question. He couldn't simply admit to using his key to get into the warehouse tonight. "I know someone who knows a guy who works out there who owes him a favor. He's going to leave a key for me at the back entrance."

"Wow, the guy must owe him a huge favor," she said.

"Houston is a small town when you lived here all of your life," he said and she nodded, but still seemed a little dubious. He sighed. "Also, I told him a little white lie about having worked there for a short period of time and that I needed to get my personnel file. I told him my boss was an ass and I was trying to get into a graduate program and I needed to make sure that personnel file didn't turn up."

"Is any of that true?"

"I had to think fast on my feet."

She smiled. "Clearly, you're good at that, otherwise who knows where I would be right now."

He felt a healthy jab of guilt. She was looking at him as if he was some kind of hero. He told himself it would be easier just to come clean and tell her who he was. Who his father was. But first he had to be sure that what he'd seen at the cemetery was exactly what he thought it was.

He needed her to trust him a little longer and then

he would tell her everything. He couldn't do anything until he knew if his father was involved.

Jack watched her drawing circles in the condensation on her iced-tea glass. From her expression, she was either reliving what had happened earlier on the street or having second thoughts. Was she suspicious of him and his explanations?

"Are you worried about us getting caught, because if you are, Cassidy—"

"No, and maybe you should call me something other than my real name."

He hadn't thought of that. "What would you suggest?"

She shrugged. "My sisters used to call me Beany."

"Beany?"

"They had this silly little rhyme that went with it." She looked embarrassed. "It was cute at the time."

"Beany it is."

Cassidy smiled that big, breathtaking smile of hers and he felt his heart do a few loop-de-loops before he told it to knock it off. He needed to keep both feet on the ground given that he was risking not only his own life, but also hers.

"You don't have to worry about me tonight," she said as if sensing his hesitation. "I won't get in the way. I might even be of some help."

Jack doubted that. He wasn't even sure exactly what he was looking for. His father had paid Ed in cash, met him in an out-of-the-way place where there would be no random video camera footage of their exchange and even set up his own alibi, putting him in another state. So why would he leave any evidence of this transaction in his office?

No reason at all.

Still, Jack had to look. He'd always thought his father was a workaholic. Now he realized he could be a criminal. The thought turned his stomach. What would he do if he found out that it was true?

His chest ached, heart racing with dread. What were they about to find out? He thought of that locked drawer that he'd been curious about for a very long time.

SARAH STARED AT the tiny dark blue velvet bag as Dr. Venable opened it and turned the contents out on the table. A small gold pendulum plinked down followed by a thin coil of gold chain.

She felt her stomach turn at the sight of it and tried to still her trepidation at the thought of what might be hidden in her memory. Since Dr. Venable had shown up at her door, he'd kept promising that he would help her remember. But he'd put her off time and time again, saying they had to take this slowly. Today he'd promised that he would provide her with what she needed before Buck got home—only because she'd dug her heels in.

She had to know why she'd tried to kill herself all those years ago. She had to know the truth. Bracing herself, she would face whatever memories were locked away. She couldn't keep putting Buck off. Just as she couldn't let Dr. Venable keep giving her the runaround.

"I have some photographs I'd like you to look at first," Dr. Venable said as he motioned Sarah into a chair at the table. He sat across from her and waited.

As she took a chair, he pushed half a dozen snapshots across the table to her. "Is this necessary?" she

demanded. The last thing she wanted to do was look
at the photographs he'd shown her once before—right
after he'd shown up at her door.

Her patience had run out. He still hadn't helped her
remember her past. And yet she'd kept him a secret
just as he'd asked—because of his promise to help her.

More and more she thought about exposing the
man. She couldn't tell Buck, but there was one person she trusted to help her whom she would call if the
doctor didn't do what he'd promised. And soon. She
would call the man who'd found her when she'd literally been dumped off near an isolated road outside of
town—retired rancher Russell Murdock.

Over the months she'd been home, she'd grown to
not just trust Russell, but also to love him. That was
why she'd agreed to marry him when it looked as if
Buck would never be free. With the death of Buck's
wife, though, she'd had to break her engagement, telling herself she belonged with Buck, the father of her
children.

Looking up now, she saw that Dr. Venable was
studying her intently. "I promise that today you will
have answers," he said as if reading her mind—or accepting that she wasn't going to wait much longer.

"Now, please," he said. "Look at these."

Sarah took the photographs he handed her and
thumbed through them. "I don't know any of these
people. I told you that before." She started to hand
them back.

"Look at them again."

She did, more slowly this time. There was one
woman in the photographs and half a dozen men. None
of them looked familiar. They all looked young and

eager and maybe a little too bright eyed. She had no idea who they were, but something about them gave her an uneasy feeling.

"Does the woman look familiar?" he asked.

Sarah looked at the redhead in one of the shots. "She has a slight resemblance to me, is that what you mean?" Her hair was dyed an awful red color. With a small jolt of memory, she realized that she'd seen a photo similar to this some time ago, but couldn't remember when or who had shown it to her. How odd that she couldn't remember something that had to have happened since she'd returned.

She frowned, the beginning of one of her headaches starting. Pushing the photos away, she rubbed her temples. "You're giving me a headache."

He nodded. "Let me take care of it." He removed the tie he'd been wearing and tossed it aside as he picked up the small golden pendulum on the slim gold chain. She felt her eyes widen, a sliver of fear piercing her skin, making her shiver as if she had reason to be fearful.

"It's all right, Sarah. You want answers. I can give them to you. Trust me."

She wanted answers, but she didn't think she should trust this man. All her instincts told her that once he gave her back her memory, she needed to get as far away from him as possible.

"I want you to relax. I can make you feel better." He began to move the pendulum back and forth, back and forth. The shine of the gold caught the light. His voice was low and soothing. Within moments, she was transfixed. Somewhere in her subconscious, she knew this was not the first time Dr. Venable had hypnotized her.

"Listen to my voice, Sarah. I am going to help you

remember everything. You do want to remember the past, don't you? You want to go back to where it all began. You want to remember that strong, intelligent, capable woman who could conquer the world. You *are* that woman. There isn't anything you can't do. You are a leader. Within you are all of the answers. Within you is a bright, beautiful tomorrow. I'm going to take you back. Back to another time. Back when you went by the name Red."

"YOU'RE PUTTING THE ranch up for sale?" Destry Grant West sounded as if she couldn't believe what she was hearing. "Dad, why? I know you haven't been happy since…"

Russell Murdock could see that his daughter didn't even want to say Sarah's name. "Since Sarah broke our engagement?"

Destry let out a breath of obvious frustration. "I'm sorry that you're hurt, but, Dad, she was all wrong for you. Surely, you realize that now."

He didn't want to get into this with his daughter. Destry had forgotten no doubt what it was like to be so in love with one person that no one else would ever do.

"You understand then why I want to sell the ranch and move away," he said. "Not too far. I have to be able to see my grandchildren."

She nodded, her smile sad. It was clear that she worried about him. Her fear, though, was that Sarah wouldn't remarry Buckmaster Hamilton. His was just the opposite.

He hoped that someday Destry would understand that Sarah was in danger as long as she was around Buckmaster. It was why he had to get her away from him for good. Why he still couldn't leave her. It was all too complicated to explain to his daughter, but still he tried.

"I know how you feel about Sarah, but a quack doctor stole her memories, replacing them with ones that terrify her."

"Dad, you don't really believe—"

"I know it for a fact. At first I was as skeptical as you that a brain could be wiped clean of memories or that false ones could be planted, but it's true. It's modern science. I believe that Sarah's husband did something so horrible that he had this doctor remove the memories and take her away from the past twenty-two years."

Destry was looking at him with a mixture of love and pity.

"I know you must think I am the most gullible man in the world…" He smiled and nodded, knowing that was exactly what she thought. "But Sheriff Curry was able to track down the doctor—or at least where he was—and verify that he was experimenting with brain wiping."

"Dad—"

"I'm the only person she can trust." His voice broke and he saw that he wasn't making any headway with his daughter. He looked to her like a man blinded by love for the wrong woman.

"She broke your heart when she gave you back the diamond engagement ring," Destry said kindly, but firmly. "She chose Buckmaster. You have to let her go."

He nodded. He was wasting his breath. "Which is why I have to sell the ranch. You and Rylan don't need the property, so I've put it on the market." He didn't add that he was planning to use the money from the sale to relocate—with Sarah.

He also didn't tell his daughter that the quack doctor, Dr. Ralph Venable, was back in the States. All his instincts told him that the doctor would be contacting Sarah—if he hadn't already.

She was going to need him—and soon. She'd been having flashbacks of memory that scared her when she was with him. And now Buckmaster had won the primaries. He had the Republican nomination.

The only fly in the ointment would be if Sarah's memory came back and she knew the truth about what had happened all those years ago—and did something... crazy.

THE RING WAS CONSERVATIVE, the diamond not too large, the setting classic and tasteful. Buck held it up to the light. The owner of the jewelry store seemed nervous. He kept watching the door as if he expected photographers to show up any minute.

"I'll take this one. I'll need it sized." Sarah's hands were small. "She wears a six." At least she used to. Surely, disappearing for twenty-two years wouldn't have changed her ring size.

"It will only take a few minutes," the owner said and hurried to the back.

Buck walked around the jewelry store. This had been impulsive. Now he wondered if Sarah would be upset with him. He couldn't imagine why. But then he couldn't imagine why she hadn't moved in with him already.

Except that she must feel that he'd been stringing her along for the past year and a half, first because he was married and even after Angelina's death, keeping her living on the ranch—but insisting she move into he main house only recently—and all because of his presidential campaign.

But what choice had he had under the circumstances, he thought with a curse. He wasn't the one who'd left, the one who'd driven into the river in the middle of winter trying to kill himself. He wasn't the one who, failing that, had taken off for twenty-two years, leaving behind six daughters. Nor had Sarah gone alone. He thought about the doctor she'd spent those years with, an older man, a man who apparently dealt in making memories disappear. And planting false ones.

Buck shook his head. At times he knew he hadn't forgiven Sarah for what she'd done. Even when he told himself that she might have been suffering from post-partum depression, that the crackpot doctor was to blame for Sarah not being able to remember the years she'd been gone, that he himself had to take some of the blame, it didn't help.

He feared he didn't know this Sarah. That fear was like a small hard stone that had settled in his belly. Usually, it didn't bother him, but sometimes…

Like when he crossed paths with Sheriff Curry, who had his own theories about Sarah. Curry thought Buck might have reason to fear for his life. The sheriff thought Sarah had returned home to harm either his campaign or him. Maybe even to possibly kill him once he was president.

"Your ring is ready," the jeweler said. He was all smiles, as if he couldn't wait to brag that he'd sold a diamond engagement ring to a future president.

Buck realized his mistake. He should have had one of his staff handle this. Now this would be all over the news before morning.

"Thank you," he said and quickly left. He still had miles to go before he saw Sarah. Too much time to second-guess what he'd done or what he planned to do.

Buck used his hands-free phone to place a call to Ainsley, his oldest. He would tell her about the engagement, ask her opinion. He depended on her for advice. Her phone went straight to voice mail.

He started to call Olivia, but knew she was busy with the baby. Bo was pregnant with twins and hadn't been feeling well. Harper had gone out of town with Brody. Kat might be around. But she wasn't a good one to ask advice from. She didn't have her sister Ainsley's diplomacy. And right now he didn't need an analytical discussion of the pros and cons.

All of his girls were busy living their own lives. He thought of Cassidy and had a strange feeling of foreboding as he tapped in her cell phone number. He couldn't remember the last time he'd talked to her. Worse, he had no idea even where she was.

The foreboding feeling was so strong that it scared him. He just needed to hear her voice, make sure she was all right. Her phone rang three times before her voice-mail message answered.

"YOUR NEW FRIEND AGAIN?" Jack asked as he drove and watched Cassidy check her phone out of the corner of his eye.

She shook her head. "It's my father."

Earlier the new friend who'd betrayed her had called.

Jack had been right. Cassidy had been on her way to meet said new friend when she was almost abducted.

The friend had left a message. "Hey, where are you? We're waiting, but getting really worried. Call me."

"Do you think it's possible she and her boyfriend weren't in on it?" Cassidy had asked hopefully. "She says they're worried. Maybe I should—"

"No, they want you to call because they need to know where you are," he said. "Believe me, your friend and her boyfriend were in on it. Sorry."

She nodded. "I guess I was just hoping it wasn't true, you know?"

He did know. Just as he was hoping that his father wasn't in on this either.

"You might want to turn your phone off or at least put it on vibrate." He didn't think anyone was tracking her via her cell phone. Not yet anyway.

She complied, her expression puzzled.

"Is it unusual for your father to call you?" he asked, guessing at what might be bothering her.

"I can't remember the last time he called before today." She looked up at him. "Odd, don't you think that he should pick now to call?"

Jack did. He wondered if whoever was behind her abduction had jumped the gun and sent the candidate a kidnapping demand. Until that moment, he hadn't really considered that this might be about money.

But it had to be about money. He couldn't imagine what other demand his father might make, but then again, if Tom Durand was behind this, he never really knew his father.

Ahead, he could see T.D. Enterprises Inc.'s main building. He pulled the pickup over to the curb.

Cassidy sat looking out into the darkness of the warehouse district. "This is where we're going?"

Jack felt jumpy, nerves like live wires under his skin. He feared what they were going to find. Worse, he felt as if he were getting Cassidy even deeper into this mess. Not to mention the lies he was telling by omission. When she found out... He couldn't worry about that now. "The office is on the top floor. Are you sure you're up for this?"

She nodded, her voice breaking when she spoke. "I'm good." She wiped her hands on her skirt as if like his, they were sweating. That she was trying to act unafraid made him like her even more.

But as he climbed out, he couldn't help but worry. This could go so badly. As they walked through the dark toward the hulking building, though, he wondered if this wasn't merely a wild-goose chase. His father was too smart to leave anything for him to find. But then again, if his father really was on Catalina Island in the Pacific, he might not know that things had gone wrong yet. Ed might have put off calling him.

Also, if his father really was miles away, he hadn't been able to come back here and hide anything he might have forgotten. There was a chance that Tom Durand thought he had nothing to worry about when he'd left for LA.

All it required at the back door of the facility was a sleight of hand in the dark. Cassidy hadn't seemed to be paying that much attention anyway as he palmed his key and pretended to pick it up from a ledge near the door.

She was looking up at the fifth floor. He followed

her gaze. A light was on—one they hadn't been able to see from the street.

Was it possible his father had lied about being on a boat on his way to Catalina Island? He didn't know why that surprised him—if true—since being a liar could be the least of his father's deceit.

CHAPTER FIVE

CASSIDY FOLLOWED JACK into the huge old building. For a while, this had seemed a game. The new haircut, the clothes, the disguise, being with this Texas cowboy. Now, though, it felt way too real. She'd done her best to forget about what had almost happened to her earlier on the street.

But the memory was still there, ambushing her when she least expected it. Like right now. She suddenly felt vulnerable. What was she doing here with a man whom, until a few hours ago, she'd never laid eyes on before?

She couldn't help questioning herself as their footfalls echoed through the emptiness of what appeared to be a warehouse. She'd always been too trusting. She hugged herself as their footfalls echoed through the hulking building.

There were huge containers and wooden crates everywhere. Only dim after-hours lights lit their way. They wound through them to a door marked STAIRS. The stairwell had even less light and a funky old-building smell.

"You're sure there's no one here?" she asked in a whisper as she heard something clank overhead.

"We're about to find out. But I think it's probably just old plumbing."

Old plumbing? Wondering what she'd gotten herself into, she followed him up the stairs to the fifth floor, where he pushed open the door cautiously and peered around it. Her heart in her throat, she listened and heard nothing.

"Come on." Jack stepped into the empty hallway and she followed. All the doors were closed except for one at the far end of the hall where the light was on. That door was partially open, a few inches of light spilling out into the hallway.

Cassidy grabbed Jack's hand, stopping him. "There's someone in there."

He shook his head and motioned for her to follow quietly.

She hadn't realized that she'd been holding her breath until they reached the office to find it empty. The light apparently had been left on by accident. Either that or the person *was* in the building and would be returning soon.

JACK MOVED QUICKLY to his father's desk. He was about to open one of the drawers when he spotted the plaque sitting on the desk with his father's name printed on it. There was also a photo of him and his father from a fishing trip they'd taken years ago.

He glanced at Cassidy. She'd come part way into the room and now stood looking around nervously. He quickly turned the plaque and photo facedown and began opening the drawers.

The top drawer had nothing interesting in it. Nor did several of the other drawers. His father fortunately was very organized, so it made the search easier. When he got to the bottom drawer, he found it locked—just as he remembered.

"How did you know there wasn't anyone here?" Cassidy asked. She'd moved over to a wall of photographs. He felt his pulse jump in concern until he realized they were all snapshots of his father with dignitaries, politicians and even one with the latest president.

"No cars outside. Nor did I see anyone moving around up here." He opened the middle drawer, hoping to find the key. No such luck. "I could have been wrong, though." He shrugged when she turned to look at him.

"Find anything?"

"The bottom drawer is locked. I'm going to have to break the lock."

She raised a brow at that.

He had hoped to get in and out quickly and not leave any evidence that he'd been here. Reconciled, he quickly stepped to the door and closed it. His father had hired a security firm that checked the building several times during the night. They came by at midnight and 3:00 a.m. Jack glanced at his watch. It was only a little after eleven.

Back at the desk, he took his father's letter opener and began to pry at the lock. Cassidy, he noticed, had moved to another wall of photos. For a moment, Jack worried that his father might have a snapshot of him. But apparently he didn't have to worry.

The lock finally gave and he pulled open the drawer, surprised to find it held only one item—a large metal box. He took it out, a little taken aback by how light it was. If his father kept a little spare money in here, it wasn't much. Something inside it gave a metallic rattle. Like the drawer, the box was locked.

"Did you hear that?" Cassidy said, suddenly next to him.

He hadn't heard anything but the noise he'd been making himself. He listened for a moment. This time it definitely wasn't the old plumbing. He knew the sound of the old freight elevator only too well. It banged and clanked and whined. Which meant someone had pressed the button on the ground floor and was now on his way up.

Jack tried to gauge if they had time to make a run for it. Unfortunately, the stairwell was at the opposite end of the hall. He couldn't take the chance.

He quickly closed the drawer with the broken lock. With luck, whoever it was wouldn't notice—assuming this office was where they were headed. It hit him that if his father had been lying about where he was, he would be the one coming up here right now.

The elevator came to a noisy stop, the doors groaning open. An instant later, Jack heard the sound of heavy footfalls headed in their direction.

SARAH OPENED HER eyes and stretched, surprised to find herself lying on the couch. Her body ached as if she'd been curled up in the fetal position for a very long time.

"How do you feel?" Dr. Venable's voice was soft and soothing. He had put the pendulum away. She had the feeling that time had passed, but she couldn't remember it passing.

She nodded, not wanting to speak, just wanting to stretch and breathe. Her headache was gone and she was thankful for that. Remembering it, though, she recalled that he had promised to restore her memory. She sat up abruptly.

"Easy," he said. "You might feel a little dizzy."

She searched her memory. She couldn't even remember how she'd gotten from a chair at the table to this couch.

"You are going to give yourself a headache if you try to remember everything at once. Take it slow. Start here." He handed her the photographs again.

"I already told you. I don't know those people." At his insistence, she took the snapshots again. She knew the headache was only an instant away if she kept trying so hard to remember even the simplest things. She closed her eyes for a moment.

When she opened them, she glanced down at the top photo and felt shock ricochet through her.

It was a candid shot of a handsome young man. His name came to her in an instant. Joe Landon. She felt her heart do a bump against her ribs. Her mouth went dry and she couldn't speak. The memories swept over her. Tangled sheets, bodies damp with sweat, skin dimpling as a breeze stirred the curtains and washed over their nakedness.

The memories brought goose bumps that raced over her as she recalled the feel of her long-lost lover's warm flesh against hers.

"Joe," she said after a moment and her eyes filled with tears.

"Yes," Dr. Venable said and smiled.

"Is he…?"

"Alive? Yes. He is most anxious to see you," he added, sounding pleased that whatever he'd done to her, she now remembered.

She looked up at him, shock rocking the already cracked foundation of her life. Earlier she would have sworn that she didn't know these people, had never seen them before.

Now she looked at the other photographs. With a start, she realized she recognized all of the people in the shots. The most terrifying was when she recognized herself. She was the woman with the dyed red hair, she was— Dropping the photos in her lap, she hugged herself against the horrible truth. "I'm Red. I *was* a member of The Prophecy. I was…"

"The leader. You still can be."

She shook her head and stumbled to her feet. It all came back to her. She'd been part of the anarchist group back in college that had led to the death of innocent people. What was even more shocking was that she had believed in what they'd hoped to accomplish. *She'd* come up with the plan. How was that possible?

"You were the leader. You and Joe. It's true."

She took a few steps away from him, hugging herself and shaking her head. Her skin felt clammy and cold. Her head whirled. She felt weak and sick to her stomach. But she remembered the names they'd used instead of their real names. Dr. Venable had been Doc. She'd been Red. Joe… Joe had been Achilles, the strongest and most fearless warrior in the Greek war against the Trojans.

A more current memory slammed into her thoughts. "John Carter and Warren Dodge tried to kill my daughter Kat!"

Doc looked sorrowful, but nodded. "Your daughter had to be stopped. She was getting too close. As it was, Joe had to scramble to protect you when they were caught. Sarah, you are still Red. You are still their leader. The Prophecy is depending on you."

"No." She turned to face him. *"No."*

"You owe the others. They have sacrificed for you. They got Virginia Handley to confess to being Red to save you."

"No." She took a step back. She wanted to run but there was nowhere to go. She was trapped because now she knew that all of it was true. The nightmares, the memories of a powerful automatic weapon bucking in her hands, the taste of vodka on her lips, that feeling of being so powerful that she believed she could conquer the world. "Why would Virginia do that?"

"You remember Virginia. She lived on your floor at college. She would have done anything back then to be in The Prophecy. She's the one who took all of these photographs. But she was wrong for us. When we found her again after all these years, she jumped at the chance to protect you. Also, she is dying of cancer. By the time her trial date comes up, she'll be gone."

Sarah stumbled to a chair and sat down hard. With her head in her hands, she said, "John is dead and Warren…"

"He will gladly go to prison. Just as Wally McGill and Mason Green have served their time like a badge of honor. We swore an oath all those years ago to give our lives to the cause. No one has broken that oath." There was a slight hesitation in his voice. "Except you."

"Even after all these years?" she cried, thinking these people must be crazy fanatics and that she was once one of them.

"Of course, after all these years. The Prophecy has been working in other parts of the world, waiting to do something big here in the States. That's why I'm here. It's time to finish what we started all those years ago."

While she had no idea what that was, she knew enough to fear it. She raised her head to look at him. He hadn't lied. He *knew* her. She could see it in his eyes. It was almost as if he could read her mind, know what she was going to do even before she did. He knew about Russell and that she'd been ready to confide in him. He also knew how she felt about Buck.

Sarah saw what he'd done. He'd given her back these memories—only to stop her from telling *anyone*. She was a murderer—just like the rest of them. Maybe more so because she'd been the leader. Unless she went along with whatever the anarchist group still had planned…

"What are they planning?" she demanded, her voice hoarse from unshed tears.

"You will know when it's time."

CASSIDY FELT PANIC fill her as she listened to the footfalls growing nearer to the room where they were trapped. Whoever it was, he was headed right for this office.

"In here," Jack whispered as he opened the door to the small closet and pulled her inside with him. The closet was tiny and lined with shelves filled with office supplies and papers.

There was little room to stand for the two of them and the metal container that he'd found in the bottom drawer. They pressed their bodies together in the cramped space as tightly as they could and yet he'd only been able to partially close the closet door.

She heard the outer door bang open and heavy footfalls as someone entered the room. Through the sliver of light from the partially open closet door, she caught a glimpse of a large man. She didn't get a look at his face as he headed straight for the desk. A moment later she heard him let out an oath and begin opening and slamming the drawers.

When he suddenly stopped, Cassidy thought for sure that the next place he would look would be the closet. She held her breath. Jack seemed to be doing the same thing. Her heart jackhammered as the man started to turn toward their hiding place.

A phone rang. The man hesitated before pulling out his cell on the second ring. "Urdahl," he said into it. He stood, apparently listening to whoever was on the other end of the line for a few moments before he said, "Well, I hate to be the bearer of even more bad news, boss, but the package you asked me to pick up is gone."

The man held the phone away from his ear until apparently the caller quit yelling. Cassidy couldn't make out the words, but she heard enough to surmise that his boss was very angry. "Like I said, this wasn't my fault. I have men at his house in case he comes back. He hasn't been back since this morning and didn't show for some appointment he had this evening. Just tell me how you want me to handle this." He listened for a moment. "Right. I'll let you know when I find her. But what do you want me to do about your son?"

"THERE'S ONE MORE thing I need to know," Sarah said as she realized Dr. Venable planned to leave without answering any more of her questions.

"In good time," Dr. Venable said.

"No," she said, digging in her heels as she stepped past him to block the door. She crossed her arms and

held her ground. "I want to know why all those years ago I drove into the Yellowstone River in the middle of winter in an attempt to kill myself. I need to know why I left six beautiful daughters. Why I left a husband I loved. I want to know now or I'm going to call the sheriff."

Dr. Venable studied her openly for a moment. "You want to spend the rest of your life in prison? Once everyone knows you're Red—"

"*Now* or I make that call."

He sighed. "All right." His face hardened along with his eyes. "You weren't supposed to fall in love with Buckmaster Hamilton. You were supposed to blend in, like the sleeper spies the Russians sent over to assimilate into our communities. Having children was fine, though we questioned why you would have so many. Six?" He shook his head. "You were supposed to…blend in until it was time. Instead, you bought into that life. You wanted to forget the past. You wanted to forget about our plans. When Joe contacted you—"

"So that was it. I wanted out of The Prophecy," she said, feeling as if things were finally making sense. "And I wanted out of whatever…plans you say I came up with."

Doc nodded. "You'd lost that fire you'd had, that desire to change the world. All you cared about was your precious family. You bought into the bourgeoisie. You had everything you wanted and you were ready to sell the rest of us out."

She frowned. "But you couldn't let that happen."

"Not me. Joe. After two of our members had spent years in prison for a cause that you said you believed in, he was determined you weren't getting out. Not after the rest of us had done our part."

Still, why would she leave her precious family and the people she loved? *"You threatened me."* With a curse, she met his gaze. "No, you threatened to use my *family* to force me…" Her hands balled into fists. Had she held one of those automatic weapons she used to fire when she believed in the philosophy of The Prophecy, she would have turned it on him.

That bonfire he talked about, that need to "do" something, burned brighter than ever inside her. Only what she wanted to do was destroy The Prophecy. Which meant destroying not only herself, but also her family. Destroying Buck.

She looked at Dr. Venable and felt a bubble of bile rise as she realized she was still between the same rock and a hard place that she'd been more than twenty-three years before. The members of her old anarchist group would never let her quit.

Taking a moment to get control, she considered the precarious position she was in. She still didn't have all the facts because she didn't have all of her memory yet. She didn't know what they had planned. But once she did…

She nodded as if coming to the decision he wanted her to. "So failing my attempt to…escape by killing myself, I called *you*."

"I was the only one who could help you and you knew it."

"I *trusted* you apparently. And your answer to my problem was to steal all memories of that life."

"You begged me to. I erased it and then took you away from here as well. We were happy in Brazil. Oh,

don't look so horrified. We weren't lovers. We were…
associates. We talked a lot about changing things—just
like we did during your college years."

"I don't understand how I came to be part of The
Prophecy." In high school, she'd been the perfect
daughter, perfect student, perfect citizen. She'd gotten a scholarship to university. What had happened
when she reached there? Had it been Dr. Venable who'd
changed her? Or had it been—

"Joe brought you in."

She nodded, closing her eyes for a moment. Of
course she'd been a vulnerable, wide-eyed small-town
girl at a big university and Joe was handsome, charm-
ing, sexy, intense, like no other man she'd ever met.
He'd been her first lover. Memories flooded her. She
shuddered at the thought that a part of her could still
be vulnerable to him.

"It wasn't an accident that you met and married
Buckmaster Hamilton," Dr. Venable said. "You chose
him as part of a plan."

She frowned in surprise. "But how could I have
possibly known he would run for president, let alone
that he might stand a chance of winning all those years
ago?" The words were barely out when she realized
her mistake. "Buck was just a way to get to Senator
JD Hamilton. As his daughter-in-law, I would have
influence over him. There was talk that he might run
for president. I was to make sure that he did, right?"

Doc nodded. "It would have worked if he hadn't
fallen in love with the young girl who lived on the
ranch next door."

"We can't help who we love," she said, thinking
of Buck.

"You and Joe seemed the perfect match."

She shook her head. "Whatever Joe and I had, it wasn't love. He indoctrinated me."

Doc bristled. "I wouldn't let him hear you say that. And you can say you were brainwashed, but you seemed more than willing to take up the cause. After all, you're the one who came up with the plan to go after Senator JD Hamilton."

"I was young and stupid."

"Your plan almost worked."

"What plan was that? The same one you have for Buck?" Sarah saw that he had no intention of telling her. "I need to know what you're going to do to him."

He quirked a brow. "What makes you think we're going to do something to him? It will be up to you what happens. But first you have to convince him that you're dying to live in the White House, *dying* being the key word."

"You would kill me—"

"Why would we kill *you*?" Dr. Venable said as he handed her back her phone. "You and Joe are going to lead us. Just like you used to. When the time comes, you'll know exactly what has to be done and you'll do it."

"Is that what you told JD Hamilton when he was ready to quit the race for president?" she asked.

"Unfortunately, JD disappointed us and had to be dealt with. You have too much to lose to let that happen."

As he heard what Ed said into the phone, Jack no longer had to wonder if his father knew that he'd helped Cassidy escape. Nor did he have to speculate on whether his father would know that he was the one who'd broken into his desk and taken the metal box he now held under his arm in the dark of the closet.

He'd been seen. Shaken, he watched Ed Urdahl through the crack between the door and jamb. When he'd told Cassidy that Ed was looking for both of them, he'd been hoping it wasn't true. But it was.

Had his father known already when Jack had called him? Had Tom Durand made up the story about being on his way to Catalina? Maybe the sound he'd heard in the background was his father's private jet engine.

Which meant his father could be back in Houston. In fact, he could be looking for Jack at this moment. Apparently, there were already men out at the ranch waiting for him to return. There was no place safe. He and Cassidy were truly on their own.

"Okay, I'll handle it," Ed was saying into the phone. "I'll let you know when I find them. I said I would find them. When I do, I'll call and then you can tell me what you want me to do with them." Ed held the phone away from his ear, but Jack could hear his father yelling, although he couldn't make out the words.

What did his father plan to do with them? He still didn't know why he had wanted to abduct Cassidy. What had he planned for Ed to do with her? And now the big question, what had his father just told Ed to do about him?

"Yes, I heard you. I'll take care of it." Ed finished the call without another word and pocketed his phone. He stood for a moment as if trying to remember what he'd been about to do before the call.

Jack didn't dare breathe. Behind him he felt Cassidy's hand rest on his back as if like him, she feared that the man would head for the closet next. He thought about pulling out the gun, but he feared he would give away their position. It was tight enough in the closet, especially with him holding the metal container.

Not only that, when Ed had reached to put his phone away, Jack had seen the gun in the man's shoulder holster. Cassidy had, too, because he'd heard her startled intake of breath behind him.

Ed stood for a moment looking down at the desk before he walked around it and out of the office. Jack listened to his retreating footfalls, still holding his breath. If Ed suspected that Jack was hiding in the building, he would wait and catch him when he came out.

The sound of the old freight elevator clanked and groaned as if rattling the entire building as it descended. After a while, the night fell silent.

"Jack?" Cassidy whispered.

He shook his head, turning only slightly to motion for her to wait.

She nodded, but her blue eyes were huge and she still had her hand pressed to his back. He could feel her trembling. He was shaking just as wildly inside. What the hell was going on with his father?

Jack didn't know how long they stood there. His mind was like a hamster on a wheel. What was his father involved in? Whatever it was, Jack and Cassidy were now up to their necks in it.

The building sounded as quiet as a tomb when he finally pushed the closet door open a little wider and looked out. Ed had left the office door open, but he'd turned out the light as he'd left. The hallway was empty.

Cautiously, he stepped out, motioning for Cassidy to stay where she was. If he got caught, he didn't want her caught as well. He moved to the doorway and looked out. Nothing moved in the dim light of the hallway. No sound came up from the floors below.

Ed had taken the elevator. That meant he hadn't expected anyone to be in the building, otherwise he would have sneaked in as they had. Jack felt a little better at that thought, which meant there was a good chance Ed wasn't waiting outside for them. Jack had parked the truck away from the building and on a side street. Ed would have taken the main street to the office, so he wouldn't have seen it.

At least that was Jack's hope as he motioned that it was okay for Cassidy to come out now. He stepped close to her to whisper, "I think he's gone, but we aren't going to take any chances." He held his finger to his lips and she nodded jerkily.

He could tell that she was scared. It had been a close call. Also, he was pretty sure that she'd heard what Ed had said. The big man was still looking for her. But now he was also looking for the boss of T.D. Enterprises' son—Jack Durand.

From Cassidy's expression, she hadn't put that part together. At least not yet. He hoped she thought that the boss's son was one of the men in the van.

"He had a gun and he knows we have the box," Cassidy whispered, eyes big and round with fear. "What do you think is in it?"

He had no idea as he glanced at the battered and tarnished metal still tucked under his arm. It was a Pandora's box. He feared what would come springing out the moment he opened it.

She still looked scared, but he was terrified of what his father had hidden inside an old locked metal container he'd kept for years inside a locked drawer. "Let's get out of here." Shifting the metal box to his hands, he heard that faint metallic rattle again from within.

Cassidy must have heard it as well. "Maybe we shouldn't take it."

Did he really believe the answer to why his father would have the probable future president's daughter kidnapped was inside this box? But he now knew that his father had secrets—and some of them were apparently in this beat-up metal box.

Jack needed to know what he was dealing with—*who* he was dealing with.

CHAPTER SIX

"How is she?"

"Sarah's shocked and confused right now," Dr. Ralph Venable said into the phone. "It's to be expected." He'd been regretting making this call, fearing the outcome, ever since he'd left Sarah. Buck would be home by now. At this point, Doc could only hope that she didn't confess everything. "She's having a tough time."

Joe Landon sighed. "You know I never stopped loving her. When she went out to Montana to meet Buckmaster Hamilton and get close to his father, Senator JD Hamilton, I almost went after her, wanting to stop her. I was ready to run away with her and put The Prophecy behind us."

He thought of the young Joe and Sarah as they had been at nineteen. Such a beautiful couple. Joe had brought Sarah into the anarchist group with his handsome face and his passion, as well as his radical ideas.

"Why didn't you go after her?" Venable asked, thinking how different things would have been if Joe had.

"Because she didn't love me enough. She wouldn't have renounced The Prophecy for *me*." Venable heard the sharp edge of bitterness in the man's voice.

"You don't know that."

Joe laughed. "Actually, I do. The night before she

left, I told her I was in love with her. It didn't make a damned bit of difference. She was determined to start a revolution and that meant going after the Hamilton who everyone thought would be the next president. And yet, years later, she tries to kill herself rather than go through with her own plan all because she's fallen in *love*. She had what she wanted so to hell with the rest of us."

Venable said nothing. There was nothing to say since it was true. Sarah had fallen for Buck and adored the children they'd had together. She had wanted to wash her hands of The Prophecy and had refused to go through with the plan.

There'd been only one thing to do after she'd failed at suicide and called him. He had wiped away the years with Buck and her children and taken her to Brazil to keep Joe from killing her.

"So," Joe said now. "Are you going to be able to control her like you said you could?"

"So far she has done exactly what you require. She's gotten close to Senator Buckmaster Hamilton again, encouraging him in his race for president."

"She was briefly engaged to some cowboy named Russell Murdock," Joe said angrily. "That wasn't exactly in the plan."

"But we took care of that when we exterminated the senator's wife, Angelina. Just as I predicted, Sarah broke her engagement and moved onto the ranch."

"I want them *married*," Joe said through gritted teeth.

"You also want him to win the election or all of this would be for nothing," Venable pointed out. "You got me back to handle this, so let me."

"Even if you can get the two of them married and Hamilton wins, I'm not convinced that you can make Sarah do what we need when the time comes. If she no longer believes in our cause…"

That was putting it mildly, Venable thought as he rubbed the gray stubble at his chin. There were days he felt just as she did. Like Sarah, he'd been on fire with fanaticism all those years ago. He'd believed that a handful of people *could* change the world. That they owed it to themselves and the world to make that change. He'd been full of confidence and brazen disregard for everything and everyone but the members of The Prophecy, the group he'd started since he was the oldest of them.

It was Joe, though, who not only adopted his radical views, but also pushed the others to do what they had to in order to get the attention they deserved.

When one of their bombs had killed innocent people and Mason Green and Wallace McGill had gone to prison, Venable had wanted to stop. This wasn't what he envisioned.

It had been Sarah who had insisted they couldn't quit. They owed it to Mason and Wally. They owed it to the lives they'd taken. They owed it to their country to try to change the things that were wrong with it but to do it peacefully.

That's when she'd come up with the plan to make a real difference from the inside. Joe had been against it, but he'd gone along thinking Sarah would come back to him.

"From my source inside Hamilton's campaign, I understand that Buckmaster is also having doubts," Joe said. "We can't let him do what his father did. He can't pull out of the race."

Venable thought of JD Hamilton. Sarah had done her part beautifully. No one could have predicted that JD would fall in love with some young girl and be willing to give it all up. Love, he thought with a curse.

"There are always variables that have to be considered. We can't control everyone," the doctor said.

"But we can control Sarah. That's why I've taken things into my own hands to make sure she holds up her end of the bargain," Joe said.

Fear wedged against his heart. Joe, bitter over how things had turned out with Sarah, had become a hothead who acted before he thought things out. "What have you done?"

"Taken necessary steps to see that Sarah doesn't weaken. Otherwise, she is going to lose one of her daughters."

"You kill one of the daughters and I can promise you Buckmaster will pull out of the race," Venable said, furious with Joe. While the doctor had started The Prophecy, Joe, who was younger, stronger, more charismatic, had taken over. Joe hadn't had the brains, but once he hooked up with Sarah, the two of them were a team and Venable had lost the anarchist group he'd founded—and any power he'd had. He had never been more aware of that than he was right now.

It made him question what he was still doing with them. He was an old man. He'd given his life to his research and The Prophecy. "You could destroy everything with this…maneuver," he said, unable to hide his anger.

"No one said anything about killing her," Joe assured him. "Unless it becomes necessary. Same with Sarah. You already protected her once. I suggest you not do that again."

Venable swore. After Sarah had tried to kill herself all those years ago, and failing, had called him, he'd saved her by taking her to Brazil. Unfortunately, Joe had found out where they were and insisted Sarah be returned to Montana because Buck was talking about running for president.

He'd had no choice but to go along with it. Joe had made it clear that he would kill them both.

Now, though, he feared Joe was going to land them all in prison. "Joe, you can't—"

"Don't worry about it, Doc. You just do your part."

He heard what Joe didn't add. "Do your part—*or else*." He hated the fear that crowded his lungs and made breathing next to impossible. He wasn't sure how many days he had left.

But he knew one thing for sure. He didn't want to die at Joe's hands. If he couldn't control Sarah, he knew Joe would. For her sake as well as his own, he had to get through to her. If he didn't, her former lover would.

CASSIDY FLOPPED INTO the passenger seat of the pickup and closed her eyes. They'd run the last block in the darkness, the only sound the pounding of their soles on the pavement.

Now she tried to catch her breath. Her heart hurt it was thumping so hard. This was too real. She'd seen the man's gun. She'd heard him on the phone. Jack was right. Nothing was going to stop them.

She opened her eyes and looked over at Jack as

he started the engine and pulled away from the curb. "What do they want with me?"

"I would imagine money. But with your father apparently a shoo-in for the presidency..." He glanced over at her as he took a turn, then another through the empty industrial area.

There weren't any other vehicles on the dark streets, making it seem even more sinister. Cassidy realized she was shaking. Nothing like this had ever happened—nothing even close. Maybe she should call her father. Or even the police.

Out of the corner of her eye, she caught the glint of the metal box Jack had found in the locked drawer. "You think the answer is in there?"

He shrugged as he took another turn. His gaze kept going to the rearview mirror.

"We aren't being followed, are we?" she asked, hating the way her voice broke as she twisted in the seat to look back. The street was black behind them. No lights of another vehicle. "Did you see someone?"

"No, just not taking any chances," Jack said, anxiety in his voice.

Once they'd left the industrial area behind and reached a busy four-lane road with other cars and lighted buildings, she felt a little safer. But then again, now they wouldn't know if they were being followed or not.

"I'm thinking I should call my father," she said.

He shot her a surprised look before he said, "If that would make you feel better." He seemed to hesitate a moment. "You might want to wait until we look in the box. Right now we don't have a lot of information to give him."

Cassidy bit at her lower lip. Jack had a point. "Where are we going?"

WHERE WERE THEY GOING? Jack would have loved to go out to his ranch, but that was out of the question. Ed had people watching it.

He glanced over at the box he'd placed on the passenger side floor at her feet. It was time to find out exactly what they were up against. He reminded himself that the box might not have anything more in it than petty cash—just as his father had said. Except there'd been that metallic sound inside it.

"Maybe we should open it now," Cassidy said, reaching for the box at her feet. Jack swung into the parking lot of an all-night diner. He parked in the back where his pickup couldn't be seen from the street. "I'm hungry. How about you?"

She looked at him as if he'd lost his mind. "You want to eat *now*? If the reason someone is trying to kidnap me is in that box, then I want to open it."

Jack saw that there was no getting around this. Whatever was in the box, she was going to find out. "Okay. I'll break the lock and then we'll take it inside so we can actually see the contents." He could see that he didn't have a choice. "I have some tools in the back."

He popped the trunk and got out. His movements felt as if he'd fallen into a vat of molasses. He found a screwdriver, stood for a moment listening to a rustling in a nearby oak tree. Taking a steadying breath, he closed the trunk. The Texas night air felt heavy with heat and dampness.

As he slid behind the wheel again, Cassidy handed him the metal container, treating it as if she thought it was a bomb that could go off without warning. Jack thought that might not be far from the truth.

"Can't sleep?"

Sheriff Frank Curry turned from a dark corner of the porch as Nettie opened the screen door a little wider. "Just counting stars."

Nettie knew her husband too well. She came outside to join him, letting the screen door close behind her. "It *is* a beautiful night all right," she agreed. The moon was a golden sphere on the horizon. More stars than a man could ever count speckled Montana's wide and deep navy velvet sky. A light breeze whispered its way out of the Crazy Mountains to rustle the leaves of a nearby cottonwood. The mountains were a violet outline against the sky.

He smiled as she glanced over at him. "Yes, it is." Frank looked like an old-timey Western sheriff with his gunfighter mustache. His blond hair was graying, the skin around his eyes more wrinkled, but he was still the big strong man she'd fallen in love with in her teens. Now both in their sixties, they'd spent a lot of ridiculous years apart because they'd married the wrong people.

Fortunately, they'd come to their senses and were now together for what was left of their lives.

"So how many stars did you count?" she asked, knowing that wasn't what he'd been doing out here. Something had been bothering her husband for months now. He'd even talked about retiring. She worried that he would. He loved catching bad guys. Frank wasn't one to retire.

"I counted a few before I started worrying about things," he admitted with a laugh.

She could pretty much guess what was bothering him, but waited for him to tell her.

"I happened to see Russell Murdock earlier today."

Nettie smiled to herself. She loved being right. But then again, while she knew her husband, this mess with Sarah and Russell and Buck had been going on for over a year and worming a hole into Frank.

"I thought he left town," she said, encouraging him to talk.

"Apparently, Russell can't leave until he's sure that Sarah is all right."

She shook her head. "Nothing like a man blinded by love."

Frank raked a hand through his hair. "You know, the closer this damned election gets, the more I worry. I'm sure you heard about what Buck told that reporter on the plane."

The reporter had been a woman sitting next to him who hadn't identified herself as being with the media. She'd weaseled information out of Buck and the damned fool hadn't suspected a thing. He'd told her how he felt about his first wife.

Nettie, who attracted gossip the way bald tires pick up nails, heard about it the moment it hit the news. Not that she was surprised. Buck was still in love with Sarah. The only thing that had been standing in their way was Buck's second wife, Angelina. With her dead and gone, Sarah broke her engagement to Russell and moved into one of the houses on Hamilton Ranch. Nettie had seen that coming for months.

Her cell phone buzzed. She pulled it out. "Mabel Murphy just texted me."

Frank groaned. "How does Mabel find time to eat?"

As robust as Mabel was, she obviously did find the time, Nettie wanted to point out, but couldn't contain the latest news. "Mabel saw on Twitter that Buck just bought Sarah an engagement ring."

"*What?* The stores have been closed for hours."

"The owner of a jewelry store in Bozeman opened as a special request for the 'presumed' future president."

The sheriff sighed. "If voters turn against Buck for this, he'll lose the election. I hate to hope for that since I think Buck actually might make a damned good president. But his being back with Sarah makes me uneasy."

Frank was convinced that Buck running for president and Sarah suddenly coming back after twenty-two years was too coincidental—and dangerously so. He worried that she had some ulterior motive that had nothing to do with love.

"If you're right, Sarah won't do anything that will jeopardize Buck becoming president," Nettie said. "So if marrying him would hurt his chances, she'll turn him down. Which could explain why she hasn't moved in with him. It's been months since Angelina's death."

"I guess we're about to find out if Buck has reasons to fear Sarah," the sheriff said. "This is one time when I wouldn't mind being wrong about someone."

BUCK FELT FOR the small jewelry box in his pocket as he got out of his SUV and walked toward Sarah's door. It was late but there was a light on inside the house.

He'd been thinking about his life all the way to the ranch. Mostly, he'd been thinking about what he would do if Sarah refused to marry him and move into the main house with him again.

Four months ago she'd been packing to do just that. So what had happened? Or maybe he should ask himself, who? She'd cared enough about Russell Murdock to agree to marry him. Had Russell come back into her life? Buck didn't believe that Russell had left town. Was the man waiting around for Sarah? Or was Russell waiting around for Buck to fail her?

That thought was the one that had hit the hardest. The Sarah he'd known, the one who had given him six daughters, hadn't been thrilled about his involvement in politics even all those years ago. Now he was running for president. Was that the problem?

He knocked since he didn't feel he could just walk in despite that he owned the house. Things between him and Sarah were too much up in the air for him to just assume he would be welcome.

His heart was pounding as he knocked again. The car he'd bought her was parked outside, but maybe she'd left with someone else. But she'd known he was coming home tonight, surely—

She opened the door and he had to swallow the lump in his throat. His love for this woman practically knocked him to his knees. He didn't need his campaign manager to tell him how dangerous that was. This kind of love could destroy a man.

He'd planned to wait, but seeing her standing there... He dropped to his knee as he dug the ring box from his pocket with one hand and reached for her hand with the other.

She looked startled and took a step back.

He flipped open the ring box. The diamond caught the light from inside the house. He looked from it to her face. He'd never been so afraid in his life. "Sarah, please marry me."

"Buck." Her voice broke. Tears filled her eyes. "Oh, Buck."

THE LOCK ON the old metal box broke with a pop. Jack put down the screwdriver he'd used to pry the lock apart and glanced nervously at Cassidy. The neon light from the diner filled the car with a sickening green glow that made them both look ghastly. She was staring at the metal box, waiting for him to open it. From her expression, she was just as anxious as he was.

"Let's go inside so we can see what's in here," he said, picking up the container and opening his car door. He knew he was stalling. Outside the car, he took a deep breath. The Texas night smelled of oak trees and marshes mixed with the cloying scent of fried food coming from the diner.

He heard Cassidy get out, close her door and come around the car to join him. He told himself he should confess all to her before they saw what was in the box. It there was anything in here with the Durand name on it, she would put two and two together and realize he'd lied to her. Even if she didn't run shrieking for help, she wouldn't trust him ever again. He hated the thought more than he should have since he'd only known her for hours. Worse, he wouldn't be able to protect her from his father if she took off on her own.

They were almost to the front door of the diner when he stopped. "Cassidy—"

"Beany."

"Okay, Beany, there's something I should—"

"Please, let's just get inside and open the box," she cried, hugging herself even though the Texas night was hot and muggy. "You're killing me."

He nodded. As he pushed open the diner door, he was glad to see that there were only a couple of old men sitting at the counter. Jack led her to a back booth and took a seat across from her, putting the box on the cracked vinyl seat next to him.

The waitress, an older woman with what appeared to be a fresh perm and wearing too much rouge, brought them water and menus. He realized that to her, they probably looked like a couple on a late-night date.

"I'd love some coffee," Jack said, looking at Cassidy, who nodded. "And..." The daily specials were on a chalkboard behind the counter. "The breakfast special." It was ham, eggs, pancakes and hash browns and a side of biscuits and gravy. It was also the first item on the chalkboard.

"Me, too," Cassidy said as if she just wanted the waitress to go away so they could open the box.

The waitress hobbled off on orthopedic white shoes that creaked with each step. Jack waited as she moved behind the counter to post their orders. A fan whirred noisily overhead. Tension hung in the greasy-smelling air.

Across from him Cassidy toyed nervously with the short hair at her neck as the woman returned with two coffees and silverware. Once the waitress wandered off, Cassidy gave him an impatient look.

He picked up the metal box and placed it on the

table. His gaze went from it to Cassidy. *Last chance
to tell her the truth.*

   "Jack," she said in a pleading tone.
   Slowly, he lifted the lid.

CHAPTER SEVEN

FOR A MOMENT, Jack only stared down into the metal container. A driver's license lay on top of the papers inside. The mug shot was a younger version of his father, but the name on the license was Martin Wagner. He picked up the license and saw that the expiration date was October of 1982.

As if she couldn't stand it any longer, Cassidy slid out of the booth and came around to his side of the table. He slid over to let her sit down.

"Who is Martin Wagner?" she whispered.

"I have no idea." It wasn't a lie. Right now he didn't even know who Tom Durand was—the man who he'd believed was his father. The man who had raised him since birth.

In a daze of confusion, he let Cassidy take the license as he began to look at the other paperwork in the box. There was a birth certificate for Martin Wagner, a social security card, even a passport that apparently had never been used from 1979. Under those items were newspaper clippings.

Pulling out one, he saw that it was about an anarchist group called The Prophecy. Cassidy took the clipping from his hand, frowning as she glanced at it.

"The Prophecy?" she asked.

He shook his head, afraid what the two had to do

with each other. Why would his father keep the clippings unless they had something to do with him?

He dug deeper, his fingers grazing what felt like card stock. As he lifted out the rest of the newspaper clippings, he saw that there were half a dozen photographs at the bottom of the box. Picking them up, he quickly leafed through them.

There were numerous photos of his father with other people he didn't recognize. From the clothes and haircuts, he guessed the shots had been taken in the late seventies or early eighties. Jack stopped to stare at one of them. Several people in the photo held automatic weapons. What the hell?

He turned the photo over. Written on the back were the words: The Prophecy 1978. Apparently, his father had been a member of this group.

Staring at the photo again, Jack couldn't help but notice something else that sent a shock of pure ice up his spine. His father was smiling at the camera in a way Jack had never seen him smile. Tom Durand looked *happy*.

Except, apparently Tom Durand wasn't even his name.

Jack thought of his serious workaholic father, a man who had apparently thrown himself into his work. Because he'd been running from something?

"Did you see these?" Cassidy demanded, holding up the newspaper clippings. She dropped her voice. "The Prophecy was some anarchist group that *blew up* buildings and *killed* people."

He saw the date. A year after that happy photo of his father. It all began to sink in. Was this what his father had been running from? He realized he didn't know the man at all. Never had. That was the thought that kept racing around in his head like a hamster wheel.

Cassidy put down the clippings and reached for the photos. Jack felt numb. He couldn't have been more shocked. He'd wondered how far his father might go if he was behind Cassidy's attempted abduction. Now he felt he had a pretty good idea of what Tom Durand/ Martin Wagner might be capable of.

He started to dig in the box again when he saw the key. That must have been what had made the rattling sound when he'd shaken the box earlier, he thought as he drew it out. It appeared to be a safe-deposit key from a bank.

More secrets, Jack thought with growing concern. Still, nothing in this box explained why his father had hired Ed to kidnap Cassidy, except for the fact that Tom Durand had been a man named Martin Wagner. And Martin Wagner had been a member of an anarchist group called The Prophecy. Was he *still* a member?

As he palmed the key, he watched Cassidy looking through the photos. Furtively, he dropped the key into his jacket pocket, telling himself it wasn't wrong to keep this from her. Whatever was in the safe-deposit box could be worse than even this. He didn't want her involved any more than she already was. Who knew what other secrets his father had that the two of them could stumble across? As it was, there was no going back from this.

But even as he thought it, his mind rebelled against all of it. There had to be a mistake. Maybe his father had an identical twin named Martin Wagner and they were separated at birth. His father couldn't have been part of this group.

Cassidy let out a cry, startling him.

He looked over, instantly afraid. "What is it?"

"That woman," Cassidy said, pointing at the only woman pictured in the group photographs that included his father.

He hadn't really looked at anyone in the snapshots other than his father. Now he took in the redhead Cassidy was pointing at. The woman stood between Jack's father and another man. They all looked to be in their early twenties, except for one tall, lean older man off to the side. They were all smiling at the camera, eyes bright. Alarmingly so.

Cassidy pointed at the woman in the photo. *"That's my mother."*

CHAPTER EIGHT

THE ENGAGEMENT RING was beautiful. Sarah stared at it on her hand. Of course Buck had remembered her size, so it fit perfectly.

He'd slipped it on before she could stop him. He'd taken her stunned, horrified reaction for acceptance. She'd broken down, sobbing her heart out when he'd dropped to his knee and proposed. He thought that this was what she'd been waiting for. That realization had only made her cry harder.

She didn't know what she was going to do. When she'd seen him down there on his knee, she'd wanted to blurt it all out, telling him everything. But the truth wouldn't save either of them.

"Do you like it?" he asked now as he came into the room with two glasses of champagne. Of course he had thought of everything.

She could only nod. Her eyes burned with fresh tears, but she fought them back as he bent to kiss her on the cheek. She closed her eyes, wanting him to take her in his arms and make love to her. She yearned for that escape. But at the same time, she felt too vulnerable. What if she *did* tell him everything?

She had to pull herself together. Before Dr. Venable had left, he'd warned her.

"The members of The Prophecy have been leading normal lives—much like yours and Buck's had been."

"Before I tried to kill myself."

He continued as if she hadn't spoken. "They aren't going to just stop because you've changed your mind or because you want to confess all. The plan *will* go on. You'll see it all happen from your prison cell, where you will be powerless to stop it—or what happens to your family."

He must have seen that she preferred that to whatever they planned to do.

"Unfortunately, your family will pay the price," Dr. Venable said. "One wrong move, and your daughters—"

"What are you planning to do?" she'd pleaded, only to have him shake his head.

"If you want to protect your family, then you have to do what I say," Venable had said. "I'm your best bet, trust me."

"But I *don't* trust you."

"As long as you keep what you know to yourself and make sure nothing keeps Buck from winning this election…"

So that was it. Buck had to win. And then what? That was why she was back here. They'd *sent* her back. Dropped her outside of town from an airplane. She'd parachuted in at night with no memory of the twenty-two missing years or why she'd tried to end her life that winter night in the Yellowstone River.

How could she doubt that The Prophecy would carry out their threats given the lengths they had already gone to? According to Doc, The Prophecy had been responsible for all kinds of terrorist activities around the world all these years. Now they were determined to use her—and her family—for some big show of their power. Joe's power.

Dr. Venable had made his threat clear before he'd left. If she confessed all, if she tried to stop this, they would still succeed, but they would go after her daughters. The thought crippled her with fear.

"I wish I'd never heard of The Prophecy," she'd said with disgust.

Dr. Venable had laughed. "Sarah, this was *your* plan. It has just taken a while to implement it. But now that your husband is so close to being our next president… The members will carry it out with you—or without you. But once your memory is completely restored you will feel differently about what needs to be done."

She'd thought she couldn't be any more terrified by what was happening until he'd said those words. "You think I'll turn back into this woman Red, the leader?" she'd asked, horrified at the thought.

Doc had smiled. "Everyone is planning on it."

Everyone? Who was left in The Prophecy? She hadn't seen the others in years. If Dr. Venable was telling the truth, they'd all still been active. She wondered how many bombings, riots, killings and maybe even wars in other countries they'd been responsible for.

She hated them for using her family as leverage, hated herself because she was responsible for at least this part of it—*if* Doc could be believed. Now they were using her family and her past to keep her in line. She wasn't fool enough not to realize that they planned to continue to use her. Use her to get to Buck, once he was the president of the United States.

If it was her plan, then wasn't there a chance that she

could stop it? Unless Doc was right about her becoming Red again once her memory was restored.

BUCKMASTER TRIED TO relax as he watched Sarah take a sip of her champagne. Her hand shook as she brought the glass to her lips. From excitement, surprise or something else?

Her reaction to the engagement ring had been more than even he had hoped for. *They were getting married.* He would have to tell Jerrod to start putting a spin on the engagement and upcoming wedding. He would balk, reminding him about lost votes if he didn't wait. Ultimately, Jerrod would go along with it, because that's what he got paid to do. But knowing the man, he would insist they get married at the ranch, do the whole photo thing for the media. Sarah would hate it.

"Have you heard from the girls?" Buckmaster asked as they sat down on the couch.

"Harper stops by occasionally." Sarah's voice sounded strange. She still looked as if she might burst into tears again. "They're all busy with their own lives."

If he had any misgivings about her mental stability, he pushed them away. This was his Sarah. He knew this woman intimately. No matter what had happened all those years ago or where she'd been and what she'd done, she was still the same woman.

He nodded, disappointed that the girls hadn't made much of an effort to get reacquainted with their mother. That would change once he and Sarah were married. A lot of things would change.

That nagging feeling he'd had earlier surfaced. "I tried to call Cassidy. Is she still in New York?"

"I have no idea. I haven't heard from her. Why? Are you worried about her?"

He was, but he shook it off. "I'm sure it's nothing. I'd just like to talk to her, make sure she's okay. I'll try again tomorrow. She's still my baby girl."

Sarah was looking at her ring again, touching it, turning it. He'd heard somewhere that people who toyed with their wedding bands were questioning their marriage. He doubted that applied to engagement rings—especially when it was new.

"I'm thinking a wedding at the ranch... Really do it up since we eloped the first time," Buckmaster said and saw her expression. "Not right away. If you want we can wait until after the election."

Sarah nodded and smiled, but the smile never reached her eyes.

"I hope you know I would do anything for you. So you need to be honest with me," he said. "If you want me to drop out of the race, you need to tell me now."

CASSIDY STARED AT the photo of her mother, her heart pounding. What was going on? None of this made any sense.

"You're sure that's your mother?" Jack whispered as the waitress approached with their breakfasts. "Didn't she leave right after you were born?"

"A few months after. The last time I saw her was at Bo's wedding, where she fainted at the reception," Cassidy said as she studied the photo, still having a hard time believing it herself. "But in the wedding pictures that Bo sent me, my mother was standing like this, toying with whatever dangled from the chain on her necklace—exactly like she's doing in this shot. There isn't any doubt, *that's her.*"

Cassidy moved the photos to one side as the waitress brought their breakfasts. Jack quickly put everything back into the metal box except the key he'd pocketed earlier and the photos.

She picked up the stack of snapshots, looking more closely now that she had recognized her mother. Thumbing through them again, she realized that she might have not recognized her mother if she had only seen the other snapshots. The woman in them resembled Sarah Johnson Hamilton, but not enough for her to think much about it since her mother was a blonde—not a redhead. And the woman in the photos was much younger.

But in the one shot, her mother was looking straight at the camera, fiddling with whatever hung from the chain on her necklace. The look in her blue eyes was so intent… Cassidy shuddered.

Jack reached for the photos and she handed them over reluctantly. As he put them into the metal box, she asked about the key he'd found.

He hesitated. "Looks like a safe-deposit key."

She could tell that he hadn't wanted to mention it to her. If she hadn't noticed him furtively putting it into his pocket, she doubted he would have told her about it. "Does any of this make sense to you?"

Again he hesitated. "Let's eat and then we'll talk."

"That sounds ominous."

He bit at the inside of his cheek for a moment before he looked around the diner. Several more people had come in, but had taken seats at the counter. "Come on," he said, trying to act cheerful. "You have to be hungry. It's been hours since we ate. I don't know about you, but all that adrenaline, I feel like I've run a marathon tonight."

She nodded and pulled her plate closer, telling herself something had changed. The moment he'd opened the box, he'd seen something in there that had upset him. She was sure of it.

Now he knew that her mother had been part of some anarchist group called The Prophecy. Was that why she felt he had pulled away from her? Not that she blamed him. She was horrified as well. Would he insist they go to the police now?

The aroma from her food reached her nostrils and her stomach growled. Jack chuckled as he took a bite. She could tell that his mind was anywhere but on biscuits and gravy. She took a bite and tried to concentrate on eating, but she could have been eating cardboard for all she tasted.

She ate, though, telling herself that whatever was going on, she was going to need her strength.

JACK REALIZED THAT if he told Cassidy that his father was one of the men in the photographs, he had to tell her everything. She wouldn't buy that it had been a coincidence that he'd saved her—and their parents just happened to be former members of the same anarchist group. They were *former* members, right?

He'd never heard of The Prophecy, but from the newspaper clippings, the group was responsible for numerous bombings. People had died. Two of the members had gone to prison. Apparently, Cassidy's mother and his father hadn't been implicated.

But that could explain why his father had changed his name.

So why was Tom Durand, aka Martin Wagner, now trying to kidnap the daughter of one of his former compatriots? It had to have something to do with the fact that Cassidy's father was running for president.

They ate in silence, both eating apparently as much as they could before pushing away their plates.

"I'll pay and then we're out of here," he said, getting up and taking the metal box with him.

"I need to go to the restroom," Cassidy said. "You'll wait for me, won't you?"

"Of course." Did she really think he might take off and leave her while she was in the ladies' room? Earlier there had been a closeness between them that he told himself he hadn't imagined. Whatever that feeling had been, it was gone. She didn't trust him. Smart woman, he thought.

At the counter, he paid their bill as Cassidy came out. She looked a little surprised to see him, as if even after his response, she'd expected him to be gone. Probably because she'd seen him pocket the key. She knew he had hoped she hadn't seen it.

Stupid on his part. Had he really thought he was protecting her? Or himself? That she thought he would abandon her made him even more angry with himself as they left the diner.

It was almost four in the morning. The sky had begun to lighten to the east through the Spanish moss hanging from the huge old oak trees. He opened the pickup with the remote a half-dozen yards from it and realized Cassidy had stopped some distance behind him.

"Tell me," she said, standing in the middle of the small parking lot as if glued to the pavement. "What are you going to do?"

He shook his head. He didn't know what she was talking about and said as much.

"Now that you know about my mother." She sounded close to tears. "I can tell that you're upset. You took the key. You didn't want me to know."

Jack groaned inwardly. She looked so vulnerable standing there, her voice tight with unshed tears. "Get in the car and I'll—"

"No," she said, hugging herself. He could see her expression in the dawn. She wasn't moving until he told her. "Tell me why you're acting the way you are. I know something's wrong."

Everything was wrong. But right now, he was more concerned that he would drive Cassidy away—and right into the trap his father had set for her.

"You can trust me," he said.

She shook her head. "I don't think so."

"Cassidy…" He stepped to the pickup, opened the door and tossed the metal box behind the seat. Turning, he took a few steps back to her as he searched for the right words. All of this would have been for nothing if he let her get into his father's hands.

It made him nervous that they were standing out here in the open. He told himself that the chances were few that Ed would drive by and see them. But still, he felt exposed. Or maybe it was because of what he was about to tell her.

"When I come to Houston, I always stop by my mother's grave," he said as he continued to move toward her. "I wasn't planning to come into town today.

It was last minute. I went by her grave even though it was going to make me late for a meeting."

She took a step back, looking wary. "What does any of that have to do—"

He stopped a few feet away from her. "I saw my father standing next to my mother's grave. Shouldn't have been strange, right? But it was because as far as I know it's the first time since the funeral that he's been there. He wasn't alone. Within a few minutes a man joined him. I was so surprised that I stayed back to watch them." Jack could see that he had her attention now. "I saw my father hand the man a thick envelope full of money. I watched the man count it and then the two parted. Not once did my father look down at my mother's grave."

"What are you trying to tell me?" she asked in a hoarse whisper.

"I recognized the man as one of my father's associates, Ed Urdahl. Ed works on the docks. The encounter was odd enough that I decided to follow him."

In the glow of the neon, Jack saw her eyes widen as she connected the name with the man who'd tried to abduct her. When Ed had answered the phone earlier at his father's office he'd said, "Urdahl."

"So you didn't just happen along earlier." She looked scared now as she glanced around. He hoped she didn't take off running because if she did, he would have to chase her down. He couldn't let her loose in Houston knowing what he did.

"That's not all," he said quickly. "Those photographs of that anarchist group called The Prophecy? The man standing next to your mother in the shot you recognized her in? *He's my father.*"

CHAPTER NINE

CASSIDY WAS TOO stunned to speak. She took a step back as Jack reached for her. All her instincts told her to run. She took another step, turning, but before she could get away, he grabbed her arm and pulled her around to face him.

"Listen to me," Jack said urgently. "I don't know what's going on. I just know that we're in trouble. It has something to do with our parents and that anarchist group that apparently they were part of. Maybe are still a part of. And your father's run for the presidency. I'd stake my life on it. Hell, I think I already am."

She tried to free herself of his grasp, but he only tightened it.

"I can't let you take off by yourself," he said, sounding as scared as she felt. "We have to find out what's going on. Because I have to tell you right now, my father knows that I have this box, that I know the truth. For some reason, he wants you abducted. I hate to think what he plans to do. Our only hope is to stay together and find a way to stop them."

"Stop them from what?" Cassidy demanded. Her head was spinning. None of this made sense. Except for the part about how Jack had come to her rescue. "How do I know that you only saved me to turn me over to your father?"

"*Seriously?* Wouldn't I have done that at my father's office when Ed Urdahl showed up?"

This was all too much for her. "You've been lying to me this whole time and you expect me to believe anything you say now?"

"I couldn't tell you the truth until I knew for certain that my father was behind your abduction. My father is a lot of things, but I never expected this. So, of course, I had to be sure first."

Cassidy hated that what he was saying sounded reasonable enough. Still… "The key in your pocket. You didn't want me to see you take it."

"At the time, I was so blown away by the rest of the papers in the box that I didn't even want to think what might be in the safe-deposit box. I was thinking I might spare you that."

"Don't do that again. If we really are in this together…"

He nodded, looking sheepish. "I won't." His gaze locked with hers. She looked into his eyes. She saw pain in them and recalled the hours they'd spent together. She had trusted him. She had felt safe. "My mother…your father…" She couldn't finish. "Who *were* they?"

He shook his head. "Who *are* they still?"

They stood like that for a few moments, just looking at each other, before Jack said, "Beany, we really have to get out of the open. We can go anywhere you want to go. But I can't let you take off on your own. I can't bear the thought of Ed finding you."

As he loosened his grip on her arm, she sighed. Earlier, she'd been ready to run, not so much away from Jack, but definitely wanting to run away from her near abduction and what she'd learned about her mother. Her world as she'd known it had shattered. "What do we do?"

He released her. "Once the bank opens, we see what this key opens. You with me?"

She was. What choice did she have? She glanced around the parking lot as the bright sun's rays fingered their way through the oaks. It was already so hot she felt as if she couldn't breathe. She thought about Montana and the cool breezes that came out of the Crazy Mountains even in the dead of summer. She wanted to go home. She *needed* to go home.

Pushing her hand into the pocket of her skirt, she protectively touched the photo of her mother that she had surreptitiously kept back. Jack wasn't the only one trying to keep secrets.

"I'm with you," she said, telling herself that once she knew what was in that safe-deposit box, she was headed for Montana—and her mother. One way or another she would find out the truth about Sarah Johnson Hamilton.

SARAH CLIMBED NAKED from the bed. She could hear Buck in the bathroom off the bedroom. She reached for her robe, her head aching as she looked down at the engagement ring on her finger.

Her heart dropped at the sight. She couldn't go through with this, not knowing who she'd been, what she'd done, what The Prophecy still had planned for her—and Buck. Her mind whirled. She'd thought the nightmares had been bad. Now the memories haunted her during her waking hours as well.

She had to find out what her plan had been all those

years ago. If Senator JD Hamilton had been her first target, what had she and The Prophecy intended to do?

She felt sick to her stomach. At her encouragement, her father-in-law had announced he would run for president. Like Buck, the general feeling at that time was that JD was a shoo-in. He would have won.

Was that when the plan would have gone into effect? She would have been the daughter-in-law of the president of the United States. She would have had access to him.

Sitting down on the edge of the bed, she put her head in her hands. Dr. Venable had unlocked part of her past and now the memories swept in, no longer letting her believe the lies she'd lived with for so long.

She'd gone after Buck. It hadn't been fate that she'd seen him that first day in the corral in Yellowstone Park. She'd planned the whole thing, even going so far as to learn everything she could about him—and his horses. She'd set him up.

Pieces of the past began to form a pattern that made her cringe. It had been *her* idea for them to elope. She had feared that he might change his mind about her. Or more closer to the truth, that his parents wouldn't approve of her and that he wouldn't go through with a wedding.

They hadn't approved. She'd managed to win JD over, but Buck's mother had hated her right up to the last few seconds of her miserable life. Sarah shuddered at that memory. Grace had seen through the facade straight into her dark soul. No wonder, her mother-in-law had done everything possible to end Sarah and Buck's marriage. Had she lived longer…

Sarah shivered and quickly turned her thoughts

away from the image of Grace reaching for her in those seconds before the woman tumbled down the stairs to her death.

What would have happened if JD had become president? If he hadn't fallen in love with the young neighbor girl, if his wife hadn't died, if he hadn't pulled out of the race?

No one knew how or why he'd lost control of his car that night and crashed into the river. Grace had been dead and buried by then, but Sarah thought that if it had been possible, the woman would have reached up and dragged JD to hell with her from the grave. Or maybe The Prophecy *had* been responsible.

She wrapped her arms around herself, fearing that Doc was telling the truth. Surely, this plan, whatever it was, wouldn't go into action until Buck was elected president. She'd encourage JD to run. But she'd had to be "programmed" to encourage Buck to run when she'd returned to Montana. Now that she knew the truth everything would progress as planned as long as Buck stayed in the race.

"What's wrong?" he asked from the bedroom doorway. "Another one of your headaches?" Buck stepped into the room to sit next to her on the edge of the bed.

She looked up at him, tears instantly filling her eyes. "I love you so much."

He seemed startled. "Sarah?"

Shaking her head, she quickly wiped her eyes and said, "I was thinking about the past."

"Russell?" She heard the jealousy in his voice.

"No," she said almost irritably. Buck's jealousy was so unwarranted. "I was thinking about the first time

I saw you." Not exactly true in the sense she knew he would take it.

But Buck seemed to relax. "In the corral in Yellowstone Park."

She nodded and reached for his hand. "I didn't expect to fall in love with you. But I did."

His eyes shone with emotion. "I love you and I'm going to remarry you and make you my wife. I've been thinking about it for some time. I also know what's been bothering you. A life as the First Lady isn't what you want. That's why I've decided to drop out of the election. Don't try to talk me out of it. I've made up my mind."

SARAH STARED AT BUCK. Weren't these the words she had desperately wanted to hear? Unlike Buck's second wife, she had no desire to live in the White House. And now that Dr. Venable was back and she knew about The Prophecy and the part she might have played, she couldn't let Buck become president.

But she also couldn't let him quit the race because if she did, The Prophecy would go after their daughters. She looked into his handsome face and felt a little piece of her heart break and fall away like a stone. He sounded so determined. He even looked a little relieved when he'd first said the words.

But now, the finality of it seemed to be sinking in. She could see disappointment in his eyes. Buck wanted the presidency. He'd worked hard for years for it. That he would give it up for her—

"You can't quit," she said, seeing how it would destroy him. And ultimately, destroy them. Even if The Prophecy had never existed, she couldn't let him quit.

She would always be the reason that he backed out of the race. She thought of her father-in-law, Senator JD Hamilton, and how the women in his life had destroyed not just his career, but his life. A part of him was already dead before his vehicle went off the road that night.

"I wish I'd never said I would run," Buck said, sounding defeated already.

Her emotions fought each other. If he became president, could she stop The Prophecy from whatever was planned? If he didn't stay in the race, could she stop the group from going after her family?

"You *did* run, you won the primaries, you're going to be our next president. I won't let you pull out of the race," she said adamantly as she stood to face him.

He smiled sadly up at her. "Nor can you stop me."

"Buck—"

"No," he said, standing up to take her shoulders in his big hands. She was small next to him. Of course he wouldn't suspect that she could be a danger to him. "I don't want to talk about this anymore. We still have champagne left. I'm going to have another glass and celebrate our engagement."

She wanted to argue, but she could see she wouldn't get anywhere with him tonight. "I'll get our glasses."

"Nope, you just sit right here and let me." He kissed her, his gaze locking with hers. "I love you, Sarah. You'll see. Everything is going to be all right."

BUCKMASTER TOOK THE bottle of chilled champagne into the kitchen of the house where Sarah had been staying since his second wife's death. He'd wanted to move Sarah into the main house right away, but he couldn't

because of the media. They would have destroyed him
in the press.

So he'd waited. Now months after Angelina's death,
he couldn't wait any longer to make Sarah his wife
again. He felt good about the engagement. He'd even
felt relieved when he'd said he'd quit. At least for a
few moments.

Now, though, in the old farmhouse kitchen, he felt
both relief and defeat. For so long his goal had been the
presidency that he felt a little lost at the thought of pulling out so late in the race. The Republican party com-
mittee would be furious with him. He was their best
hope of winning against the top Democratic candidate.

He found the drinking glasses he'd used earlier and
thought of all the beautiful crystal at the main house.
Angelina had liked pretty expensive things. If Sarah
wanted to, she could get rid of it at a garage sale for all
he cared. Just as long as she was happy.

Working the cork out of the champagne, he started
to pour when he noticed a tie balled up in the corner
of the kitchen counter. He didn't remember leaving a
tie here.

Putting down the bottle, he picked up the end of the
tie. It unfurled like a snake coming out of a den. He
held it with two fingers, staring at the design, knowing
it wasn't his from the moment he'd spotted it.

So whose tie was it? Not Sarah's former fiancé, Russell Murdock. Murdock was a rancher. He doubted the
man even owned a tie.

Bringing the cloth to his nose, he sniffed it and
quickly held it away from him. Spearmint. He tossed
the tie back into the corner as if it really was a snake
he wished he hadn't bothered.

Ask Sarah about it.

And ruin the evening?

He shook his head as he went back to the champagne bottle and finished pouring. She would have a good explanation for it, he told himself, even though he couldn't for the life of him think of one.

It doesn't matter. Sarah was going to be his wife. He wasn't going to have any misgivings about her past, not even a recent one. He was going to trust her and...

Swearing under his breath, he picked up the two glasses and walked back into the bedroom. She was sitting where he'd left her. She looked up as she heard him approach, but he'd seen her expression seconds before that.

She'd been frowning and now quickly pocketed her cell phone. Had she texted someone? Or had someone texted her?

"Champagne," he said with more cheer than he felt. He handed her a glass and touched his glass to hers with a clink. "To us."

CHAPTER TEN

Tom Durand cursed into the burner cell phone. "Did he *say* he was pulling out of the race?"

"Not yet, but I can tell he's definitely leaning that way," Buck's campaign manager, Jerrod Williston, said. "I sent him home to Montana. I hope you're right about Sarah being able to convince him not to. He seems to think that the reason she is holding him at arm's length is because she doesn't want to be a First Lady."

Damn Sarah. He feared they couldn't depend on Sarah, no matter what Dr. Venable said. If anything, he feared she would try to get the senator to quit the race, thinking she could foil the plan. No wonder Joe had ordered Cassidy Hamilton's abduction. He didn't have any faith in Dr. Venable or Sarah either.

But what would Joe do when he heard that Cassidy had slipped the net—and Tom's own son was behind it? His stomach roiled. He reached into his pocket for his antacids.

Once he had Cassidy... His son had screwed up things, but he still had faith that Ed would find both the girl and Jack. But if Ed and his boys didn't find her soon, they could always grab one of the other sisters. Cassidy had been the obvious choice because she was the most vulnerable. He'd had someone tracking her for a while now. Being single and way too trusting and gallivanting all over the globe made her an easy mark.

Getting her to Houston had been child's play. Like right now, she was no doubt trusting his son. Tom swore at the thought, but assured himself it would all be sorted out soon. Hopefully, soon enough.

"I just don't want him going to the press before we can stop him," the campaign manager said.

That was Tom's fear. Buckmaster had been wavering according to inside sources for some time. That was why Joe had ordered the abduction. But then Ed had blown it. No, he thought with another curse, his son had decided to play hero. How, though, had Jack even gotten involved?

He scrubbed a hand over his face and then let out a curse. The cemetery! Why the hell had he picked it for a meeting with Ed? It was private with no video surveillance, isolated with lots of trees and if anyone saw him, he'd have the perfect cover since his wife was buried there.

Jack must have seen him. Must have witnessed the money exchange. He cursed his bad luck. What was Jack doing there anyway? He was supposed to be at the ranch.

"You just do your part on your end," he told Jerrod now, anxious to get off the phone. "Don't let him announce anything for forty-eight hours. Tell Joe that I'll make sure the senator stays in the race." He disconnected and put away the phone.

Pulling out his usual cell phone, he called his son. The phone rang only once before going to voice mail. "We need to talk," he said through gritted teeth. "Call me." He disconnected before he said more than he had intended.

He tried to imagine what Jack would do now as he poured himself a stiff drink and wandered to the window of his penthouse suite in his high-rise condo that overlooked downtown Houston. Jack hadn't gone to the police, or Tom would have known about it by now.

So where was Jack, he wondered as he sat down to enjoy the view he'd paid a fortune for. The booze would play hell with his stomach, but he didn't care. He needed a drink desperately.

Where was Cassidy Hamilton? He had no clue. Unfortunately, Jack had taken after his mother. Tom had never understood his son, so it was hard now to conceive of what he would do next.

What had Jack thought of the contents of the box he'd taken from the locked desk drawer? Given what was inside, he imagined that his son had been righteously appalled. Jack had never had any idea what his father was capable of, but he did now. So what would Jack do?

The realization came out of nowhere like a bullet. Spilling his drink, he shot to his feet with a curse. The safe-deposit box! Jack had the key.

ED URDAHL'S PHONE vibrated in his pocket. He'd been staking out the ranch, waiting for Jack to return. In the perfect scenario, Jack would return, the girl with him and this would be over quickly.

But so far all Ed had done was swat mosquitoes and sweat in the summer heat. At some point he'd fallen asleep, only to wake to the sun shining in his car window.

"What?" he asked petulantly into the phone without checking to see who was calling.

"That's what I'd like to know," Tom Durand snapped, making him sit up straighter.

"Sorry, it's hot out here and the damned mosquitoes—"

"If you hadn't blown it in the first place, you would be home in bed," his boss interrupted. "Where are you?"

"At the ranch. He didn't come home."

"He's not stupid."

Ed wanted to say he hadn't been able to think of any other place Jack might have gone last night after the break-in at the office, but Durand didn't give him a chance.

"I need you back in the city. I think Jack is headed for my bank, if he isn't there already." He rattled off the name of the bank. "Don't try to apprehend them there. Follow them and wait for a less public place. I assume you know what to do once that happens."

Picking up the gun from the opposite seat, Ed said, "I can handle it. But what if your son—"

"Do whatever you have to do to get the girl."

"Even if it means killing Jack?" He was no bleeding heart. His ex-wife told him he lacked compassion for other people. But he still wouldn't tell someone to kill a son of his—even if he didn't like the kid.

"Just get the girl," Durand snapped again. "Let me know when you have her. I'll deal with Jack."

With that, the line went dead, leaving Ed shaking his head. "What is wrong with this world anymore?" he muttered to himself as he disconnected, started his car and headed for downtown Houston.

EVEN AFTER JACK had released Cassidy's arm, he'd been half-afraid she would try to run. He could see in her eyes that she was now wary of him. He couldn't blame her. He'd lied to her. If he'd been in her shoes, he would have wanted to get as far away from him as he could.

While she'd finally agreed to go with him, he knew she could take off at any point. He glanced over at her now as he drove. She had her head turned facing out the side window. He caught glimpses of her reflection and tried to read her expression. Was she having second thoughts? Was she planning to jump out once they reached a more hospitable part of the city? Or was she, like him, trying to make sense of all this?

"Our parents knew each other," she said, turning to look at him.

"So it seems." He recalled one of the photos. Sarah Hamilton had appeared to be with the man on the other side of her from Jack's father. But how well had his father known her? Had they been in touch all these years? Was Cassidy's mother in on this abduction?

"Do you think they're behind this now?" she asked, as if her thoughts had taken the same path as his.

He shrugged. "I'm hoping whatever is in the safe-deposit box will give us a clue. All I know is that apparently my father changed his name to Tom Durand and kept his other life a secret all these years."

"You don't think your mother knew?"

"No." He let out a laugh. "Trust me, my mother would have never stayed with him if she'd known." He drove aimlessly around Houston, waiting for the bank to open, his thoughts a maze with no way out.

"There is no way my father knows either." Cassidy turned her face away again. He could tell she was scared. He knew the feeling.

His father's bank was a large branch in downtown Houston. He was hoping that meant that Tom Durand wasn't that well-known there. It would make it easier for them to get into the safe-deposit box.

Moments before it opened, he parked in the lot behind the bank and got out. Cassidy followed just as quickly. He could tell she wanted to get this over with. Then what? Jack suspected she planned to split on him and swore softly under his breath at the thought. Now that he knew how deceitful his father could be, he wouldn't put anything past him. Who knew what resources Tom Durand had through the anarchist group or what he would do now to stop his son—and Cassidy.

"Just act nonchalant once we get in here, okay?" he said, seeing how nervous Cassidy looked.

She nodded, lifted her chin and let out a breath. When she turned to face him, she looked cool and calm. He envied her ability to do that. But then again, she was Senator Buckmaster Hamilton's daughter. It wasn't her first rodeo being in the limelight and having to play a role.

They found the clerk who handled the safe-deposit boxes. "I'd like to get into my box, please," he said to her, brandishing the key and holding his breath. If she knew his father—

But she hardly looked at him as she shoved a ledger toward him. "Sign here."

In high school, he'd been adept at forging his father's signature on everything from report cards to absence notes. He picked up the pen and glanced at his father's signature from the last time he'd been here.

Jack signed, noting the date. His father had opened
the box a little over a year ago—the same month Cassidy's mother had returned from the dead, he realized
with a start.

The clerk glanced at his signature before retrieving
a second key and leading them back into a large room
full of shiny security deposit boxes. She found the one
she was looking for, a large one, inserted the key and
reached for his key.

Jack watched as she inserted his key, turned it and,
after pulling out the box, handed both the container
and his key to him.

"There is a room over there if you want privacy. Re-
place the box when you're finished. It will automati-
cally lock." With that she left.

"Privacy," Cassidy whispered after the woman had
gone. Jack nodded and led her into the room and closed
the door. Her gaze went to the ceiling. "No cameras.
You don't think they can hear us, do you?"

"I don't think so." She was as paranoid as he felt.
He put the box down. It was heavier than he'd antici-
pated. Apparently, whatever his father had hidden in
here wasn't snapshots and old newspaper clippings.

After a glance at Cassidy, he opened the lid and
heard her gasp.

JERROD WILLISTON GOT the call he'd been fearing not
long after he'd hung up with Tom Durand.

"I need to talk to the Republican campaign commit-
tee. I'm going to pull out of the race," Senator Buckmaster Hamilton said.

"You can't do that." It was the first words that came
to his lips.

"Of course I can. We'll announce that I'm withdrawing for personal reasons."

"Sarah." Jerrod swore.

"We're getting married. She has no interest in being First Lady and she's been through enough. I'm doing this for my family."

"What happened to your need to help your country?"

"I will still help my country any way I can, but I need to take care of my family first," Buck said irritably. "I don't expect you to understand."

Jerrod understood too well. "All right," he conceded. "But give me a couple of days before we make the announcement. Can you do that?"

"If this is merely a stall tactic on your part—"

"It's not. There are things that have to be done. People on your campaign are now going to be out of work."

"Yourself included."

He held back a retort. "Don't worry about me. I'll be fine."

"I'm sure you will. Forty-eight hours. That's all you get." Buck hung up.

Jerrod stared at the phone a moment before he disconnected. He'd been expecting this and yet it still made him weak with worry. Joe would be furious.

He quickly made the call. "Buck's bailing just as I feared. He said he'd wait forty-eight hours but I wouldn't bet on that. He sounds way too determined to get it over with. I need to call Joe."

"No." Durand let out a string of curses before he calmed down and said, "I have it under control. The senator will *not* be leaving the race."

"ARE THOSE THOUSAND dollar bills?" Cassidy asked in a whisper.

There appeared to be stacks of them. Jack stared down at the contents of his father's security deposit box. He picked up a rubber-banded pile of papers that had shifted to one side of the bills. There were a half-dozen bank books with offshore accounts, the balances astounding. No way had his father's business made this kind of profit.

Jack felt a tremor move through him. What had the man calling himself Tom Durand being doing all these years to accumulate this kind of wealth?

In the stack of papers, he also found a half-dozen passports. He flipped several of them open. Each had a photograph of his father, each had a different name.

"What do we do now?" Cassidy asked, still in a whisper.

It seemed clear enough. "Apparently, my father thinks he might have to leave the country," Jack said as he looked through the rest of the passports. And soon. All of the passports were up-to-date—all issued a little over a year ago. Again about the same time that Cassidy's mother had returned to Montana after everyone thought she'd been dead for twenty-two years.

He stared at the passports, not realizing at first what was bothering him about them. They were also all for his father. None for his mother, who would have been alive at the time. None for Jack. Apparently, his father hadn't been planning to take either of them with him when he skipped the country.

Sickened, he put everything back into the box and started to shut it, when he realized what he was doing. "I'm going to need your bag." He'd picked up a quilted bag for her at the used-clothing store yesterday. The clerk had said it was a Mondo bag, whatever that was. All he'd known was that it was large and went with the Bohemian look he'd chosen for Cassidy.

"You sure this is a good idea?" she asked, sounding scared as she took her designer purse out of the bag and handed it to him. "I mean, when your father finds out all this is gone…"

Jack knew she was right. But he figured his father was already losing his mind over the missing metal box with his past in it.

"He's already looking for us. This is our bargaining chip. He'll want this back," he said as he began to dump the contents of the safe-deposit box into the large quilted bag. He stopped to look at her. "This is good news. We have something we can use to negotiate."

She didn't look convinced and he couldn't blame her. It was either daring or suicidal. If they got caught with the contents on them, it would be for naught. Which meant he had to find a place to hide the stash before his father or Ed caught up with them.

He emptied the box and closed the lid. His father didn't have a key to the box now. By the time he was able to get another one… He realized that the man might not even bother. He would know that Jack had taken everything.

Jack swallowed. If things went badly, he and Cassidy would be dead. All he could hope was that they could stay one step ahead until… Until what? It would help if he knew why his father had wanted to abduct Cassidy.

CASSIDY REALIZED SHE was shaking. "I don't understand what's going on," she said as she watched Jack put the safe-deposit box back and reach for the filled-to-overflowing quilted bag. "We're just going to walk out of here with all that?"

"With luck, we are." He glanced at his watch.

She could tell he was anxious to get out of the bank. Was he worried that his father would have realized they'd hit the bank this morning? Was that Ed person already out there waiting for them?

Cassidy felt tears burn her eyes. Her life as Senator Buckmaster Hamilton's daughter hadn't prepared her for this. Nothing had. She'd always been coddled, pampered, treated like rare crystal. Now someone was trying to abduct her, maybe even kill her.

"It's all right," Jack said, quickly moving to her as if seeing how close she was to breaking down. He put down the bag and pulled her into his arms. She pressed her cheek against his strong chest and breathed in the male scent of him. "I'm going to do everything possible to keep you safe." He drew back to meet her eyes. "You believe that, don't you?"

She looked into his handsome face. As her gaze locked with his, she felt as if she were diving headlong into a Caribbean sea. A feeling of warmth spread over her. Still wired on fear and lack of sleep, she closed her eyes and sighed, resting against his warm, hard body. She could feel the thunder of his heart against her own pounding chest.

He touched her cheek with his large hand, lifting her face to look down into her eyes. She heard his sharp intake of breath. A shiver tap-danced up her spine as he lowered his head, brushing his lips tentatively over hers. And then his lips were on hers, parting them, drawing out a ragged breath from her as he deepened the kiss. She clung to him, lost in the feel of his mouth on hers, his body molded to hers.

The door opened behind them. Startled, they jerked apart as the clerk came in with another safe-deposit key and another bank customer.

"We're finished," Jack told the clerk. Jack had put down Cassidy's bag, but quickly picked it up from the floor and whispered, "Let's get out of here," his voice rough with emotion.

As the bank clerk and the customer disappeared into the maze of the expansive vault, Jack started to push open the door to leave. Cassidy touched his arm and whispered, "What if they're waiting out there for us?"

"They aren't going to try anything in public. Once we reach the car, I'll have my gun." His hand on the doorknob, he seemed to be waiting for her to ask more questions.

"Then there is nothing to worry about," she said, her voice cracking.

He smiled at that before reaching to brush a lock of her now-dark hair back from her forehead. "Nothing to worry about at all," he said. And taking her hand, they walked through the bank toward the exit.

CHAPTER ELEVEN

IT WAS EARLY enough that Ed managed to get a parking spot across the street from the bank. He'd recognized Jack's ranch pickup the moment he'd seen it.

Durand had been right. Jack was at the bank. But was the young woman with him? Ed could only hope.

He waited patiently, angry with himself. He'd done other jobs for Durand, but none as demanding as this one. Before, he hadn't given a moment's thought to roughing up competitors or even taking a few out in the gulf for a concrete-shoe dip in the middle of the night.

But this was different. This was some nice-looking young woman. This was Durand's son. Ed didn't like anything about this. It made him nervous, not a good sign. Nor was he getting paid enough if he was going to have to take out the two of them.

He was sweating even with the air conditioner blasting when he saw Jack come out of the bank, the girl with him. Jack was carrying what looked like a large purse. Whatever was in it, it looked heavy.

Durand wasn't going to like this, he thought as he watched the two cross to Jack's pickup. They looked nervous. They should have been.

The girl climbed in as Jack lifted the heavy bag behind the seat and then went around to slide behind the wheel.

When Jack pulled out into the growing traffic, Ed let a couple of cars go by before he followed. All his instincts told him this wasn't going to end well.

JACK GLANCED OVER at Cassidy. She was watching the side mirror as if she couldn't believe they'd gotten away from the bank without being confronted.

He couldn't either. She touched the tip of her tongue to her upper lip for a moment and he saw her smile. Was she thinking about the kiss? He couldn't get it off his mind. It had felt so…natural. And yet, it had shocked him by the intensity of it.

A car honked, making him jump and reminding him he needed to get his head back where it belonged. Glancing in the rearview mirror, he caught sight of a green car behind them and swore under his breath.

"What?" Cassidy demanded, turning to look behind them. "Are we being followed?"

"I can't tell. There's too much traffic. So I'm going to assume we are. Hang on," he said and sped up, running a red light to the blare of horns and barely missing a bread truck that was pulling out.

"Where are we going?" she asked as he hung a right, then a left, then got caught in traffic at a light.

He had no idea where to go or how many people might be looking for them at this moment. Maybe his father had hired more than Ed and his goons. It still felt unreal. He was being hunted by his own father?

"We need to hide what's in your bag and then get out of Dodge," Jack said as he stared into his rearview mirror. Would Ed still be driving his green car? Or would he have picked up another vehicle that Jack wouldn't recognize?

He hadn't seen any cars that seemed to be following them, but he couldn't shake the feeling that Ed or someone else his father had hired had followed them from the bank.

The traffic finally began to move and he hung another right.

"I want to go to Montana," Cassidy said, determination in her voice. "I have to confront my mother." He started to mention how dangerous that could be, but she cut him off. "I can't just wait for these people to find me."

"Confronting your mother, though, doesn't that seem like a bad idea?"

She turned to meet his gaze. "You have a better idea?"

He didn't. He hadn't gotten any further than staying out of Ed Urdahl's sights and possibly trying to make a deal with his father. Neither of his ideas were worth mentioning. Ed would continue to look for them. As for trusting that his father would keep his end of any bargain—

"My father owns a large ranch outside of Big Timber, Montana."

"Cassidy—"

"I'm not suggesting going to the main house or letting my family know I'm in Montana, but there are houses hired hands use during calving and roundup that came with property my father has acquired. No one would know we were there. I was thinking of one in particular… We can stay there until we can confront my mother."

He glanced over at her as the traffic stopped again. There was a stubborn set to her jaw and a look in her eyes that told him her mind was made up. "But we can't get on a plane with all that money even if my father didn't have men watching the airports."

"We could take a private jet," she said.

"A private jet?" The light changed. The car behind him honked, startling him. He hurriedly stepped on the gas and took another right turn and then a left as they moved away from the downtown area. "I'm afraid I don't have a private jet." He'd been a rich kid by most people's standards, but he didn't even have friends who had their own jets.

"I could call my friend Evan."

She knew someone with his own jet? Of course she did.

"I HAVE TO take care of some things at my campaign office in Helena," Buckmaster said early the next morning after Sarah had made him breakfast. He almost choked on the lie. He hadn't been able to sleep last night. Just the thought of that damned tie that smelled like spearmint had kept him awake.

"I thought you were staying here longer," she said, looking at him in surprise. "We really need to talk about this decision you've made. I heard you on the phone this morning. It's too quick. It's wrong. Please—"

"That's one reason I'm going to the capital. I need to talk to my staff in Helena and see what kind of repercussions this might have on the party."

"Do you want me to go with you?" she asked.

"No, it would be too boring for you and I need to do some thinking on the drive. I promised Jerrod I wouldn't announce anything for forty-eight hours."

She seemed to relax, which confused him even more. He'd thought she would be happy about him quitting the race. But then again, he hadn't expected to find another man's tie in her house either.

"I'll be back this evening," he said. "We can talk then." All his instincts told him that starting an engagement by lying was bound to jinx the marriage.

The thought almost made him laugh. Nothing about his relationship with Sarah had been normal since the night she'd driven her car into the Yellowstone River and let him believe she was dead for twenty-two years.

It was clear that she wasn't exactly being honest with him. Not that he'd asked about the tie. He'd been riddled with doubts for too long. Wasn't that why seeing the tie had felt like the last straw?

And he wasn't the only one with doubts about Sarah, he reminded himself. The sheriff thought she was dangerous and questioned why she'd come back when she had.

Buck kept telling himself that the Sarah who had come back to him was the same woman he married. But not even he believed that.

It was her timing. She'd reappeared in his life right when he was ready to run for president. Why then? The sheriff had his own theories, one of them involving Sarah killing him apparently.

He pushed that thought away as he kissed her goodbye and drove down the dirt road from the farmhouse. Jerrod had taken his quitting better than he'd expected. No doubt his campaign manager had been expecting it. Buckmaster still had mixed feelings about his decision. But after finding that tie in Sarah's kitchen…

Looking in his rearview mirror, he could still see

the farmhouse in the distance as he drove down the road. He dropped over a hill and then took an old logging road up into the pines. He hadn't gone far when he parked, got out and, taking the binoculars he kept in his glove box, walked the rest of the way up the hill.

A cold wind blew out of the Crazies. It whipped his clothing, making him aware of the fact that he was still in one of his good suits. He could drive down to his ranch and change, but he didn't want to take the time. Nor could he chance that he might miss something.

From the top of the hill, he had a good view of the farmhouse through the pines, but Sarah—and whoever he expected visited her—wouldn't be able to see him. He settled in to wait as long as it took, hating his suspicions and praying that he was wrong.

It wasn't forty-five minutes later when a car came up the road and turned into the yard. Buckmaster held his breath, his heart aching. He hated that he'd been right and cursed under his breath as a man climbed out.

Lifting the binoculars, he focused on the figure walking toward the house. To his shock, the man was much older than himself. The man knocked once and opened the door as if it wasn't his first time visiting Sarah. Before he closed the door, he looked out as if sensing he was being watched and Buckmaster got his first good look at the man's face. It was Dr. Ralph Venable.

He'd only seen the doctor in a photo that the sheriff had shown him. It had been a snapshot of Dr. Venable and Sarah taken in Brazil, where apparently Sarah had spent the twenty-two years she'd been believed dead.

Why hadn't Sarah told him that the doctor was back

in the States? Not just back in the States, but was now more than a casual visitor?

Or was Dr. Venable doing more than visiting her? Buckmaster thought about what Sheriff Curry had found out about the doctor. Venable had been experimenting with brain wiping. According to the sheriff, there was a good chance Sarah had called Dr. Venable that night after surviving the freezing river. So was it as the sheriff suspected? Was the doctor responsible for stealing Sarah's memory?

Then why would she let the man back into her life unless there was more to the story?

CASSIDY COULD STILL feel the effects of the kiss. A warmth coursed through her veins. She hugged herself. Not even her very first kiss had stirred such longing in her.

She glanced over at Jack, studying the solid line of his stubbled jaw, the shape of his mouth, the tiny laugh lines around his blue eyes. Desire burned low in her belly. She quickly looked away. They were running for their lives. Was that why this need had felt so powerful?

With regret, she worried that she would never get to kiss him again or find out because they would be killed before it could happen. She looked out at the passing city. They'd left the commercial area behind and now seemed to be in a deserted warehouse district. It reminded her of the one they'd broken into last night.

Or at least she'd thought that had been what they'd done. Jack had lied. He'd known all the time that they were entering his father's building. That the man after them was Tom Durand. But what Jack hadn't known was the connection between his father and her mother. That had come as a shock to them both.

A part of her didn't want to believe it. Her mother was petite, waiflike. No one would believe she'd been some anarchist member of a group calling itself The Prophecy. Cassidy fought the urge to pull out the photograph she'd stuffed into her pocket.

But why would her mother's former partner in crime want to kidnap her daughter? She would ask when she confronted her mother.

SARAH STARED AT the engagement ring on her finger again. It wasn't that long ago that another man's ring had been there. Agreeing to marry Russell Murdock had been impulsive. She'd been heartbroken over Buck remarrying. Not that she blamed him since she had been gone twenty-two years. She couldn't really expect him to stay single all that time—even though *she* had apparently.

When Russell had asked her, Buck was still with Angelina. Sarah hadn't seen any possible way she and Buck could ever be together again—not if he wanted to stay in the presidential race. If he had left Angelina, the scandal would have killed his chances.

Angelina's car accident and subsequent death had reopened a door Sarah had thought closed forever. Russell had understood why she'd broken off the engagement. She'd been honest with him from the start—she would always love Buck, the father of her six daughters.

But she'd also loved Russell. She missed talking to him. He'd told her to call him if she ever saw Dr. Venable again. He'd predicted the doctor would come back into her life. He'd warned her to call him because he feared she would be in danger.

What a laugh. She couldn't bear to think what Russell would think of her if he knew that she was the one who was dangerous. She was the ringleader of The Prophecy with her lover, Joe Landon. She shuddered at the thought. Russell, like Buck, believed her to be someone she clearly was not. She could no more tell Russell the truth than she could tell Buck.

"Having second thoughts?"

She swung around to see Dr. Venable standing in the doorway. She hadn't heard him come in. "Buck *just* left."

"I saw him leave about forty-five minutes ago."

So he'd been watching the house. Her irritation bumped up a notch. "Don't you knock?"

"I did. I saw you through the window," he said as he moved to her. "You seemed to be lost in your own world." His gaze went to her left hand as she brushed back a lock of her blond hair.

Catching her hand, he studied the ring. "Expensive enough, but not too expensive. Your husband definitely knows his voting public."

She bristled at his words. "It isn't always about politics."

He laughed. "Of course it is. Buckmaster Hamilton was a born politician."

That didn't sound like a compliment. "I'll have you know, he's pulling out of the race."

"No, he's not. You're going to keep him in the race."

"Just so you can use me to get to him once he's president? I have every reason to let him quit the race."

Doc shook his head. "Do you still not comprehend

how far The Prophecy will go to make sure not only that Buck wins the race, but also that you are there by his side when he does? Sarah, I just got a call. They have Cassidy. If you want to see her alive again, you will make sure that Buck not only stays in the race, but also that he wins as per plan."

TOM DURAND HAD run his fair share of bluffs in his time, but none were as dangerous as this one. He'd called Dr. Venable and told him he had Cassidy. Technically, he had her in his sights. At least Ed did. It wouldn't be long and it would be true.

He was betting everything on this bluff. Anything could go wrong. Jack could up and decide to go to the authorities not only with what he'd found in the metal box from the office, but also from what he'd apparently taken from the bank. Or Cassidy could call home before she could be stopped.

He paced, unable to sit still as he waited for Ed to call letting him know that Cassidy was in his possession and that Jack had been…neutralized.

Jack. His stomach burned like the fires of hell at the thought of his son. It had been his dream from the moment the kid was born to bring Jack not only into the business, but also into The Prophecy—just as Jerrod Williston had been brought in.

But even at an early age, Jack had proved to be too much like his mother. Kate had been a do-gooder who worried about global warming, saving the whales and feeding starving children in some godforsaken country on the other side of the world.

The truth was, she'd been embarrassed by her husband's success. It still appalled him that she wanted to give away his money to make herself feel better. If she'd known where the money had really come from, she would have had a coronary.

"There are poor people who can't afford to buy food while we…" She'd opened her arms to encompass the palatial penthouse he'd bought for her. He'd thought her ungrateful even while a part of him had understood. He'd loved her, though. Just as he loved Jack.

And now, like his mother, Jack knew too much about Tom's past. He didn't have to ask himself what his son would do with the evidence he'd found. Jack wouldn't hesitate to bring down his own father. There would be no explaining why Cassidy Hamilton had to be kidnapped. No explaining about The Prophecy and what they planned for the country.

He *knew* his son. Jack would do what his mother would have called the "right thing." He'd sell out his own father.

That's why Tom had had to make the hard decision. Jack couldn't be allowed to take what he knew to the police.

He put those thoughts out of his mind, the same way he'd put his former wife out of his mind. He had known that he could no longer trust her. And like her, Jack had to be taken care of as well. That's just the way it was. But he hadn't expected it to hurt so badly. First Kate, now Jack?

He paced the floor, his stomach a ball of fire. He told himself that once he had Cassidy, everything would fall back into place. No reason to dwell on things he couldn't change.

His cell phone rang. He snatched it up, praying it was Ed with good news.

"Do you have her?" a male voice demanded.

Tom groaned inwardly at the sound of Joe Landon's voice. He'd changed his name, of course, and had assimilated into society like the rest of them. For years, Tom hadn't heard from him. Not until it had been time to send Sarah back to Montana, back into Senator Buckmaster Hamilton's loving arms and for the newest plan to begin ticking down.

"It's taken care of." He couldn't quit bluffing now. Especially to Joe.

Joe had been the face of The Prophecy. Until he met Sarah and brought her in. She'd taken to it with a tenaciousness that had surprised them all. It wasn't long before The Prophecy really took off and it became clear that she was the true leader.

Sarah had planned it all. Unlike Joe, who was a hothead, she had been cool and calm when the group had needed it most. It had been Joe's stupid idea to dynamite the building that killed the two innocent people inside. That move had gotten two of their members caught and imprisoned.

After that, Sarah had been determined that nothing like that would happen again unless it served a purpose other than to make a name for The Prophecy. Sarah had seen the bigger picture unlike Joe, who'd simply liked seeing The Prophecy in the news.

When Sarah had faltered twenty-three years ago, Joe began giving orders again. Just as he was doing now. His former love for Sarah had turned into a finely honed hatred. Tom was glad he wasn't in Sarah's shoes. Once this was over… He didn't like to think what Joe would do to her. Admittedly, Sarah had a few weak moments—like now. But she didn't deserve what he figured Joe had planned for her.

All he could hope now was that Sarah would remember the woman she'd been, the leader who'd believed in The Prophecy and an adaptation of the plan she'd come up with all those years ago. If she tried to let everyone down... Well, Joe would make sure her daughters paid the price.

"You better be telling me the truth," Joe said now. "You promised to handle this."

"It's handled. You just worry about yours and Doc's part," he said, sounding more confident than he felt.

"It's you and Doc I worry about."

"I thought Doc was replacing her memory."

"He is. But he says he has to take it slowly. Apparently, she's balking and wants to know everything right now. You know Sarah."

He heard the bitterness in Joe's voice. "Yes, I know Sarah." And Joe would be a fool to underestimate her.

Getting off the line as quickly as possible, Tom began to pace again as he willed the phone to ring and Ed to give him the good news. Otherwise, he might get a surprise visit from Joe.

CHAPTER TWELVE

"You bastard," Sarah spat as she grabbed for her cell phone. She was fumbling for Cassidy's number when Dr. Venable reached over and took the phone from her. "Give that to me."

"You need to listen to me," he said as he pocketed her phone.

She wanted to lunge for the man's throat. She could have ripped out his eyes she was so angry. Had she been holding the pistol Buck had bought her, she would have emptied it into the man without hesitation.

"You. Kidnapped. My. Daughter?" she demanded from between her gritted teeth.

Dr. Venable took a step back and raised both hands as if he knew what she was capable of. "Not me. The Prophecy."

"Don't you dare try to hide behind that," she snapped. "You *are* The Prophecy."

"No more than you are. This was your plan originally, Sarah."

His words blew out the anger like a gust of wind extinguishing a fire. She could pretend she was nothing like the members of The Prophecy, but the truth was, she'd been one of them. She'd been responsible for the deaths of two innocent people. She *was* The Prophecy in the eyes of the law. Because of her involvement her entire family was at risk.

Sarah fought to remain calm. If she had any hope of rescuing her daughter, she had to be strong, to be patient, to find out the truth about the woman she'd been. The woman she *still* could be.

"All this will be easier when I restore the rest of your memory," Dr. Venable said.

She shook her head. She didn't believe him. He was stringing her along. Buck was determined to quit the race and now The Prophecy had abducted their daughter to force him to stay in?

"What are you planning to do with Cassidy?"

"Joe is running everything now. I'm just a small cog in a big wheel."

What surprised her was that she actually believed that might be true.

But did he have the answers that she desperately needed if she was going to keep their big plan from happening? At the back of her mind was the fear that if she remembered, she might become again the fanatical anarchist she'd apparently been. That she might become Red, the leader of The Prophecy, again and destroy not only the lives of her family, but also possibly bring down the country, terrified her.

She took a few deep breaths. If she hoped to get any of them out of this alive, she had to calm down. "I want to speak to my daughter."

Dr. Venable shook his head. "I doubt that's possible."

"I either speak to my daughter to make sure she's all right or I call the sheriff and end this all right now."

"You really need to quit making threats, Sarah," he said, enunciating each word.

Her laugh came out hard and brittle. "You're the one not only threatening me but also my children. I want to talk to Cassidy. *Now,* Doc. If they really have her—"

He pulled out his cell phone, but didn't dial the number. "This is a mistake. Joe won't be happy. Aren't you worried about what The Prophecy will do to your daughter as retribution for your...demands?"

She was petrified of what they would do, but she couldn't let him see it. Years ago, she *was* Red, she reminded herself. Apparently, nothing had scared her then. If there was a time that she needed to be stalwart and daring, it was now.

"I have *six* daughters," she said in answer to his question. "I don't doubt you would use all of them to try to manipulate me. But I can bring The Prophecy down with one call. You want Buck to be president? He won't be if I make that call to the sheriff."

Doc sighed. "I don't think you realize who you're dealing with if you try to go against The Prophecy."

She stared him down, while quaking inside.

"All right," he said after a moment. "I'll see what I can do. But I would be reasonable if I were you." His gaze grew almost sympathetic. "We all want the same thing here. Once you remember—"

"Make the call."

She turned and stepped away from him. Her anger was so intense that her palms itched for the feel of a weapon in her hands. The .22 pistol Buck had bought her was in the bedroom. She knew she could get to it before Doc realized what was happening.

That she thought she could kill him should have shocked her. It didn't.

She told herself that Doc was only the messenger. Killing Doc would be like cutting off one small tentacle of an octopus. She had to think about her daughters and Buck. She couldn't let The Prophecy make her so angry that they took it out on her family. That fire of fanaticism he talked about, that need to "do" something burned brighter than ever inside her. She would destroy The Prophecy or die trying.

Taking a moment to gain control, she reminded herself of the precarious position she was now in. They said they had Cassidy. Buck wanted to quit the race. She only had part of her memory back. She needed all the facts, all her memory. But once she did…

Jack still questioned if going to Montana and confronting Sarah Johnson Hamilton was a good idea. But he could tell that Cassidy was determined. He couldn't let her go alone. And her idea to have someone take them by private jet would help erase their trail out of Texas—and get everything they'd taken from his father out of the state as well.

"This Evan is someone we can trust?" Jack asked as he kept winding his way through the maze of streets. It made him even more nervous having all that loot behind the backseat of the pickup.

Cassidy nodded. "I broke up with him before I went to Europe, but I think I can talk him into taking us to Montana in his jet."

Jack hadn't realized until that moment the kind of boyfriends she would have had. Superrich ones. One's who had their own jets apparently.

"You sure you want to call him?" he asked, thinking about the kiss earlier. It was ridiculous under the circumstances, but he wasn't sure he wanted to meet one of her old boyfriends—even though the private-jet idea was a good one.

She reached for her phone. "He won't mind. We left it fairly civil."

He didn't think he would have taken it well if Cassidy had been his girlfriend and she'd broken things off.

Jack realized that he hadn't been paying attention to where they were going. He'd hoped that by taking a lot of turns they would have lost anyone following them since he hadn't seen a tail. Now he saw that he'd driven into a maze of narrow streets in a run-down, deserted-looking industrial area.

Cassidy had pulled out her phone and was thumbing through her contacts. How many old boyfriends did she have anyway?

Unfamiliar with this area of Houston, Jack pushed the button on his GPS, hoping for a route out. At least there was little to no traffic.

Just as he thought it, he heard the beep-beep-beep of a commercial vehicle backing up. He looked up an instant before a delivery truck backed into the street, blocking them. Hitting his horn and his brakes, he skidded to a stop only a few feet from the side of the huge delivery truck.

The delivery truck's engine had died apparently when the driver stopped. As Jack rolled down his window to yell at the driver, he could hear the driver trying to crank the motor over. He honked again but got no reaction. Squinting, he could see the driver. Young, tattooed, wearing headphones and rocking out behind the wheel. No wonder he couldn't hear Jack honking.

With a sigh, Jack looked over at Cassidy. When he'd hit his brakes so suddenly, she had apparently dropped her phone. She was fishing for it on the floorboard when he happened to catch movement in his rearview mirror. His head snapped up to the mirror, where he saw the car speeding toward them. He had wondered if Ed would change cars. He hadn't.

In that split second before Ed came roaring up behind him, a half-dozen realizations came to him. There was no way the man could have tailed them unless Ed had put a tracking device on Jack's pickup. With a curse, he realized his father would have known he would head for the bank with the safe-deposit key. Ed would have recognized Jack's truck in the lot. Jack couldn't believe how stupid he'd been. He'd underestimated his father and his resources.

And now they were screwed, he thought as Ed jumped out of the car, weapon in hand and walked toward them.

Cassidy was still fishing for her phone. Ed had reached the back of the pickup. The driver of the delivery truck was still rocking out and grinding the starter on the engine, completely oblivious of what was happening only yards away.

Ed raised the gun, ready to fire.

"Stay down," Jack yelled as he grabbed his own weapon, threw open his door and tumbled out.

CHAPTER THIRTEEN

ED CHARGED THE PICKUP. Jack was behind the wheel, but he couldn't see anyone in the passenger seat. Where the hell was the girl?

He'd only taken a few running steps when the driver's side of the pickup flew open and Jack dived out, hit the ground and rolled. Something flashed in the light. Ed saw the weapon too late. He swore as the air between the run-down buildings filled with the echoing report of the shot.

Suddenly, his right leg was on fire, but he was still moving, his gun raised. He got off one shot, but heard the crack as the bullet bounced off the pavement inches from Jack's head.

His left leg went out from under him at the same time he heard Jack's second shot. His own shot went wild, pinging off the truck blocking the street as he fell. The pavement rushed up at him. One knee hit the hard surface as he tried to block his fall. He lost his grasp on the gun. It skittered across the pavement only seconds before he heard the sound of Jack's boot soles moving swiftly toward him. From the ground he watched Jack pick up the gun and approach.

"You don't want to kill me," Ed said through his pain. Both his legs were on fire, the hot pavement under them slick with warm blood. He pushed himself up on one arm, rolling to his side, his legs like dead wood attached to his body.

Jack squatted a few feet away, a gun in each hand. "I'm not going to kill you unless I have to. Why does my father want Cassidy Hamilton?"

Ed hadn't known her name. Now that he did, the name didn't ring any bells. "I don't know anyone by that name."

Jack poked at the wound in his right leg with the barrel end of the gun, making him cry out in pain. "He paid you to abduct her. Why? Where were you taking her?" He jabbed at the wound again without even waiting for Ed to answer.

"I'm going to kill you," Ed gasped from between his gritted teeth.

"Where were you supposed to take her?"

As Jack started to prod the wound again, Ed raised a hand to stop him, promising himself he would make Jack suffer if he ever got the chance. "I was to call him when I had her and then he would tell me where to take her."

Jack studied him for a moment. "And you have no idea why he wanted her?"

He shook his head and closed his eyes for a moment, half expecting Jack to finish him there in the street. "I didn't even know her name until you told me." In the distance he could hear the driver of the delivery truck still cranking at his engine. The smell of diesel fuel filled the air an instant before a loud boom made him start. He'd thought for sure that Jack had shot him again.

He opened his eyes, realizing with relief that it had only been the delivery-truck motor backfiring. He could see the driver still trying to get the delivery truck backed around on the one-way street. Even from where he lay, Ed could hear the hard rock music that escaped from the young driver's headphones. The dumbass apparently hadn't witnessed any of this as he got the motor going and drove off.

Jack stepped around him to walk back to his car. Ed had left the door open, the engine running. Jack turned off the motor. He heard him pull the keys. He tried to sit up, his legs on fire. There seemed to be too much blood on the pavement. Hell, had one of the bullets hit a major artery? Was he going to bleed to death in this dirty street?

"I have to get to a doctor," Ed called to him as Jack withdrew the device he'd used to track him and stomped it to rubble under his boot heel. "If you take my keys, I'm going to bleed to death."

Jack walked toward him, the keys jiggling in his hand. Ed saw that his gun was tucked into the waist of Jack's jeans. The other gun was still dangling from the fingers of Jack's right hand.

"Don't let me see you again," Jack said as he hurled the keys into the open doorway of a nearby abandoned warehouse. Ed's gun followed.

Ed heard both hit and then fall as if tumbling down into a hole. He swore, groaning in pain as he watched Jack walk back to the pickup. The engine turned over and he sped off down the street.

Praying he didn't bleed to death before anyone found him, he pulled out his cell phone and hit his brother's number.

"I WANT TO talk to Cassidy," Sarah said again to Dr. Venable. He'd pulled out his cell phone but he hadn't made the call.

"What if I can't make that happen?" He looked from the phone to her. "I know you don't believe it, but I'm just an old man whose time has passed."

True or not, he would do as she said. "You want me to convince Buck to stay in the race? Then you fix it so I can talk to my daughter and make sure she is all right. If something happens to her—"

"You are threatening the wrong person for three very important reasons. One, I have no power in this organization anymore."

"So you say."

"Two, while it is true that I have no power when it comes to making decisions within the organization... I alone hold the key to your memories."

"And three...?" she asked impatiently.

"The Prophecy can pull off the plan without you. But more people will suffer in retaliation because of it. Do I have to spell out how far these people are willing to go?"

No, she thought. *They've kidnapped my daughter. They've tried to kill another of my children.* Sarah swallowed the lump in her throat and fought not to show her fear. "Once I talk to Cassidy—"

"I told you—"

She swallowed her fear and drew on her anger. "Make it happen. Or I will take my chances with Sheriff Curry."

CASSIDY COULDN'T MOVE let alone speak as Jack slid behind the wheel and, after pocketing his handgun, drove on down the street as if nothing had happened.

He'd driven several blocks before she found her voice. *"You shot him. Twice."*

He glanced over at her, looking surprised. "What did you want me to do? Let him kill us both? I only wounded him. He'll live."

The coldness in his voice shocked her. What had made her think she knew this man? What had made her trust him? Quaking inside, she tried to catch her breath.

"I'm sorry you had to witness that," he said after a moment. "But if I hadn't wounded him, he would have killed me and then gone after you."

She could feel him looking over at her every few seconds as he drove.

"You do understand that these people mean business, right?" he asked. "It's like being in a war. You can't hesitate or you're dead. You can't think about the person coming at you with a gun as a man with a wife and kids and dreams. He is just the enemy and it is do or die."

Her voice sounded small, but calmer than she felt when she spoke again. "You make it sound as if you deal with this kind of thing all the time."

"I've had to deal with these kinds of circumstances before, if that's what you're asking."

She finally faced him again, surprised to find him frowning as if confused by her reaction.

"Who are you?" she demanded.

"I told you—"

"You told me you worked on a ranch."

"I do."

"But you carry a gun and I just saw how quick you are to use it."

Jack looked over at her. "I spent four years in the military. I was a sharpshooter."

"A sniper?"

He nodded.

"But why do you still carry a gun?"

"When I worked for my father, I often handled the payroll deposit late at night, so I started carrying a gun. This city can be dangerous."

He didn't have to tell her that.

"I didn't mean to scare you back there, but Ed was armed. He would have killed me and taken you if I hadn't stopped him."

"I don't understand how he could have followed us. I didn't see any cars behind us."

"He didn't follow us. He tracked us. He put a tracking device on my truck probably when it was parked at the bank. I didn't want to shoot him. But I had to stop him and I had to make sure he didn't come after us again. At least for a while."

Cassidy considered his words. She'd never been in a situation like this. She'd never had to resort to violence. Nor had anyone around her. Growing up in Montana, she had learned to shoot a variety of her father's guns. Guns didn't scare her. Men who used them so easily did.

What did she really know about Jack Durand? Only what he'd told her.

And yet she'd trusted him from the moment he'd come barreling into her life.

"Did you get hold of your friend with the jet?" he asked. "Or have you changed your mind about me going with you?"

She looked out her side window. *Jump out of the car at the next red light and run.* But as Jack slowed for the light ahead, she looked out at the run-down neighborhood and asked herself what she would do then. Call her father? Her older sister Ainsley?

"Beany, if you want to bail on me, I understand. Right now, I suspect you want to call your father, have him call in the secret service or the National Guard to protect you. But there's something you should know. My father has friends high up in the government. Right now, I don't think we can trust anyone, especially anyone in the FBI."

She looked over at him in surprise. He knew what she'd been thinking of doing. "You can't really believe that your father has men in the FBI."

"You don't know my father. Do you recall when we were at his office before you knew who he was? You were looking at the photos of him with dignitaries, presidents and other famous people."

She swallowed the lump that formed in her throat at the memory.

"You also saw what was in the safe-deposit box. A man who can accumulate that much wealth has friends in high places. Which is another reason why, if you decide to call your…friend Evan, you won't want to involve him in this and put him in danger."

This thing with The Prophecy couldn't be that big, that widespread, she told herself. But then her father was running for the highest office and most powerful position in the world and yet these people had dared try to kidnap one of his daughters. The man who sat in that chair at the White House would have his finger on a button that could destroy the world.

So did she really think that her father's enemies wouldn't use everything at their disposal? Even one of his daughters.

She looked over at Jack, studying his handsome face for any sign of deceit. He looked as tired as she felt. That man back there had tried to kill him. That man who worked for Jack's father. Her heart broke for Jack. Had his father ordered the hit on him? Had her mother ordered the men to kidnap her?

They were in this together. Jack had shot the man to save her. If it wasn't for him, she would be locked up somewhere—if not dead. Not to mention, Jack was the one who had found information about her mother—and his father. If she wanted answers that could make this all stop, then she couldn't bail on him.

"I'm sorry I questioned you about what happened back there," she said. "You were just doing what you had to."

He nodded, but she could see that he was anything but complacent about it. His voice was rough when he spoke. "When I left Iraq, I thought I would never have to shoot another human being."

Leaning down, she picked up her cell phone from the floorboards, having forgotten all about it when the shooting started. She'd been reaching for the phone when Jack had ordered her to stay down. Seconds later she'd heard the loud reports of gunfire. She'd frozen, heart in her throat. When she'd finally braved a look, she'd been transfixed by what was taking place in the street and too paralyzed with shock to move.

Now, with trembling fingers she keyed in Evan's number. It rang three times before he answered.

WHEN HIS PHONE RANG, Tom Durand snatched it up. All he wanted to hear right now was that Ed had Cassidy Hamilton. He had a place all ready for her. It would be just a matter of waiting for Joe to give him the order as to what to do with her.

"Tom?" The voice was old. It cracked with a tension that instantly set his nerves on end. "It's Doc."

Dr. Venable? What the devil was he calling for?

"I have Sarah here," the old man said. "She demands to speak to her daughter. Otherwise, she says she is going to the sheriff."

Durand swore silently. "Have you called Joe about this?" He heard the old man hesitate.

"I thought speaking to you would be preferable under the circumstances."

He almost laughed. Even Doc didn't want to deal with Joe. But he was grateful. All he needed was Joe calling him and wanting to speak with Cassidy.

"Well, I can't get a phone to her right now. In fact, it could take at least a day."

"That long?" The doctor sounded disappointed to hear that. "Sarah is quite adamant. What shall I tell her?"

"That if she wants to see her daughter alive again, she will sit tight and wait. And if she puts up a fuss, we'll take her daughter Ainsley. I have a man in position who can take her out as well. Or there is always Bo. She's pregnant with twins. Doesn't seem like a good time to take her under the circumstances. Tell Sarah, it's entirely up to her."

Silence, then "I will relay that message to her."

Tom had disconnected with a curse and quickly keyed in Ed's number, unable to wait any longer. If Joe found out that he didn't really have Cassidy...

Ed sounded breathless when he finally answered.

"What's going on?"

"I can't talk right now."

"The hell you can't," Durand said. *"What's going on?"*

"I've been shot."

The words reverberated in his skull for a few moments. "Who shot you?"

Silence, then he heard Ed talking to someone. "That was the nurse," Ed said after a moment.

"Who shot you?" he demanded, fearing he already knew. He cursed the day he taught Jack to shoot. He'd been surprised how the kid had taken to it. Even at a young age, he'd been a crackerjack of a shot. It was no wonder that he had excelled in the service.

Tom had been so proud of him. That small accomplishment had given him hope that his son would turn out all right. But he'd turned into a rancher instead of a partner in The Prophecy.

"Jack," Ed whispered into the phone.

Swearing, the questions piled up before spilling out in a rush. "Jack shot you? How could that have happened? He went to the bank, right? You didn't have this shoot-out at the bank? You better be dying, otherwise—"

"He went to the bank, just like you thought. I put the tracking device on his pickup. I followed him and when a delivery truck blocked him in on a street in some run-down industrial area, I got out to get the girl and take care of Jack."

"But instead he shot you and got away with the girl. Wait a minute, did you say *nurse*? You let them take you to the hospital? The cops will be called. What the hell were you thinking?"

"I almost bled to death," Ed barked, then quickly lowered his voice. "I told them here it was a drive-by shooting since I was found in an area known for drugs. I called my little brother, Alec. He'll find them."

Durand nearly crushed his phone in his fist. "I want results and if I don't get them immediately—" He disconnected, too angry to speak further. He needed Cassidy locked down. As for his son still being alive, he couldn't help feeling relieved. No matter what, Jack was his blood.

He tried to calm down and think. First things first, he told himself. Check the safe-deposit box at the bank. Maybe Jack hadn't been able to get into it. Tom knew he was clutching at straws, but he had to know just how deep his son was in all this.

If worse came to worst, he would have to handle this himself.

CHAPTER FOURTEEN

SHERIFF FRANK CURRY sat on the picnic table outside the Beartooth General Store watching two young crows playing keep-away with a leaf. The birds had always fascinated him because of their human characteristics. They were smarter than most people thought. Smarter than any cat or most children he'd met.

His cell phone rang. He hit Accept without looking to see who was calling.

"This is Dr. Ken Iverson at the state hospital. I'm calling about your daughter, Tiffany Chandler."

Frank felt that old ache, as painful as the bullet that had been meant to kill him. "Tiffany isn't—" He had started to say that she wasn't his daughter. That it had all been a lie, a revenge plot by Tiffany's mother. But he stopped, unwilling to get into that with the doctor. "What about her?" he asked, feeling suddenly drained.

An older bird cawed down from a pine bough off to his right. Neither of the young crows paid attention until the older one cawed again, changing the tone. The older one scolded the two young ones.

"Tiffany wants to see you." The doctor's tone made it clear that he couldn't understand why a father would go so long without visiting his daughter. Clearly, Tiffany had pulled the wool over the man's eyes. The doctor had no idea what kind of psychopath Tiffany was beneath that sweet, innocent-looking face of hers.

One of the young crows reluctantly dropped the leaf. The other started to grab it, but changed his mind. Both took flight, joining the older crow.

Frank had learned from his own family of crows that had taken up residency at his ranch house that crows have a vocabulary of thirty or more unique calls. He knew when they were upset or when they were simply saying hello to him. He could even tell the crows apart by their calls, each unique to the bird.

"Did you hear what I said?" the doctor asked, sounding even more perturbed.

He looked away from the crows. "Did she happen to mention what this was about?"

"I'm sorry but I don't understand your reluctance to—"

"I'm sure you don't understand. Tell Tiffany I'll think about it." He disconnected and went back to watching the crow family for a moment. The older authoritative figure was giving the two young crows hell, no doubt for not coming when they were called.

All three flew away as Frank's wife joined him with two small brown paper lunch bags and two cans of orange soda. He'd lost his appetite after the call from the mental hospital, but he took the bag she offered him and smiled as she sat down.

"Are you all right?" she asked, studying him.

"I was just watching the crows," he said. One of their first dates was crow watching. "They are so much like us and yet they seem to have a lot more figured out than we do."

She raised a brow. "I've seen them attack one of their own and kill it."

He nodded. "I'm sure they have their reasons, probably their form of crow justice. Less inhumane than ours. But I was thinking more of how they form families, adopting loners and orphans. They don't care so much about blood as we do."

"You're in a strange mood," she commented as she took out her sandwich. She was eyeing him curiously. He studied his wife for a moment. Everyone called her by her nickname, Nettie, but he preferred to call her by her given name, Lynette. It was something he'd started years ago when they were both kids and it had stuck over the years.

"Frank, what's going on?" she asked, pulling him out of his musings.

"Tiffany wants to see me."

She had just started to take a bite and now stopped in midmotion. "Why?"

He shook his head. "The doctor either didn't know or didn't say."

"You told him that Tiffany isn't your daughter, right? That her mother was a lying, murdering psychopath and that the crazy nut didn't fall far from the tree?"

He smiled over at her. Lynette's dyed red hair shone in the sunlight, her face was animated, her eyes bright. "I love you," he said with a sigh.

"So you didn't tell him."

"Enough of my dirty laundry has been hung up for the world to see, and what would be the point? Daughter or not, Tiffany isn't through with me."

"With us."

Silence fell between them. The crows had come back. Now there were three young ones. They were teasing each other with a twig and jumping around having fun. The older crow watched from a tree limb.

"Are you going to go see her?" Lynette finally asked.

He saw that she'd put her sandwich down. "I don't know. Probably not."

That seemed to relieve her. He dug out his sandwich. It could have been made of cardboard for all he tasted. But he ate it so his wife would eat hers. As he chewed, he thought about the day Tiffany had come out to his ranch and told him that she was the daughter his ex had kept from him for almost eighteen years.

He'd been so excited to have a child that he'd tried hard to overlook the…warning signs. Instead, he'd tried to make it up to the girl, thinking that maybe love could fill whatever dark hole her mother, Pam, had bored into her.

Ultimately, he hadn't been that surprised the day Tiffany had come to the ranch and killed one of his crows out of sheer meanness before turning the gun on him. One of the crows had dive-bombed her. He'd survived the wound. But his family of crows had left. He'd feared they would never return.

It had taken a long while, but finally they had come back. Like his wound, the bond between them had healed.

"You're sure there is no chance of Tiffany getting out of the mental hospital?" Lynette asked as she put her half-eaten sandwich back into the bag.

He wished he hadn't said anything. He'd spoiled their lunch. "I don't want you worrying about that.

Even if she found a way…" He let the rest of the thought hang in the air. "I will protect you to the death. You know that."

"Even if it means killing her?"

Frank nodded solemnly. "I just hope to hell it never comes to that."

AFTER CASSIDY MADE the call to Evan, they went to a restaurant, though neither of them had much appetite. Evan called back to say he'd made the necessary arrangements and gave directions to a private airstrip where they could meet later in the day. Since it wasn't far away, they only had a few hours to kill.

They shopped for new clothing in the swanky outskirts of Houston before they'd meet Evan. Jack bought a couple pair of jeans, some shirts and underwear, unsure how long he would be gone.

Cassidy insisted he also buy some warmer clothing. "You've never been to Montana, right?"

He admitted he hadn't.

"Then you're in for a surprise even though it is summer there," she said. "It gets cold at night. Especially for a Texas boy." She was trying to make light of what came next. But he could see how vulnerable she was. He wanted to take her in his arms and hold her, but she was more distant since their encounter with Ed Urdahl. Not that he could blame her. Nothing like this had ever happened to her before. He forgot sometimes how other people lived. Not everyone had to carry a gun. Not everyone had ever had to worry about killing before being killed.

As they headed for his truck after buying clothing, he asked, "Do you have a plan for when we land in Montana?"

She looked surprised by the question as if it was obvious. "Just confront my mother."

"It will be late by the time we get there. You're sure your father won't be with her? Or even another member of The Prophecy?"

She wasn't sure, of course. He could see that she was winging this—just as he had been.

"For all we know, she was behind your kidnapping," Jack pointed out. "If my father was willing to have me killed for whatever this anarchist group is up to, then why wouldn't your mother be just as dangerous?"

Cassidy bit her lip. "What choice do we have?" She sounded scared, tired and discouraged.

"We could take the money and run."

Her smile was knowing. "Is that really what you want to do?"

"I just don't want anything to happen to you." They rode the rest of the way to the airstrip in silence.

When they arrived, they unloaded their shopping bags and made their way across the tarmac. Jack felt the weight of the world on his shoulders as they walked toward the plane.

Evan Chadron was just as rich and good-looking and well-groomed as Jack had expected him to be. It was also instantly clear that Evan hadn't gotten over Cassidy.

"Like your new look," Evan said, leaning in to give her a kiss on her cheek.

She beamed at him and touched her hair. "Just trying something different."

Evan's gaze shifted to Jack, his expression making

it clear that he thought Jack was also something different she was trying. Clearly, Evan didn't think either the hairdo or Jack would be staying around long.

Unlike him and Cassidy, Evan Chadron didn't appear to have a care in the world. "When you called and asked for a lift to Montana, I was thrilled," he said as they boarded the plane. "I was planning to head back to Virginia tomorrow, so you caught me at just the right time."

"Lucky that you just happened to be so close by," Jack agreed.

"I was in New Orleans on business," Evan said. "I'm sorry, what kind of business did you say you were in?"

"I didn't."

"Jack is a rancher," Cassidy said. "He's been a lifesaver. I was mugged and Jack saved me. And now you're saving me by giving me a ride back to Montana."

Evan's eyebrows shot up. "Well, I'm glad I could be of service." His gaze shifted again to Jack. "So you're seeing her home safely?"

"He's never been to Montana."

That didn't answer the real question Evan was asking, but Cassidy quickly changed the subject as they settled in by asking about old friends they had in common.

Jack only half listened to the two of them chat on about beach parties in the Hamptons, spring breaks in the French Riviera and who was with whom as they waited for their flight plan to be cleared.

He couldn't help worrying about what his father would do once he found the empty safe-deposit box. Scrap the whole abduction idea? Not likely. Ed was out of commission, but Jack was sure there were other men willing to do his father's bidding for a price.

With targets on his and Cassidy's backs, the question was what to do once they reached Montana. Cassidy was determined to confront her mother. Was she looking for answers? Or was she hoping that she was wrong about her mother being a member of The Prophecy?

No one wanted to believe that their parents could hurt them, but Jack had been around long enough to know it happened all the time.

As he tried to concentrate on what lay ahead, he found his attention drawn to Cassidy. She was playing her part. She was laughing at something Evan had said, her blue eyes bright and shiny, her lips parted. He felt a pang of jealousy as he thought about their kiss.

Her gaze shifted to his. For a moment, the sadness and fear in her eyes lifted. Her lips turned up at the corners and something like a thunderbolt seemed to pass between them before she turned back to Evan.

Jack had warned himself not to fall for this woman, but he felt as if he'd just taken a tumble. He would give his life to keep Beany safe.

Stepping away from them into the ultraluxurious jet's private cabin, Jack made the call he'd been dreading. His father answered on the first ring.

"JACK." It was his father's patient voice, the one Jack had grown up with. The calm but disappointed, on edge but not-quite-going-to-explode voice.

Now that he had him on the phone, he didn't know where to begin. Unlike his father, he wanted to blow up. He wanted to demand to know what the hell Tom

Durand, or whatever he called himself, was doing paying a dockworker to kidnap the apparent future president's daughter.

"We should meet," his father said. "Somewhere quiet so we can have a civilized conversation. There is a lot I need to tell you."

"*Meet?* Do you think I'm stupid?"

"No, I think you're very bright and that I've underestimated you. You've proven yourself to be more like me than I ever thought possible."

"I. Am. Nothing. Like. You. I don't even know who you are. You're certainly not the man I thought you were."

"You know me. Isn't that why you're calling?"

"I'm calling because I have everything that was in your safe-deposit box from the bank and I'm assuming you want it back."

Silence, then "That money's not mine and if it doesn't get to the person it belongs to—"

"I don't want to know what you're involved in. I just want you to leave Cassidy Hamilton alone."

"What are we talking here? A *deal*? You're my son so of course I don't want anything to happen to you or the girl. Once we talk—"

"Let's start with why you paid Ed Urdahl to kidnap Cassidy Hamilton," Jack said. "And please don't waste my time by lying."

"Fine. Cassidy's father is thinking of dropping out of the presidential race. My friends don't want that to happen."

Jack frowned. "So this is about…*leverage*? That's it?"

"These kinds of things happen all the time in politics. You just don't hear about them because they're handled…privately."

He'd never heard such bull. "So once Hamilton agrees to stay in the race, you let his daughter go?"

"Of course."

"Why am I having a hard time believing this? Oh, I know. It's because Ed Urdahl just tried to kill me."

"He is no longer a problem."

"Only because I put a bullet in each of the man's legs."

"Look, Jack. I'm assuming you have Cassidy with you. I just need her to stay out of sight for a few days until an arrangement can be made with her father. It's that simple. No more violence. I will call you when it's over and you can see that she gets home safely. After that, we can talk about your future."

His father sounded so reasonable. "Why do you want Hamilton to be president so badly that you would kidnap his daughter?"

"As president, he'll see that businesses like mine can still make a profit. If the damned Democrats get in—"

"What kind of business is that?" Silence. "Is this about The Prophecy?"

Tom Durand sighed. "That was a long time ago. I was more radical in my thinking when I was younger."

"I guess killing innocent people *is* more radical than kidnapping."

In the silence that followed, he could almost see his father mashing his teeth. "Jack, you know so little about the way the world is run. I'm sorry that you had to find out this way."

He would just bet his father was. "I'm going to contact Senator Buckmaster Hamilton and tell him that his daughter Cassidy is fine. Whatever game you're playing—"

"If you do that, one of his other daughters will be

taken. I understand Bo is pregnant with twins. It could be disastrous to abduct her in her fragile condition."

Jack swore under his breath as he heard the jet engines start up. "I didn't want to turn everything over to the FBI, but I can see that is the only way to stop you." He was bluffing. Just as he told Cassidy, he didn't trust the FBI at this point.

"You can't stop The Prophecy, but you can get Cassidy and her entire family killed if you do something impulsive."

"You're a monster."

"It wouldn't be my doing. Like I said, I'm not as radical as I used to be. But some of the other members—"

"Like Cassidy's mother?"

His father sighed. "She was the leader of The Prophecy back when she went by the name Red. So see, son, you really have no idea what you've stepped into. Please don't do anything that can jeopardize your life and that girl's any further."

Jack hung up as Cassidy opened the door to tell him that they were about to taxi and he needed to take his seat. "Is everything all right?" she asked as he put his phone away.

"Fine. I was just making arrangements for a car once we reach Montana." He'd already seen to that earlier when she'd been trying on clothes.

She nodded, but when her gaze met his, he felt that connection again. It was clear that she knew he was holding something back.

DR. VENABLE HAD promised that he would pass on Sarah's message to Joe. "But as I mentioned, I'm not sure continuing to threaten to go to the sheriff will be helpful."

"If I don't talk to my daughter—"

"I heard you clear as a bell," Doc had said as he left. "But she isn't where they can get a phone to her right now. You'll talk to her tomorrow."

She'd been so shaken that she'd collapsed the moment the door closed behind him. Her mind raced as to what she could do to save Cassidy, to stop this insanity. Had she really come up with some doomsday plan? Had she been that fanatical, that crazy?

Doc hadn't been gone long when Sarah heard a vehicle and looked out, shocked to see that it was Buck. He'd said he had to go to Helena. But surely he hadn't had time to go all that way and already return. What if he'd returned minutes ago and caught Dr. Venable leaving?

She quickly moved away from the window, scanning the living room as if searching for any evidence that anyone had been here. She was still shaking inside with fury and fear. The Prophecy had Cassidy. The last thing she could do was the one thing she desperately wanted to do—throw herself into Buck's arms and plead for his help.

He couldn't help her. Not against The Prophecy. If he thought there was a chance he might be blackmailed once in office, he would quit the race, get the FBI after The Prophecy and risk everything—including Cassidy's life—to bring an end to this. He didn't know these people. Sarah knew them from the nightmares that had plagued her since her return. They would kill Cassidy and then go after her other daughters.

After that, Sarah would be arrested. That's if The Prophecy hadn't killed them all.

As she heard Buck on the front stoop, she rushed

to the door and threw it open. "Did you forget something?"

He had a strange look on his face as he glanced past her. "Actually, I did. I can't find my phone. I thought I might have left it in the bedroom."

"Do you want me to look?" she asked, opening the door wider and stepping back.

"No, I can." He moved past her and headed for the bedroom. She saw him looking around and then sniffing as if testing the air.

She took a whiff and caught the scent of spearmint. Dr. Venable chewed the mints when he was nervous. He'd had a mint before he'd left. She picked up the cell phone Doc had taken from her hand earlier. He'd left it on the end table. She thought maybe her and Buck's phones had gotten switched. But it was her phone.

Pocketing it, she followed Buck as far as the kitchen. *Tell him everything. Maybe you're wrong. Maybe he can save Cassidy and destroy The Prophecy and make all of this go away.*

"Buck?" Her gaze wandered to the kitchen counter as she heard him moving around in the bedroom. With horror, she saw Doc's tie. He'd left it there that one day. She recalled the way he'd tugged it off and tossed it aside. She'd found it later and had balled it up, thinking to toss it in the trash in the kitchen she'd been so furious with him for coming back into her life.

Instead, she'd balled it up and stuck it in the corner, not wanting to look at it.

Now she saw that the tie was no longer balled—nor was it where she'd put it. Buck. Her heart hammered so hard, she thought it might rip its way out of her chest.

Her cell phone vibrated in her pocket, startling her.

With trembling fingers, she fumbled it out. When had she put it on vibrate? She hadn't. With a shock, she recalled Dr. Venable asking for a glass of water earlier. She'd left him alone in the living room with her phone. Had he done something else with her phone besides putting it on vibrate?

The words of the text swam before her eyes. Make another demand and Cassidy dies.

She stared in horror at the words.

A photo popped up on the screen. It was of Cassidy coming out of a building in some city. Another photo popped up of what appeared to be the pale blue sweater Cassidy had been wearing in the earlier photo. Only it had a large dark stain on it. Blood?

Sarah hurriedly tried her daughter's cell phone. It went straight to voice mail. She was about to try again when Buck walked into the room.

Buck came out of the bedroom holding his phone. She jumped, startled as if she'd forgotten he was still in the house. "Is everything all right?"

She swallowed the bile that had risen in her throat and tried to calm herself. She knew what Buck would do if she told him. He'd have the National Guard out looking for Cassidy. But it would be too late.

There was only one way to save Cassidy. Buck had to stay in the race for president. And yet, if he won...

Sarah realized she still had her phone in her hand. "I got a text from Cassidy," she said, quickly improvising. "She's met some man and is flying back to Europe for a few days. That's why we haven't been able to reach her."

He looked relieved. "Then she's all right. But I was hoping she would come home for a while."

"I'm sure she will soon. Buck, we need to talk. I don't want you to quit the race. I *won't* let you quit. Our country needs you. I need you to follow your dream." She brightened as she stepped to him and put her arms around him, kissing him before he could argue. "I will be right by your side. I want this for us, please, Buck, reconsider quitting."

"Sarah—" The phone in his hand rang and he swore as he glanced at the screen. "I came back to tell you that I have to return to Washington." He met her gaze. "Tell me you're going to marry me."

She nodded, smiling through the burn of tears. "I can't wait to marry you."

"And you'll come with me on the campaign trail?"

"I'll have to buy some new clothes and get my hair done, but of course I will."

He let out a laugh and she felt herself relax a little. "Spoken just like a woman." He sobered. "Seriously, if you want me to quit—"

"I don't know where you got that idea. Yes, I was hesitant for us to get too involved, but only because I thought it might jeopardize your chances of being president."

He was studying her as if trying to tell if she was lying. He knew her well enough to know that she was holding back something. He got another text.

"You should get going so you don't miss your flight."

"If you're sure…"

"I'm sure." She held his gaze.

"Then start planning the wedding. We're getting married as soon as possible. I need you on the campaign trail with me." He sounded relieved. Almost happy. Something was still bothering him, though. If he only knew…

He leaned in to give her a quick peck. "I'll call you later and we'll talk."

And he was gone. She listened to the sound of his car engine die off in the distance, telling herself he didn't know anything. If asked, she would come up with a story for the tie, for the smell of spearmint. Or she wouldn't mention either.

Breathing a sigh of relief, she told herself to plan a wedding. She had to concentrate on keeping Buck in the presidential race for Cassidy's sake. For all their sakes. Later she would worry about finding a way to destroy The Prophecy.

Unless Dr. Venable gets into your head and brings back Red, the terrorist woman from your nightmares. Who knows how you will feel about any of this then.

CHAPTER FIFTEEN

WHEN THE JET landed at the Bozeman Yellowstone International Airport, Evan offered to hang around for a few days in case Cassidy wanted to go somewhere else. Clearly, he couldn't understand what she was doing with Jack.

"Thanks, but I think we can take if from here," Jack said, picking up their bags and ushering her toward the door.

She hid a secret smile. Jack was acting like a jealous boyfriend. Any other time, she might have resented his behavior. But she'd never felt as close to Evan as she did Jack. There was something about him. Or maybe it was something about the way she felt when she was with him.

"Thank you so much for the plane ride," she said to Evan and gave him a hug.

"Call me," he whispered loud enough for Jack to hear.

Jack mugged a face, shaking his head as they exited the plane. "You actually *dated* that guy?" he said after they were on the tarmac headed toward the small private terminal.

"What's wrong with him?" she asked innocently. Raised in Montana on a ranch, she'd grown up around cowboys, so they had become her image of "real men."

That image didn't fit any of the young men she'd dated. That's why none ever lasted more than a few months tops.

"Just because a guy looks good on paper…" Jack muttered under his breath.

She laughed. "Give me some credit. There's probably a reason Evan is an *ex*-boyfriend, don't you think?"

Jack glanced over at her. He might be a Texas cowboy, but he fit right in here in Montana. He also fit right in to her image of a real man, she thought. He wasn't just handsome. She liked the confident way he carried himself, the way he sized up people and the way he came to a woman's rescue.

But there was also a dangerous side to Jack, she reminded herself, still shocked how easily he'd been able to shoot the man who'd come after them. Strange, but maybe that was part of the appeal. Jack would do whatever it took to protect her. How could a woman not swoon over a man like that?

Careful, she warned herself, and balked at the thought of falling for Jack. Even if their lives weren't so tangled in this mess with their parents, she wasn't one to fall in love after just one kiss. And yet even as she thought it, she felt a connection to Jack that felt deeper than what had brought them together.

Jack went to get the SUV he'd called for, and feeling nervous and at loose ends, Cassidy had walked into the gift shop to wait. Impulsively, she bought Jack a T-shirt with mountains and Montana printed on it.

As she stepped out of the shop, she saw Jack pull up. She hurried outside and stopped to breathe in the cool, sweet air. She'd been gone so long that she'd forgotten this. Forgotten the way the sun shone on the pine-covered mountains. Forgotten Montana's big sky's deep blue color. Forgotten the way it smelled.

"Memories?" Jack asked as he opened the driver's side door and glanced over the top of the vehicle at her.

She nodded, oddly feeling close to tears. "I've been away at school for years now, coming home only for family events and leaving again. I'd forgotten what I love about being here." She smiled through fresh tears. "It's nice to be home."

It wasn't until they were on the highway headed for Beartooth that she finally asked, "Are you going to tell me who you called from the plane before we took off?"

He didn't even pretend surprise that she'd known he was lying earlier. "My father."

She felt her eyebrow shoot up. "Was that wise?"

"We were sitting at the airport outside of Houston. Even if he could trace the call, which he might have, he wouldn't know where we were going. He told me why he'd paid Ed to snatch you. It was just as we suspected. Leverage. Your father apparently has been thinking about pulling out of the race."

Cassidy shook her head in disbelief. That was news to her. "So he was going to kidnap me to keep my father from doing that?" She couldn't help being appalled.

"He said I was naive not to know that it is the way politics are done. Believe me, I've been hearing versions of this my whole life. All's fair in love and war and business with him."

"Did you ask him about The Prophecy and my mother?"

JACK CONCENTRATED ON his driving as Highway 191 began to climb toward the Bozeman Pass. This was once the route that the first settlers had taken when they'd brought cattle up from Texas to settle the Gallatin Valley.

Before her question, he'd been admiring this wild, beautiful country with its towering pine-clad mountains and clear running streams. He'd never been to Montana before but he could see why it was called the Big Sky Country.

"I told him if he wanted what was in that safe-deposit box from the bank, then he needed to call off his goons."

"And if he didn't?"

"I was going to take the box and everything else I knew about him to the FBI."

"But you said we couldn't go to the FBI."

He nodded.

"So it didn't scare him," she said, sensing that the call hadn't gone well.

"He said that if they don't have you, they'll take one of your sisters."

"No!" She stared at him and then shook her head. "That's why I have to confront my mother."

For once, he thought she might be right.

"She's my *mother*. She gave me and my sisters life. She wouldn't hurt us."

"And Tom Durand aka Martin Wagner is my *father*." Ahead, the highway climbed up over the mountains.

"I don't know what else to do," she said in a pleading tone. "I don't know what to believe."

"I haven't known what to believe or do since the moment this all began," he said. The highway dropped down through the foothills, then wove through lush green countryside as it followed the Yellowstone River.

Cassidy shook her head as if in frustration either

with him or the situation before turning to look out at the passing scenery. "I want to look her in the eye and ask her. If she's behind my kidnapping…"

"I guess we'll know soon enough," he said. "This is a no-win situation. My father said that if I go to the feds, they will take one of your sisters. Bo. Apparently, she's pregnant with twins?"

Cassidy looked horrified. "We can't let them win."

Jack rubbed the back of his neck as he drove. "Let's stop and get some supplies, then go to this house you said we could stay in. I don't know about you, but I'm exhausted. Maybe after a night's sleep…"

Cassidy nodded and he saw that she had her phone in her hand. "My mother's called four times. She left a message." She played it for him.

"Cassidy, I have to talk to you. I have to know you're okay. Please. Call. Me."

Sarah sounded scared and worried. But was she scared and worried that her daughter had been abducted? Or that she hadn't?

"There is something else my father told me that I think you should know," Jack said. "He said your mother was the leader of The Prophecy. That she went by the name Red. And that we have no idea what we've gotten ourselves into. I think he's at least right about that."

RUSSELL MURDOCK OPENED his front door late that night to find the last man he would have expected standing on his front step. *"Buck?"*

The senator had been staring toward the Crazy Mountains behind the ranch house. As he turned his attention to Russell, it was clear this was the last place he wanted to be.

"We need to talk."

Russell didn't like the sound of that. There was no love lost between them since they'd both fallen for the same woman. "If this is about Sarah—"

"Of course it's about Sarah." Buck snapped. "Are you going to let me in or are we going to have to do this standing out here on your doorstep?"

Russell wasn't easily intimidated, even by a man who might become his future president. "I guess it depends on what you have in mind," he said, but stepped back to let Buck come in on a gust of mountain air.

Once in, Buck stood in the center of the living room as if suddenly unsure.

"If this is about my seeing Sarah the other day—"

"So you're seeing her, too." Buck didn't sound happy about that, but not surprised.

"I just went by to check on her."

"You think she needs checking on?"

Russell sighed. "What is it you want? Sarah made her choice and it was you. So what are you all riled up about now?"

Buck cleared his throat, his expression changing from anger to almost embarrassment. "I'm sorry, but I didn't know where else to go. I don't want to be here any more than you want me here. I need your help. I understand you did some checking into her memory loss."

It was clear that Buck was anxious. Russell chose his words carefully. "It wasn't memory loss per se. Her brain was wiped of…certain memories."

The senator met his gaze. "I know you think I had

something to do with that, but you're wrong. It's that doctor."

"Dr. Venable?" The man had his attention now.

"I saw him going into her house today and it didn't look as if it was the first time."

"What?" Russell couldn't believe this. "You're sure it was him?"

"He's older, but he looks like the photograph the sheriff showed me months ago. It's the doctor she apparently was with in Brazil during the twenty-two years she can't remember."

Russell shook his head. "I knew he was back in the States. I warned Sarah. I don't understand why she didn't call me."

"She doesn't want us to know that she's seeing him," Buck said as he looked around. "I don't suppose you have anything to drink?"

"Bourdon."

Buck nodded as Russell went to the kitchen and poured them both a glass. He handed the senator his and took a chair. Buck sat down heavily in a chair opposite him.

"I just don't understand it. She knows how dangerous this man is," Russell said more to himself. Then it hit him. "She thinks he can restore her memory." He swore, something he seldom did. "But doesn't she realize he might implant false memories? *Dangerous* memories?"

"Maybe he already has," Buck said with a sigh as he looked down into the dark amber of his drink. "She isn't the same woman who left me." Russell could tell the admission came hard for him. Buck looked up as if surprised that he'd just admitted it to a man he didn't like, a man he'd been in competition with. "Something is definitely going on with her. I thought she just didn't like my running for president, but I suspect it's much deeper than that. So you didn't know about this?"

Russell shook his head and took a drink, needing to feel the alcohol burn down through him. He was angry and disappointed in Sarah. He couldn't help but think of the first time he'd laid eyes on her. He'd almost run her over that day over a year and a half ago when she'd come stumbling out of the trees along the deserted road north of Beartooth. He'd had no idea how she would change his life.

She'd seemed so vulnerable and yet at times, he glimpsed another woman, a woman who even he suspected might be dangerous. The more he'd learned about her, the more he'd wanted to save her. It hadn't helped that he'd fallen in love with her, almost married her. "I still can't believe she'd let a man like Dr. Venable near her again."

Buck shoved to his feet. "Well, I'm putting a stop to it right now. I'm going to the sheriff and have him arrested."

"On what charges?"

"He wiped her brain of memories of her own children."

"Not sure that one is on the books," Russell said. "Don't you think you'd better talk to Sarah about this before you do anything rash?"

Buck slowly sat down again. "I could kill the bastard with my bare hands."

He felt the same way. "I think Sarah's in trouble," he said after a moment. "If you had nothing to do with this—"

"I sure as hell didn't. If I was guilty, would I be here now?"

"Then we have to assume Sarah contacted Dr. Venable the night she tried to kill herself all those years ago. What is their relationship that she would trust such a man not only back then, but again now?"

"WHAT ARE THOSE MOUNTAINS?" Jack asked, in awe. Against the evening sky, they were a jagged deep purple that seemed to rise straight up out of the ground.

"The Crazy Mountains, or the Crazies, as we call them," Cassidy said as she opened the bag from the airport gift shop. "I bought you something at the airport."

"You did?"

"Something to always remind you of Montana." She pulled out a T-shirt with the word Montana scrawled across mountains. In small print under the mountains were the words *Crazy Mountains*.

He laughed, touched by her thoughtfulness. "I love it." His gaze me hers. "Thank you. Whenever I wear it I will think of Montana. And you."

His gaze locked with hers for an instant. She looked embarrassed and pulled away first. "Keep going on up the road. We're almost to the ranch."

Minutes later he drew up in front of a small older ranch house that stood against the backdrop of the towering toothed mountain range.

"These mountains are incredible. Is that snow up there this time of year?"

She laughed and opened her door. "At one time or another, it has snowed in every month of the year in Montana."

Jack stepped out into the cold night air. He was

YOUR PARTICIPATION IS REQUESTED!

Dear Reader,

Since you are a lover of our books – we would like to get to know you!

Inside you will find a short Reader's Survey. Sharing your answers with us will help our editorial staff understand who you are and what activities you enjoy.

To thank you for your participation, we would like to send you 2 books and 2 gifts – **ABSOLUTELY FREE!**

Enjoy your gifts with our appreciation,

Pam Powers

SEE INSIDE FOR READER'S SURVEY

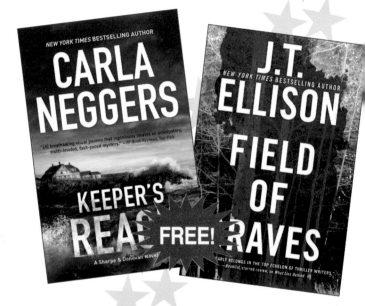

YOUR READER'S SURVEY
"THANK YOU" FREE GIFTS INCLUDE:
- ▶ **2 FREE books**
- ▶ **2 lovely surprise gifts**

PLEASE FILL IN THE CIRCLES COMPLETELY TO RESPOND

1) What type of fiction books do you enjoy reading? (Check all that apply)
- ○ Suspense/Thrillers ○ Action/Adventure ○ Modern-day Romances
- ○ Historical Romance ○ Humor ○ Paranormal Romance

2) What attracted you most to the last fiction book you purchased on impulse?
- ○ The Title ○ The Cover ○ The Author ○ The Story

3) What is usually the greatest influencer when you <u>plan</u> to buy a book?
- ○ Advertising ○ Referral ○ Book Review

4) How often do you access the internet?
- ○ Daily ○ Weekly ○ Monthly ○ Rarely or never.

5) How many NEW paperback fiction novels have you purchased in the past 3 months?
- ○ 0 - 2 ○ 3 - 6 ○ 7 or more

YES! I have completed the Reader's Survey. Please send me the 2 FREE books and 2 FREE gifts (gifts are worth about $10) for which I qualify. I understand that I am under no obligation to purchase any books, as explained on the back of this card.

191/391 MDL GLDN

FIRST NAME	LAST NAME

ADDRESS

APT.#	CITY

STATE/PROV.	ZIP/POSTAL CODE

SUS-816-SFF15

READER SERVICE—Here's how it works:

Accepting your 2 free Suspense books and 2 free gifts (gifts valued at approximately $10.00) places you under no obligation to buy anything. You may keep the books and gifts and return the shipping statement marked "cancel." If you do not cancel, about a month later we'll send you 4 additional books and bill you just $6.49 each in the U.S. or $6.99 each in Canada. That is a savings of at least 18% off the cover price. It's quite a bargain! Shipping and handling is just 50¢ per book in the U.S. and 75¢ per book in Canada.* You may cancel at any time, but if you choose to continue, every month we'll send you 4 more books, which you may either purchase at the discount price or return to us and cancel your subscription. *Terms and prices subject to change without notice. Prices do not include applicable taxes. Sales tax applicable in N.Y. Canadian residents will be charged applicable taxes. Offer not valid in Quebec. Books received may not be as shown. All orders subject to approval. Credit or debit balances in a customer's account(s) may be offset by any other outstanding balance owed by or to the customer. Please allow 4 to 6 weeks for delivery. Offer available while quantities last.

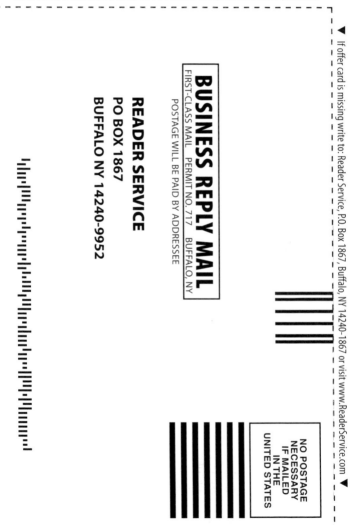

▲ If offer card is missing write to: Reader Service, P.O. Box 1867, Buffalo, NY 14240-1867 or visit www.ReaderService.com ▲

BUSINESS REPLY MAIL
FIRST-CLASS MAIL   PERMIT NO. 717   BUFFALO, NY

POSTAGE WILL BE PAID BY ADDRESSEE

READER SERVICE
PO BOX 1867
BUFFALO NY 14240-9952

NO POSTAGE
NECESSARY
IF MAILED
IN THE
UNITED STATES

used to Texas summers with their muggy, hot, breath-less nights. He took in the chilly sweet scent of pines as he turned to look at the valley below them. "This is your father's ranch?"

"Pretty much as far as you can see," she said.

He thought of his own ranch, which would have looked like a postage stamp in comparison. Dusk had settled over the valley. The pines left long dark shadows as the breeze whispered in the branches. "It's more beautiful here than even the photographs I've seen."

Cassidy nodded as she stood next to him in the growing darkness. "This is where I grew up."

"Not a bad place to grow up," he said, glancing over at her. "Come on, you look as tired as I feel. At least I got a little sleep on the plane."

She laughed. "You really are jealous of Evan," she said, turning on her heel and heading for the house.

"I'm not jealous of that..." He shut his mouth before he pushed his boot in farther and followed her.

Cassidy retrieved a key from a ledge around the side of the house and opened the door. A gust of stale air escaped as they entered. She snapped on a light. "The ranch uses this as a bunkhouse at different times of the year. So there is bedding. We can get whatever else we need. If we're here that long."

Jack carried their belongings in and looked around, wondering how long they *would* be staying here. The old ranch house with its dated wallpaper and linoleum flooring had a lost century feel to it. "It's homey," he said as he closed the door behind him.

"The bedrooms are upstairs," she said and put what supplies they'd bought in the refrigerator. "Take your pick." He heard the kitchen faucet spew water in stops and starts and then run for a few moments before she turned it off. "All the comforts of home," she said as she came out of the kitchen.

Jack suddenly felt awkward. The house felt too intimate here with her. He'd had relationships but he'd never let anyone move in just as he had never moved in with a woman. He liked his space.

"I'll take these upstairs," he said, picking up the two duffel bags with their clothing. He hesitated, wanting to warn her again about contacting her mother. "Try to get some sleep."

She nodded. "Jack," she said as he started up the stairs.

He stopped halfway to look back at her.

"Thank you. I've put you in danger and I'm sorry, but we'll figure this out."

"We're in this together, remember?" Then he repeated something his mother used to say. "Things will look better in the morning." He just wished he believed it.

CHAPTER SIXTEEN

"WE NEED TO talk to you."

Sheriff Frank Curry recognized the voice as that of Senator Buckmaster Hamilton. Frank raked a hand through his graying blond hair. "We?"

"Russell Murdock and I."

Frank blinked. He couldn't imagine what the two of them were doing together. Whatever it was, he was betting it wasn't good.

"Shall we come by your house or would you prefer to meet us?" Buck asked.

The sheriff had just gotten home, barely had hung his Stetson up on the hook by the door and was about to open a beer and relax. He glanced over at Lynette, who, not surprisingly, was all ears. "Tell me where you are and I'll come to you," he said, reaching for his hat.

He heard his wife put the beer back in the fridge and turn down whatever she had going in the oven. She'd been married to him long enough already that she'd learned that his job was never eight to five. Another reason retirement had its appeal. He felt often lately that he was getting too old for this.

Disconnecting, he called to the kitchen, "I'll be back as soon as I can."

Lynette peered through the doorway. "Everything

all right?" Which was her way of asking what was going on.

"Everything is fine. I shouldn't be long." He turned and left, his crows calling goodbye to him as he climbed into his patrol SUV and headed for Russell Murdock's.

BUCK WAS TOO anxious to sit. Russell had poured them another drink and then put the bottle away as if afraid they might finish it off.

At the sight of headlights coming up the road, he tried to relax, but it was impossible. He knew Russell thought he was wasting his time talking to the sheriff about this.

"He isn't going to arrest the man, if that's what you're hoping," the rancher had said.

"No, but at least he can talk to him, let this…doctor know that we're aware he's in town and visiting Sarah," Buck had argued.

"Wouldn't it make more sense to talk to Sarah yourself?"

Buck had sighed. "Do you really think she is going to tell either of us the truth?" He'd seen that Russell thought she might tell him. That didn't help his already furious disposition. He wished he hadn't come here on impulse, and yet he had needed someone to talk to who understood. He was just glad that Sarah hadn't been lying by omission only to him. She'd kept her former fiancé in the dark as well.

"I heard you bought Sarah a ring," Russell said from the corner where he'd been sitting, thinking and waiting.

Buck shot him a look as he heard the sheriff park and get out. "I want my family back."

Russell nodded, but the truth hung between them. Sarah wasn't the woman Buck had married. That family he'd had more than twenty-three years ago was gone the minute she'd driven her car into the icy Yellowstone River hoping to die. Or hoping to escape. Either way, she'd been gone and Buck's wife hadn't come back.

Buck jumped at the sheriff's knock on the door. He rushed to it and swung the door open wide. "'Bout time," he said under his breath.

Frank didn't react, just wiped his boot soles on the mat and took off his Stetson as he stepped in. His gaze went to Russell, who had gotten to his feet. "What's this about?" He sounded worried.

"Sarah," Buck snapped. "Who the hell do you think?"

CASSIDY COULDN'T SLEEP. She felt wired, her head aching with every kind of crazy thought. She still couldn't believe what was happening to her, let alone that Jack was up to his neck in this as well.

Stepping out onto the ranch house porch, she stood at the railing and watched as a huge orange moon seemed to rise from the valley floor. Hugging herself, she stood looking out across Hamilton Ranch. Tears burned her eyes. She felt as if she'd never appreciated any of this until now. True, her tears were partly from exhaustion. The adrenaline rushes she'd felt over the past forty-eight hours had depleted her energy.

She couldn't seem to control her thoughts—or her emotions. She knew she should go to bed. But the air out here felt good and seemed to help clear away some of the static in her brain. The night was infused with the scent of pines, the smells so familiar that they made her ache. She could hear an owl hooting softly from the trees. A slight breeze rustled the boughs, sounding like a contented sigh.

Cassidy thought of her mother. She'd had little contact with her since Sarah's return, but then again, the woman was a stranger to her. Intellectually, she knew that Sarah had given birth to her and her twin, Harper. But she had no memory of her.

And yet there was a tenuous connection that she could feel blood deep. Was that why she had to confront her? Because she believed that if she felt that mother/child bond, then surely her mother would have it even stronger.

Willing to bet your life on that? asked a small voice at the back of her mind.

The moon rose, seeming to set the horizon on fire with a blaze of color. The breeze picked up, sending down a chill from the snowcapped Crazies.

Go to bed, Cassidy. You can't figure out anything as tired as you are.

She thought of Jack's words. Would everything be clearer in the morning? She could only hope because the one thing she did know was that she couldn't hide out the rest of her life. While she appreciated her education, she hated that she hadn't accomplished anything yet in life.

Being back here made her more aware of an old dream she had of starting a commercial organic garden on the ranch. Her father had all this land, why not put it to use other than just feeding cows and horses?

She'd never mentioned her dream to even her sisters. They would all laugh. She hadn't wanted to think about what her father—a hard-core rancher—would say about it. But being back here made her yearn for that dream—or any one that promised her a future.

She was tired of bumming around the world telling herself she was getting an education. This was where she belonged. This was where she would make her mark on the world.

Unless her mother—and The Prophecy—had other plans for her. With a shudder, she went back inside and, doing something she'd never done on the ranch, she locked the door behind her. It felt foolish, given the age of the lock. Any fool could break in.

But she knew that even if the door had a half-dozen dead bolts, she wouldn't feel safe. What would it take to feel safe again, she wondered as she started up the stairs.

At the landing, she listened to Jack's rhythmic breathing from the open doorway of his bedroom. A feeling of peace washed over her as she made her way to her own room. After stripping off her clothes, she pulled on the white cotton gown she'd bought and slipped between the cool sheets.

Her head had barely touched the pillow when her eyes closed and she felt herself falling asleep as if tumbling down into a deep black hole.

FRANK PUT HIS Stetson aside and took the chair he was offered. He didn't need to wait long.

"That doctor, Dr. Ralph Venable, he's back and he's seeing Sarah," Buck bellowed. "You know damned well that he's messing with her memory again and only God knows what else. What are you going to do about it?"

Frank looked over to where Russell sat in the corner.

He had an empty drink glass in his hand that he turned in his fingers as if his mind was a million miles away.

"Russell?" the sheriff said. "You have something to say?"

He looked up in surprise, then slowly took a breath and let it out before he spoke. "Sarah's going to do whatever it is she wants to do." He shrugged and Frank got the feeling the rancher had already drunk more alcohol than was normal for him.

Buck waved a dismissive hand at Russell and his comment. "You have to run him out of town."

Frank laughed and shook his head. Was this what had brought these two adversaries together? A mutual hatred for Dr. Venable?

"This isn't the Old West, Buck. We don't tar and feather people we don't like and send them out on the rails. As long as the doctor hasn't done anything illegal—"

"Well, how would we know that?" Buck demanded.

"Also, if Sarah is seeing him of her own free will—"

"He's messing with her mind. She probably doesn't even know her own free will," the senator snapped.

"Have you talked to Sarah about this?" the sheriff asked and saw the answer right away. "But you know for a fact that Dr. Venable is in town and has had contact with her?"

"I saw him going into her house as if it wasn't his first time there and he…he left his tie there," Buck said and drained his glass to look around for the bottle. Russell sighed and got up to retrieve it from the kitchen, where he'd put it earlier.

Frank ran a hand through his hair. "I would suggest that you talk to Sarah before you—"

Again Buck interrupted him. "Damn it, Frank, I need *you* to talk to her and if all you can do is talk to this doctor, then do it."

The sheriff sighed as Buck poured himself a drink from the bottle, put it aside and stared down at the amber liquid. Getting to his feet, Frank picked up his hat. "This is not my affair," he said and instantly wished he'd chosen his words better.

"We pay you to keep this county safe," Buck said, still holding the drink he'd poured.

"In that case, if you're going to drink that, I would suggest you not drive. As far as Dr. Venable, it doesn't appear that either he or Sarah have done anything to make the county unsafe," Frank said. "You know I have my suspicions about Sarah's return and your election, but that's all they are. You said yourself that you don't believe Sarah has any involvement in anything we should concern ourselves with."

Buck swore. "I'm telling you, he's messing with her mind."

"Talk to her, Buck. That's the best advice I can give you," the sheriff said as he settled his Stetson back on his head and opened the door to leave. He stopped in the open doorway to glance back at Russell. "Or let Russell talk to her. Maybe she'll be more forthcoming with him." He managed to get the door closed behind him before Buck went off, but he could still hear him cussing as he got into his patrol SUV.

It wasn't that he didn't share Buck's concern about his first wife. He would have bet his ranch that they all had reason not to trust Sarah. What woman parachuted from a plane at low altitude and at night to return to the family she'd left? There were too many questions and Sarah wasn't apparently capable of answering any of them.

Frank worried that Sarah wasn't just dangerous. He believed that she would be the death of Buck—if he was elected president—and bring harm to the entire country.

But without any evidence, his hands were tied.

JACK WOKE TO SCREAMING. He lurched from the bed, confused and disoriented as to where he was, let alone what was going on. He grabbed his jeans and hopped on one foot and then the other before he got them pulled on and partially buttoned. Picking up his gun, he hurried out the open doorway of his room.

The moment he stepped into the hall, he realized that the screaming was coming from the room Cassidy had taken. Rushing down the hallway, he tried her door, praying it wasn't locked. It wasn't.

As he threw open the door, he saw the room cast in moonlight. There was no one in the room except Cassidy. She lay thrashing about on the bed, still screaming. The sound ripped at his heart as he crossed the space in three long strides.

"Cassidy." He reached to touch her shoulder, half-afraid to wake her too suddenly and yet unable to stand seeing her so obviously terrified.

The moment his fingertips touched her heated skin, she flinched and struck out at him, her screams rising in pitch.

"Cassidy!" He stuck the gun into the waist of his jeans and grabbed her shoulders, shaking her gently as she tried to fight him off. She was gasping for breath, her eyes open, but focused on something in her nightmare. Was she reliving her attempted abduction?

She was stronger than he'd imagined. One of her blows hit him in the eye, another caught his nose, making him wince in pain.

He shook her harder, calling her name until he saw her blink and look wildly around the room. He could see that she was still caught in the darkness of her nightmare.

She gave a violent shudder before her gaze focused on him. "Is she still here?"

"Who?"

"My…mother."

He thought of the empty room he'd entered. "Your mother isn't here."

She swallowed, taking another gasp of air as her body seemed to go limp.

Jack released her shoulders, letting her fall back against the pillows. Was it possible her mother had figured out where Cassidy had gone and paid her a middle-of-the-night visit? Not likely. "I think you just had a bad dream."

Cassidy shook her head as if dispelling the last remnants of the nightmare. Her gaze took in the room. Sitting up, she pulled the quilt on the bed up to her throat and held it there clutched in her two fists. He could see that she was shaking in the moonlight.

"Your nose is bleeding," she said, frowning as she finally settled her gaze on him.

He chuckled and reached for a tissue on the nightstand. "You have a mean right hook."

"I'm sorry. I…" Her gaze went again to the moonlit room. "I must have scared you. Was I screaming?"

"You sounded terrified."

She nodded. "I haven't had that dream in years. This time it was so real that I thought…"

"Do you want to tell me about it?" he asked as he sat down on the edge of her bed. She still looked scared. He didn't want to leave her alone. Not yet.

"It's one of those dreams that doesn't make any sense," she said, looking embarrassed. "I'm in my room at the ranch and I wake up to find my mother standing over me." She gave a shiver as if the image still held her worst fears. "She is covered with dirt and her face…" Cassidy looked away as if fighting tears. "She says she's come from her grave for me. Her hands are covered in dirt as she starts to reach for me. But it isn't to pick me up. Her hands grab my throat…"

Jack pulled her to him. She came easily, curling against his chest as he rubbed her back through the thin cloth of the cotton gown she wore. On his bare chest, he felt the heat of her through the gown. Her back was damp with perspiration. She shivered and he pulled her closer.

For a moment he didn't speak. He was too shocked by her account of the dream. Or a premonition? Sarah Johnson Hamilton coming back from the grave for her daughter.

"How old were you when you first had the dream?" he asked, as nonchalantly as he could.

"Three or four. It was so real that the next morning I expected to find dirty footprints on my bedroom floor." She shivered and he tightened his arms around her, pressing his lips into her short dark hair.

After a moment, she angled her head to look up at him. Her blue eyes were huge in the moonlight. One tear still clung to her lash, looking like a shining jewel. He touched it with his fingertip and it dissolved, warm and wet into his skin. His gaze shifted to her bow-shaped mouth. Her lips trembled, then parted. A soft mew of a sound escaped them.

There was nothing to do but kiss her. He lowered his mouth to hers, tasting the salt of her tears, then the sweet soft interior as the kiss became more demanding.

She pulled him down beside her. He felt himself being drawn into the sensual heat of her mouth, her body beneath the thin cotton gown, as the quilt fell away. Her breasts were round and full, her nipples hard and taut against his bare chest.

Jack pulled back from the kiss to look into her eyes. They shone in the moonlight, bright as blue diamonds. "Are you sure about this?"

She cupped his jaw with her hand and gave him a tremulous smile before she drew his mouth down to hers again.

CASSIDY BRUSHED HER fingers over Jack's stubbled jaw, her fingertips tingling from the touch of him. His mouth devoured hers, as hungry as she was for him. As the kiss broke off, she leaned her head back against the pillow. His lips trailed tantalizing kisses down her throat to the rise of her breasts.

With warm fingers, he slowly slid down one strap of her gown to expose the dark hard nipple of her breast. His mouth dropped to it, his tongue lathed it to a peak so erect that she arched against his mouth, wanting more. Sliding down the other strap, he latched onto her other nipple. She let out a moan, desperate to rid herself of the gown and him of his jeans.

Fumbling, she managed to undo what few buttons he'd closed on his jeans to find him naked under the denim. Her fingers brushed the crisp, tight dark curls beneath before pressing her hand against his male hardness.

She had never wanted a man as she wanted him now. She lost herself in the heat of his touch, the solid warmth of his body, the pressure of his mouth as it moved over her skin.

But as she reached to free the last buttons on his jeans, he covered her hand to stop her. She pulled back to look into his eyes questioningly.

"I don't want it to be like this the first time we make love," he said quietly. "You're still scared from the dream. This isn't the time."

She stared at him in disbelief as he pulled up the straps of her gown, then rose to close the buttons of his jeans. "Jack," she cried. "You can't be serious. You can't..." Her gaze went around the room. She hugged herself, aware of how cold the room was without him next to her.

"I'm not leaving you," he said as he crawled back into the bed beside her and pulled the quilt over them. "I'm just not making love to you. It would be too easy to take advantage of the way you're feeling right now."

She wanted to start screaming again. The way she felt right now was as turned on as she'd ever been in her life. "You are the most, the most—"

"Chivalrous man you've ever met?"

"That wasn't exactly what I was going to say."

But as he snuggled against her, his bare chest warm and reassuring against her, she closed her eyes and felt her pulse return to normal. The exhaustion that she'd gone to bed with earlier returned almost immediately and she felt herself drifting toward sleep.

As she did, Cassidy realized she'd never felt as safe as she did in Jack's arms.

RUSSELL LISTENED TO the sheriff leave and then the breeze in the trees outside his window. The moon had come up and now cast the night in gold. What a waste of a beautiful summer night, he thought as he listened to Buck cuss first the sheriff and then the crazy doctor. He'd picked up his drink and drained it and was now pouring himself another.

"You might not want to—" But Buck downed it before he could tell him that getting picked up driving half-drunk would only make matters worse.

"You stay away from Sarah," Buck said, slamming down his glass and pointing a warning finger in Russell's direction.

He had to laugh as he got up from his chair. "Seriously? After you came out here asking for my help?" He and Buck weren't that different in size and stature. As angry as he was, Russell knew he could take the senator in a fair fight. But right now he didn't want to fight fair.

Sarah was in trouble, just as he'd known she was the moment he laid eyes on her. Unfortunately, she was still in love with this fool. Worse, she'd let Dr. Venable back into her life. What was she thinking?

"You're not good for her," Buck was saying. "You confuse her."

"Or maybe she knows that marrying you again is a mistake."

Buck glared at him and took a threatening step toward him.

Bring it on, Russell thought. He'd never been a brawler even in his youth. He knew how foolhardy it would be to take it up at his age, but he clenched his fists anyway and took a step toward the man. He'd been wanting to hit Buck for a long time.

At the sound of a car engine, they both froze and then exchanged a glance.

"You don't think…" Buck said and turned toward the door at the sound of someone roaring up, car door slamming and then the stomp of footfalls on the porch.

Russell flinched at the loud banging on the door. Buck was closer to it. "You might want to open it. Or not."

The senator stepped over and swung the door open. *"Sarah? What are you doing here?"*

"I got Russell's text." She looked mad enough to chew nails.

"You texted her?" Buck demanded.

Russell shrugged. "I thought she might want to know why her ears were burning."

"What's this about?" she demanded. "He said the two of you were having a…meeting about me?"

"You and Dr. Ralph Venable," Russell said.

Her gaze shot to him and her mad seemed to drain out of her. She looked down at the floor for a moment. Looking up finally, she said, "Neither of you could possibly understand what I've been going through. Dr. Venable is giving me back my memory." Her gaze shifted from Russell to Buck and back again. "You both have to trust me."

"Sarah—"

"She's right," Russell said, interrupting Buck. "If you love her, you have no other choice."

Sarah gave him a grateful look, then turned to Buck. "I know what I'm doing."

The senator shook his head and looked around for his Stetson. His movements were those of a man who'd had too much to drink.

Russell hadn't moved. As Sarah's shoulders slumped and tears bloomed in her blue eyes, he started to step to her.

But she held up her hand to stop him. "Please don't." Her gaze met his. "I can't explain, but I don't have a choice."

He nodded. "I'm here if you need me."

Her tears spilled over her cheeks. Her smile broke his heart. "I'm counting on that."

Buck found his hat and slapped it down on his head angrily. "Great. Well, let me know where I fit into all this. If I even do." He headed for the door.

"You aren't driving," she said after Buck. "We'll pick up his rig in the morning," she added over her shoulder as she followed Buck out, leaving Russell alone with his unbearable pain.

CHAPTER SEVENTEEN

SHERIFF FRANK CURRY had made the trip up to the state mental hospital so many times he swore he could do it blindfolded. He thought of all the other times he'd driven up here, hoping and praying that Tiffany would be better.

He'd believed back then that she was his flesh and blood. Had he really thought that whatever she had inherited from him could combat the evil genes her mother had given her?

For years he'd followed the debates on nature versus nurture. In his ex-wife Pam's case, Tiffany had gotten not only her mother's "crazy" genes, but also she'd been brainwashed in hatred. He still had dreams of locking his big hands around Pam's throat and crushing the life out of her.

Unfortunately, someone else had gotten to her before he had. It had saved him a prison sentence, but left him feeling...helpless. He hadn't been able to stop Pam. Nor had he been able to help Tiffany.

It had been strange the day he realized Tiffany wasn't even his. There'd been that pure, hot rush of fury against her and her mother, quickly followed by a drowning sense of relief. Tiffany wasn't his problem anymore.

But he'd only been kidding himself. The young girl

had been programmed to hate him, hell, to kill him. How could he simply wash his hands of her and walk away knowing that if she ever got out, she'd come after him and Lynette?

Tiffany blamed him for hurting her mother. It wasn't anything he'd done intentionally. When Frank had married her, he hadn't realized that Pam had been an empty well of need, which he'd done his best to fill with love. But it had never been enough. She'd grown to hate him, blaming his love for Lynette as the reason for their failed marriage.

It was true. A part of him had still been in love with Lynette. But Lynette had married Bob Benton. He had married Pam. He had wanted children, but Pam kept putting him off. At some point, he knew it was never going to work for either of them. They'd divorced.

He'd had no idea that she was pregnant at the time—just not with his baby. Of course, he hadn't found that out until recently. He hadn't known Tiffany existed before she'd turned up at his ranch one day. He'd been overjoyed to hear that he had a daughter—even a teenaged one. He had been shocked that Pam had kept something like this from him, though. He had wanted to wring Pam's neck for keeping the girl from him.

Then Tiffany had tried to kill him and many months later he'd found out that she wasn't even his blood and genes. The day he'd found out, he'd seen Tiffany with her real father at the mental hospital—and she'd seen him. She'd given him that pleased, hateful smile of hers. He hadn't even needed to check the DNA test that he'd refused to open before that. But he had opened it, confirming what he then knew was true. Tiffany and her mother had both lied to him.

He'd thought he would never return to the hospital. He'd told himself he was through with her forever. That the hell she and her mother had put him through was over.

Now as he parked in the lot outside the mental hospital, he knew he'd only been deluding himself. Even though she wasn't his daughter, Tiffany still had a hold over him. Her hatred was like a noose around his neck. She wanted him dead. He could probably live with that, but she also wanted Lynette dead. For that reason alone, he had to make sure this crazed young woman never saw the light of day beyond these walls.

CASSIDY FOUND JACK standing out on the porch looking off into the distance. At the sound of her joining him, he turned to smile.

"How are you this morning?" he asked.

"Better than I was last night. I'm sorry—"

"No apologies. We've all had nightmares." He looked as if he were living one right now.

"Were you thinking about your father?"

He turned back to the view. "It's hard not to." Glancing over at her as she joined him at the rail, he said, "What about you?"

"Am I still determined to see my mother?" She nodded. "If she's behind my abduction, then I guess I'll know quickly enough. I was thinking it might be safer if I went alone."

He shook his head. "Not safer for you. Sorry, but there isn't a chance that I'm letting you face her alone," Jack said and touched the pistol tucked into the waistband of his jeans. "Remember? We're in this together."

She started to open her mouth to protest, but he stopped

her. "I'm not letting you out of my sight until this is over."

"This might not be over until my father is elected president."

"I guess you'd better get used to having me around, then." He turned back to the house. "I made coffee. Want some? Also, I make the best French toast you've ever tasted."

She smiled and followed him back into the house. A gun-toting, rugged maverick who also cooked. "How did I get so lucky?" she joked as she poured them each a cup of coffee and watched as he went to work on the French toast.

Taking a chair at the table, she marveled at how normal this all felt. She'd never played house with any man, but as the old ranch house was quickly suffused with the wonderful scents of frying bacon and sizzling French toast, she thought she could. With the right man.

Jack was singing a country song along with the music on the radio and doing a little Texas two-step as he cooked. She knew the song and began to sing along. His face lit up and he turned, pancake flipper in hand, to grab her hand and pull her into his arms. As they danced a few steps, she fought the irresistible desire to run her fingers through his hair and to pull him down into a kiss. To forget breakfast, forget the reason they were here, to forget everything and go back to bed.

He looked down into her face. She saw desire spark in his blue eyes. A tremor moved through her. His gaze moved from her eyes to her lips. She felt them part as if preparing for his kiss. Her eyes started to close as she relished the memory of his last kiss.

"Got to save your bacon," he said as he let go of her.

The kitchen instantly felt colder.

"Want to set the table?" he asked, his back to her.

She didn't want him saving her bacon, so to speak. She wanted to lie in his arms again. She wanted him to make love to her.

But he'd turned her down last night. He'd said the timing was all wrong. Cassidy knew he was right. But under the circumstances, she doubted the timing would ever be right.

Her body ached, her eyes burning with unshed tears. She yearned to complete this connection she felt between them. It would be so easy to lose herself in his big, strong, solid body. But was that what he was afraid of? That she was only trying to do anything but think about what was happening to them? Was that why he hadn't made love to her last night? Why he was now busying himself with breakfast instead of taking her upstairs?

"Jack—"

"I've been thinking," he said as he pulled down a plate, slid two strips of bacon and three thick slices of French toast onto it. He turned to hand it to her. Their eyes met. He slowly shook his head as if fighting his own need to lose himself in her.

She saw the determination in all that blue. She took the plate and watched him fill another one before he joined her at the table.

"We need to go see your mother," he said. "But first we need to know everything we can about The Prophecy. We need to be as prepared as possible so we know what we're walking into."

"WHAT'S GOING ON?" Kate French asked as she slid into the booth across from Lynette "Nettie" Curry early the next morning. The Branding Iron Cafe was fairly quiet this weekday morning since it was still early. Several couples were sitting in front of the window. Nettie didn't recognize them and wondered if they'd spent the night at the hotel next door.

The Beartooth Hotel had finally opened after months of construction to restore it. Nettie had been watching the progress, anxious for the big open house that was planned. It would be the biggest event that the small old mining town had seen in a hundred years, she thought.

"Nettie?"

She focused on the pregnant owner of the cafe. Kate had given birth to a baby girl and was now pregnant with twin boys. She glowed with happiness except when one of them would give her a swift kick.

"I asked you what was going on," Kate repeated. "I've never seen you this distracted." She was eyeing her quizzically. "It isn't like you not to share whatever it is. Unless… Is it Frank?"

Nettie shook her head, only a little amused that she was still thought of as the worst gossip in the county. Mabel Murphy had taken over that title and then some.

"I've just had a lot on my mind, that's all," she said and saw at once that Kate wasn't going to let her off that easily. "I suppose you heard about the ring Buck got Sarah?" Kate nodded. "There is talk of a quickie wedding."

"What's the hurry?"

"Apparently, Buck wants to be married right away so she can join him on the campaign trail."

Kate raised a brow. "Do you think voters will like that? How long has if been since his wife was killed?"

"Almost a year." For a moment, Nettie watched her friend gently caress her protruding stomach. Nettie had never gotten to feel what it was like to have a baby, let alone two, growing inside her. So many times she wished that she had married Frank back when they were young. They would have had children, probably a half dozen, then Frank wouldn't spend so much time with his birds and she would… Nettie felt tears burn her eyes.

Kate looked up as if sensing her distress and reached across the table to take her hand. Theirs was an odd friendship because of their age difference and also because when Kate had first come to town, Nettie had been convinced the woman had a secret. Of course, she hadn't sat still until she'd learned what it was.

"Talk to me," Kate said quietly.

Nettie cleared her throat. "The mental hospital called to say that Tiffany needed to speak with Frank. I didn't want him to go. I just have this…bad feeling." She looked up into Kate's sympathetic gaze. "He said he was done with Tiffany when he found out that she'd been in on the scam to make him believe she was his daughter."

"He still feels guilty because of his evil ex-wife, Pam," Kate said with a shake of her head as she let go of Nettie's hand to cut herself a piece of the homemade cinnamon roll they'd been sharing.

"Pam poisoned Tiffany against him to get revenge so he feels responsible for what the young woman has become."

"Revenge is one thing. Pam programmed Tiffany to kill Frank. That's a whole different level of retribution."

"Tiffany is as crazy as her mother and that's what

scares me," Nettie said, shaking her head when Kate offered her a buttered bite of roll. "She's so manipulative, just like Pam was."

"You don't know what she wants?"

Nettie shook her head. "She wouldn't tell Frank. I suspect it has something to do with her getting out of the mental hospital."

"That can't happen, can it?" Kate asked in horror.

"If a doctor says she's competent to stand trial, they might let her out until her trial date."

Kate shook her head, eyes wide with fear. "But if she gets out…"

"She would come after Frank and me. Tiffany has already said she would kill us both. Pam blamed all her misery on me and Frank, and now her daughter does, too."

Kate shuddered and took a sip of her coffee before she spoke. "Did you ask…?" She indicated Nettie's purse.

Nettie shuddered as she thought of the pendulum. She wished she'd never bought the darned thing. It had been on impulse after she'd learned that Sarah Johnson Hamilton had a pendulum tattooed on her butt.

Curious, she'd ordered one and, after reading the directions, had begun to ask it questions. The astonishing thing was that it was always right.

She lowered her voice as she leaned toward her friend. "It said Frank's in danger. I couldn't bring myself to ask if he… I have to believe that he'll be all right. He came home last night and announced he was going to drive up to the mental hospital today. He says he knows what Tiffany's capable of, but I'm afraid he'll underestimate her and…" She caught her breath.

"If she got the chance, she would kill him right there in the hospital and we all remember that she managed to get hold of those scissors that time and cut most of her hair off—"

"Frank will be fine," Kate said, putting a hand on her arm. "He knows to be careful. You can't let yourself worry. Frank is trained for this."

Nettie took a deep breath and let it out slowly. Tears stung her eyes. "That's just it, I'm terrified of what Frank might do. He told me last night that he would never let Tiffany hurt me, no matter what he had to do."

TO THE SHERIFF'S SURPRISE, Tiffany was waiting for him in the visiting room. All the other times Frank had driven up to see her, she'd made him wait. It was another way of controlling him.

Her blond hair was even longer than it had been before that incident when she hacked it all off with a pair of scissors she'd gotten her hands on.

"How did she get scissors?" he'd demanded of the doctor overseeing her care. But he'd known. Tiffany was resourceful. Resourceful with no compassion for other people. That's why she'd broken out of the place once—injuring two staff in her attempt—before she was caught.

She rose, meeting his gaze with a blue-eyed one he'd once thought was so like his own. One of the reasons she was able to fool people was her innocent face. She was slight in build, her blond hair so light it fell in wisps around her heart-shaped face.

"I'm surprised you came," she said and gave him a tentative smile.

"No, you're not." He noticed that there was an orderly standing near a door on the other side of the room. At least they were smart enough to know that Tiffany shouldn't be left alone in a room with him.

Her smile widened for a moment before she bit down on her lower lip and gave him her most innocent look. He'd fallen for that look, for that smile, for that young girl whom he'd actually thought that he could save.

"What do you want, Tiffany?"

"I know you're angry with me—"

"No, I'm not. I *was* angry when you killed one of my crows. I *was* angry when I realized that you'd lied to me about being my daughter—"

"I honestly didn't know until Mom—"

"Don't bother. It's way too late for me to believe anything you say. Just tell me why you had to see me."

Tiffany got a self-satisfied look on her face as if just getting him to come when she demanded was enough for her. "I know I have no right to ask for your help, but—"

He laughed. "If this is about getting you out of here…" He shook his head. "Not. A. Chance. In. Hell."

That wiped the smile off her face. Some of her true feelings burned bright in all that blue. Tiffany wasn't just a psychopath, she was evil. She took pleasure in hurting other people. The last doctor here at the hospital had been convinced she was getting better. The stupid man had actually worked toward getting her released. He'd even hooked her up with a lawyer who thought he could get her off the attempted murder charge and the other charges dealing with the two staff members she'd almost killed.

But then Frank had heard that the doctor had quit without warning. There was talk of him being brought up on charges of his own involving trying to rape one of his patients.

The sheriff didn't need to guess who that young female patient was. Nor did he believe for a moment that the doctor had tried to rape her. What the doctor had done was fall for Tiffany's lies. When he couldn't get her out of the mental hospital, she'd turned on him, taking him down without an ounce of conscience or regret. Tiffany would do whatever it took to get what she wanted. Just like her mother.

And right now she wanted out of the hospital so she could finish getting revenge against him and Lynette. It was her one single motive for everything she did. He found that to be the most horrendous thing Pam had done. Because of her mother, Tiffany had nothing else to live for.

"I don't blame you for the way you feel," she said, trying another tactic.

"Good, then you'll understand why I won't be driving up here ever again at your beck and call. It's over, Tiffany. You had a good run, but I'm out. I don't plan to ever see you again." He turned to leave.

"You'll see me again!" she cried. He heard her advance on him from behind. He also heard the orderly beating a path toward her.

Frank turned, half-expecting to see a pair of scissors clutched in her hand arcing toward his heart. If she'd managed to get them once, she could again.

But her balled-up hands held no weapon.

She stopped short of him as if she, too, heard the rapid approach of the orderly. She dropped her voice to a hoarse whisper that turned his blood to slush. "You will wake up and find me standing over your bed. You will see the flash of a blade before I plunge it into your heart. My face will be the last thing you ever see." Her contorted features softened back into the young innocent-looking girl who'd broken his heart and who now wanted to cut it wide open.

"But first you will watch your precious wife die," she whispered with a smile before the orderly reached her.

"Is everything all right, Tiffany?"

She nodded, looking close to tears. "I'm okay, Jerry. Daddy's just leaving." Her gaze met Frank's. "He said he's never coming back." Her voice broke.

The orderly looked at him as if he couldn't believe anyone would say something like that to this girl.

"Jerry, this probably won't save your life," Frank told him. "But if you trust this young woman, she'll cut your throat when you least expect it." With that he turned and started out of the hospital, swearing he would never enter it again.

Behind him he could hear Jerry trying to comfort his sobbing hysterically pretty young patient. Jerry didn't have a clue that he was being set up. He wouldn't remember Frank's warning until he felt the cold steel of the blade when Tiffany plunged it into him. Frank knew it would be a knife because Tiffany had just told him what she had planned.

He put in a call to Dr. Iverson, her latest champion, as he drove away from the mental hospital. "Tiffany Chandler has gotten her hands on a knife."

"What?" the doctor demanded. "How is that possible? Did you see this knife?"

"Just listen," Frank said impatiently. "I'm telling you, she has a knife hidden somewhere. You need to find it. Turn the whole place upside down if you have to. But she is going to use that knife if you don't find it." He hung up, the doctor still wanting to argue. Dr. Iverson better hope Tiffany made her move on his day off.

She might not be his daughter, but she was Pam's and he had known his ex-wife intimately. She'd loved to play ruthless games with people's lives. So did Tiffany. She was already reeling in Jerry and whoever else fell for that "poor little girl" act of hers.

Frank could see the future but there was nothing more he could do. He'd always known that it was just a matter of time before Tiffany would be coming for him and Lynette.

CHAPTER EIGHTEEN

"THERE HAS BEEN only one mention of The Prophecy in over thirty-five years," Cassidy said between bites of French toast and bacon as she put down her cell phone. "This recent article didn't even make the front page of the local paper when one of the members was killed and another is awaiting trial. How dangerous can they really be?"

"We know the answer to that," Jack said. "I understand what you're saying. They seem…harmless. No one cares about them anymore. They're history."

"Sure seems that way. They're all…" She hated to say old, but they certainly weren't anything like the photographs from the metal box. "Older." They'd aged. "They don't look like terrorists."

"Which is to their advantage. If they've been active, they've kept it quiet. They've probably also brought in new blood."

She tried to imagine anyone her age getting involved with them. Then again, she'd never been very political. She'd left that to her father.

She and Jack had done independent searches online to familiarize themselves with everything they could find about the anarchist group. There wasn't a lot since the group hadn't apparently been active except in the latter 1970s.

The music was still playing on the radio, reminding her of earlier when they danced and she'd been in his arms. "So what now?" she asked, pushing her plate away.

"We pay your mother a visit. We have the element of surprise," he said as he stood to take their plates to the sink. "Also, I will be armed. But I think you need to be ready for what she might tell us."

"We already know she was a member of The Prophecy."

He nodded. "What if she still is? What if the group has been working behind the scenes? If what my father said is true…"

"I'm sorry, but I don't believe she's so determined to keep my father in the presidential race that she would have her own daughter kidnapped."

"I didn't believe my father could do what he's done either, so I understand."

Cassidy rose to help clean up, knowing he was right. The thought of facing her mother paralyzed her. During the few times she'd been around Sarah, she had felt her mother's frustration. The woman seemed to want to reconnect, but none of them really knew her, especially Cassidy and Harper.

"You aren't getting cold feet, are you?"

She looked up at him, swallowed back the lump in her throat and said, "No. I just want this over."

"Me, too." His gaze locked with hers for a moment before he seemed to drag it away. He glanced toward the bag full of money. "I need to do something with that." It was sitting on one of the spare chairs. The metal box with all the information about The Prophecy was at the other end of the table, open and some of the contents lying on the table's surface.

"Maybe we should have had Evan take us to Europe," Cassidy said, suddenly feeling overwhelmed. She'd led too pampered a life to have to face kidnappers, let alone killers.

A muscle jumped in Jack's jaw. "You can always give him a call," he said without looking at her. "Maybe you should." His gaze rose to hers again. "In fact—"

"No," she said quickly. "I'm not leaving you. Like you said, we're in this together."

His gaze softened. "This is dangerous business, Beany."

She smiled, warming at the use of her nickname.

"Maybe we should just tell your father what's going on. With the evidence we have in that metal container—"

"Do you think that's enough proof to have the people in those photographs arrested?" She could see his doubts. "I can tell you right now that my father would never believe Sarah was a member of The Prophecy let alone that she is still the leader. He loves her. He's blind and deaf when it comes to her. Do you doubt that The Prophecy will harm my family—just as your father threatened?"

He hesitated too long.

"My father would try to protect all of us, but do you really think it's possible to keep us all safe? And for how long? The only hope I see is confronting my mother. If she is behind having me kidnapped…" Cassidy couldn't finish. She couldn't imagine any mother doing that to her child.

With a sigh, Jack raked a hand through his dark

thick hair. His look was sympathetic. "You really think she's going to confess everything?"

"No, but I want to see her face when I turn up at her door. From there I guess we play it by ear."

"Just as we have so far," Jack agreed. "Let's see what your mother has to say."

TIFFANY WATCHED AS the orderlies tore her room apart looking for the knife. She sat in the corner, her arms around her knees, hiding her gleeful expression as she watched in mock surprise and anguish.

They hadn't mentioned a knife, but she knew that was what they were searching for. Inwardly, she smiled. She'd known Frank would pick up on it and tell. The lawman thought he was *so* smart. Tiffany loved that she could run circles around him.

"I am so proud of you," her mother whispered next to her. Since her murder, Pam Chandler Curry had begun visiting her. At first Tiffany had been a little frightened to wake up and see her dead mother. In life, Pam had wanted nothing to do with her after Tiffany had failed to kill Sheriff Frank Curry—her ex.

But in death, Pam was like she'd been when Tiffany was a child. She would sit with her for hours and tell her how proud she was of her, how she would help her grow into a strong woman who no man could ever hurt.

"You have fooled them all," Pam whispered. "Look at them making idiots of themselves looking for the knife. Once they don't find it, they will think Frank was just trying to make trouble for you and them. They'll trust you even more."

Tiffany smiled inwardly since that was exactly her plan.

"You are your mama's girl," her mother whispered. "It won't be long now. I want to be there when you kill Frank and Nettie. Write my name on the wall in their blood, will you?" Her mother laughed softly. "I want everyone to know, I may be dead, but I'm not forgotten. You'd do that for your mama, won't you, Tiffany?"

"I will," she said quietly under her breath as the orderlies finished and left her alone in her room. They hadn't found the knife because it wasn't there. But it was close by. "Won't be long now, Mama."

THE HOUSE WHERE Sarah Johnson Hamilton lived wasn't far down the road. Jack was struck by two things as they drove. Hamilton Ranch lay in the shadow of the Crazy Mountains, an incredible, rugged snowcapped range. He couldn't get over how beautiful the area was.

And all of it, according to her, was owned by her father. Apparently, he'd been buying up smaller ranches for years.

Jack thought of his own father and his need to buy and own and conquer. He wondered if Buckmaster Hamilton and Tom Durand weren't all that different.

Cassidy had been right. A person could get lost here it was so vast and isolated. He wondered if they should do exactly that, as they came over a rise and she pointed down to what had once been someone's small ranch before it had been gobbled up by the Hamilton Ranch.

The house was larger than the one he and Cassidy were staying in. There were several old barns and outbuildings behind it, then nothing but green valley that ran to the Yellowstone River.

"As I drive past, see how many cars are parked outside her house," he told Cassidy.

"I see only one, the SUV my father bought for her."

He drove farther up the road and then turned around in a wide spot. He didn't go far before he stopped in the shade of a grove of huge cottonwoods along the creek. "I'm thinking we'll park here and walk back to your mother's. If we drive in—"

"She might have time to make a call," Cassidy agreed.

Jack was glad to see that they were on the same page. No matter what Cassidy said, she didn't trust Sarah any more than he did. "There is an animal trail that leads back that way," he said as he checked his gun. He'd reloaded it after their run-in with Ed. Now he tucked it into his jeans, covering it with the jacket he wore. "Ready?"

Her expression was one of determination, but he could see a tremor of fear beneath it. "If you'd rather stay here—"

"No." She shook her head. "She has to see *me*. She has to look me in the eye."

He wasn't so sure it would be that easy. If Sarah was the leader of The Prophecy as his father had claimed, she probably had lying down to an art form. But he wasn't about to argue with Cassidy.

Confronting Sarah would tell them what he needed to know, he feared. But he wasn't planning to go by what he saw in her eyes—even if he held a gun to her head. If she lied, he would demand to see her cell phone—where he suspected he would find his father's number and real proof that she was part of all this.

THE KNOCK AT her door made Sarah jump. She leaped up from where she'd been sitting cradling a hot cup of coffee in her hands for warmth. She hadn't seen Buck since she'd confronted him at Russell's house. He'd insisted she drop him off at the main ranch house. Not wanting to argue, she had. Now he wasn't answering his cell phone. She'd left a message, but he hadn't called.

A chill had filled the house at the thought that it might be over between them. She shouldn't have kept the news about Dr. Venable from him.

She glanced at the engagement ring. It felt too heavy on her finger. Or maybe that was just her conscience making her feel that way, she thought as she rushed to the door. She'd locked it last night, in no mood for a visit from Dr. Venable. But she hadn't heard from him either.

Filled with hope that Buck had returned, she opened the door expecting to see him on her doorstep. He wouldn't have liked the way he'd left things with her. It would be just like him to surprise her.

And she *was* surprised. Shocked in fact. *"Cassidy?"* Heart in her throat, she grabbed her daughter and pulled her into her arms. Tears blurred her vision so much that she didn't even notice that Cassidy wasn't alone.

Nor had she felt at first that her daughter had stiffened in her arms. As she let go of her, Cassidy stepped past her into the house. "So you're alone?"

She frowned at her daughter's words. Who had she expected to find here? Her father? "Yes." She looked to the handsome cowboy standing in the doorway and thought for a moment that he was the man The Prophecy had hired to kidnap her daughter. She frowned because there was something familiar about him.

Belatedly, Sarah realized she shouldn't have opened the door so hastily. She wished she had her gun. But it was too late now. "And you are?" she asked.

"Jack. Jack Durand." He said it as if he was waiting to see if she knew the name. She didn't. He had a Southern accent. She was sure that she'd never seen him before and yet there was something about him.

Turning back to her daughter, her mouth went dry at the expression on Cassidy's face. "I don't understand. I got a call that you'd been kidnapped."

"Who called you?" Cassidy asked.

"I...I didn't know the voice." She took a step toward her daughter, feeling off balance and half-afraid. The air around them sparked with a tension that had her on edge. "I'm just so glad to see you." Behind her, she heard the cowboy step in, close the door and lock it.

She stopped a few feet from her daughter, desperately wanting to take her in her arms again, but seeing that was the last thing Cassidy wanted. Her hand went to the small silver horse on the necklace at her throat. She touched it nervously as she asked, "What's going on?"

"Why don't you tell *me*, Mother?" she said and thrust a crinkled photograph at her. "Or should I call you Red?"

NETTIE COULDN'T STAND it any longer. She opened the kitchen drawer and took out the tiny box she kept hidden in the back of the cabinet. She often carried it in her purse, especially when she went to see Kate at the cafe.

But not today. She'd left it at home in the drawer,

afraid to ask it anything. Even though she'd confessed to Frank about what was inside the box, she still kept it hidden. Often the contents felt almost…evil. It was definitely dangerous since she'd become addicted to its use.

Stepping to the kitchen table, she removed the lid and took out the small felt bag. Her fingers shook as she undid the drawstring and carefully poured out the contents into her palm.

The pendulum gleamed in the overhead light. Hurriedly, Nettie picked up the thin strap, letting the pendulum swing free. As it dangled from her trembling fingers, she closed her eyes, waiting for it to slow and finally stop.

Opening her eyes, she stared at it and asked the question that was killing her. "Is Frank all right?"

For a moment, the pendulum didn't move. Her heart lodged in her throat and she almost cried out when she heard the sound of a vehicle coming up the road. Hastily, she tossed the pendulum back into the box, hid it again and rushed to the door in time to see Frank getting out of his patrol SUV. Her relief made her sway and grab the doorjamb.

From the slump of his shoulders, she knew that his visit with Tiffany hadn't gone well. But he was alive! She'd had the worst premonition that something was going to happen to him. Throwing open the door, she rushed to him.

"What's this about?" he asked in surprise as she threw herself into his arms.

She couldn't speak her throat was so choked with tears of relief.

Frank's family of crows began to caw down to him

from the telephone line. They were worse chatterboxes than Mabel Murphy, Nettie thought.

Her husband called greetings to the crows. She heard his voice break and frowned against his broad chest. Had Tiffany threatened the crows again? Or was he still regretting what that girl had done to one of them?

Her husband hugged her tightly for a long while before holding her at arm's length. "Lynette?" he asked, studying her face.

She made a swipe at the errant tears on her cheeks. "It's nothing. I just had a bad day." She could see that he knew what it was. "I was worried about you."

"Well, I'm fine." He wasn't, but whatever had happened, he wasn't ready to talk about it. "What's for dinner?" he asked jovially as he put his arm around her and ushered her toward the house.

"I made your favorite, pot roast."

He took a deep breath as if he could smell it cooking and sighed. "Bless your heart. That is exactly what I need right now. Pot roast and you," he said with a laugh. One of the crows tried to imitate his laugh, making him laugh harder.

Nettie luxuriated in the warmth of that laugh and his strong arm around her as she tried to tell herself that everything was fine now that he was home.

CHAPTER NINETEEN

CASSIDY WATCHED HER mother toy nervously at the charm at the end of her necklace. Her heart was pounding like a war drum. She realized that a part of her had wanted to believe it was all a case of mistaken identity in her mother's case.

But the woman standing before her was Red, the alleged leader of The Prophecy. She was the woman in the photo. Cassidy felt sick to her stomach as her mother took the photograph she handed her and glanced down at it.

She saw her mother's expression change. She became guarded. She looked from the photo to Cassidy then to Jack and back. For a moment, Cassidy thought she would try to lie her way out of it.

"Where did you get this?" she asked.

"From an old metal box that my father kept locked up in a drawer in his office," Jack said.

Sarah looked at him in surprise. *"Your father?"*

"Tom Durand. You knew him as Martin Wagner. I'm his son, Jack."

Her mother said nothing, but she'd visibly paled.

"Along with photographs of all of you, there were newspaper clippings of The Prophecy's…accomplishments," Jack said with obvious revulsion.

Sarah stepped back to drop onto the edge of a chair.

As she lowered her head, her trembling hand went again to her necklace—just as it had in the one photo that Cassidy had recognized.

"Did you give the order to have me kidnapped?" Cassidy demanded.

Her mother's head snapped up, her blue eyes wide with alarm. "No! Of course not."

"Why should we believe you?" Jack asked. He was still standing by the door. Cassidy knew that if her mother made any kind of move to get a weapon, he would pull his gun. She hoped it didn't come to that as she stared at the woman who'd given birth to her and wondered if she could trust anything she said.

ALL THE WAY into Big Timber, Montana, Russell Murdock told himself that the best thing he could do was wash his hands of the whole mess. The whole mess being Sarah and the way he felt about her. He'd warned her not to trust Dr. Venable and yet she had. He'd warned her not to trust Buck and yet she had. He told himself there was nothing more he could do. She'd made her choice when she'd chosen Buck over him.

He'd tried to help her. He'd put his ranch up for sale, but only because he knew that he and Sarah would need money to get out of the country once... Once whatever was going to happen happened.

This morning at the ranch, the idea had come to him after pacing the floor for an hour. Dr. Venable had to be staying close by, probably in Big Timber, the closest town with a motel. Since there were only a few motels there, how hard would it be to find the man? Not that hard at all since he knew what the man looked like.

Now, as he pulled up in front of the motel he thought

Venable was most likely to stay in, he saw that there was only one vehicle still parked in front of the last unit. It had local plates. A rental car, he thought with satisfaction.

Parking, he got out and walked along the sidewalk that linked the units to number eleven. He actually thought about breaking down the door like he'd seen in the cop movies. His love for Sarah had made him do things he'd never imagined. But he reminded himself that he was a rancher in his fifties and while in good shape, breaking down the door was a bad idea.

Russell knocked and waited. The curtain on the window next to the door twitched and he realized that if there was a back way, Dr. Venable might be headed for it right now. This was why the cops kicked in the door, so the bad guy didn't get away.

He was debating running around back to cut the doctor off, when the door opened. Dr. Venable was much older than the photograph Russell had seen of him, but there was something keen in his blue eyes—and cold.

"Hello, Russell. I wondered how long it would be before we met," Dr. Venable said as he pushed the door open wider. "Please, do come in. We need to talk about Sarah. That is why you're here, right?"

"I DON'T KNOW what you want me to say," Sarah said, stalling for time to think. She couldn't believe what was happening and yet, hadn't she known it was going to come out the moment Dr. Venable had returned those memories?

The members of The Prophecy had protected her so far. That was what scared her the most. They had already proved how far they would go to make sure nothing stood in the way of the plan. Not only would they use her family, they would kill them if they got in the way.

And now her daughter knew. She felt sick. Fear had curdled her stomach. What if Cassidy and Jack foolishly went to Buck with this? She couldn't let them do that because they would be risking not only their own lives, but those of her sisters and their families.

"Seriously? You don't know what to say?" Cassidy cried as she stepped to a chair near her and sat down on the edge. She leaned forward, her beautiful face contorted in anger. "Some men tried to *kidnap* me!"

"I'm so sorry. Thank God you managed to get away."

Her daughter shook her head in obvious aggravation before looking to the man with her for help. Martin's son. No wonder he had looked familiar.

"We *know* that you're involved," Jack said as he, too, moved closer. "That you may even have told them to abduct your daughter—"

"No," she cried. "I didn't have anything to do with it. I swear."

"But you're a member of The Prophecy," Cassidy said. "So you do have something to do with it."

She couldn't argue that.

"We have killers after us," Jack said slowly as if she was hopelessly stupid. "We need you to call them off."

Sarah looked into his blue eyes, eyes so like his father's. He made it sound so simple. He thought she was the leader. No doubt his father had told him that.

"How long have you known about your father?" she asked Jack.

He told her how he'd seen his father at his mother's grave giving another man an envelope full of money. When he'd followed the man, he'd been able to foil the kidnapping. It wasn't until he'd gone to his father's office that he'd found out about The Prophecy—and his and Cassidy's connection.

"I see." What had Joe been thinking ordering that Cassidy be abducted. She balled her hands into fists, hating this man she had apparently once loved. Now her daughter and Martin's son knew the truth. It was over. Once they told… "I don't know what I can do. I have no control over these people. Instead, they are the ones controlling me through my children."

"You're one of them," Cassidy snapped. "You are their leader."

Sarah cleared her voice, swallowing down the bile that had risen in her throat. This was all her fault. She'd chosen the Hamilton family to go after. This had once been her plan. Had it also been her plan to have six children with Buck so The Prophecy could use them later? Apparently, the only part she hadn't planned on was falling in love with him and her children.

"I won't lie to you. I'm told I was the leader," she admitted.

Cassidy groaned. "Not this 'I can't remember anything' story you came back here telling."

"It's true, I can't remember a lot of it, but I was a member of The Prophecy. Possibly the leader all those years ago. But I'm not now. I'm a pawn, just like you. They're using me to get what they want."

"What do they want?" Jack asked, finally taking a seat.

"They want your father to be president," she said to her daughter.

"Why?" Cassidy asked frowning.

"That part is unclear. Maybe just so they can control him through me and all of you."

"Or?" he asked.

"Or they have something more...violent planned."

"LEAVE SARAH ALONE," Russell said as he stepped into the motel room and turned to face Dr. Venable. The man was much shorter and slighter in build than he'd thought Venable would be. He had to be in his seventies and yet he looked stronger and more vital than he should have for his age—and his size.

"Why don't you sit down so we can discuss—"

"I won't be staying long enough to sit down or to discuss Sarah with you," he said. "Either you stay away from her or the next time I come by—"

"Please, no threats. They are wasted on me. I came back to help Sarah. Not hurt her."

"The way you helped steal twenty-two years of her life?"

"Those years weren't stolen," Venable said. "The memories are still there. That's why I've come back. To retrieve them for her."

Russell shook his head in disbelief. "She missed seeing her children grow up. You stole her life."

"That was her choice."

Russell tried to control his temper. "*Her* choice?"

"She knew I'd been experimenting with brain wiping. She begged me to take away those memories because she couldn't live with them. *She'd tried to kill herself.* This was a woman who needed my help."

He shook his head. "And your answer was to erase her life and take her to Brazil."

The doctor said nothing for a moment. "She was happy in Brazil, maybe happier than she'd ever been. But ultimately, she needed to remember. I am giving her back her memories. It's a gradual process, but soon, she will remember everything. I know you care about her, but interfering will only make things worse for her and certainly for you."

"Now that sounds like a threat," Russell said. He'd removed his Stetson when he'd stepped in the door. Now he put it back on as he faced Venable. "You've messed with her mind enough. Who knows what you're putting into her head. I want you gone. I'm going outside. You pack up. You're leaving town one way or another. *Your* choice." He pushed past the doctor and out the door.

SARAH WATCHED JACK rake his fingers through his thick dark hair as he got to his feet.

"Violence? It wouldn't be the first time The Prophecy had resorted to that, would it? So if you're just a pawn like us, how do we stop them, Sarah?"

He looked so much like his father with that gesture that she had a flashback. She felt herself standing in some old building where they'd gathered. The sun was coming through one of the dirty windows. Joe was complaining that they weren't getting the kind of attention they needed. Martin was arguing with him. In his agitation he reached up with his hand… The image was gone as quickly as it had come.

"If Daddy doesn't become president…"

Sarah cut her daughter off. "He can't pull out of

the race. I know you probably won't believe me, but if he does that our family will pay dearly. The only way I can stop any of this is to get my memory back so I know what The Prophecy's plan is."

"Which means *what*?" Jack asked.

"I have to make sure Buck stays in the race. If he does, he'll win."

"And then what?" Cassidy asked. Her blue eyes were wide with alarm.

Sarah reached for her daughter's hand and squeezed it, quickly letting go when she saw Cassidy's revulsion at her touch. "Then I will stop it and bring The Prophecy down."

Jack let out a sigh. "And why should we believe you?"

Tears blurred her eyes. "I know now why I drove into the Yellowstone River that night all those years ago. I had been contacted by one of the members of The Prophecy. It had been so long since I'd heard from any of them that I guess I'd hoped they'd—" she let out a bitter laugh "—forgotten all of those crazy plans from back in college, especially after the tragedy and several members going to prison."

She took a breath and let it out, trying hard to control her emotions. She was running scared. If she couldn't convince Cassidy and Jack…

"I begged and pleaded with them to let me go. I had made this amazing life for myself." Her gaze fell on Cassidy. "I had these children I adored and a husband who I loved more than life."

"But they wouldn't," Cassidy said.

She shook her head. "I realized they were going to

use me. I wasn't thinking clearly. I thought if I was dead…"

"But you weren't dead," her daughter said.

"No. When I survived the river, I called one of the members I thought I could trust to help me, a doctor. His idea of help was to erase the memory of my husband and my children."

"So you really didn't know about us?" her daughter asked, sounding shocked and hurt.

"Not for twenty-two years. I apparently lived in Brazil and worked with this doctor. He was doing experiments on helping people who had traumatic memories that were keeping them from leading normal lives."

"That is just sick," Cassidy said. "But…wait. You came back so you must have remembered…something."

"Now I realize that the doctor gave me back some of those memories. I found myself in Montana again, dropped by parachute at night in an isolated area. I didn't know how I'd gotten there. I thought no time had passed. I thought you and your twin, Harper, were still babies."

She saw compassion in her daughter's expression. "That must have been horrible to realize you'd missed so much."

"It was." Her voice broke. "I've been so confused. I didn't remember The Prophecy at all. Then things began happening…"

Jack walked to the window and peered out. "So how do you get your memory back so you can stop this?"

Sarah hesitated, but only for a moment. "The doctor who stole them is slowly returning them."

He turned to stare at her. "You trust him?"

She shook her head. "No, but I have no choice. He swears he will provide the rest when I need to know."

"What about in the meantime?" Jack asked. "My father's men are looking for us. I'm not sure what they planned to do with Cassidy, but it was real clear they plan to take me out."

"Apparently, they were going to use Cassidy to force me to convince Buck to stay in the race," she told them. "But that isn't necessary any longer. I've agreed to do whatever they ask."

"What about us?" Cassidy demanded.

"I'll let them know you're here and that there is no need for them to take any further action," she said.

"You're sure you can convince them?" Jack asked.

She wasn't.

"My father said they would take Bo if they didn't get Cassidy," Jack said.

Sarah felt a wave of panic wash over her. "Bo is pregnant with twins. She isn't doing well. If they…" She couldn't finish. "I will contact them and tell them that I have the two of you."

"*Have* the two of us?" Jack asked.

"Where are you staying now?"

"At one of Dad's houses, the one closest to the Crazies," Cassidy said.

Jack shot her a look as if he wished she hadn't told her that.

"If you stay there and out of sight until I can talk to them—"

"Wouldn't it be better if you just told your husband and he pulled out of the race?" Jack asked.

"The Prophecy would retaliate," she said quickly.

"But your husband could hire people to protect you."

Sarah shook her head. "You've seen how patient the members of The Prophecy can be. Not even Buck would be able to protect his family from them. But he's stubborn enough to try. He would quit the race if he knew what was going on and it would be the worst thing he could do."

Jack stepped away from the window. "Are you sure about that? Maybe the worst thing he could do is win this presidential race."

DR. VENABLE GLANCED out the window, not surprised to see the big rancher leaning against his pickup, his arms folded over his chest and his gaze on this motel room.

He let the curtain fall back into place and reached for his phone. "I have a small problem. Actually, a large problem by the name of Russell Murdock."

On the other end of the line, Joe Landon swore. Not that that was the name Joe went by now. Part of the plan was that they each didn't know how the others had assimilated into society or what they did for a living or what new names they were using. It would make it easier for them to avoid arrest should something go wrong. Their only way of connecting was by throwaway cell phones.

Except for Doc, who had kept his real name.

"I thought Russell was out of the picture?" Joe demanded now.

"He's in love. You remember what it was like being in love with Sarah."

Joe let out an angry growl. "You would be wise not to bring that back up."

Doc knew he was right. But some days, he felt old and tired and even though he'd started all this, sometimes he forgot why. "Russell is running me out of town."

"What does that mean?"

"He's standing out by his pickup. He says if I don't leave, he'll bodily see that I am gone."

Joe laughed. "Does he have any idea who he is dealing with?"

"He seems to. He's the one who found me and has been busy putting all the pieces together. He knows I've contacted Sarah."

"How?"

"Maybe she told him. More than likely, he's been watching her house."

"That pathetic fool. She broke up with him. Why doesn't he…leave town himself?"

"He's apparently staying to protect her and possibly win her back. I don't believe he thinks much of Buck. I get the impression he thinks he'll be around to pick up the pieces."

"Well, he's wrong," Joe drawled. "He's dead wrong about that."

CASSIDY FELT NUMB.

"What do you think?" Jack asked as they drove away from her mother's house.

"I don't know what to think," she said. Her throat closed with unshed tears, her chest aching with unreleased sobs. She was holding it all in, trying hard to be strong. "It is all so…surreal. I wanted her to tell me she wasn't one of those…anarchists. I wanted to believe it was all a mistake—including the attempt to kidnap me and having some…killer after us. But it's *real*."

"Can we trust her?" Jack asked.

She met his gaze. "I…" Swallowing, she said, "I don't know. I want to. I think she was telling the truth." Cassidy could see that he looked skeptical. She let out a sigh that came out sounding like a sob. "What choice do we have? If she calls your father and says that she has us…"

"I'm not sure he'll believe her—let alone be content with it."

"Do you think he'd come to Montana?" she asked, suddenly concerned at just how many people were after them.

"I wouldn't be surprised. My father is a hands-on kind of businessman. I suspect he'd be even more that way with this…organization he's involved in."

"We could make a run for it, but you heard what my mother said. If they think that she's lying about having us under wraps, they'll go after Bo."

He glanced over at her. "Then let's hope she convinces my father that she has everything under control." He reached over and took her hand, his large and warm. She closed her eyes as the rental SUV bumped along the gravel road in a familiar rhythm that almost soothed her.

"If this had to happen, I'm glad you were the one who—" she opened her eyes and swallowed "—saved me."

He squeezed her hand, keeping his eyes on the road. "Me, too."

Jack let go of her hand to steer around a sharp curve in the road. They were almost back to the old ranch house. Behind it, the Crazies gleamed in the sunlight against a sky so blue it hurt to look at.

"I can't understand why anyone would ever leave

here," he said as if as captivated by their surroundings as she was. "It's...breathtaking." He pulled up to the house and cut the engine before he looked over at her. "Just like you."

Her heart did a little bump. The heat of his gaze scalded her bare skin. His smoldering look burned into hers. "I'm scared that I'm not going to be able to protect you."

She shook her head. "It's going to be all right." She wished she could believe that. From his expression, he definitely didn't. But then again, he knew his father better than she did. She was depending on her mother, a woman she barely knew.

He reached for her, his hand curving around the back of her neck to draw her close. His mouth brushed across hers to plant a kiss at the corner of her lips.

She felt a feverish heat rush along her veins as his other hand cupped her cheek. With agonizing pleasure his rough thumb pad skittered over her lips, opening them to get at the tender flesh of her mouth.

Drawing her even closer, he gently kissed her mouth. A tremor moved through her as he parted her lips with his tongue. She opened to him, wanting this more than her next breath.

"We should go inside," Jack said, drawing back from the kiss.

All Cassidy could do was nod, her heart pounding at the look he gave her. They got only as far as just inside the door before he grabbed her and pulled her to him. He buried his hand deep into her hair as his arm encircled her waist. Her body collided with his, her soft curves to his large, rugged, muscle-hard frame. A slow burn of desire spread through her as she clung to him.

"Beany." His voice sounded ragged with longing. His eyes blazed with a fire matching her own. His mouth dropped to hers and he drank her in as if dying of thirst. She moaned in answer to the assault on her senses as he explored her mouth with quick flicks of his tongue against her sensitive skin.

She wanted his hands on her, her hands on him. Pulling back from the blistering kiss, she grabbed the front of his Western shirt and jerked. The snaps sung. Her palms pressed against his warm smooth chest. His nipples were erect. She bent her head to touch her tongue to one.

Jack groaned. "If you don't stop, we'll never make it to a bed."

She smiled as he swung her up into his arms and took the stairs with her as if she were weightless.

JOE WAS SURPRISED and a little wary when he saw who was calling him on his private cell phone. He had been standing at the window when the phone rang. Since it seldom rang, it took him a moment to pull it out of the inside pocket.

"I have Cassidy." It had been so long since he'd heard Sarah's voice that he felt momentarily stunned. Just the sound of it pierced his soul, bringing back pleasurable memories that made him ache. He lowered himself into a chair. "I also have Jack. *Martin's son*."

He couldn't speak for a long moment. "Sarah? Is this really you?" He knew what he was asking. She must have, too.

She laughed at his surprise. "You know it is. I wanted to call you personally and tell you that I have taken care of everything. Just as we planned."

He had dreamed of this moment. But even now he couldn't believe it had actually happened. He'd told himself for years that once Sarah regained her memory she would come back to him and only him. Once she remembered their shared passion, she would *beg* to come back.

After another stunned silence, he ventured, "I'm not sure I understand, though."

"You understand. I *remember.* I remember *everything.*"

This *was* a dream. This couldn't be happening. Not after all these years. Not after the last time they'd talked and she'd made it clear that she wanted nothing to do with him ever again. His stomach roiled at the memory. "I thought...you'd—"

"Forgotten *us*?" Her laugh, like that one word, was achingly sweet and laced with sexual subtext. He was struck by the memory of them tangled together, their bodies scalding with the heat of their lovemaking, the painful, pleasurable release...

"I don't know what to say," he finally managed.

"That's a first."

Joe put one hand on the window for support, telling himself this was no dream. He could hear it in her voice. And yet, another part of him knew better than to trust this. Knew better than to trust the Sarah who'd fallen for Buckmaster Hamilton. That memory burned in his belly like acid.

He realized there was only one way to find out if she'd truly come back to him. "When can I see you?"

"Wouldn't that be too dangerous under the circumstances?"

So like Sarah to point that out.

"But once we know that Buck is definitely going to win the election…"

He heard it in her voice and felt himself react as he always had. His need for her burned so hot that at that moment he would have given up everything for her.

"What do we do in the meantime?" he asked, his voice rough with the desire that had him in physical pain.

"You can start by calling off Martin so he doesn't ruin *everything*. He stupidly tried to kidnap my daughter Cassidy, thinking I needed extra…incentive."

Joe instantly withered. "I thought we were talking about us?"

"There is no us if all of this blows up in our faces."

He nodded to himself. "Putting The Prophecy first. Just like the old Sarah."

"The *old* Sarah was *your* Sarah. That is what you wanted, isn't it?"

A cold chill moved over his skin. His laugh hurt deep down. "I wouldn't have you any other way." And have her he would. Soon.

CHAPTER TWENTY

CASSIDY LAY IN bed spooned against Jack, sated and reveling in the cocoon of pleasure she felt. She never wanted to leave this bed. Their bodies fit together perfectly as if they'd been made for each other, that connection between them even stronger. When they'd come together earlier—

Her cell phone rang, dragging her back to reality.

Reaching for it, she saw it was her mother and forced herself to sit up to take the call.

"I wanted you to know, I've taken care of everything," Sarah said. "The two of you just need to stay where you are. You trust me, don't you?"

What choice did she have?

"I love you, Cassidy. I would never let anything happen to you if I could help it."

"I know," she said, praying it was true.

"Stay close to the house. I promise this will be over soon."

Cassidy turned as she disconnected to see Jack was awake and watching her expectantly.

"Your mother?"

She nodded and swung her legs over the side of the bed. Those earlier moments of contentment were gone. She felt restless, uncertain. Worse, for a while she'd forgotten that she and Jack were in danger. She'd been able to dream that what they had was something lasting.

Now she feared that after finding each other, they would be torn apart. Or worse, killed. "Want to see a favorite place of mine?"

"Is everything all right?" he asked as he got up and pulled on his jeans.

She turned to look at him. He was so handsome, so tender. Tears welled in her eyes. Was he serious? Everything was far from all right. "It will be," she said, praying it so. "I assume you know how to swim?"

He chuckled as he reached for his shirt. "Swim?"

The day was warm, the breeze sweet with the scent of pine. She led him down a path through tall cottonwoods with green leaves that rustled overhead. They walked through the shadowed coolness until they reached a barbed wire fence.

Jack held the strands of barbed wire apart so Cassidy could step through and then she did the same for him. She could smell the water before she heard its soft roar.

"Where are you taking me?" Jack asked, sounding excited.

"You'll see," she said with a grin. They'd been through a lot in a matter of days. The man had saved her life. Wasn't that enough reason to feel so incredibly close to him? It was odd but she felt as if they had been destined to meet.

As they moved through a tunnel of new cottonwoods under a canopy of old cottonwoods, she glanced over at him. Wasn't it possible there was another reason she felt close to him? That their lives were on a course where they would always be together?

Her heart swelled at the thought.

Jack let out a cry of pure pleasure next to her as the tree branches parted and the creek came into view.

"I thought you might like this," she said, pleased. "The water's cold compared to that in Texas, but—"

"But this is a swimming hole and we're going in, right?" He turned to look at her, grinning.

"Last one in," she said and began to strip down to her underwear. Again, she felt shy as she looked up to find him watching her undress, desire warm in his gaze.

"Sorry," he said quickly after being caught. "It's just that you are so beautiful. I can't stop looking at you."

"Especially when I'm half-naked?" she joked.

His grin widened. "Especially."

She laughed and ran through the grass to the edge of the creek. Water pooled in an oxbow, deep and green. Someone, long before her father had bought this addition to the ranch, had tied a rope from a large old cottonwood branch. It was neatly tucked behind the trunk of the tree.

She unhooked it after climbing up on the large rock next to the creek.

Jack had stripped down and now stopped at the edge of the shore to watch.

She held tight to the rope and leaped off the rock to sail out over the water. It had been so long since she'd done this. It brought back memories of her and her sisters playing here as children. At the perfect apex of the pendulum swing she let go, dropping through the sunlight and warm air.

Her feet broke the surface of the water and she plunged in. Water rushed up over her head as she descended into the dark depths. The cold of the water shook her to her core.

She surfaced with a shriek of laughter and, grabbing the thin retrieval rope dangling from the end of the swing rope, quickly began to swim toward the shore. "Your turn."

"You are covered in goose bumps," he cried, but took the rope from her.

Her body felt alive from the cold and the burst of adrenaline.

"I'm from Texas. You do realize this could kill me."

That struck them both funny since they were much more apt to die a completely different way given what was going on in their lives.

Laughing, Jack took the end of the rope and mounted the rock to stand at the edge. He wore a pair of expensive navy briefs. His skin was dark from the sun and he was beautiful, a sculpted Adonis.

He was still laughing when he swung out, caught for a moment suspended over the creek.

"Let go!" she called and he dropped, his body perfectly straight, into the emerald green.

He shot back out moments later with a shriek. "You didn't tell me it was this cold," he said between chattering teeth. He rapidly swam to the shore, threatening what he was going to do to her.

Laughing, she tried to get away, but he caught her in the sun-warmed green grass at the edge of the creek, pulling her to him for a kiss. They were both trembling from the cold, but only as long as it took for the kiss to warm them. They shucked off their wet clothing and pressed their naked bodies together. One kiss led to another. They made love slowly, tenderly, the rest of the world forgotten.

The summer sun glowed on their skin as the breeze in the high tops of the cottonwoods sighed and the creek hummed along as it flowed past.

"I've never felt this way about anyone," Jack said as he looked down into Cassidy's eyes. "I know it's happening too fast—"

"It doesn't feel like it. Not to me. Do you believe in soul mates?"

He smiled. "I didn't. Until I met you."

"My father would say we are too young to feel like this. But he and my mother fell in love at this age." She groaned. "And look how that turned out." Flopping back down, her laugh held no humor.

He pulled her close again. "Maybe there will be a happy ending for us.

Cassidy smiled at him. "You really are a romantic."

"Am I?" He leaned closer until their lips were only a breath apart. "No matter what happens, I know I want to spend every moment with you."

"A *hopeless* romantic."

They lay in the grass, staring up at the big sky overhead and talking about movies, books, silly things that had happened to them at college or since they'd been out.

They didn't talk about the trouble they were in now. Instead, they pointed out different shapes as clouds drifted past on the breeze. For a while, it was just a summer day and they were just twentysomethings enjoying each other.

Neither mentioned love. It was too early for that and they both knew it. They'd had other relationships, but nothing like this. Mostly, Cassidy thought they didn't want to jinx it.

"Neither of us has mentioned the future," Cassidy said finally. "Is it because we're terrified we don't have one?"

Jack said nothing for a long moment. "Do you know what you want to do with the rest of your life?"

She wanted to lie here in the grass with him beside her after swimming in the creek and then making love. But that seemed impossible given the way they'd met.

"You mean a career?" she asked. "I had a dream to start an organic farm here on the ranch. But I don't feel ready yet. It's like there is something else I need to do first, but I have no idea what it is."

"I feel the same way. There are things I know I don't want to do, like take over my father's business—even before this. But I'm like you. I feel there is something I need to do." He shrugged.

"I know I want to live here in Montana. My sister Olivia owns a boutique in town, but now that she's married she spends very little time there. Maybe some of us just aren't cut out for the usual careers."

Jack laughed. "Mine as well. I keep thinking that something will happen and I'll know and when I do…" He shrugged. "I don't think we're alone. A lot of people our ages don't have clear career goals."

"I have a confession." She picked a piece of grass and played with it for a moment. "I've never had a job. I've never had to *have* a job."

He laughed. "The only job I've had—other than in the military—was either on the ranch or at my father's business."

She pushed up on one elbow. "We sound spoiled."

He turned toward her, picking a four-leaf clover and handing it to her. He'd grown somber. "We've been sheltered and maybe a little spoiled. Until now."

They grew quiet for a long time. Cassidy finally said, "It's crazy, but it's as if we were meant to meet." She glanced over at him, trying to gauge how he took her comment.

He laughed. "I was just thinking the same thing. That even if things hadn't happened the way they did, we would have met somehow." His gaze shifted to hers and held it. "I keep thinking about our parents. Maybe they just wanted to change the world they lived in and went about it all wrong."

They both lay back, their faces turned up to the deep blue of the sky and the clouds drifting past.

"What if we are the generation that will make things better in the world?" he said quietly without looking at her. "Maybe we're supposed to make up for what our parents did."

"I love you, Jack." The words were out before she could call them back.

He rolled over again on his side and drew her close as he kissed her and looked into her eyes. "I love you, Beany. No matter what happens, more has brought us together than our parents and their pasts. There is a reason I was at the cemetery that day, that I followed Ed, that…that I'm here with you."

She felt her heart soar at his words because that, too, was what she believed. They were in this together. Nothing could tear them apart.

SHERIFF CURRY GOT the call in the wee hours of the morning that a badly beaten man had been found beside the river road.

"I thought you'd want to know. It's Russell Murdock," his deputy said.

"Russell?" he said, sitting up in bed.

"We found his pickup parked at the fishing access."

Frank rubbed a hand over his face. "What does he say happened?"

"He's in a coma. The EMT said he is in critical condition."

"I'll be right there." Swearing under his breath, he got out of bed, not bothering to turn on a light.

"What is it?" Lynette asked drowsily.

"It's nothing. Go back to sleep." He pulled on his jeans and boots, then searched around in the dark for his uniform shirt. Finding it, he moved out of the bedroom, closing the door behind him.

All he could think about was his "meeting" with Russell and Buck. This had something to do with Dr. Ralph Venable, sure as hell. After his discussion with the two, Frank had found out that the doctor was staying at a local motel.

He'd talked to the motel owner, a woman by the name of Iris. Apparently, the doctor had been pleasant, paid in cash and had told them he was on vacation. Iris had said, though, that she found it strange how little time he spent away from the motel.

"He stays in his room most of the time except to get something to eat, which he usually brings back to the motel," she said. "He goes out, but isn't gone all that long. I feel sorry for him. He seems so…lonely. I was thinking of maybe trying to fix him up with Ethel Anderson."

She hadn't asked Frank why he was interested in the man's comings and goings. Apparently, it had never crossed her mind that Dr. Venable was anything but a nice lonely old man.

Frank had wanted to speak with the doctor, but it had been one of those rare occasions when he was gone.

When he reached the hospital, he found Russell was still in a coma and doctors weren't giving him much chance to recover. He hesitated for only a moment before he called Sarah Hamilton.

"I'm sorry to wake you," he said when she answered. "I thought you would want to know. Russell Murdock is in the hospital."

He heard her come fully awake. *"What happened?"*

"Someone apparently assaulted him. He's in a coma and critical."

She let out a painful cry. "Do you know who did it?"

"Don't you?"

CHAPTER TWENTY-ONE

"I SPOKE WITH Sarah earlier."

Dr. Venable tried to wake up. What was worse than being awakened in the middle of the night? Hearing Joe Landon's voice on the other end of the line, he thought.

"She called me. I was curious how she got my private number," Joe was saying.

Doc froze, his mind racing. He hadn't given it to her. The only way she could have gotten it was from Martin or— He bit back a silent curse. Somehow she'd gotten it from him. But how?

"She says she remembers everything and she is the old Sarah," Joe was saying.

He was hardly listening. How had she gotten Joe's number? He racked his brain. Was there any chance she had gotten it from him without his knowing it?

The memory came in a hot flash. The only time he'd left his phone to go into the other room was when she'd been upset and asked for a glass of water... The bitch. He'd been buying into her helpless, confused, desolate act. Maybe the old Sarah really *was* back.

Joe hadn't waited for an explanation of how she'd gotten his number. Doc decided confession might be good for the soul, but it would play hell with Joe Landon.

"Sarah says that she has her daughter Cassidy and

Martin's son, Jack, with her," Joe was saying. "I've spoken with Martin. He's not happy. Apparently, Jack cleaned out his safe-deposit box at the bank, money earmarked for The Prophecy, and has some incriminating evidence in his possession. We need it back. At any cost."

Doc shook his head, but held his tongue. Joe's plan to kidnap the girl had blown up in his face. He was murderous and not thinking clearly. Surely, he realized the blowback should they kill Jack and Cassidy.

"What do you want me to do?" he asked.

Joe's hesitation made him even more anxious. "Is it possible Sarah really is her old self? I thought you said you hadn't returned her memory that far back."

He hadn't. "It's possible. She was bound to start remembering once I began to give her back the puzzle pieces of her life."

"Find out if it's true. You can do that, can't you?"

"No problem," he lied.

"Also, you got the help I sent you?" Joe had sent two burly thugs with lots of muscle but little brains. He'd questioned them when they'd called. Apparently, they'd nearly killed Russell Murdock. As it was, he still might die. Or if he did wake up, he would probably be nothing more than a vegetable, they said.

If they'd just knocked him out and thrown him in the river like he'd told them... But apparently Russell had put up more of a fight than they'd been expecting of someone in his fifties. The two had then reacted like the savages they were, beaten him to a pulp and dumped him beside the road.

He'd told them to go back and get rid of the body. They said that they'd realized they should have done that. But when they started to go back, they saw flashing lights from across the river. Now the sheriff would be involved.

Joe was still talking. "If you really are as talented as you've led us all to believe, then you will get Sarah to tell you where you can find Jack and Cassidy. You'll have help."

Doc hesitated, but knew he had to say something. "We can't have any more bodies, especially two young people. We already have an old rancher in critical condition in the hospital and the sheriff—"

"Did I say kill them? Find them and put them somewhere…safe. Martin is on his way to Montana. He'll take his son back to Houston and deal with him there. I want to be sure that Sarah is really back with us before I decide what to do with her daughter. I'm not the fool you think I am, you old quack. Remember that."

The connection was broken. Doc put down his phone and lay back onto the bed, but he knew he wouldn't be able to sleep. Sarah had stolen the number off his phone and called Joe. That had taken some balls to do that. But pretending that she remembered everything? Did she not know how dangerous this game was that she was playing?

He sat up thinking about Joe and Sarah. Joe had often been derisive about Sarah and the family she'd made for herself. "Love apparently addled her so much that she became a broodmare," he would lament. "What happened to that woman we all knew and trusted? Now she says she loves Buckmaster Hamilton?" He had scoffed. "I think perhaps she wasn't the woman we all thought she was after all."

Every time Joe mentioned Sarah, Doc heard what the man didn't say. Joe was still in love with her. But it was a mean, resentful kind of love. Doc hated to think what her life would be like if the two reunited—as they had planned all those years ago. Sarah might be better off dead when this was all over.

From the nightstand, he picked up the velvet bag that held the pendulum and his way into Sarah's mind. He dropped it into his black doctor bag next to the drugs he also carried.

She would resist even if she was her old self, which he doubted. He would need something stronger than hypnotism to convince her to give up the location of her daughter and Martin's son.

CASSIDY WOKE TO an empty bed. She felt for Jack in the dark. The sheets next to her were cold and even colder the farther she reached. She sat up in alarm.

"Jack?" Her voice sounded too high. "Jack?" As her eyes adjusted to the darkness, she saw that the room was empty.

Getting up, she quickly pulled on his shirt that had been discarded earlier at the foot of the bed. The floor was cold against her bare feet as she padded to the doorway and looked down the stairs. No lights burned below in the darkness.

"Jack?" She started down the stairs, when the front door opened, startling her. She grabbed the stair railing as a hulking dark figure filled the doorway. Her breath caught in her throat.

As the man stepped into a shaft of moonlight, she saw his face and let out a cry of relief. Jack, wearing only jeans and boots, looked up and saw her. His gaze softened. She caught her breath as he closed the door behind him and quickly took the stairs.

"I woke up and you weren't here," she said in a rush, releasing the panic she'd felt only moments before.

"I'm sorry. I thought I'd be back before you missed me." He held her at arm's length for a moment. "Damn, but you look better in that shirt than I do." He kissed her neck, working his way from below her ear down toward the open neck of the shirt.

Cassidy felt herself giving in to her desire for this Texas cowboy. But even as she did, she noticed that he had the quilted large bag that had held the contents of his father's safe-deposit box. The bag was now empty. "Is everything all right?"

"Couldn't be better," he said as he picked her up and took her back to the bedroom. He lowered her to the bed and turned to go into the bathroom to wash his hands. "I'm sorry if you woke and were worried."

She watched, surprised that his hands were covered with dirt. A bad feeling had settled into the pit of her stomach. "You hid the money."

He glanced back at her as he began to dry his hands on the towel. "Don't ask where. This way…"

She swallowed the lump in her throat. This way no one could ever torture the location out of her. Would it come to that?

"Everything is going to be all right," he said as he took her in his arms again. She didn't believe that any more than he did. But as he slowly began to unbutton his shirt that she wore, the world seemed to shrink to only the touch of his skin against hers, the whisper of his mouth as it moved over her, the feel of him as he slowly joined their bodies.

SARAH HAD JUST started out the door to go to the hospital when Dr. Venable stepped from the moonless shadows. She jumped, instantly regretting that she hadn't thought to grab her gun. But who grabs a gun to go to the hospital to see an injured friend? Any woman involved with The Prophecy, she thought belatedly.

"What do you want?" she demanded. She'd known that Joe would call him, but she hadn't expected him to show up in the middle of the night.

"Spare me just a few moments of your time."

"I'm on my way to the hospital. Russell Murdock…" Her voice broke. A well of fury rose in her. "But I suspect you know all about that. It was you…people who did this, wasn't it?" She sounded close to tears.

"You people?" Venable chuckled. *"You* are one of us, Sarah."

She shook her head adamantly and tried to step away from him, but he grabbed her arm. The pinprick of pain surprised her.

"At least now I know that you aren't the old Sarah as you tried to get Joe to believe," Doc said. "That was very foolish of you. When he realizes that you lied…" He let go of her arm and she stumbled back.

She stared down at her arm, suddenly aware of what he'd just done. "You didn't…" But that was all she got out. Her body suddenly felt as if made of water.

He caught her as she staggered. If he hadn't taken her weight, she would have slumped to the ground. The drug he'd injected into her made the moon swim dangerously in Montana's big sky. When she tried to talk, her words were slurred. "Why?"

"Did you really think you could fool Joe?" Doc shook his head as if disappointed in her as he helped her back inside the house, and locked the door behind them, before helping her over to the couch.

"What are you going to do to me?" she asked, her words badly slurred.

He looked almost compassionate. "I'm going to help you, Sarah. That's all I've been trying to do since I came back, but you've been fighting me. That has to end or we're both dead."

"WHAT IS IT?" Cassidy asked, startled awake. She'd been sound asleep when Jack had suddenly sat up. Now she touched his back and felt him tense. He seemed to be listening to the night.

"Get dressed," he whispered.

"Jack, tell me what's wrong."

He turned to hold a finger to his lips. "I heard something. Downstairs." He swung out of bed and grabbed for his clothes, hurriedly pulling on the Montana T-shirt she'd bought him. "Hurry."

"My mother wouldn't…" The words seem to freeze in her throat. Quickly, she dressed and began to pack her things. "She *promised*." She glanced over as Jack finished dressing and threw everything into his duffel.

He looked at her, his expression sympathetic. "Let's just get out of here, okay?"

She nodded numbly. The wind had come up. She could hear it whistling past the eaves. Pine trees swayed, becoming dark moving shapes beyond the window. Something scraped against the house. A shutter or maybe a limb? Surely, that's what had wakened Jack and nothing more.

But now every creak and groan of the old house

seemed ominous. Jack hadn't wanted to stay here. He hadn't trusted her mother. But she'd been so sure…

As they started toward the open bedroom doorway, Jack pulled the gun and motioned for her to stay behind him. As they reached it, Jack stopped. She could tell he was listening. The wind seemed louder now. She could hear a shutter banging somewhere on the lower floor.

Please let that be all it is.

Faint moonlight knifed through a gap in the drapes. Cassidy fought to get her eyes to adjust to the dim light. Dark shadows seemed to move restlessly as Jack began to descend the stairs, her right at his back. She heard nothing except the wind and the complaints of the old house. A stair creaked under Jack's weight and he stopped suddenly, on alert again.

She caught an odd smell. Sweet. And for the moment she couldn't place it. Spearmint. She frowned as she heard what sounded like a floorboard creak.

CHAPTER TWENTY-TWO

SARAH WAS TORN between anger and heartbreak as she looked down at Russell's battered body lying in the hospital bed. His head was bandaged. Both eyes were black with bruises. But that would heal. It was all the tubes and wires hooked up to him that worried her. This was serious.

She would kill whoever did this.

Most people said things like that but didn't mean them. She'd never meant anything more in her life. She was also more than capable. Stepping to the bed, she leaned down to gently kiss his cheek. "I will get them for this. I promise."

Russell didn't move, didn't make a sound.

She clung to the edge of the bed, still feeling woozy. Earlier she'd awakened on the couch, having no memory of how she'd gotten there. Her last memory had been of getting ready to go to the hospital to see Russell. The memory gaps scared her. Dr. Venable's doing? Or was it true what he told her that her memory would come back but that there would be side effects like short-term memory loss?

"How did you get in here?" came a strident voice behind her.

She turned to see the ICU nurse's surprise. Sarah had startled her. "You can't be in here. Only family members are allowed in and only during visiting hours." The nurse moved to the side so Sarah could leave.

Ignoring the woman, she turned back to the bed, placing her hand on Russell's arm and giving it a squeeze. "I'll be back," she said to him. "You just get well. I'll take care of everything."

"You need to leave," the nurse said.

Sarah finally turned her look at the woman. She wanted to bat her away like a pesky fly. Smash her under her shoe sole. *I wouldn't mess with me right now.*

But the last thing she needed was to get arrested for making a scene in ICU.

"I'll be back," she said to the nurse.

"Not if you aren't family," the woman said as if needing to get the last word.

Sarah glanced over her shoulder as she left to give the woman a withering look. The nurse had the good sense to keep her trap shut.

It wasn't until she pushed out the door of the hospital that she let the raging emotions hit her. She gulped the cold night air, sucking it in as if suffocating. Her hands balled into fists. She wanted to wail at the moon. Instead, she staggered to her car and leaned against it until she got control again.

Her right arm ached. She touched it and pulled back in surprise. There was a tender spot. She couldn't remember hurting it. Frowning, she got behind the wheel and turned on the interior light. As she pushed up her sleeve, she saw the needle mark. It was red around it.

It wasn't short-term memory loss. She'd been drugged. It explained why she still felt disoriented. But why?

Her mind seemed to clear of her earlier fury. She sat for a moment before the truth hit her like a tire iron between the eyes. With a wave of horror, she knew that Russell being attacked was only the first part of the message that had been sent expressly to her.

She started the engine and threw the car into gear. She had to get to Cassidy and Jack before it was too late.

THE FIGURE CAME out of the darkness to Jack's right. Another to their left. Jack got off a shot, but it went wild. He'd been expecting an attack, just not one from both sides. He felt a blow to his solar plexus. All the air rushed from his lungs. He was taken down hard, the gun wrenched from his grip, as he fought to get the two large, powerful men off him.

"Run!" he managed to cry out, knowing it was Cassidy's only chance. The men who had him were too big, too strong and too determined. They'd also gotten a jump on him. In a fair fight, he thought he could have taken them. But not like this.

Cassidy's scream pierced the night air, sending a terrified chill through him. Jack fought harder, heartsick at not being able to protect her. He heard a struggle ensue off to his left, which meant there were at least three assailants, maybe more.

Her scream seemed to wind down, slowing, trickling into a mew of a cry. He knew that she'd been drugged with something fast and powerful as he felt the needle bite into his thigh. He kept struggling even as the drug raced through his veins and took all the fight out of him.

The two burly men who'd attacked him dropped

him to the floor without ceremony. Jack felt something warm run down into his left eye. Blood. He thought his ribs might be cracked, his whole body ached, but the real pain was in his heart.

"Cassidy?" His voice came out in a whisper. She didn't answer. Jack tried to fight the drug but it was useless. He couldn't get up. He couldn't move. His body seemed to be sinking into the floor. The dark night around him was getting blacker. Cassidy. They had her.

SARAH DROVE TOO fast to the old ranch house, no longer worried about leading anyone to Cassidy and Jack. She watched her rearview mirror, though, almost hoping someone *was* following her, because that would mean that she hadn't given up Cassidy's location.

But there was nothing but dust and darkness behind her. They hadn't been waiting at the hospital for her so she would lead them to Jack and Cassidy. They were already at Jack and Cassidy's, she thought with growing panic.

The sun rose, a bright blinding orange that foretold of the summer day ahead. She could feel the heat of it coming in the car windows, but it did little to chase away the chill that had settled in her.

All her instincts told her that she'd misjudged her power over Joe. Then again, he'd misjudged her. Did he really think she'd take this lying down? He had all the control. At least for the moment, she assured herself. She had to hold herself together. She had to think smart. She had to save Cassidy.

As she came over a rise, she saw the ranch house ahead. The rental vehicle was gone. She had told Jack and Cassidy to stay at the house. Maybe they hadn't listened and had gone somewhere. For once, she hoped that was the case.

Parking, she jumped out and ran up the steps to the porch. There was a wet spot on the worn wood decking where someone had recently wiped up a spill. It had left a dull red tint to the wood.

Heart in her throat, she tried the door. It came open, the door creaking into the cool, musty room.

Sarah stood for a moment feeling her age. She wasn't that gun-toting teenager anymore. But she'd stayed in good shape, secretly doing aerobic workouts at night when she was alone. Even before she'd gotten back her memory, she'd exercised as if it was something she'd always done.

Clearly, a part of her brain had known that one day she would need all the physical strength she could muster.

She took a step into the house. More spots on the floor where something had been wiped up. Her gaze went to the stairs. No spots. No glint of recently washed wooden steps. No reason to go upstairs. Jack and Cassidy weren't here. Whatever had happened, had taken place right here in front of the door.

Her cell phone rang. It made a hollow, eerie sound in the empty house. She let it ring four times before she picked up.

"I'm going to cut you some slack," Joe said without preamble. "You haven't regained your memory, so don't bother to lie. Because of that, you're behaving with emotion instead of good sense."

She waited, not giving him the satisfaction of asking what he'd done with her daughter. Or Martin's son.

"You need to take care of business. No more distractions. That's why I had your daughter taken. As long as you hold up your end of things, she will be fine."

If only she could believe that. Still, she didn't speak.

"Martin is coming to take care of his son. In the meantime, you do whatever you have to do to convince your husband you want nothing else but for him to be our next president. Otherwise—"

"You don't have to bother with more threats," she said, finally speaking. "You think I don't remember you?" She let out a chuckle. "Oh, I remember *you*. I look forward to when we finally get to see each other again."

He let out a surprised laugh. "Why do I feel like *I'm* the one being threatened? Bring it on, Sarah. You and me. Just the two of us. In the meantime, you aren't in a position to—"

She disconnected. Her legs felt wobbly and weak beneath her, but she managed to turn and walk back off the porch steps to her car. He was right. She shouldn't waste her time trying to find her daughter. Joe was no fool. Cassidy could be anywhere by now.

For so long now, she'd been stalling for time. She'd told herself that she couldn't marry Buck because it would be playing right into The Prophecy's hands. But now that they had kidnapped Cassidy, Sarah knew what she had to do. It was the only way she could save her family and Buck—and her country—from The Prophecy.

Once behind the wheel, she called Buck. "Let's get married. Right away."

CHAPTER TWENTY-THREE

CASSIDY SURFACED AS if swimming up from the deep dark bottom of a lake. She opened her eyes, sitting up and gasping for breath. Her head swam and she had to lie back down as she took in her surroundings. Her breathing quickened with fresh anxiety as she looked around the strange room. There were containers of food and water on shelves against one wall. A toilet like ones she'd seen advertised for camping sat in one corner behind a folding screen.

"Jack?" Her voice echoed in the small chamber. "Jack!" she called more shrilly. She heard nothing. The walls seemed to be super insulated. Either that or she was underground.

That thought sent a shock of terror through her. Her gaze shot to the door. She knew it would be locked. Still she slipped her legs over the side of the bed where she had awakened and stumbled to it. Handle in hand, she tried to turn it. Locked, just as she'd expected and yet she felt a wave of disappointment that turned to panic. She felt as if she'd been buried alive.

"Jack!" she screamed and had to cover her ears from the loud echo. Tears blurred her eyes. She swayed, still feeling the effects of the drug she'd been injected with.

As she dropped to the bed again, she put her face in her hands. She'd trusted her mother. Worse, she'd

talked Jack into trusting her. What had they done to
him? She couldn't bear to think.

She became aware of a fan whirring softly and felt
the faint air around her stir. Some of her panic eased.
She had oxygen, and plenty of food and water. She
could survive for weeks, maybe even months. That
thought only made her panic kick in again.

THE IMPROMPTU WEDDING of presidential candidate Buckmaster Hamilton and his former wife, Sarah Johnson
Hamilton, was all over the news. Nettie had released
the information the moment her friend at the clerk and
recorder's office had called.

"Are you sitting down?" the friend had whispered.
From the background sounds, it appeared she was in
the ladies' room at the courthouse. "Buckmaster Hamilton just paid $53 for a wedding license." Her excite-
ment seemed to make the phone hum. "He's marrying
his first wife again!"

"Sarah? He's marrying Sarah," Nettie had said more
to herself than to her friend. Hadn't she suspected this
would happen?

She got off the phone as quickly as possible and
called her husband.

"Sheriff Curry," he answered gruffly. If he was having a bad day, it was going to get worse with this news.

"Buck is marrying Sarah. They just bought the license."

Frank was silent for a moment. "What the hell is
Buck thinking?"

"He's in love."

"If that's it, then love is blind *and* stupid," her husband said, irritating her.

"Except in our case, you mean?"

He chuckled. "Except in our case."

"Does this make you more worried?" she had to ask. Frank had called in the FBI to investigate Sarah when she'd mysteriously returned to town. He'd been worried about her timing, coming back right as her former husband had thrown his hat into the presidential race.

The mystery surrounding Sarah had only grown over the past year and a half. While Frank had no proof of any wrongdoing, he was convinced that Sarah had been a member of an anarchist group that called themselves The Prophecy.

To Nettie's surprise, Frank had let her help in the unofficial investigation after the FBI signed off on it. She and Frank had been able to find the sanitarium where Sarah had allegedly gone after she'd driven her car into the river in an apparent suicide attempt. From there, Nettie had talked to a nurse's aide who'd worked there and been able to track down the doctor who had allegedly treated Sarah.

Dr. Venable had been experimenting with brain wiping. Nettie had tracked him to a clinic in Brazil and talked a worker there into sending a photo of the doctor—and his assistant. The assistant who had been working for Dr. Venable had been none other than Sarah Johnson Hamilton.

But still there was no proof that Sarah had done anything illegal.

"Everything about Sarah Hamilton worries me," her husband said now. "I don't like that she'll be right by his side when Buck wins the election."

"Unless, because of his marriage, he doesn't win."

"He'll win." Her husband didn't sound glad about that.

"If you're right and Sarah is dangerous, nothing will happen until he's president, right?"

The sheriff sighed. "I'm just hoping I'm wrong. But there's not much we can do now."

"Any luck on finding Russell Murdock's attacker?" she asked hopefully. She'd heard about it through the usual gossip network. Russell was a nice man whose good luck had changed the day Sarah had stumbled out of the trees in front of his pickup, Nettie thought now.

"No. I talked to the hospital this morning. He's still in a coma. It doesn't look good."

"You think it has something to do with Sarah?"

"Seems like everything bad for the past year and a half ties back to Sarah's return to Montana." Frank had been in law enforcement long enough that he was seldom wrong, she thought as she disconnected and went back to work at her part-time job at the Beartooth General Store. She touched the pendulum in her pocket. She'd given up keeping it in a drawer at home or even in her purse. She'd started carrying it with her.

Now she couldn't wait to be alone. There were several burning questions she wanted to ask it. So far, the pendulum had been right every time.

JACK HURT ALL OVER. He opened his eyes and everything came back in a rush. He sat up. His head swam. Beany.

"Cassidy," he called, but wasn't surprised when all he heard was the echo of his own voice. One look around and he frowned. He appeared to be in a root cellar. Or a bomb shelter, he thought.

Getting up, he stumbled to the supplies stacked on the shelves. His father had had a bomb shelter built years ago on the ranch, back when some apocalyptic religious group was calling for the end of the world. Hadn't that group settled somewhere around Big Timber, Montana?

He noted that some of the items on the shelves had been purchased in Bozeman. So he was still in Montana? The drug he'd been injected with had left him feeling fuzzy headed, but he was pretty sure that not a lot of time had passed.

What had they done with Cassidy? He moved to the door and tried it. Locked. It also felt solid, not that he was up to using his body as a ramrod to try to bust of out of here right now.

He sat back down on the cot and waited for his head to clear a little more. They hadn't killed him. That was something. But that didn't mean they wouldn't at some point.

His gaze took in the space. It was smaller than some college dorm rooms. Good thing he wasn't claustrophobic, he thought, and wondered if Beany was. He hoped not. That was assuming she was in a room like this, which would mean...

Jack got up again. Most bomb shelters were larger than this one with enough places for an entire family to sleep. Or in the case of that religious group, one of their bomb shelters was said to hold twenty-two-hundred people.

As his head began to clear, his reasoning returned with it. This room had to be one of numerous ones underground. He quickly searched for what he was looking for and was rewarded when he found the panel behind a framed prayer on the wall.

He pushed the first button and spoke into the intercom. "Cassidy, are you there?" No answer. He tried another button with the same results. There were a dozen buttons. He was losing hope when static suddenly filled his room.

"Jack?" Her voice was tremulous but he'd never heard such a wonderful sound.

"Beany." His own voice was choked with emotion. "Are you all right?"

"Yes. But where are we?"

"I think we're in a bomb shelter. It's all right. They aren't planning to leave us here," he said even though he had no intention of waiting to see if that was true.

BUCK LOOKED OVER at his wife and felt as if all was right in the universe—finally. He'd been overjoyed when she'd called and said she wanted to get married right away.

"But don't you want our girls there?" he'd asked, a little wary. Not only did she want to get married right away, she sounded excited about the prospect.

"They're all busy with their lives. Anyway, I don't want to make a huge deal out of this and they'll want a real wedding. I've thought about it and there is no reason to wait. I love you. I want to be your wife. We need to be together. The girls will understand."

Buck knew part of the reason he'd agreed to it was that he was afraid she might change her mind. He hated that he would even fear that. It hadn't been his only fear. When he'd heard that Russell Murdock had been assaulted and now lay in a hospital bed near death, he'd worried that Sarah would go back to him.

"There is no required wait period in Montana. We can be married by a judge I know right after we get the license. If that is really what you want."

"I was afraid I would hurt your career by marrying you with all my…baggage."

"How *is* Russell? Or was that the baggage you were referring to?" He'd said it like a joke, but he knew that his jealousy had come out instead.

"Bad. They aren't sure he'll ever wake up. That's another reason I want to marry you and not wait. Life is too short. At the thought that I might lose you…"

"You aren't going to lose me, Sarah. I'm sure whoever hurt Russell will be caught and punished."

"I'm planning on that."

He hadn't wanted to talk about Russell. He didn't want to think about him or anyone else other than Sarah.

Now they were cuddled up in bed, husband and wife. His campaign manager had been upset at first when he told him there would be no big showy wedding.

"Sarah and I are married."

"What? You got married?"

"That's right and she is going on the campaign trail with me. Deal with it." He'd hung up, pleased with himself.

Pulling Sarah closer, he breathed in the scent of her, telling himself that everything was going to be all right now. Jerrod had called back, saying he wouldn't have done it the way Buck had, but he approved and was now putting a positive spin on the marriage. Actually, he sounded pleased almost as if this had been his plan all along.

With Sarah at his side, there was nothing Buck couldn't do, he told himself. He was excited about the election again. Excited about making his country strong again. Sarah was going to make a great First Lady.

There was only one fly in the ointment, he thought. Dr. Ralph Venable. Sarah had promised she would no longer attempt to get her memory back. She would tell the doctor that she couldn't see him again if she heard from him. Buck would make sure of that, no matter what he had to do.

SARAH HAD GOTTEN Buck off to Washington, DC, closing the door behind him with relief. She couldn't believe how well she'd been able to hold up under the circumstances. Their precious daughter had been taken by The Prophecy. For all Sarah knew, Cassidy was dead.

With Buck gone, she could finally express all the warring emotions she'd been feeling. Fear and fury. They burned through her like acid. She wanted to hurt someone and that, too, scared her.

Buck had wanted her to go with him, but she'd reminded him that she would have to buy clothing and get her hair done and he'd laughed.

"I'm sorry. Of course you'll want to get ready. There will be lots of photographers and reporters." He'd frowned. "Are you sure you're ready for this?"

"I am," she'd said with false enthusiasm. "I'm your wife. The next First Lady. I have to look the part."

"So you'll join me soon?"

"I will. I'll move into the main house right away and get ready to go on the campaign trail with you."

He'd been happy with that and had left in better spirits than she'd seen him in a long time. As soon as he'd driven away, she'd broken down, crying and raging until she had enough of it out of her system to make the call.

"I did what you asked," she said between gritted teeth the moment Doc answered. "Now I want to see my daughter. And Martin's son as well. And you'd better hope that they are both fine."

"You really have to quit making demands," he said.

"I don't think so. If I really am Red, then you should all be afraid. Very afraid. I've held up my part of the bargain. Now it is time for Joe or whoever is running this show to do the same. One word from me and Buck will pull out of this race so fast that it will make your head spin like a top."

"They are both safe. Trust me."

"*Trust you*? The man who drugged me so he could kidnap my daughter, who—"

"Fine, don't trust me. But, Sarah, you have to start going along with things. You can't keep balking at every turn. Do I have to remind you what Joe is like?"

"Apparently, I have to remind you what I was like and what I apparently am capable of being again?"

He sighed. "For your sake and Cassidy's, don't push this."

She thought of the Joe she remembered, her lover. But that wasn't the Joe she'd seen in the photo Cassidy had left with her. A too-handsome man with blue eyes that seemed to look through her. His smirk of an arrogant smile told her he thought he was smarter than most people. And yet, according to Doc, she'd been the true leader—not Joe. But it was the cold, intense look in his eyes that told her more than she wanted to know. Joe was a killer. She shuddered. Had she not seen that side of him? Otherwise, how else was it possible that he'd been her lover?

"When will you let her and Jack go?" she asked, too angry to back down.

"As soon as we know your marriage hasn't hurt Buck's chances of winning."

"But you're the ones who insisted I marry him!"

"You have to be with him when he wins," Doc said simply. "We weren't sure what was the best course of action. This is the one you chose."

She let those words sink in with a premonition that shook her very foundation. Whatever they had planned, it would be after the election.

"We'll know in a matter of days. The polls right now aren't a good indicator yet."

"What about Jack?" Her question was met with silence. "What are you going to do to him?"

"Nothing. His father is coming from Texas to deal with him."

"Kill him?"

"Don't be so dramatic."

"What are you saying, then?" she demanded.

"I don't know. You seem to think that I know more than I do. I have no say over what happens."

She ground her teeth for a moment before she snapped, "Tell me you didn't have any say about what happened to Russell."

Doc sighed. "He came to see me. I was planning to handle it, but Joe—"

"Joe." She said the name like a curse, promising herself she would take it up with Joe and praying that day wasn't far off.

NETTIE HAD A long day at the Beartooth General Store. She was glad when she got home to find Frank was still at work and she would have a little time to herself. She hurried toward the house, saying a quick hello to his crows that cawed greetings to her from the phone line. There seemed to be more crows on the line than usual. Uncle, as Frank called the head of the crow family, must have adopted more strays.

"You crows are as bad as Frank," she said to them, thinking of Tiffany. There was a stray for you, she thought. Look how quickly Frank had adopted her.

Something glittered on the porch in front of her door. She stopped short. Maybe it was because she'd just thought of Tiffany that a ripple of fear moved like a wave through her.

She stepped closer, frowning as she saw that it was a tiny pile of shiny things—pieces of broken bracelet, an old key, a sparkly piece of tinsel from Christmas, a shard of weathered glass, a balled-up candy wrapper.

Behind her, the crows began to caw. Nettie couldn't keep from tearing up as she turned back to the birds. They all seemed to be waiting for her reaction to the gift they'd left her.

"Thank you all so much!" she said, her voice breaking with emotion. When she and Frank first married, the crows hadn't been happy about her moving in. They'd pooped on her car. Not exactly the welcome she'd been hoping for. But Frank had helped her befriend them. While they often greeted her, they'd never left her presents like they did Frank.

This was a first and it touched her heart more than she could tell them. "Thank you," she said, her voice breaking again. She was rewarded with a cacophony of caws from the telephone line. Scooping up the present, she waved to the crows and went inside.

Once in the house, she hurried into the kitchen to put her present in a small baggie. Hands washed, she took the pendulum out of her pocket. The gold coating of the pendulum caught the light as she sat down at the table. She put her elbow on the table and dangled the pendulum a few inches over the surface.

The waiting for the darned thing to stop moving was the hardest, she thought. When it finally stopped, she took a breath and, steadying her arm, asked, "Did Sarah have something to do with Russell's attack?"

The pendulum began to move back and forth. No. It stopped more quickly than usual and it didn't make a very wide arc, she noted.

She frowned. "Did Buck?" The pendulum moved in a wider swinging arc, making her eyes widen with interest. So Buck wasn't involved, but maybe Sarah was in some way?

The pendulum stopped again. Nettie swallowed, her throat dry. "Will Sarah kill Buck when he's president?"

The pendulum didn't move. She stared at it, trying to make sense of what it was attempting to tell her—and feeling foolish. Half the time she didn't believe any of this. The other half—

Nettie felt a jolt. "Will Buck be president?" she asked, but didn't get to see the answer as the sound of a vehicle door slamming made her jump. Frank was home. He knew about the pendulum, but she had a feeling he was in no mood tonight for "hocus-pocus," as he called it.

"Wait until he sees what I got from his crow family," she said, putting away the pendulum and picking up the baggie proudly as she went to meet him.

CHAPTER TWENTY-FOUR

JACK HAD BEEN young when the bomb shelter was built on the ranch, but his father had insisted he learn everything about it. Tom Durand was convinced that one day they would have to use it—and that that day wasn't far off.

At the time, he'd thought his father was simply being either cautious or paranoid. Now, though, he wondered if his father wasn't involved in some crazy plot to cause the end of the world. He pushed that too-scary thought away as he searched the rest of the room he was being held in.

He had no way of knowing how sophisticated this bomb shelter was. His father's had a fail-safe backup. In case of the apocalypse, the idea was to get to the bomb shelter, lock the doors so no one else could get in and wait until it was safe to venture out.

So there had to be a way to open the door and escape—without electricity, assuming that everything aboveground had been destroyed.

"I'm so sorry I got you into this," Cassidy said through the intercom.

He stepped to his. Just the sound of her voice made him feel hopeful. "We were destined to meet, don't you think? Anyway, there is no one I would rather be in this with than you," he said. "We're going to get out of here. It's going to be all right. I promise." He cringed at his own words because he knew that he had no way to promise such a thing.

Cassidy said nothing at her end. She knew where his heart was, but she didn't have much faith that they would ever see daylight again. He couldn't blame her. But he was damned sure going to do everything in his power to make it happen.

"How big is your space?" Her estimate definitely made it sound a lot larger than his. She had a larger bed in her unit, while his had bunk beds. "Do me a favor." He explained what he was looking for. "See if you can find anything like that in your unit."

Jack waited, praying silently that she was in one of the units for adults. His room, he suspected, was for a child or two given the bunk beds, so there wasn't any way to open the door once it was locked from the outside.

"I think I found the panel!" Cassidy cried. "Tell me what to do."

TIFFANY CHANDLER SAVORED this moment as she let her thumb pad move teasingly over the sharp blade of the knife. It had been a long time coming. For a while, she'd actually thought that one day she would walk out of this place a free woman.

"It isn't going to happen," her mother had told her from the grave. "At best you will go from here to a prison cell. There is only one way to end this, the way we always planned."

Now as she tested the blade, she realized her mother was right. Her mother was always right. "I couldn't have done this without you," she said to her mother.

Pam Chandler sat on the small bed in the mental hospital's violent offenders' wing beaming up at her, pride in her expression. "You're my daughter. My blood courses through your veins. You make me proud."

Tiffany felt her throat tighten. All she'd ever wanted to do was make her mother proud. She tried not to dwell on the fact that it hadn't happened until after Pam's death. It still bothered her. Not only had her mother not come to visit her before, but Pam had washed her hands of her, saying she never wanted to see her again.

Tiffany had been devastated that she'd failed her mother. Now she quickly shoved that memory into a dark corner of her mind. That had been the most heart-breaking moment of her life. She'd failed her mother. Failed to kill Sheriff Frank Curry, her mother's former husband. Failed to kill Nettie, the sheriff's true love. Failed.

But then one night her dead mother had come to her room when everyone else was asleep and told her what had to be done. Pam had married Frank Curry years ago, but belatedly she'd realized he was still in love with his ex-girlfriend, Lynette "Nettie" Johnson. Nettie had married a man named Bob Benton and broken Frank's heart. On the rebound, according to her mother, he'd married her.

When her mother had first begun visiting after her death, she'd been disappointed in Tiffany and taunted her.

"I give you one thing to do and you can't handle it. You had the gun in your hand. All you had to do was pull the trigger," her mother would say.

"I *did* pull the trigger. I hit him. I just didn't kill him before he got the gun away from me."

"I'm sick of your excuses. You should kill yourself. Or maybe you would bungle that, too."

It had been her mother's idea to get hold of the scissors. Pam had wanted her to stab herself, but the scissors were dull. Tiffany had been so upset at failing once again that she'd chopped off all her pretty blond hair. Her mother said she deserved much worse.

"When Frank comes to visit you, tell him that you will kill yourself if he marries Nettie," her mother said one late night.

She'd done as she'd been told, but Frank had married Nettie anyway.

"Please," she'd begged her mother. "Give me another chance. I can get out of here. I can still make you proud. I promise."

Her mother had finally relented. "But if you fail this time…"

"I will kill myself and we can be together."

Pam had smiled. "But if you fail, I will have nothing to do with you even in death."

"When will you do it?" her mother asked now. Pam had been nagging Tiffany night after night. But Tiffany'd had to wait until Jerry was on duty. She'd had to wait until she could get the knife from where she'd hidden it. She'd had to wait until the time was right.

"When?" her mother demanded.

"Tonight."

Her mother's smile broadened. "Make your mama proud."

CASSIDY STARED AT what appeared to be some kind of control panel. Her fingers trembled. What if she hit the wrong one and made matters worse?

She took a breath and flipped the switch. Nothing happened. She took another breath and tried the next one and then the next one.

Her door let out a clank, startling her. She quickly tried the handle, her heart soaring as it turned and the door swung outward. "It's open," she cried as she stepped back in to press the intercom button. Holding it open, she glanced out into a dim, narrow hallway with a half-dozen other doors. "How do I find you?"

"I'm sure there is a master release of the door locks somewhere, but let me try tapping on my door."

She waited until she heard the faint *tap, tap, tap* of something metallic on steel. Letting the door close behind her, she moved toward the sound. The bomb shelter was a maze of rooms connected by a series of narrow hallways. She felt her claustrophobia kick in. Her breathing quickened along with the frantic beat of her heart. She had to find Jack and quickly.

Turning down one hallway, she realized the tapping had grown fainter. She swung around and hurried back. Suddenly, there didn't seem to be enough air in the hallway. Gasping, she fought to hear Jack over the rasp of her breathing.

Miraculously, the tapping sound was growing stronger. She practically ran. Stopping next to a door where the tapping was the loudest, she tried the handle. To her relief, the door opened. She fell into Jack's arms.

"What is it?" he cried in alarm as he saw the shape she was in. "You're shaking."

"I have to get out of here," she said. "Please. The walls are closing in."

"It's all right. I've got you now. Come on." He took her hand and led her back the way she'd come.

She tried not to think of anything except the moment when she could breathe fresh air again, when she could see blue sky, when she would no longer be closed up so deep underground.

They hadn't gone far when Jack stopped so suddenly she plowed into the back of him. That's when she heard it. A sound over their heads. She felt the panic and frustration rising in her. She couldn't bear being trapped down here any longer.

"This way," Jack said, motioning for her to keep quiet.

She was breathing hard again, gasping for air. He pulled her close, cradling her head against his chest. She took in the now-familiar male scent of him and felt herself relax a little. Her breathing slowed some.

From somewhere in the distance came the clank of metal stairs as two sets of feet descended. Cassidy tried to close out the sound. If they were caught down here—

"Which rooms are they in?" a male voice asked and she felt Jack tense.

Raising her head, she looked into his eyes. He'd recognized the voice. *His father?* The thought terrified her even more.

"You told me to separate them so I did," a different male voice said. "I put them down here somewhere."

"You don't remember which rooms they're in?" There was a curse and then the voices grew fainter.

"Come on," Jack whispered. He ushered her along the hallway. The light seemed to get bright at the end. They turned a corner and she saw stairs next to a small elevator. "Take off your shoes. We can't make a sound," he whispered.

She did as he ordered and began to climb the stairs

quickly. The two men had left the hatch above open. She could see blue sky and sunshine. She caught a whiff of fresh Montana infused with the scent of pine and began to cry.

There was a noise like the sound of running feet on the concrete and then she was out, Jack right behind her. She heard angry shouts come up the shaft, but they were quickly muffled as Jack dropped the steel hatch.

The two men had left a Land Rover parked nearby. Cassidy stood for a moment, sucking in air as she looked at her surroundings. She'd thought she'd never see any of this ever again. But where were they? They seemed to be on a knoll above a river valley surrounded by mountains. It looked vaguely familiar.

Jack ran over to the vehicle. "They left the keys in it," he called back to her.

Cassidy's legs felt like water as she tried to run. She managed to get into the passenger side as he slid behind the wheel. "Those men down there... Was one of them your father?"

He nodded as he turned the key and the engine jumped to life. "Do you have any idea where we are?"

"I think we're in Paradise Valley. Head down that way," she said, pointing to the river. "If I'm right we aren't that far from Livingston." She turned to look back as dust rose from the tires. Two men emerged from the bomb shelter. One had a gun drawn, but before he could aim it, the Land Rover dropped over a rise.

Cassidy turned back to Jack. "Now what?"

His cell phone rang, making them both jump. He glanced at it. "It's my father."

THE BLOOD HAD dried on her hands a dark red. Tiffany picked at it as she drove. The knife lay on the seat next to her. It was still wet and had already left a mark on the leather upholstery. Dr. Iverson would have been so disappointed in her, she thought, and had to laugh. He often told her how disappointed he was. She was going to be his perfect patient, the one he saved from crazy. He was going to write a paper about her for some medical journal and make a name for himself.

Well, he was really disappointed with her now, she thought.

Jerry had come through for her, just as she'd known he would. All she'd had to do was pretend to pout and he was putty in her hands.

"I would kill for a hot fudge sundae," she'd said right before he'd gone off duty.

He'd chuckled. "Best not let the head shrink hear you say that."

"I know it's too much to ask, but I'm serious. There isn't *anything* I wouldn't do for one."

Jerry had met her gaze, his burning with his need for her. She'd been teasing and tempting him, never letting him get everything he wanted from her. Tonight, though, could be the night, her look had promised. If he brought her the sundae.

He'd looked around. The hospital was quiet in the hour after dinner. Whatever they put in the food seemed to knock out the patients. Soon, though, there would be moaning and groaning, crying and screaming. Often Tiffany had to put her pillow over her head to drown it out before the staff finally came around with the meds.

"You could sneak the sundae to me later in between

shifts," she'd tempted. She gave him a wicked look. "I'll even share my sundae with you."

He had grinned at that. He'd brought her ice cream one other time, but it had melted before they'd gotten to it. That had been the first time she'd coaxed him into her room late at night with the promise of a "surprise." Neither of them had been surprised by what she had to offer, but he'd definitely enjoyed it and she could tell he would do most anything to have more of her.

"All right," he'd finally agreed earlier, his eyes gleaming at the thought of what they would do when he returned. "I just can't get caught and lose this job."

"I won't let that happen." After tonight, she'd thought, he wouldn't be needing a job.

Jerry had been most accommodating. She'd left him in her blood-soaked bed, his pants down around his knees, his throat cut—just as the sheriff had predicted. She'd eaten some of the hot fudge sundae but left enough for evidence of what Jerry had bribed her with, before she'd covered him up. Wouldn't want him to be found too quickly, she'd thought.

She'd taken Jerry's keys to let her out of the hospital—and provide her with an escape vehicle. With a quick glance at her watch, she'd seen that it was the time the staff met to discuss the patients before meds. She'd had only about twenty minutes before they would be coming around.

Using Jerry's keys, she'd slipped down the hallway to the staff section of the hospital and helped herself to clothing from one of the lockers. Fortunately, one of the nurses was her size. Also, Tiffany liked the way nurse Elle Thompson dressed when she wasn't on duty. She knew that Elle always kept a change of clothes in her locker because she went out a lot after work.

Tiffany had slipped into the designer jeans, a long-sleeved silky T-shirt and nice leather sandals before pulling on the matching blue-jean jacket. It had been so long since she'd worn anything but the lightweight cotton pants and tops the hospital provided. The fabric felt so good, she had wanted to pet it.

Pulling her hair up, the way Nurse Thompson did hers, she'd checked herself in the mirror. They were both blonde and both the same size. Elle often stopped in even on her days off to change before hitting the bars. This way her husband didn't have a clue what she was up to.

Tiffany had just hoped she didn't come in tonight and ruin everything. She'd checked herself in the mirror. She even had down Elle's cocky way of holding her head. If any of the patients happened to see her, they wouldn't think anything of it. Nor would any of the staff if they happened to get a glimpse of her when she left.

She'd walked down the hallway as if she owned it. No one had made a stir. As she'd neared the main desk, she'd seen that it was empty. She'd heard the murmur of voices from the staff room behind it.

Tiffany had kept walking, right past the main desk without looking in the direction of the staff meeting. She knew that a lot of the staff didn't like Elle, didn't like her running around on her husband. She pretended to be in a hurry and merely gave a distracted wave when several of them looked in her direction.

Still, she'd half expected one of the nosier ones to come out of the room. That's why she'd had the knife tucked up under the sleeve of the jean jacket. Lucky for them, none of them had.

As she'd left, the door closing behind her, she'd let out the breath she'd been holding and had tried to relax. Almost home free.

Walking to the parking lot, she'd looked for Jerry's beat-up old car. It wasn't there. She'd felt her first wave of panic.

She'd stared at the keys she'd taken from Jerry's pocket and realized that he had driven his pickup back to the hospital tonight instead of his old car. The pickup was a stick shift and she had no idea how to drive it.

"Elle!"

She'd recognized the voice. Dr. Iverson. She'd thought he'd left for the day, but apparently he'd come back for something.

"Elle! Wait up."

She'd stepped deeper into the parking lot as if she hadn't heard him. Assured she was out of sight of the hospital windows, she'd stopped to wait for him.

"Hey," he'd said, coming up behind her. "I thought you were off today."

She'd pulled out the knife as she'd turned to face him. His expression had been priceless. There was that moment of confusion as he'd stared at her face followed by that instant of realization even before he saw the knife.

For months he'd been telling her that he would help get her out of the hospital. Right then, she'd thought, he finally would.

Now as she drove his nice car, she concentrated on Frank and Nettie Curry. It wouldn't be long. She glanced at the knife. It would be all she needed to take care of the two of them. But she would need to take the sheriff's gun to finish what she planned.

Bitterness made her grimace as she thought about the way Frank felt about his "real" family. Before she left the Curry house, she planned to kill all of his precious crows.

CHAPTER TWENTY-FIVE

"PICK UP, YOU LITTLE son of a b—" Tom Durand clamped his lips closed as he heard his son's voice. He took a breath and let it out slowly as he tried to rein in his fury—and his fear. Jack had outwitted him again. Maybe the kid had a hell of a lot more of his genes than he'd originally thought. But it was also going to get him killed. He just hoped he could talk some sense into him.

"You still there?" Jack asked. There was an insolence to his tone. The kid had the upper hand and he knew it.

"We need to talk."

"Isn't that what we're doing?" Jack asked.

He could hear traffic occasionally, which meant they were on the highway. But headed where? "Talk face-to-face."

His son laughed. "Do you really think I'm that stupid?"

"We need to come to some sort of agreement."

"I can't see how that is possible anymore," Jack said. "I think it's time to let the sheriff handle this."

"You want to go to prison for impersonating me and stealing from my bank's safe-deposit box?" he snapped.

Jack laughed again. "I was just trying to get the

proof I needed to have you arrested. I think I'll take my chances with the sheriff."

"If you do that, I can promise you that Cassidy's family will pay."

"You won't have much luck killing anyone from jail." Jack didn't sound so sure of himself.

"But I am only one member of The Prophecy. If I went to jail, someone else would handle it. You have to believe me. The only way to keep Cassidy and her family safe is to play ball with me."

"That's a funny expression since you seldom played ball with me when I was a kid," Jack said. "You were too busy."

"Really? You want to dig up a bunch of old crap? I was busy making a good life for you and your mother."

"You're breaking my heart. Maybe that will work for you on the witness stand at court, but I'm not buying any of it. Remember, I know what was in that bank box."

"Listen to me. You're my son. I don't want to see anything happen to you. Jack." His voice broke. "I love you. If you go to the sheriff—"

"We're going to the sheriff."

He swore as he realized Jack had hung up.

IT HAD BEEN almost thirty years since Sarah had seen Martin Wagner. He'd aged well. If he hadn't been so flushed with fury, he would have been handsome. He called himself Tom Durand and from what she could gather, he'd been successful, funding much of The Prophecy's work all these years.

She'd gotten the call from him and come at once to pick him up. It was late afternoon. The sun had dropped behind the mountains. A cool breeze moved through the pines as dusk settled in the deep green branches. She found him and another man waiting on the side of the mountain next to a large bomb shelter from when a religious group built them all over the area in preparation for the end of the world.

When the world didn't end, a lot of the group moved on, leaving behind these underground bunkers.

Sarah marveled at how pretty the surrounding area was. Below her, the Yellowstone River made lazy turns through the valley in a ribbon of glittering emerald. In all that beauty and calm, Sarah felt a volcano brewing inside her.

"I had this handled. If you had stayed out of it. Now where is my daughter?" she demanded as she approached the two men. The man with Martin was apparently a paid thug from the looks of him.

"Your guess is as good as mine," Martin snapped and motioned the thug out of hearing distance. "Don't blame me for this. If my son hadn't gotten involved and then Joe decided to take over and *fix* things…"

"Cassidy could go to her father now. Or the sheriff." She shook her head angrily. "What was the point of taking them? I'm married to Buck and he's staying in the race. I'm moving into the main house. I will be campaigning with him. Isn't that what Joe wants?"

Martin looked over at her. "It's gotten more… complicated. Surely, you realize that. Your daughter and my son know about The Prophecy. They know about us. You think they are just going to keep their mouths shut?" He shook his head. "Joe can't let them live."

Sarah felt as if the ground under her was no longer solid. "If he hurts my daughter—"

Martin shook his head, his eyes filling with tears. For the first time, she saw how upset he was. Like her, he loved his son. "Joe can't let them go to the sheriff." He sounded as desolate as she felt. "You know what happens now."

"No!" Sarah pulled out her phone and dialed Doc's number. She quickly told him what had happened. "Do something, damn it."

"If I go against Joe—"

"You really are just an old coward," she snapped. "Save my daughter and Martin's son and—" she looked at Martin and continued "—and we'll do whatever you want."

"Sarah, they know too much. Surely, you realize—"

"If anything happens to Cassidy, I'll destroy The Prophecy and its plan. Are you listening to me?"

"I told Joe that would be your reaction. Fortunately, for you and Martin, I believe you. That's why I told Joe I would take care of it."

"What does that mean?" she demanded.

"That you are going to have to trust me. Pray that I am as good at what I do as I think I am."

Her heart leaped to her throat. When she spoke the words came out in a hoarse whisper. "What are you going to do to them?"

"I suggest the two of you sit tight. You'll be told what you need to do next. You owe me, Sarah." And he was gone.

"What?" Martin demanded.

She was trembling so hard she could barely get her phone back into her pocket. "Doc—" She couldn't bring herself to say the words. She was only too aware of how Dr. Venable *handled* things. Sobs filled her throat. She turned away, not wanting the men to see her cry.

She'd been telling herself that she wasn't one of these people. That she'd never been. But, like something hard to swallow, the lie wouldn't go down.

What had she done? Unfortunately, she knew perfectly well.

CHAPTER TWENTY-SIX

THE SHERIFF CHECKED with the hospital to see if Russell Murdock's condition had improved. It hadn't. Angry with himself as well as Russell, he turned to his computer and clicked on the photos taken at the crime scene.

Russell had gotten involved with Sarah Johnson Hamilton from the moment she stepped in front of his pickup almost a year and a half before. He'd come to her rescue and foolishly fallen in love with her. After that, he'd been obsessed with proving that someone had stolen her memories from the twenty-two years she'd been missing.

Frank had to hand it to the man—he'd been the one to track down Dr. Ralph Venable. But even after Sarah had broken her engagement to Russell and gone back to Buck following his second wife's death, Russell hadn't quit snooping around in Sarah's past.

That, the sheriff was sure, was what had gotten him almost killed at the fishing access site. Russell had been convinced that Senator Buckmaster Hamilton was behind the "brain wiping" that had taken Sarah's years away. Frank wondered if that was still the case after seeing Russell and Buck together the other night.

He was flicking through the photos from where Russell's body had been found, when something caught his eye. He turned back to the photo and stared at something on the ground. At first it looked like a penny. Since they were worth so little, often people tossed them. Or didn't bother to pick them up.

But this wasn't a penny. It was a token and it appeared to have been dropped recently given how shiny it still was. He'd seen one like it recently and realized where. Big Timber Java, the coffee shop on the main street.

"DID YOU SEE that car?" Cassidy asked, turning in her seat to look back. "The driver seemed to—"

"Recognize us. Or more than likely the car," Jack said as he glanced in the rearview mirror.

"He's turning around!" she cried. "He's coming after us."

Jack sped up as much as he could. The highway through Paradise Valley followed the winding Yellowstone River. To make matters worse, it was summer and tourist season, which meant traffic on two-lane Highway 89 between Livingston, Montana, and Yellowstone Park.

The dark-colored car was behind them with several vehicles in between. The driver had made several attempts to pass, but had been thwarted by all the traffic.

"I'm not sure I can lose him," Jack said. Ahead he saw a junction for secondary East River Road. At least there wouldn't be as much traffic, he thought, as he slowed enough to make the turn at Tom Miner, according to the sign. This highway was narrower, but had very little traffic. He sped up, glancing back and seeing no one following them. At least not yet.

"I don't see the car," Cassidy said, turning in her seat to look back. "Maybe we lost him."

Jack doubted that. The driver of the dark car would have seen them turn, but if they knew the area, they might have realized that the two-lane blacktop ran adjacent to the main highway on the opposite side of the river.

"Were you serious about going to the sheriff?" Cassidy asked as she turned to him.

"I don't see any other way out of this. They aren't going to stop looking for us. We know too much."

"You aren't suggesting that they'll *kill* us," she cried.

"What other choice do they have? It isn't like we can promise not to tell and they'll agree to that. These people are fanatical killers."

"These *people*, as you call them, are our *parents*," Cassidy cried.

He glanced over at her as he took one of the sharp turns. "I'm not sure that makes a difference." Had she really believed that once she talked to her mother this nightmare would end? The highway now ran along the side of the mountain overlooking the river. The pavement was patched and full of potholes. Jack had no choice but to slow down. There was no guardrail on the road or shoulder. On the left side, the land dropped off in a steep cliff to the river. On the right side of the road, the mountain rose in a wall of rock.

Glancing back in his rearview mirror, he was surprised to find the highway still empty. "This highway?" he asked. "Do you know if it connects to the other one at some point?"

"If I'm right about where we are, there are several

places along the river where there are bridges and other roads that connect with it before we reach Livingston."

He nodded. That was exactly what he feared. If the driver of the vehicle that had spotted them called ahead...

They came up over a rise. Jack had only seconds to react. A van swung in front of them, blocking both sides of the road. His choice was the cliff to his left or the rock wall to his right.

Jack slammed on the brakes. The SUV skidded toward the van as he fought to get stopped.

FRANK CALLED BIG TIMBER JAVA and was told that the owner, Alex Ross, would be in soon. He drove downtown, parked and walked a half block to the coffee shop. As he entered, he saw Emily Calder and her daughter Josie sitting at one of the tables. Apparently, he wasn't the only one who was looking forward to seeing Alex this morning.

He noticed that Emily still had a variety of tattoos and piercings, but she didn't have that rebellious chip on her shoulder like she had when she'd first come back to town. Emily had gone a little wild after her parents had died. Her older brother, Jace, was still in high school at the time so he hadn't known how to handle her. She'd left town, fallen in with the wrong crowd and even done some jail time.

But after a while, she'd returned to the area, gotten a job at the Sarah Hamilton charitable foundation started by Buckmaster, and was doing well. Frank suspected her relationship with Alex Ross hadn't hurt either. Alex was as straitlaced as Emily was rebellious. He figured the two were good for each other.

"Good morning, Sheriff," Emily said, her daughter echoing her words.

He stepped to their table, ruffling the little girl's hair as he said hello. "How are the nieces coming along?" he asked. Her brother, Jace, and his wife, Bo, were expecting twin girls.

"Poor Bo. She's as big as a barn," Emily said with a laugh. "She's so uncomfortable and the doctor has her on bed rest. But it won't be long now." She smiled. "We can't wait." Josie seconded that.

As Alex came in through the back, Frank excused himself, saying he needed a word with him. They stepped into Alex's office.

"Tell me this isn't about Emily's ex," Alex said, looking worried.

"Sorry, no. Harrison Ames is still locked up. No more trouble from any friends of his?" Last year one of Ames's former prison buddies had been stalking Emily.

Alex let out a relieved breath. "No trouble. In fact, everything's been…" He couldn't seem to suppress a grin. "Great."

Frank had to smile as well. "I'm glad. I won't keep you from Emily and Josie. I don't know if you heard, but Russell Murdock was attacked."

"I heard. Out by the fishing access site."

The sheriff nodded. "I found this close to where Russell had been found." He handed Alex the token. Before he'd come by, he'd had the lab try to get a clear print off the token but it was too smudged. "This might not even belong to the attackers but I thought I'd give it a shot. I'm thinking whoever worked him over was from out of town." Those kind of men often stood out in a small town like Big Timber.

"I haven't been here much, but I can ask my cousin Jeff."

Frank followed him out to the counter.

Jeff nodded when asked. "Couple of rough-looking dudes have been in a few times." He laughed. "They ask for the kind of coffees that women like. Sissy drinks." He provided a pretty good description of the two.

"Any idea where they might have been staying?" the sheriff asked.

"Actually, I think I do. They were driving a big SUV." He described it, but hadn't noticed the license plate. "I happened to see it parked at that motel on the edge of town, the old one with the row of units. Can't think of the name." Frank provided the name and Jeff nodded. "That's the one. Haven't seen them today. Hope that helps."

"Definitely does." He noticed that Alex had joined Emily. Josie was busy telling him about a butterfly she'd caught in the net he'd given her and how her mother had made her let it go.

"Some things are just for looking at, not keeping," Alex said. "Some things are for keeping," he added and his gaze locked with Emily's.

Frank felt himself smiling as he left. Lynette would tease him for being such a softy, but he was happy for Alex and Emily, and especially for Josie.

Armed with a description of the two men and the SUV they'd been driving, he drove by the motel only to find that they had checked out.

"They paid in cash. Said they were brothers here visiting Yellowstone," the clerk told him. "They paid a security deposit since they said they didn't believe in credit cards. They didn't cause any trouble or break anything."

"Have they picked up their security deposit?" Frank asked.

"Afraid so. They said they were headed home."

He asked to see the form they'd registered on. One glance at it told him they'd lied about everything on it. Still, he had the owner make him a copy. Back at the office, he put in the names. Nothing came up, just as he'd figured.

JACK HAD BARELY gotten the car stopped within inches of colliding with the van in the road, when two men emerged from the other side of the van. Everything happened so fast that he didn't have time to pull his gun before the men smashed the side windows.

Glass exploded over him and Cassidy. She screamed. He was trying to get the car into Reverse and pull his weapon, when his head was slammed back and the keys were ripped from his hand.

A moment later, he and Cassidy were dragged from the SUV at gunpoint. Their wrists were bound behind them with plastic cuffs, their ankles also bound, before being dumped unceremoniously into the back of the van. Jack's mind raced as he tried to think of a way out of this.

Just when he thought it couldn't get any worse, they were both jabbed with hypodermic needles again.

One of the men slid behind the wheel and the motor revved. The van began to bounce along the highway. Jack sat up enough to look back through the dirty rear window to see the other man behind the wheel of the SUV they'd stolen from his father.

As the drug began to take effect, Jack lay back down next to Cassidy, his gaze going to her beautiful face. He feared that this time they wouldn't just be locked up. This might be the last time he saw her, the last time he got to look into those blue eyes. His throat closed at the thought. "I'm so sorry."

Tears welled in her eyes. "No matter what happens, these days with you have been the best of my life. Jack? I love you."

He smiled, choked up at her declaration. "I love you, Beany," he said, moving closer to her so he could kiss her one last time.

SARAH WATCHED MARTIN pace in the large cold warehouse. They'd been told to come here, but given no other information. Through the dirty barred windows, she could see nothing beyond the darkness. She'd lost track of time.

"Do they have Cassidy?" she'd demanded when Martin had gotten the call. She'd watched his expression as he listened to whoever was on the other end of the line.

He'd nodded. "We'll meet you there. You know what I have to have."

"Is this about the money they took from you?" Sarah had cried as Martin disconnected. "What about our children?"

"Settle down. They're fine. And yes, I need the money. *We* need the money."

"To finish this…plan," she said irritably. "After everything Joe has done, you're still going along with it?"

"What choice do we have? You've seen what happens if you fight them."

She knew he was right, but that didn't make it any easier. "How did we get involved in this?"

He shook his head. "I just know there is only one way out."

Sarah hugged herself and looked toward the closed door at the end of the large warehouse. "You know what Doc's doing to them."

"This way is better than what Joe had wanted to do," Martin said. "Just hope to hell it works. Otherwise…"

She felt numb from the cold, numb from where her life had taken her, and maybe even more numb to where it was headed. All her thoughts were with Cassidy, the child she hadn't gotten to see grow up because of her poor choices.

Now she waited, watching Martin pace and listening to the low murmur of Dr. Venable's voice in the room beyond them where he had Jack and Cassidy. "Tell me about your life."

Martin stopped to look at her as though he was deciding if she was serious. "What's the point?"

"Humor me. I'm going crazy here. Unless you want me to start pounding on that door down there…"

"I have an import/export business in Houston and a few other businesses on the side. I've done well."

That wasn't what she was asking. "You were married?"

He nodded and looked away. "Marriage is required so we can blend in like Russian spies who were imported years ago. But it is risky in this business making a family. It is hard to keep our two lives separate. But I guess I don't have to tell *you* that."

"What happened to your wife?" she asked, a bad feeling in her belly.

He avoided her gaze. "She found out."

Sarah felt sick to her stomach. "You let them—"

"You don't *let* them do anything. They just do it. Good God, woman, look what they've done to you."

She said nothing for a long moment. "Didn't you ever want out of The Prophecy?" she asked hopefully. And yet she knew even by broaching this subject she was taking a horrible chance. If Martin told Joe—

"This has been my sole purpose for years." He frowned at her. "What else is there? What is the point of making money if not to change the world?"

That sounded like tired rhetoric to her, something he'd said to himself too many times over the years. "I just question how much we're going to change anything," she said, looking toward the closed door again. She couldn't hear Doc's voice.

"That attitude will get you killed, you know."

Sarah turned to look at him. "Blowing up buildings, killing people, I'm sorry but doesn't that just make us terrorists? Isn't there a better use for your money than putting it into anarchism? You could have run for office. You could be changing things from the inside."

Martin laughed. "You *really* have bought into the bourgeois bullshit." He shook his head. "That kind of talk makes me think that you've become a liability to our cause."

She met his gaze. "I will do whatever I have to do to keep my family safe. Never doubt that. But I'm not one of you anymore."

"I can see that. Which tells me that you can't be depended on to make the right decision when compromises have to be made."

"*Compromises?* Like when they killed your wife? Did you love her at all?"

He made a pained sound. "How can you ask that? That's why I have to see this through. Otherwise, it was all for nothing."

Sarah felt a shudder move through her. "What if what Doc is doing in that room doesn't work and your son remembers everything he's learned about you and The Prophecy?" she asked, knowing that she was digging her own grave asking such things.

"Don't forget, your daughter also knows."

Sarah turned as the door opened at the other end of the warehouse. As she started in that direction, Martin grabbed her arm, shaking his head as he said, "If Dr. Venable can't fix this, then I am going to have to take care of both of them. If you try to stop me, Sarah—"

CHAPTER TWENTY-SEVEN

TIFFANY HAD ALWAYS used the way she looked to get what she wanted. She'd learned that from her mother. Pam could look as innocent as a summer day. No one had seen the dangerous storm lurking behind that face.

If they had, they would have run away in horror, Tiffany thought now. She remembered her own fear of her mother when she was a child. The first time she glimpsed the real Pam Chandler. She shuddered now as she drove. She'd been no more than five at the time. She'd wanted to tell someone, to warn someone, but there had been no one she could turn to.

From the time she could remember, it had just been the two of them. "I'm all you've got," her mother used to say. "You ever turn on me and you'll have no one. No one. And I will be coming after you. You never want that."

Fortunately, most of the time, all Tiffany saw was her mother's sweet face and the disguise that went with it. Pam had loved that they looked alike, both blonde, both blue-eyed.

"See this face?" her mother used to say, cupping Tiffany's face in her hands. "It is your greatest asset. Just blink those big blue eyes of yours and look slightly confused," Pam would say. "You'll be amazed what you can get away with."

Her mother had been right about that anyway. Tiffany smiled to herself now as she drove toward Beartooth and the small ranch where Sheriff Frank Curry and his wife, Nettie, lived. She'd stopped at a cafe, ducking into the bathroom to clean up. Fortunately, she'd found a coat in the back of Dr. Iverson's car and was able to cover the bloodstains he'd gotten on her Elle outfit.

Once she was presentable, she ordered a large dinner, ate every bite, and then when faced with the check, suddenly broke down in tears claiming she'd lost her purse.

Seeing her inconsolable, several of the other patrons had chipped in to buy her meal. The waitress even gave her ten dollars to make sure she had enough gas to get home. The kindness of strangers always amazed her. Or as her mother said, "A sucker is born every second for women like us."

Tiffany had waited patiently for night. Driving through that darkness now, she felt anxious to reach the ranch. And yet she wanted to savor every moment because these would probably be her last. Full and content, she drove with her window down. The cold night air made her feel more alive than she'd felt in a very long time.

Every once in a while she would look over at the passenger seat. Somehow she'd thought her mother would have come along. She hadn't thought Pam would have wanted to miss this. Maybe she would show up later when the fun started. It was late enough that Frank and Nettie would be asleep in their bedroom.

Word wouldn't have gotten out yet that she'd escaped. Even if the staff found Jerry in her room the way she'd left him, there would have to be a search of the hospital, then the grounds, before the alert was called.

Dr. Iverson's body might be found during the search of the grounds. She'd rolled his body off into a nearby ditch. If only it would rain tonight and wash away the blood from the pavement. But she couldn't depend on that.

At some point, Sheriff Frank Curry would be called, since everyone at the hospital still thought that he was her father.

Which meant that she had until daybreak to accomplish everything she'd come to Beartooth, Montana, for in the first place.

"OH, MY GOD, what have you done to my daughter?" Sarah cried as she pushed past Dr. Venable and into the room. Cassidy lay on the floor. Her face was white as if in pain. Her eyes were closed and for a moment, Sarah wasn't sure she was still breathing.

She turned, advancing on the doctor, her fingers aching to close on his scrawny throat. Martin restrained her, pulling her back as Doc snapped, "She's fine." He sounded exhausted and irritable. He immediately turned to Martin. "You said you could get them on a plane back to Houston?"

"The plane is standing by," Martin said. "You want me to take both of them?"

"If we get them out of here now and on a plane, everything should be fine since Houston will be their last memory," Doc said with a sigh and handed Martin a slip of paper. "This is where you'll find your... *property* Jack hid."

"You're sure they won't remember anything?" Martin asked as he looked at the slip of paper.

"Trust me, they won't remember any of this. The clinic in Houston is standing by for both of them with cover stories. If I did my job, they won't remember any of this." Doc shifted his gaze to her. "Go home. The hospital will be calling with news about your daughter. I implanted a suggestion that she come back to Montana. If anything, your relationship with her should be better."

"What about my son?" Martin said to Doc's retreating backside.

"The last thing he will remember is visiting his mother's grave days ago. You're both in the clear. Don't screw it up." With that he was gone.

Sarah looked at Martin as two large men pushed past with gurneys and loaded Jack and Cassidy for the waiting van. Martin looked relieved and yet worried.

"It was bad enough when Doc messed with *my* mind," she said between gritted teeth. "Now my daughter's? And all because of you and Joe."

He spun on her. "No, Sarah, this is on you. You knew what you had to do and you fought it. If you haven't realized it by now, nothing is going to stand in the way of The Prophecy's plan. Get with the program or the consequences will be much higher next time. If Doc did his magic and it works, we both got lucky this time."

IT WAS ALMOST two in the morning by the time Tiffany neared the Curry ranch. The moon peaked in and out of the low clouds. The breeze coming out of the Crazies was cold. It reminded her of the short period of time when she had been living over the Beartooth General Store. That was before the mental hospital, before she'd failed to kill the sheriff.

She felt a sudden pang recalling the artwork she used to do. She'd loved to draw. There had been days when she'd dreamed of being an artist, even though she'd known that wasn't her destiny.

When she'd failed to kill Sheriff Frank Curry as her mother had instructed her to do from the time she was ten, she'd quit drawing. At the mental hospital, they encouraged her during arts and crafts hour. She couldn't bear to draw.

Instead, she'd sat cutting paper into tiny pieces with the dull rounded scissors that made her feel like a kindergartner.

All that was behind her now, she told herself as she parked a half mile from the ranch. Before her attempt on Frank's life, she'd spent a lot of time around the ranch when he was gone. She could find her way, even in the dark.

Taking the shortcut across a pasture, she reached the trees. Several of the horses in the pasture near the house picked up her scent and began to snort, ears raised, as they moved away.

The house was a ranchette and only one story. Frank's bedroom was at one end. She hadn't been here since he'd married Nettie. She was assuming they would be together since they'd fought so hard to be that way. Seemed fitting that they should die together.

His patrol SUV was parked in front of the house beside the smaller SUV that Nettie drove. Tiffany felt as if she knew Frank well enough that they *could* have been father and daughter. She wished it had been true.

He'd been kind to her. Something inside her ached at the memory of riding horses with him.

Unfortunately, he'd been the man who'd broken her mother's heart. Frank had always been in love with Nettie, her mother had told her—even when he was married to her. That was what had broken Pam Chandler Curry's heart. She'd known she hadn't been his first choice and couldn't live with that.

But she'd also known that he was still in love with Nettie and that he could never love her as much as he had his first love. That's when she'd decided he had to die and that it would be her daughter who killed him.

"What mother brainwashes her daughter into being a murderer?" Frank had often demanded on his visits to the mental hospital before he'd realized she wasn't his daughter. "Pam was a monster who used you. Tiffany, work with the doctors. You deserve a life, not to be used in some horrible revenge scheme."

Clearly, he didn't understand. He thought that when Pam died that she wouldn't come around anymore. He didn't know that she would never be free of her mother—even in death. Frank just never knew what Pam was capable of, otherwise he would have known from the beginning that Tiffany wasn't his.

That's why she had to finish this. She couldn't bear waking in the middle of the night to find her dead mother standing over her bed, her face filled with hatred and telling her what she was going to do to her if she didn't finish what they'd started.

Frank Curry didn't know what it was like being that terrified.

Better to finish this even knowing that her mother would make her kill herself once it was done.

As she neared the patrol SUV, she knew it would be locked. Just as she knew the front door of the house would be as well. Frank knew she was coming. He hadn't known when or exactly how she would pull it off, but he would be ready.

She also knew that he would underestimate her.

She worked her way down the side of the house to where she had hidden the key. Getting copies of his keys had been child's play. That was back when she had the run of the place; back when Frank thought his love could heal anything Pam had done to her.

Fortunately, the patrol SUV was the same one Frank had been driving when she'd been sent to the mental hospital. She took the key she'd had made and moved toward the vehicle. She knew exactly where she would find what she needed.

From the telephone line, one of the crows roused and let out a squawk. Frank had told her stories about crows. He swore that crows recognized people, people they liked, people they hated. Also that the birds passed that information on to other crows.

She wasn't sure she believed they would remember her, but she wasn't taking any chances since the last time she was here she'd killed one of them. She now had her head covered with an old towel she'd found in the back of Dr. Iverson's car. Keeping the towel's edges so the birds couldn't see her face, she unlocked the patrol car.

Another squawk from the telephone line. "Shut up you stupid bird," she muttered under her breath. She couldn't wait to kill the whole bunch of them.

Joe Landon slammed his fist into the wall. He'd never been so furious.

"I handled it," Doc said on the phone. "Isn't that why you pay me the big bucks?"

The old man's sarcasm was irritation enough. "You don't have the authority to take things into your own hands. Those two young people are a liability. I want them both killed." That would show Sarah just how serious he was.

"Haven't we had enough bodies as it is?" Doc questioned. "Let's not forget that we lost John Carter and Warren is now in jail awaiting trial. Do you really want to call more attention to us right now, especially when we are this close to our objective?"

He hated how reasonable Doc sounded. When this was over… "What if they remember everything and go to the authorities?"

"They won't. If that becomes the case, though, I will personally see that they never reach the authorities. You have my assurance."

Joe scoffed at that now as he hung up. He was the *leader*, not that old man. How dare he take things into his own hands? "If I want those two killed, by damned they will be killed if I have to do it myself," he said to the empty room.

Doc had told him that the two were headed for the clinic in Houston. Joe picked up the phone. Unlike Martin, he didn't have a private jet. But he still could get to Houston before either of them left the clinic.

The thought of Martin made him even more angry. He'd given the man an order and he'd blown it. He shouldn't have let his son get involved.

The idea had been to blend into society and wait.

That meant acting normal. Normal for most of the others was getting a job, finding a wife, having children. But a wife and children had proved to be a problem. Wives become suspicious and had to be dealt with, like Martin's wife.

And children... Well, they grew up. They asked questions. They noticed things. Simply put, they couldn't be trusted.

That was one reason he was so furious with Sarah. Six children? What had she been thinking? Worse, she'd fallen for Buckmaster, fallen for that "fake" life.

Well, he would deal with her when the time came. Right now, he thought, as he threw a few things into a suitcase, he had to deal with her daughter and Martin's son. He would show them all who was in charge of The Prophecy. It would be a lesson he knew at least Sarah wouldn't forget.

THE TASER FELT light as a feather in Tiffany's hand. She'd spent time online studying how Tasers worked. If one of the staff happened by, she would switch to Pinterest and pretend to look at hairstyles. Frank's Taser gun was ready to go.

She'd also taken his extra Glock. She'd put both the handgun, fully loaded, and the knife with the now-dried blood in Dr. Iverson's backpack she'd discovered in the rear of his SUV. She'd bought the duct tape with the ten dollars the waitress had given her.

"Some things are meant to be," she'd said to herself when she'd discovered the coat, towel and the backpack after a potty break at a gas station. "Thank you, Dr. Iverson," she'd said with a laugh.

Now, as she crept back to the side of the house, she

feared things were almost going too well. The crows were watching her through the ambient glow of the large old yard light. She pulled the towel across most of her face. Was it possible they recognized the way she moved? The one with the loud mouth let out another squawk.

"I'll be back for you," she said under her breath as she rounded the corner into the darkness that hunkered behind the house.

The night felt colder back here away from the light. She shivered, adjusted the backpack she had slung over one shoulder and stuffed the towel into it. Standing perfectly still, she listened. The only sound was the breeze in the nearby pine trees. It sighed almost impatiently as if saying, "Get on with it."

Scuttling along the back of the house, Tiffany stayed in the deepest of the shadows until she reached the back door. She'd learned from experience that people in these parts, especially rural residents, didn't lock their doors. Half of them couldn't even remember where the keys were for their houses.

She also had a duplicate of that key. Her mother had taught her to always be prepared. As she pulled it out, though, she hesitated. Frank hadn't changed the key for his patrol SUV since he didn't know that she'd copied his extra key he kept in a drawer in the house. But what if he'd had the locks changed on the house?

Suddenly, she feared that he might be one step ahead of her. After all, everyone knew Frank had a crazy daughter by his first marriage who would give most anyone nightmares—and reason to have their locks changed.

Then again, as far as anyone knew, poor sick Tiffany

was locked up in the criminally insane ward of the state mental hospital with no chance of ever getting out.

She stood for a moment before she reached for the doorknob and tried her key. It fit into the lock. She turned it. There was a soft click. As she turned the knob, the door swung in. She stepped into the quiet predawn darkness.

CHAPTER TWENTY-EIGHT

THE SUN WAS just coming up over Texas. Martin rode in the ambulance that took them to the back entrance of the clinic, where Jack and Cassidy were put on stretchers and wheeled to separate rooms.

"There is nothing more for you to do here," the head nurse, a stout older woman with short gray hair, informed him. "Come back during visiting hours."

He felt at loose ends as he exited the clinic to where his car and driver were waiting behind the ambulance. Getting in, he told himself he was too anxious to go about his day as if nothing was happening. What would Jack remember when he woke up? *Would he wake up?*

Both Cassidy and Jack had looked like death warmed over. He realized how close he'd come to losing his only son. It had shaken him more than he had wanted to admit to Sarah. And it wasn't over. If Jack remembered—

He shoved that thought away. The best thing he could do was go to work. Business as usual. Until he got the call from the hospital, then he would charge down there, praying that whatever Doc had done had worked.

He thought of his wife and felt tears fill his eyes. He told himself he was exhausted and yet his hands

shook as he tried to pull out his cell phone to call his
secretary at the office.

Maybe Sarah was right. Maybe there was something
deeply wrong with them. Did he even still believe in
this cause that he'd given his life to? He'd been so busy
protecting The Prophecy, so busy making money to
keep the cause going, so busy hiding behind the mask
of Tom Durand, did he even know who he was anymore?

"Where to, boss?" his driver asked, dragging him
from his thoughts.

"My office," he said and leaned back as the luxury
car purred away from the clinic. Out the window, he
could see the Houston skyline in the distance. This
was his city, his life, if not his dream. He'd always
wanted to make a mark on the world. He had rebelled
at the thought of being a car salesman like his father.
A nobody. He had wanted to accomplish something.
He couldn't bear the thought of dying like his father
and no one would remember him except someone he'd
once sold a car to.

He was still looking out the window when a car
whizzed past them. All he saw was a glimpse of a familiar face—and a flash of white against black.

Turning in his seat, he craned his neck to watch the
car turn into the front entrance of the clinic.

"Stop!" he yelled at his driver. "Go back. Hurry."

THE SHERIFF WOKE with a start. He lay in bed listening,
unsure what had brought him out of his nightmare so
suddenly. He didn't move, afraid he would wake Lynette, as he tried to still his racing heart and calm his
breathing. He was perspiring heavily, his pajama top

drenched, making him aware that he'd had the same nightmare again.

He turned down the comforter and sheet only to have the night air coming in through the open window send a chill through him. He got up and closed the window a few inches as quietly as possible. He and Lynette both liked the fresh air. He didn't want to wake her. She'd be worried about him. Worried that he'd had that nightmare again.

He unbuttoned the pajama top and slipped it off, dropping it beside the bed as he gently pulled his dresser drawer open and pulled out another top. He'd have to remember to pick it up before she saw it in the morning.

So far he'd been able to keep how often he had the nightmare a secret from Lynette—which was no easy task. The woman was a bloodhound if she thought he was keeping something from her.

But he hadn't wanted her to worry. And she would if she had any idea what haunted him most of his nights. *Tiffany*. It was always the same. In the nightmare, he woke to find her standing at the end of his bed holding his gun in her hand. He would raise his right hand, try to say something, but before he could, she would pull the trigger.

He rubbed the palm of his right hand, assuring himself there was no bullet hole. Just as he always assured himself there was no Tiffany standing at the foot of his bed when his eyes finally adjusted to the darkness. It was just a bad dream.

Frank almost laughed at that. It was a *nightmare* like none he'd ever experienced even in his childhood when everyone knew there were bogeymen under their beds.

The worst part of the nightmare was what happened after the first shot. He shook his head, refusing to go back to that part, the part where Tiffany killed the only woman he'd truly loved, his Lynette.

He eased back into bed and closed his eyes, letting the night air chase away the dampness on his skin until he shivered and pulled the sheet up. Turning on his side to face Lynette, he listened to her soft breathing and smiled to himself. As long as she was safe, everything was all right. But if anything ever happened to her…

Not letting his mind go down that particular path, he breathed in the sweet, clean scent of Lynette's face cream and pictured her putting it on each night before bed. Smiling, he let sleep take him again.

MARTIN WAS OUT of the car before his driver even brought it to a complete stop. "What are you doing here?" he demanded of the man who was headed for the front door of the clinic.

The priest turned, looking surprised as he cupped one hand against the rising sun to stare at him. "I'm sorry, do I know you?"

For just a moment, Martin thought he'd made a mistake. He stepped closer. The priest's face was in shadow, but now he was near enough that there was no doubt. "Joe."

The priest's eyes narrowed to dark blue slits. "Sorry? I don't know a Joe. My name is Father John David Williams."

Now that he'd confronted him, Martin wasn't sure what to do. Joe was still handsome, actually distinguished. He'd always carried himself like a man who knew who he was and where he was going. A man who wasn't going to let anything stand in his way.

The fact that Joe was here now didn't bode well. Wasn't that why Martin had accosted him? One of the rules they'd had when they'd parted all those years ago was that they would keep their "fake" lives separate so there would be no connection. But never in a hundred years would Martin have dreamed that Joe would become a priest.

He thought of his son and Cassidy inside the clinic. "Where are you going, *Father*?"

"To see some of my parishioners. Do you have a problem with that?"

The contents of his stomach began to roil at the look Joe gave him. It was an are-you-sure-you-really-want-to-do-this look. He reminded himself how dangerous this man was. *Don't let the priest getup fool you*, Martin told himself. *This man standing before you would kill you without batting an eyelash.*

Martin swallowed. "I can't let you do whatever it is you've come here to do."

Joe raised an eyebrow and smiled. "I'm curious. How do you intend to stop me?"

"I'm hoping with reason. Doc says he has this covered."

Joe stepped closer, his priest garb rustling softly and yet it was a sound that sent ice water down Martin's spine. "Doc isn't running this show."

"You got what you wanted. Sarah is back in line. Now it is just a sprint to the finish line. But if the presidential candidate and his wife lose a child…"

Joe's jaw tightened as he looked away. "And if Doc is wrong?" he asked, turning that laser gaze back on him.

Martin met the man's eyes with an even more intense look. "Then I will do whatever has to be done."

With a sigh, Joe said, "You're out of line here today, *Martin*. I'm not leaving the city until I am assured this has been contained. Oh, and Martin, never confront me like this again." He turned on his heel and headed back toward the car he'd arrived in.

Martin stood watching the priest go. His legs quivered under him as he realized that he was a dead man. Joe wouldn't forget this. He stumbled to a bench along the sidewalk and sat down for a moment as he watched Joe drive away. Joe Landon had become a priest? Somehow that made him even more terrifying.

THE BEDROOM WAS still dark but Tiffany could see faint light to the east as she stepped in. The sun would be rising soon. She stood listening. Both the people in the bed were snoring softly. It gave her an odd feeling. This peaceful scene felt so normal.

She wondered what it would have been like to have a mother and father growing up. She imagined what it would have been like if Frank had loved Pam more than Nettie. Maybe they would have had a child together. Maybe it would have been her. She shoved that thought away, surprised by the well of sentiment that kept surfacing. Was it because tonight would end it all, she wondered as she stepped to the end of the bed.

The sheriff stirred. Tiffany smiled to herself. He had sensed something wrong. Maybe he even sensed her.

He sat up suddenly, blinking. Even when he saw her standing there, it was as if he couldn't believe his eyes. She wondered how many times he'd thought he'd seen her here only to realize it was only his worst nightmare.

As he started to get up and reach for something in the bedside table, Tiffany squeezed the trigger. Two charged electrodes at the ends of long conductive wires shot out, launching through the air. The attached wires trailed across the bed as dozens of confetti-sized identification tags filled the air.

The barbs of the electrodes caught on Sheriff Frank Curry's pajama top, sending current through the fabric to his flesh. In the predawn light coming through the window, she saw his eyes widen as his body began to quiver. He tried to get up, only to fall on the floor on his side of the bed.

She knew she had only one shot and for a moment, she thought it wouldn't incapacitate him. But once on the floor, he didn't move.

Nettie had come awake, sitting up and staring for a moment as if seeing a ghost. Tiffany smiled. "Hello, Nettie."

As the woman scrambled from the bed to get to her husband, Tiffany snapped on the light and drew the gun. "Stop!" she ordered.

Ignoring her, Nettie dropped down beside Frank. Tiffany ground her teeth. She couldn't wait to kill this woman. But this was not the way she had it planned. What had Frank seen in this woman anyway? Pam was much prettier.

Frank began to twitch on the floor.

"Get away from him," she ordered, motioning with the gun. "Now!"

Nettie rose slowly. Her original fear and horror had been replaced with anger. Her eyes blazed. "You're just like your mother."

"I'll take that as a compliment."

"Don't. She was a selfish, manipulative—"

"Don't talk about my mother," Tiffany snapped, pointing the gun at Nettie's heart.

That's my baby girl, her mother said as she materialized beside her. *Kill them*.

"Not yet."

I said kill them.

"No, this is my plan."

"Who are you talking to?" Nettie asked in a whisper. She didn't look as angry. She looked worried.

"Mother wants me to kill you both."

"I'm sure she does," Nettie said.

Frank was getting stronger. She couldn't wait much longer. But she wanted to be sure he got to see Nettie die. Then he would get to see her kill his precious crow family—every last one of them.

Nettie had sat down on the edge of the bed with Frank still at her feet.

Get on with it. Pam was next to her demanding she finish it. *What are you waiting for?*

Frank managed to pull himself up into a sitting position, his back against the wall. She thought he might beg her to reconsider. She thought he would at least say something. Instead, he looked resigned as if he'd been waiting for this day, knowing she would come, knowing she would kill them both.

Tiffany realized that she wanted to see panic in their eyes, fear, not the pity she witnessed in Frank's. Not the resignation and sadness she saw in Nettie's.

She'd dreamed of this moment. It would be so easy to pull the trigger. Kill Nettie and empty the rest of the shots into Frank.

And then what?

Steal Nettie's SUV and go anywhere she wanted. She had the money her mother had left her. She had moved the account out of the country in a place where there was no extradition. She could live on that for a long time. If the money ran out, she could get a job. She could make a life for herself.

Her mother laughed. *Stop kidding yourself. They will catch you and this time you will never get out of the loony bin. You should save one bullet for yourself and finish this. It is the only peace you will ever get.*

Tiffany could feel Frank watching her as if he could see the struggle going on inside her. She shook her head. He'd thought all it would take to cure her was listening to the doctors at the hospital. He didn't know that her mother would never leave her alone.

Outside one of the crows began to caw again. She had the extra clip in her pocket. Enough firepower to kill the crows and then herself. It was the only way to escape her mother. Hadn't she always known that was the way it had to end?

Frank was still sitting on the floor. He hadn't tried to get up. He hadn't tried to rush her. This wasn't going the way she'd planned it and that made her angry and worried. She felt off balance. She had envisioned this so many times. Why wasn't it going like she'd seen it in her head?

Just then, Nettie lunged toward the door—and a shotgun leaning against the wall in the corner.

Her mother screamed a warning. *The knife! Use the knife!*

CHAPTER TWENTY-NINE

CASSIDY WOKE SICK to her stomach. She rolled to her side, her eyes flying open as she felt an arm come around her. An older nurse dressed in white said, "There, there, sweetie," as she produced a small container. Cassidy was trying to make sense of her surroundings when the meager contents of her stomach roiled up and out.

She lay back as the nurse wiped Cassidy's mouth, murmuring soft words. The woman had a kind face and what appeared to be a sweet disposition as she smiled down at her. "Feeling better now?"

All she could do was nod as she took in the room and the nurse beside her bed.

"You're in a hospital in Houston," the woman said as she tidied up the area next to Cassidy's bed.

"What's wrong with me?" Her voice came out in a whisper.

"Here, have a little drink. You must be parched." As she took a sip through the straw, she saw that the woman's name was clipped on her uniform. Susie. No last name. "You've had a rough time of it. Some kind of flu bug that knocked you off your feet. It's something that's been going around, I'm afraid. You've been down for a few days now."

A few days? Cassidy stared at her in surprise. "I don't remember coming here."

"Your friends brought you."

"My friends?" she repeated.

The nurse frowned. "You were staying with one of them, I believe. You've been so sick. You don't remember? Well, she remembers *you*. She's right outside your room and anxious to see you. Feeling up to it? I won't let her stay long."

Cassidy nodded, needing to understand how she'd gotten here. "Thank you." She felt better since she'd thrown up. Mostly, she felt weak and confused. Houston? A friend? Her memory felt blank, like a deep dark hole.

The door opened again shortly and a young familiar-looking woman came into the room. "Hey, we were so worried about you, but you finally have some color. Remember me? Taylor Scott. You've been staying with me in my brownstone?"

A piece of memory clunked into place. "You invited me to Houston."

Taylor smiled and nodded. "Glad to see you're better than you were when I first brought you in here."

Chattily, she sat down on the edge of Cassidy's bed and opened her large purse. "I wasn't sure how long you were going to have to stay so I brought you some magazines, a hairbrush—though with that hairdo, you shouldn't have to do much."

Her hand went to her hair. She pulled it back in surprise to find her long locks gone. "I got it cut?"

"Cut and colored." Taylor shrugged. "You said you needed a change." She studied Cassidy openly for a moment. "It looks good on you. You've never had it short before?" Not giving her a chance to answer, Taylor chatted on until Cassidy found an opening.

"I don't remember coming here."

The young woman stopped and looked at her. "What's the last thing you remember?"

Cassidy tried to recall, but it only made her head ache.

"You were supposed to meet me and Peter for dinner at a restaurant not far from my apartment. Do you remember that?"

She did. Just being able to retrieve that memory made her feel a little better.

"But when you got there, you were complaining that you didn't feel good. Whatever it was hit you hard. You were so sick." Taylor mugged a face. "It scared us so we brought you to this hospital. Peter knew someone who worked here and had heard it was the best in Houston." She shrugged again. "I'm just glad that you're doing better."

"Has my family been told?"

Taylor frowned. "I didn't know how to reach them. You never told me anything about them. There were a few numbers in your purse, but I was hesitant to call them. When we met, I got the feeling that you weren't close to your family."

Cassidy nodded as Susie came back into the room.

"Let my girl get some rest now," the nurse said as she chased Taylor off her bed and began to smooth the sheets. "I bet you've talked her arm off and worn her out."

Taylor laughed. "I'm just glad she's feeling better. Also, I needed to tell her my news. Peter and I are headed for South Padre now that you're all right. If you feel up to it, you could join us there…"

"No," Cassidy said. "I need to go home for a while."

"You never said where home is."

"Montana. I've been gone too long," she said, thinking how true that was. She had a deep yearning to go home.

FRANK FOUGHT HARD not to react as Tiffany grabbed Lynette. It all happened in an instant. Now a crazy woman had a knife to his wife's throat. He caught the gleam in Tiffany's eyes. She would delight in slitting Lynette's throat. He could see that she'd already nicked it. A trickle of blood ran down to the neckline of Lynette's nightgown, where it formed a dark stain against the white fabric.

Now what? He thought. How long were they to stay like this before Tiffany did what she'd come here to do?

Frank had known this day would come. As he tried to get feeling back into his body, he told himself that he'd been waiting for it. So had Nettie. Neither had believed it wouldn't come. Tiffany was too smart. Of course, she would escape and of course, she would come here.

But as months had gone by, he'd become lax. He'd apparently left the patrol unlocked. How else had she gotten the Taser and his gun? Had he really thought she wouldn't have studied up on how to use the weapons he kept there? He'd underestimated her, a huge mistake.

But he hadn't been a complete fool. He'd prepared. There were weapons hidden all over the house. Nettie didn't even know all the places he'd put them for this very occasion.

He stalled, waiting for his body to stop trembling. He would need to be steady because he would get only one chance.

It hadn't been a coincidence that when he'd been able to move after the Taser shot that he'd propped himself up on this wall with the bedside table off to his left, his boots to his right.

He would have to move fast, something he wasn't sure he could do just yet.

Tiffany was arguing with the empty space next to her as if her mother was standing there. He could well imagine what Pam was saying to her. It appeared that Tiffany was trying to ignore her—just as she probably had her whole life. But it wasn't working. The Pam in her head was clearly making her nervous and anxious. Earlier he'd seen confusion in the girl's face. She had been having doubts about what she planned to do.

Not now, though. She wanted to get it over. He could see resignation in her expression. She thought she had no choice. Dead or alive, Pam had never given her a choice.

He had to do it, even if he wasn't sure his motor skills had completely returned. Otherwise, Lynette was about to die. If that happened, he didn't care what Tiffany did to him. But he also had to end this here tonight. He couldn't let her loose on society. Not with her dead treacherous mother in her head.

He watched her. He knew better than to try to reason with her. He'd tried that for years now. It only made her madder and more hateful.

"Stop it," Tiffany snapped, turning her head to look

at the spot next to her. "I'll do it. Just let me do this in my own way."

Pam was encouraging her to kill—just as she had done most of the poor girl's life.

He met Lynette's gaze, saw her eyes widen in alarm as she, too, realized it was time. It was only a matter of time before Tiffany did as her mother ordered.

Minutes ticked off. He could feel his strength coming back, though slowly. Part of it was his age, he knew. The Taser had left him weak and shaking. He watched Tiffany's face. Apparently, Pam was doing all the talking. Tiffany was shaking her head as she listened to the one-sided conversation.

Pam, even dead, was still tormenting her daughter. He wondered if crazy was hereditary. Maybe all the doctors in the world couldn't have helped Tiffany. Maybe she had always been a lost cause and only fools like him had thought he could save her.

If he failed to end it here in this bedroom… He hated to think what would happen. After this, Tiffany would never get out of the criminally insane ward. Once they caught her. *If* they caught her. But like her mother, she might be elusive for years. What damage could she do in all that time? He hated to think and knew he couldn't let that happen.

But he feared if he made a move, Tiffany would cut Nettie's throat before he could stop her.

Right now it was a stalemate. He didn't dare move. He could hardly breathe.

NETTIE FELT NUMB. It surprised her. She'd gone through such a mix of emotions in a nanosecond. Surprise, fear, anger, resignation and now a numbness. This was how it was supposed to end, she thought. At least she and Frank had found their way back to each other and had this time together. She was grateful for that.

She'd never thought about life after death, but a warm feeling now moved through her that wherever she and Frank were headed, they would be together.

She felt the knife blade prick her skin again and closed her eyes, telling herself it would be over soon.

JACK WOKE WITH the worst headache he'd ever had. He tried to sit up, but everything spun.

"Take it slow," said an unfamiliar female voice next to his bed.

A wave of nausea hit him when he turned his head to look at her. The nurse had apparently been sitting there, waiting for him to awaken.

Now she rose and came to him, taking his wrist in her cool fingers as she apparently checked his pulse.

"Where am I?" His voice came out a croak.

"You're in a private hospital in Houston."

"Houston," he repeated under his breath as if the word was alien to him.

"Do you remember what happened to you?" she asked as she removed some apparatus from his arm and then moved to turn off a monitor next to his bed.

He searched his mind. The last thing he recalled was visiting his mother's grave. "No."

"I can only tell you what I was told. Apparently, you stepped off the curb and were nearly run down by a utility truck."

He lifted the sheet to look down at his legs, worried how badly he might have been injured.

She noticed and shook her head, "Your only injury was from the fall. You struck your head."

His hand went to his head and felt the rough cotton of a bandage.

"You have a concussion so your memory might be a little fuzzy."

A little fuzzy? He didn't recall any of this. "Was anyone else hurt?"

She looked a little surprised at the question. "No, you were alone."

He lay back on the pillow, not sure why he had asked the question. He'd been alone at the cemetery.

"Try to get some rest," the nurse said.

"Has my father been called?"

"He's the one who had you sent here to our private hospital. I'm sure he will be stopping by to see you soon. He's been here since it happened. I sent him home this morning. He was looking worse than you."

"How long have I been here?" he asked.

She seemed reluctant to answer for a moment. "A few days. Don't concern yourself about that."

A few days? He wanted to ask her more questions, but she left, closing the door behind him. A deep lethargy seemed to descend over him. He closed his eyes.

The dream came almost at once. Mountains, a stream, a beautiful young woman smiling up at him from deep green grass. A woman he'd never seen before.

CHAPTER THIRTY

THE GUN WAS in Frank's boot where he put it each night. He finally spoke as he tried to get up. "Tiffany—"

She reacted just as he feared she would. She jerked Lynette back against her and dug the knife into her flesh. Another bead of bright red appeared on her throat and began to run down, this one larger than the last.

He reached for his boots as if trying to steady himself and fell back, landing with a groan as he pulled one boot to him. He closed his eyes, his head against the wall. She wouldn't kill Lynette unless he was watching. He knew her that well. He hadn't suffered enough.

"Do that again and I will cut her throat from ear to ear," Tiffany said from between gritted teeth.

"You're going to do that anyway," he said, not opening his eyes. His hand slipped into the boot, his fingers closing around the stock of the pistol. "So what is stopping you?"

"You ruined my mother's life," Tiffany cried. "I want to ruin yours."

"Haven't you already done that?" he asked still without opening his eyes. "For years now I have lived in fear of this night."

He heard her make a satisfied sound. She wanted to

hear about his anguish, she fed on it. And so did her insane mother.

"You have no idea what it's been like knowing how smart and capable you are. I knew you'd get out. I knew you'd come here." He opened his eyes. Just as he knew, she was hanging on every word. "I've been beside myself. Did you know I thought about retiring and moving to Arizona or maybe Florida or another country to get as far away as I could?"

She liked that. A slow smile curved her lips. She really was a beautiful girl, so sweet looking like chocolate candy that looks so delectable only to take a bite and find out it's full of maggots.

He closed his eyes again, resting his arm on the boot as if for support. She needed to believe that he was too weak to get up. She needed to believe that she'd outsmarted him.

And it was true, he had suffered waiting for this night. He'd been afraid he couldn't save Lynette. It had been his only fear. That fear had his blood humming right now. He still wasn't sure he could save her.

But he would die trying. He could see that Tiffany was unraveling. She kept talking to the spot beside her, becoming more agitated as her dead mother nagged at her. Pam had always been relentless. He hated to think what it must be like for Tiffany to have that woman in her head. He knew he couldn't wait any longer.

He squeezed the pistol inside the boot tighter. He'd always been a good shot. But tonight, he had to be a crack shot or the woman he loved would be dead.

JACK COULDN'T SLEEP. Getting up, he wandered into the bathroom. He felt stronger, less confused, not so weak. After using the facility, though, he didn't want to go back to bed. He was hungry, hungrier than he felt he'd ever been.

Opening the door to his room, he stepped out into the empty hallway. Before that moment, he hadn't given any thought to how large this private hospital was—or how many patients there were.

He saw now that the place appeared to be very private. A dozen rooms ran along the hallway, most of the doors open, the rooms empty. Each was made up to look like a pretty bedroom. No wonder he'd been confused when he'd awakened. He hadn't realized he was in a hospital.

He could hear faint voices at the end of the hall, the farthest away from the exit at the other end of the hallway.

Moving toward the sound, he was thinking how different this concussion felt from his last one. His last one was why he'd given up bucking broncos and the rodeo circuit. Now he'd had another one? He really had to be more careful. He didn't want to turn out like one of those football players who'd been hit in the head too many times.

The voices were getting stronger. He was thinking that he must be the only patient they had right now when he saw her.

She was curled up in the bed, her face turned toward him. He recognized her at once. The girl from his dream! He stumbled to a stop and stared, struck dumb. He'd dated his share of women, but there was something about this one that made his heart beat a little faster.

Her big blue eyes were open. He knew she'd seen

him when she let out a chuckle at his sudden stop. He smiled, wondering what she was doing here.

She had short dark hair that made her blue eyes look even larger. Unlike him, she didn't have a bandage on her head. But her face was pale. He hoped whatever was wrong with her wasn't serious.

He realized he must have seen her before. Why else would he have dreamed about her?

Just as he was about to say something to her, his nurse, a woman named Rene, appeared. "What are you doing up?" she demanded.

"I got hungry." He was still trying to see the young woman in the bed, but the nurse had stepped in front of him. She took hold of his arm and was turning him back toward his room when another nurse hurriedly closed the young woman patient's door.

"You should have rung the bell for me," Rene scolded. "You're not that steady on your feet yet."

"I feel…better. The walk did me good. I could eat a bear," he said.

Rene chuckled. "I'll see about cooking you up one. If not a bear, maybe some beef?"

Remembering the blue-eyed patient, he asked, "That young woman back there…" He half turned.

She still had hold of his arm. She pulled at him. "We're very strict here about our patients' confidentiality."

"Just tell me. Is she going to be all right?"

Rene looked at him for a long moment as they walked. "She's going to be fine. As a matter of fact, she's scheduled to leave tomorrow morning. Now don't ask me any more. I've said too much already."

He smiled. "I'm glad she's going to be all right."

"You act as if you know her," Rene said.

"No, but…" He grinned. "I liked her smile."

CASSIDY COULD SEE that her nurse wasn't happy with her. "I told you that keeping your door open would disturb your sleep," Susie chastised Cassidy as she clucked around her like an old mother hen.

"I like hearing voices," she said. "It's too quiet in here. I've had too much time to think."

"Thinking isn't a bad thing, unless something is bothering you," Susie said, then eyed her closely.

"I just haven't been home in a long time. The truth is, I was distancing myself from my family. I guess I'm feeling guilty about that."

"Family is nice to have. Do you have a large one?"

"Five sisters."

"My heavens! How lucky. I was an only child. Count your blessings." She straightened the sheets, patted Cassidy on her arm and then said, "Get some sleep. You're going home in the morning."

Susie had made arrangements for a taxi to pick her up to take her to the airport. She'd even gotten her a flight to Montana.

"Thank you for your help. For everything."

The pleasant-looking nurse smiled. "I'm so glad you're better. You have the whole rest of your life. Make the most of it."

Cassidy was surprised to see the nurse so serious and almost sad. As Susie started to leave the room, she asked, "That man in the hallway…"

"Another patient and no one to concern yourself about. People come here who want privacy."

Cassidy recalled how quickly the other nurse had

ushered him away and Susie had closed her door. She nodded and closed her eyes as the nurse left.

But she found sleep elusive. There was something about that man. She would have sworn she'd seen him before. Maybe when she'd been brought into the hospital.

NETTIE SAW WHEN Frank reached inside the boot. It came to her in an instant what he was reaching for. She could feel the sharp cold steel against her neck and feared that if she tried to move to give him a shot, Tiffany would slice her throat just as she'd said she would.

The girl was trembling as if under unbearable stress and talking crazy to her mother as if Pam was in the room. The numbness Nettie had felt earlier left her the moment she saw Frank reach into the boot.

She had to do something. Anything. And she had to do it quickly. Tiffany was losing it.

Nettie said a silent prayer, then in one swift movement, she reached up, grabbed the girl's arm holding the knife to her throat and kicked back at Tiffany's legs. The movement threw the girl off balance. But only a little.

Her fingers bit into Tiffany's arm as hard as she could. The knife slid across her throat, stinging like a paper cut as she stumbled forward. Two gunshots, one after the other exploded in the small bedroom.

Nettie shoved the knife away from her, but Tiffany's body pushed her to the floor. She sprawled, the breath knocked out of her, as she was bathed in hot red liquid.

Then Frank was shoving Tiffany's dead body off her and pulling her into his arms, crying, "Are you hurt badly? Lynette, are you hurt?" There was so much blood, Lynette couldn't be sure what was hers.

The next thing she remembered was Frank carrying her out to the ambulance and then holding her hand as they raced toward Big Timber and the hospital.

AFTER CASSIDY'S PHONE CALL, Sarah dropped into a chair, buried her face in her hands and sobbed until she had no more tears to cry. Her daughter was coming home.

"I assume everything is all right?" Doc asked when she finally dried her tears and looked up.

All Sarah could do was nod. "Thank you."

"I did what had to be done. Now there is nothing standing in the way of your husband winning this election."

She swallowed, nodding again. "You're so subtle," she said, getting to her feet. She'd heard the warning in his words. Nothing else better go wrong.

Sarah thought of the young woman who Sheriff Frank Curry had once thought was his daughter. The news was all over the county. He'd had to kill the girl after she'd escaped from the mental hospital and tried to kill him again. Nettie was in the hospital from a knife wound but expected to live. Frank, according to the nurses at the hospital, had stayed by her side, refusing to leave.

"You spared my daughter," Sarah said now to Dr. Venable. "Don't you think I know at what cost?" Joe would make the older man pay for going against his orders and they all knew it.

Doc got to his feet, picking up his bag with the pendulum inside it. "My work here is done, then. For now."

He didn't need to remind her that he would be back. There was a chunk of her memory missing. The woman she used to be, Red. The Prophecy. And the plan.

That was why Doc was still alive. Joe couldn't kill him. Not until Doc turned her back into Red. Could he do that? Sarah lived in fear that he could. Just as he had made Cassidy and Jack forget everything that had happened to them.

After Doc left, she looked at her meager belongings packed in suitcases by the door. Buckmaster would be calling soon to find out if she had moved back into the main house.

She forced herself to rise and pick up the suitcases. With a final glance at the house she'd been living in, she headed for the SUV Buck had bought her months ago.

Loading the suitcases was no problem. Doc had offered before he'd left, but she'd said she could manage.

Behind the wheel, she drove toward the main ranch. Buckmaster had built the house for her and their children. She'd never dreamed of living in such a beautiful home.

As she came over a rise and saw it in the distance, she thought of more than twenty-three years ago when she'd left it in the middle of the night. A defeated woman, destroyed by her past, she'd thought the only way out was to kill herself. But she hadn't even gotten that right.

Now she drove toward the house with a new kind of desperation. She would have to outwit The Prophecy. If she had really been the mastermind behind the anarchist group, then wouldn't she be able to foil their plan once she remembered everything?

Which meant she had to bide her time. After almost losing Cassidy, she knew she had to do whatever was asked of her until the time came.

She and Buck were married again. It was where she'd always belonged. She was his bride. A second time. Fate, and of course, The Prophecy, had given her this second chance with Buck. Damned if she wasn't going to make the most of it.

Sitting up a little straighter, she turned into the entrance to the house. The guard nodded at her as she drove in and parked in front of the big house.

For a moment, she sat merely looking at it. Buck had built the girls a separate addition off to the left. Now it was empty since all of them were busy living their lives.

But Cassidy would be here soon. Buck would be flying in tonight. All of them would be together again. Sarah hugged herself at the thought. Buck was determined that once they were a family again, the girls would warm to her. She prayed that was true.

Getting out, she didn't bother with her suitcases—just as Buck had told her. There was staff to do that. She walked to the house, her hand hesitating only a moment on the door before she turned the knob and stepped in.

Home. Tears flooded her eyes. She was finally home.

"LAST NIGHT I dreamed about this girl I saw in the hospital," Jack said when his father picked him up that afternoon.

"Oh?" Martin asked.

"I went by her room but she was already gone," his son said with a shrug. "I was worried about her."

"Did you know her?" he asked, his heart in his throat.

"Naw, there was just something about her." He shrugged again, then stopped in the hallway on the way to the door.

"What is it?" Martin asked as he saw Jack look down as if remembering something. He felt his heart take off like a rocket. "Something wrong?"

"This shirt." His son turned and Martin saw with a shock that Jack was wearing a T-shirt with Montana printed over snowcapped mountains. Why hadn't anyone noticed what Jack had been wearing before he was brought to the hospital?

"I wonder where I got this," Jack said, sounding confused.

"I would suspect that whatever you were wearing was covered in blood, maybe even torn. The nurses probably dug up the T-shirt so you'd have something to wear to go home. I hadn't thought to bring you clothes."

Jack nodded, frowning. "They really do seem to think of everything at this hospital."

Martin said nothing as he ushered his son to the car. "This way," he said when they reached the exit. "I'm parked out back."

"So you already checked me out of the hospital?"

"All taken care of." He'd stopped at the desk to pay and also to talk to the nurse who'd been assigned to Jack.

She'd assured him that his son was fine. "The last thing he remembered was visiting his mother's grave."

Martin wanted to kiss Doc on the top of his balding head. He'd done it. He'd pulled this off.

"Will be nice to get back out to the ranch, I would

imagine," he said as his driver jumped out to open their door.

His son only nodded and looked toward the Houston skyline.

The nurse had warned him that it would take a few days for the drugs to wear off. "He'll seem confused, but the symptoms are the same as a concussion. Didn't you say he had one during a rodeo? Well, then, he won't have any reason to question what happened to him since he's been there before."

Martin tried to keep his eyes on the road ahead as they left the hospital. But he found himself glancing over at Jack. He had an almost sadness to him.

He thought of the girl, Cassidy Hamilton. Had there been something between the two of them besides trying to destroy their parents?

"I was watching the presidential debate on TV last night," Jack said as they drove through the streets of Houston. "I really like Buckmaster Hamilton. I think he'd make a good president."

Martin said nothing.

"As a matter of fact, I was thinking this morning that I'd like to get involved in his campaign."

What had precipitated this? Martin could only wonder. His son seemed excited, though, for the first time in a very long time. His mother's death had been hard on him. Also, Martin had to admit, his insistence that Jack join him in the business hadn't helped.

Jack needed to find his own path. After the past few days, he understood his son better. Jack was a lot stronger and more capable than he had imagined. He had a newfound respect for his son.

"If that's what you want to do, then I give you my blessing."

Jack looked at him in surprise. "I thought you'd..." He shook his head and smiled as if he was not going to get into what he thought. They had both changed.

"I know you don't understand. But you've always been involved in politics behind the scenes, right?"

Martin was surprised that Jack had known that. He kept wondering if small memories weren't surfacing.

"I know you were disappointed when I wasn't involved in college politics. So you should be glad that I'm finally taking an interest."

"Does this have something to do with a girl?" Martin asked.

His son laughed. "No, but it's interesting. That Montana T-shirt I wore home from the hospital? Those mountains on it are the Crazy Mountains. Candidate elect Buckmaster Hamilton lives at the foot of those mountains."

"And you see that as a sign that you should join the man's staff?"

"I told you, I heard him speak. I liked what he had to say."

Martin nodded. He could see that Jack had made up his mind. All the ramifications of that weighed on him. What were the chances that Jack would be there the night Hamilton gave his acceptance speech? Too damned good for comfort.

But the election was still a long way off. A lot of things could happen in the meantime. And if he tried too hard to change his son's mind, he might alienate him again. Or force him to remember something he shouldn't.

"Son, I'm proud of you. I'll miss you, but if this is something you feel you have to do—"

"It is. I haven't felt this strongly about anything in a long time. I've always been interested in politics," Jack said with a grin. "I've just never agreed with yours."

Martin managed a laugh. "What if I told you I planned to vote for Hamilton?"

Jack looked over at him in surprise. "He's pretty liberal for you, Dad. I think I'll give his campaign office a call and see if there is some way I can help."

Martin watched the city he knew so well blur past the window. He told himself not to worry. But that was like telling himself not to breathe.

"Sweetie, don't worry," Sarah said when she saw Cassidy staring into the mirror. She'd picked her up at the airport and brought her to the main house and one of the guest rooms. "We can make you a hair appointment in town. Once you're blonde again and your hair grows back—"

"I don't want to change it," Cassidy said, still staring at her image in the mirror. "I like it, though I don't remember doing it."

"That flu you had must have been awful. I hate that you were so far away from home when it happened." She smiled at her daughter in the mirror, just thankful she had Cassidy back, although she still seemed confused. Doc had said she should be her old self soon. "I'm just glad you're home."

"I was going to talk to you about that," Cassidy said, finally turning from the mirror. "Dad mentioned something about you joining him when you could on the campaign trail. Are you just staying here because of me?" Sarah started to open her mouth, but Cassidy cut her off. "That's what I thought. You need to go join Dad."

"I don't want to leave you just yet."

"You won't have to." Her daughter smiled, blue eyes shining. "I want to go along."

Sarah hadn't expected this. "I'm not sure—"

"Dad needs us. I can help out. I've done nothing with my life thus far. I want to do this. I want to support Dad like he's always supported me."

She studied her daughter, thinking how much Buck would love having the two of them with him. "All right." She smiled. "Your father will be delighted."

"We're going to need new clothes," Cassidy said, making her laugh. Maybe her daughter was going to be all right if she was thinking of shopping.

"Yes, we will," she said, giving her a hug. "That sounds like your father now. Why don't you tell him the good news."

Cassidy ran downstairs. Sarah joined them to find Buck looking more than a little pleased.

"Did she tell you the news?"

Buck nodded. "But I have to ask. You've never shown an interest in politics before. What brought this on?"

Cassidy shook her head and shrugged. "I don't know. I want to help. Since I woke up in the hospital, I feel…different. I missed all of you and Montana. I think I've selfishly been angry about you running for president because it inconvenienced me," she confessed. "I want to make up for it."

Buck looked to Sarah. His eyes were bright. "What do you think about this, Sarah?"

She couldn't help but wonder if this sudden interest in politics had something to do with what Cassidy had learned about her mother. She pushed that thought away, telling herself she was being paranoid.

"I think it's going to be fun to have Cassidy working with us." She knew part of the reason was that she could keep an eye on Cassidy. Not that she thought she might remember. But just in case she did, Sarah would have to take care of it.

Buck looked again at their daughter. "Well, whatever your reason, I'm delighted." He pulled them both into a hug. "My girls with me? I couldn't be happier."

EPILOGUE

"THIS IS THE young man I was telling you about, Jack Durand," Buckmaster said. "He's been a godsend for our campaign."

Those words hung in the air as Sarah turned to see Jack Durand come into the room.

Shock quaked through her, rattling her for a moment. She quickly smiled, praying he hadn't seen her shock—or her fear—at the sight of him. She'd known he had joined the campaign, but she'd thought he was in Houston working with the staff there.

"It's so nice to meet you," Jack was saying. "And belated congratulations." She must have looked confused. "On your wedding," he added.

"Oh, thank you," she said with a nervous laugh. She knew she'd been staring at him, fearing that he had remembered and that was why he was here. But as her gaze met his, she saw nothing but sincerity.

"My husband has told me wonderful things about you," she said, needing to fill the silence. She was still so shocked that the young man her husband had been bragging about was Jack Durand. "Is this your first campaign?"

"It is. I've never gotten involved in politics before, but I saw one of your husband's debates. I was so impressed that I felt I had to be part of him becoming our next president."

"That's wonderful," Sarah said, wondering if his interest was some residual memory from what he'd learned about his father and Cassidy's mother. The mind was a strange thing. Where did those lost memories go? It wasn't as if they could be eradicated, pulverized into dust. They still had to be there, just inaccessible. Unless someone unlocked them.

She thought of her time in Brazil and the deep longing she'd had for something she'd never been able to articulate. Now she knew it had been for her husband and children. For twenty-two years she hadn't known they existed, and yet she'd *missed* them.

Doc had taken her family away, wiping out their memory, and yet something had stayed. A deep longing. So who knew what was going on in Jack's mind, let alone Cassidy's? She was just glad that her daughter wasn't here. Maybe with luck, the two wouldn't cross paths.

Not that there should be a problem, according to Doc.

AT THE CAMPAIGN office in Helena, a song came on the radio as country as rural Montana. Cassidy began to dance without even realizing she was doing it. These months working on her father's campaign had been the happiest of her life. She was finally doing something that felt right.

Her father was talking about keeping her on in some capacity after he was elected. He said he had another volunteer he wanted her to meet sometime.

"I think you'll like him," her father had said with a gleam in his eye.

"No playing cupid," she'd warned him. "When the right man comes along, I'll know it."

As she was swaying to the music, she was surprised when a young man came through the door, caught her hand and pulled her into a cowboy jitterbug. She laughed as he twirled her out and pulled her back into his arms. Someone turned the radio up and other members of the staff joined in. She looked into his handsome face and felt a start.

"I know you," she said, smiling.

He met her gaze. "You do look familiar. Ever been to Houston?" He swung her around. Expertly, she came back to him.

"On occasion."

"Jack Durand," he said, smiling as he swung her out again and caught her by the waist.

"Cassidy Hamilton."

His step faltered only for an instant. Cassidy had grown up dancing to Western music in Montana. What surprised her, though, was how easily they fell into step together.

"Not…"

"Buckmaster is my father." She said it with a sense of pride.

Jack shook his head. "That must be why you look so familiar. Maybe I saw a photograph of you. Not that it matters. It will eventually come to me. It always does."

BUCKMASTER WATCHED FROM the doorway as his daughter and Jack Durand danced. Cassidy had her head thrown back, her face glowing with pleasure. Jack's gaze was on her, his expression one of wonder. Buckmaster figured the young man had to be questioning how he'd gotten so lucky.

Cassidy looked happy. It radiated from her. Buckmaster thought he couldn't have picked a better man for her. Jack reminded him of himself. He would go far. Everyone liked him.

The song stopped on the radio. His staff laughed breathlessly and started to go back to work when they saw him. Someone quickly turned off the radio and they scurried back to their desks.

"No need," he said, although they clearly thought otherwise. "I was enjoying watching you all." He couldn't wait to tell Sarah that Jack and Cassidy had finally met and from what he could tell, they'd hit it off.

"WHAT ARE WE going to do?" Martin demanded when Sarah called him with the news weeks later.

"Nothing. Jack hasn't mentioned some girl that he's met and fallen for?"

Martin groaned. "I've heard it in his voice, but he didn't mention any names. He sounds…"

"Happy?"

"You don't think—"

"They *aren't* remembering," Sarah assured him.

"How can you know that? Come on, they both decide they are suddenly interested in politics and just happen to cross paths? What do you call that?"

"Fate. They believe they just met weeks ago. If you saw them together… They are so much in love."

Martin swore. "What does Doc say?"

"That more brought the two of them together than us and our…secret. He called them star-crossed lovers."

Martin was quiet for a moment. "And Joe? What does he have to say about this?"

"Doc hasn't said. If anything, Joe is probably waiting to see what happens like the rest of us. The election isn't that far off now."

"So you haven't heard from him?" he asked.

"No." She wondered if Martin was having his doubts. Their children were in love. They were excited about their future, while their parents were planning... What exactly would it be? Something big. But what if it was a big sizzle instead? She prayed that at least at her end that would be the case.

But she knew this wasn't over. Jack and Cassidy were in love. Would at some point one or both of them remember? Doc didn't think so. Right now, they were blissfully happy.

Buckmaster was also happier than she'd ever seen him. The campaign was going better than expected. He would be the next president of the United States—unless something or someone stopped him.

Inside her a tiny voice at the back of her mind whispered that it might be her. It was the fear she lived with as the days counted down to election night. A fear that a switch could be thrown in her mind and she would become Red, a ruthless murderer.

* * * * *

*Read on for a sneak peek of
the next installment in*
New York Times *bestselling author
B.J. Daniels's*
THE MONTANA HAMILTONS *series
HONOR BOUND
Available November 2016*

CHAPTER ONE

Election night 2016

IT WAS THE old priest's limp that caught Ainsley Hamilton's attention as the presidential election results were announced over the loudspeaker. A deafening roar rose from the bundled-up crowd gathered at the Sweet Grass Fairgrounds outside Beartooth, Montana, that November night.

Her father, Buckmaster Hamilton, had just been announced the winner. Music began to play loudly as the throng cheered. She watched the priest, hunched over his cane, edging ever closer to the platform where her father would be giving his acceptance speech soon. Ice crystals danced in the night air against the backdrop of the Crazy Mountains. Millions of stars twinkled in the velvet of Montana's big sky overhead. There was an excitement in the air as well, an electricity that had her feeling warm inside.

Ainsley felt her heart surge. She was so proud of her father, so happy for him. This was his night. He had worked hard to get here. She told herself that nothing could spoil it for him, especially her sister Kat's concerns about security. The fairgrounds were crawling

with secret service agents, sheriff department depu-
ties and even the sheriff himself was here somewhere.

Her gaze went again to the priest as he limped forward. The crowd parted for him, no doubt seeing his
determination to get closer. When he finally reached
the elevated platform where she was standing with her
family, he leaned heavily on the cane as if trying to
catch his breath. Like her, he must have wanted to be
part of this history-making night.

Another roar erupted from those gathered as her
father strode out onto the stage. He smiled and nodded, then turned to motion to his wife and six daughters. They had been waiting in the wings out of the
cold breeze for this moment. Ainsley looked at her
five sisters.

Bo smiled in her direction. The twins, Harper and
Cassidy, were holding hands, both crying. Olivia was
dabbing at her eyes as well. It was clear that they had
all been moved to tears, all except sister Kat, who
looked nervous as their mother led the way across the
stretch of red carpet to her waiting husband.

Out of the corner of her eye, Ainsley saw that the
old priest was straining to see. His limp looked painful, she thought as she saw him clutch his cane with
both hands.

His limp reminded her of another man, a man she'd
given her heart to recently only to have it broken. As if
she needed a limp to remind her of Sawyer Nash and
what a fool she'd been. Thoughts of him were never
more than a heartbeat away.

Ainsley fell back, letting the others go out ahead of

her. Too many emotions had her feeling vulnerable. She wasn't ready to face all these people right now.

Her sisters started down the carpet to join their father, and Ainsley had no choice but to join them. She took a deep breath, reminding herself that this night was for her father, the first Montanan to be elected president. The sound of the roaring crowd seemed to fill her heart to bursting.

Standing on the platform, she smiled at her father through her tears. Her pride in him closed her throat as she tried not to cry with this many people watching.

Fortunately, the cameras—just like the secret service agents—were trained on the future president as he hugged each of them and then stepped to the microphone to make his acceptance speech. She and her five sisters and mother moved back on the platform into the shadows again as he took his place to the applause of the massive crowd. Buckmaster Hamilton had won by a landslide, and no one within four hundred miles wanted to miss this even on such a cold night.

Ainsley had been making her way back, willing herself not to cry, when the priest looked up and their eyes met. Recognition made her stumble. She would have fallen if her mother hadn't caught her arm.

But Ainsley hardly noticed. She was staring down into the priest's face. He wasn't as old as he had seemed when she'd first spotted him moving through the crowd, leaning heavily on his cane. Even more shocking was that she *knew* him. A childhood memory long buried surfaced in a wave of guilty emotions. The man had been younger back then, but so had her mother.

She'd seen the two of them out by the stables from her bedroom window.

Even from that distance, Ainsley, barely twelve, had known that something was wrong the moment the man approached her mother. The man had grabbed her mother's arm. Sarah was struggling to get free of him. Ainsley couldn't hear them, but she could tell that they were arguing.

She'd rushed down the stairs in time to get a good look at the man. He let go of her mother's arm when he saw Ainsley. His last words were "This isn't over, Sarah." Then he walked around the back of the stable, but not before his gaze had bored into Ainsley. She'd known she would never forget those eyes. An electric blue that felt as if they had branded her.

"Who was that?" she'd demanded of her mother, recalling how he'd said her mother's first name.

"No one." Her mother had quickly wiped her eyes. "A stable hand. I had to fire him."

"Did he hurt you?" Ainsley had cried, seeing where the man's fingers had bit into her mother's arm.

"I'm fine," she'd said, pulling down her sleeve to hide it before she took Ainsley's shoulders in her trembling hands. "You can't tell anyone about this, not your sisters, especially not your father. It will only upset him. I've taken care of it. The man won't be back. Do you hear me? Promise you won't ever tell."

"But he said—"

"Please."

It was the word *please* that came out almost a sob that had made Ainsley make a promise she'd guiltily kept from all those years ago. Weeks later her mother would drive her SUV into the Yellowstone River. When her body wasn't recovered from the iced-over river, she'd been assumed drowned. For twenty-two years her mother would be dead—until recently, when she returned from the grave with no memory of where she'd been.

Now those electric-blue eyes from her childhood burned into hers for one startling instant before they shifted to where her mother was standing next to her. Her mother, who had grabbed her arm to keep her from falling when she'd stumbled.

Later Ainsley would remember it all happening in a split second. But in truth it felt like slow motion. The man's hands twisting the top off the cane. Even when he raised what looked like a toy pistol, she knew it wasn't. Even as her mind argued that he would have had to go through security to get in here tonight, she knew he'd somehow avoided detection. Just as she knew he'd come here not to kill the new president— but the woman he'd argued with all those years ago.

As he raised the weapon, pointing it at her mother, Ainsley cried out. But her voice was lost in the roar of the crowd. All eyes, including those of the secret service agents, were on the president, not some old priest.

Ainsley didn't remember pushing her mother aside to launch herself at the priest. She didn't hear the weapon discharge. She hadn't even been sure he'd fired until she felt the burning heat an instant before she crashed into the priest, taking them both down. She hit hard, heard screams around her and a struggle.

The cold November night and the canopy of stars seemed to move in and out. Her chest burned while the rest of her felt as if she were freezing. Sounds were indistinguishable. Above her she would see faces. They seemed to sway in the breeze.

Arms came around her and a male voice cried, "She's hit! Get an ambulance! Hurry! Ainsley, can you hear me? Stay with me, sweetheart."

"Sawyer?" She blinked, thinking she must be hallucinating or dying. She tried to bring the man's face into focus, but the darkness closed in and she dropped into it.

Find out what happens next in
HONOR BOUND
by B.J. Daniels.
Available November 2016 wherever
HQN books and ebooks are sold.

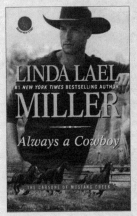

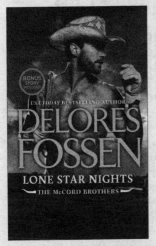

INTRIGUE

EDGE-OF-YOUR-SEAT INTRIGUE, FEARLESS ROMANCE.

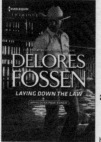

Save $1.00

on the purchase of
LAYING DOWN THE LAW
by *USA TODAY* bestselling
author Delores Fossen,
available August 23, 2016, or on any
other Harlequin® Intrigue book.

Available wherever books are sold, including most
bookstores, supermarkets, drugstores and discount stores.

- ✂

Save $1.00

on the purchase of any Harlequin® Intrigue book.

Coupon valid until November 30, 2016. Redeemable at participating outlets in the
U.S. and Canada only. Not redeemable at Barnes and Noble stores.
Limit one coupon per customer.

52614040

Canadian Retailers: Harlequin Enterprises Limited will pay the face value of
this coupon plus 10.25¢ if submitted by customer for this product only. Any
other use constitutes fraud. Coupon is nonassignable. Void if taxed, prohibited
or restricted by law. Consumer must pay any government taxes. Void if copied.
Inmar Promotional Services ("IPS") customers submit coupons and proof of
sales to Harlequin Enterprises Limited, P.O. Box 3000, Saint John, NB E2L 4L3,
Canada. Non-IPS retailer—for reimbursement submit coupons and proof of
sales directly to Harlequin Enterprises Limited, Retail Marketing Department,
225 Duncan Mill Rd., Don Mills, ON M3B 3K9, Canada.

5 65373 00076 2   (8100)0 12195

U.S. Retailers: Harlequin Enterprises
Limited will pay the face value of
this coupon plus 8¢ if submitted by
customer for this product only. Any
other use constitutes fraud. Coupon is
nonassignable. Void if taxed, prohibited
or restricted by law. Consumer must pay
any government taxes. Void if copied.
For reimbursement submit coupons
and proof of sales directly to Harlequin
Enterprises Limited, P.O. Box 880478,
El Paso, TX 88588-0478, U.S.A. Cash
value 1/100 cents.

® and ™ are trademarks owned and used by the trademark owner and/or its licensee.

© 2016 Harlequin Enterprises Limited

DFCOUP0816

REQUEST YOUR
FREE BOOKS!

2 FREE NOVELS
FROM THE SUSPENSE COLLECTION,
PLUS 2 FREE GIFTS!

YES! Please send me 2 FREE novels from the Suspense Collection and my 2 FREE gifts (gifts are worth about $10). After receiving them, if I don't wish to receive any more books, I can return the shipping statement marked "cancel." If I don't cancel, I will receive 4 brand-new novels every month and be billed just $6.49 per book in the U.S. or $6.99 per book in Canada. That's a savings of at least 18% off the cover price. It's quite a bargain! Shipping and handling is just 50¢ per book in the U.S. and 75¢ per book in Canada.* I understand that accepting the 2 free books and gifts places me under no obligation to buy anything. I can always return a shipment and cancel at any time. Even if I never buy another book, the two free books and gifts are mine to keep forever.

191/391 MDN GH4Z

Name   (PLEASE PRINT)

Address   Apt. #

City   State/Prov.   Zip/Postal Code

Signature (if under 18, a parent or guardian must sign)

Mail to the **Reader Service:**
IN U.S.A.: P.O. Box 1867, Buffalo, NY 14240-1867
IN CANADA: P.O. Box 609, Fort Erie, Ontario L2A 5X3

Want to try 2 free books from another line?
Call 1-800-873-8635 or visit www.ReaderService.com.

* Terms and prices subject to change without notice. Prices do not include applicable taxes. Sales tax applicable in NY. Canadian residents will be charged applicable taxes. Offer not valid in Quebec. This offer is limited to one order per household. Not valid for current subscribers to the Suspense Collection or the Romance/Suspense Collection. All orders subject to credit approval. Credit or debit balances in a customer's account(s) may be offset by any other outstanding balance owed by or to the customer. Please allow 4 to 6 weeks for delivery. Offer available while quantities last.

Your Privacy—The Reader Service is committed to protecting your privacy. Our Privacy Policy is available online at www.ReaderService.com or upon request from the Reader Service.

We make a portion of our mailing list available to reputable third parties that offer products we believe may interest you. If you prefer that we not exchange your name with third parties, or if you wish to clarify or modify your communication preferences, please visit us at www.ReaderService.com/consumerschoice or write to us at Reader Service Preference Service, P.O. Box 9062, Buffalo, NY 14240-9062. Include your complete name and address.